Touched by Thorns

LOVESWEPT ®

Doubleday
NEW YORK LONDON TORONTO SYDNEY AUCKLAND

Touched by Thorns

Susan Bowden

*...the heart that is soonest
awake to the flowers
Is always the first to be touched by the thorns.*

Thomas Moore

LOVESWEPT®
PUBLISHED BY DOUBLEDAY
a division of Bantam Doubleday Dell Publishing Group, Inc.
666 Fifth Avenue, New York, New York 10103

DOUBLEDAY and the portrayal of an anchor with a dolphin
and the word LOVESWEPT and the portrayal of the wave device
are trademarks of Doubleday, a division of
Bantam Doubleday Dell Publishing Group, Inc.

Except for certain actual historical personages, all of the characters
in this book are fictitious.

LIBRARY OF CONGRESS CATALOGING-IN-PUBLICATION DATA

Bowden, Susan, 1936–
Touched by thorns / Susan Bowden. — 1st ed.
p.   cm.
"Loveswept ®"
I. Title.
PR9199.3.B628T68   1991
813'.54—dc20   91-8821
CIP

ISBN 0-385-42145-1

Copyright © 1991 by Susan Bowden Twaddle

All Rights Reserved

Printed in the United States of America

October 1991

First Edition

*For my sisters,
Geraldine and Penny,
and my brother, Robin,
and in loving memory of our grandmother,
May Barron (née Fitzgerald)*

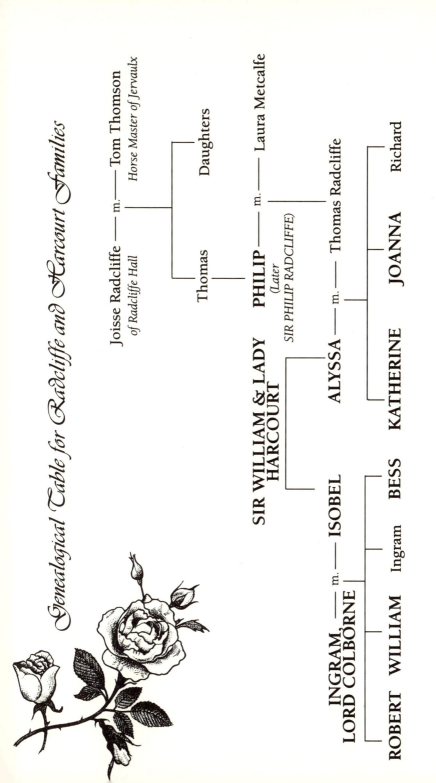

Part 1
1581

Chapter 1

A thin blanket of snow covered the moor above Radcliffe Hall, softening the harsh outline of Penhill against a brooding February sky, stilling the sounds of birds and animals as they sought shelter.

But inside the Hall, all was noise and bustle and laughter, as everyone prepared for the arrival of the long-awaited guest.

At the very center of this activity was the bedchamber of the two Radcliffe sisters, where Katherine Radcliffe was dressing or, rather, being dressed, for it seemed that every female member of the household was gathered in the chamber, some to help, some to hinder. There was no doubt, however, that all were there for the same reason, to share in the happiness of their beloved Mistress Kate.

She stood now, surrounded by all her admirers, the skirts of the green damask gown swaying over the farthingale, the low-cut bodice displaying her white skin and curving breast.

"Will it do?" she asked anxiously of them all. An assuring babble greeted the question.

"Th'art even more beautiful than thy mother on her wedding day," Dame Joan, her mother's old nurse told her.

Katherine bent to hug her. "But it is not my wedding day," she declared, blushing.

Old Joan pinched her cheek. "Not yet, 'tisn't. But it will be very soon, my pretty."

The lights in Katherine's dark eyes sparkled even brighter at this. She spun around, giddy with happiness, her hair, burnished like ripe chestnuts, rippling to her waist. Having just turned seventeen, she was part-child, part-woman. But there was no denying, not even by her enemies—and, with her quick temper and pride, she had made a few of them in her short life—that Katherine Radcliffe, the elder daughter of Alyssa Radcliffe, was beautiful.

Joanna, Katherine's sister, who had most cause to be her sister's enemy, for she was short and plump and lacked Kate's fire, was in truth her most ardent friend and supporter. In their childhood, she had often tried to take the blame upon herself when Kate had become entangled in some outrageous escapade. Of course it had never worked. However much she was loved, everyone at Radcliffe was wise to the ways of Kate Radcliffe.

"Edward will be quite dazzled by you," Joanna whispered in her sister's ear, as she gave her a hug.

Katherine returned the embrace. "Oh, I do hope so."

It was more than a year since she had last seen Edward Carlton. All that time her greatest fear had been that he might have fallen in love with some older and more experienced woman in London. Thanks be to God, there was no longer any cause for fear on that account.

Now that she was dressed, her grandfather, Sir Philip, was called for. When he entered the chamber, leaning heavily on his ebony walking stick, he joined in the general praise. "Edward is a most fortunate man," he told Katherine, his blue eyes twinkling, but Katherine sensed a hint of disapproval as his keen gaze traveled over her new gown.

She turned in sudden panic to her mother, her hands at her bodice. "Edward will not think me immodest, will he, Mother? He has never before seen me in such a gown."

"No, dear heart, he will not think you immodest. Your gown is eminently suitable." Alyssa Radcliffe took Katherine's elbows and stood on tiptoe to kiss her cheek. "How I wish Dickon could have been here for the occasion. Then the family would have been complete."

Katherine's face clouded. She wished her mother had not spoken what everyone was thinking, for her young brother had been sadly missed by all at Radcliffe since he had joined Lord Scrope's service at Carlisle.

"I wish he were here, too," Katherine whispered.

Her mother stepped back. "But we will not be sad today," she said briskly. "I know that I speak with prejudice, but I believe that there is no more beautiful lass in all the ridings of Yorkshire than Kate Radcliffe."

Laughing with delight at this uncommon praise from her mother, Katherine gathered her little body against hers. Today, she was so happy she could forgive even her mother *anything*.

Dear God, she prayed, *make this day the most perfect one of my life, I beg you*. For today, Edward, her darling Edward, was coming to Radcliffe to ask her to marry him. Their fathers had been talking of marriage between them since Katherine was an infant. But Edward Carlton, being eight years older than she—and a younger son—had first had to make his way in life before thinking of marriage.

Three years ago, when Edward had left to study law in London, Katherine had thought her heart would break, but he had assured her that, when the time was right, he would ask for her hand in marriage. Since then, whenever he returned to the Dales, he had renewed that vow, his love for her increasing as she grew to maturity. Now the time was right—and ripe—for them to wed.

Edward had written to her grandfather to say that he was riding down from London and would be at Radcliffe within the week. He had made no mention of marriage, of course. Edward was too correct to speak of such weighty matters in an open letter, but both families knew the reason for this unexpected return to Yorkshire. This afternoon she would hear the words from his own dear lips and, before the summer was out, she would be wife to Edward Carlton, fourth son of Sir John Carlton of Langthorpe Hall, in Swaledale.

The messenger rode fast along the frost-hard bridlepath, his breath hanging white before him like the low cloud that had engulfed him on Bowes Moor that morning.

"Mind you stop only to change horses," Lord Scrope had warned him. "The news must reach Radcliffe by nightfall."

Already the pale February sun was beginning to sink behind the snow-specked moortop, yet still the messenger had not reached the turning to Richmond. The wind blew keen as a new-whetted knife on the open moor. Despite his fleece-lined cloak and riding boots, he was chilled to the very marrow. His fingers could barely feel the reins they clutched.

"Iffen his lordship wishes thee to reach Radcliffe at all, never mind tonight,

lad," he muttered to himself through wind-chapped lips, "tha'd best take a warm by the fire and summat to heat thine innards at Richmond."

• • •

The soughing of the evening wind through Radcliffe Hall's many chimneys reminded Alyssa of a woman's keening over the body of her husband when the plague had destroyed the town of Wensley. A shiver ran across her shoulders.

"Tobias. I think we should have the shutters closed. It is already dark."

The black-garbed steward rose from his seat by the hearth, setting his chesspiece down on the board.

"Do not think you can escape that easily, my friend," said Sir Philip, bending over the chessboard. "I have you at my mercy now."

"Then it is useless for me to continue, is it not?" Tobias Ridley told him with a glimmer of a smile.

"Ah, but you must not deprive me of the pleasure of the actual kill, old friend." Philip flashed a smile at his steward and then waved a thin hand at him. "Go, give your orders. It is always duty before pleasure with you, Tobias."

As the steward hurried away, Alyssa bent to tuck a shawl about Philip's legs. "You treat me as if I were an ancient invalid," he told her with a rueful smile.

"That wind is cold," said his daughter-in-law.

"But the fire is warm." Philip stretched his long-fingered hands out to its blaze. He cast a glance to the far end of the parlor and, seeing that the two other occupants were in close conversation, took Alyssa's hand in his.

It was not only the warmth of the fire that set Alyssa aglow. "Take care," she whispered, eyeing Katherine and Edward, sitting stiffly across from each other at the small table.

"Kate and Edward are too immersed in themselves to notice us. My poor little Kate." Philip drew in a long breath and shook his head. Having gently pressed Alyssa's hand, he released it. Still, she knelt at his side, his proximity a solace in her sadness.

She gazed up into Philip's eyes, their brilliance dimmed a little by age and adversity. They smiled gently at each other, as always reading each other's thoughts.

He laid his arm gently about her small shoulders. "Even at this unhappy time, we must remember that we have been the most fortunate of people. Each day I kneel to thank God for his amazing kindness and goodness. I have you, my dear Alyssa, continually at my side, and my three healthy grandchildren: two fair granddaughters and

Richard, the Lord of Radcliffe, to whom God has granted both good looks and wisdom."

Alyssa's smile was one of unabashed maternal pride, her sadness for Katherine's bitter disappointment forgotten for a moment. "He has a wonderfully enquiring mind, does he not? It gave me such pleasure to hear the two of you conversing so easily in Latin when he was at home at Christmastide. I never did master Latin well, yet Richard, who is but ten years old, seems perfectly at ease in it."

"Before we know it, Richard will be Secretary of State," Philip said, smiling at her. "Or Archbishop of York."

Alyssa smiled back at him. "You may mock me as much as you please, sir, but I believe that Richard is destined to be a great man."

"We shall see. It is in God's hands. I pray that it will be so. Perhaps that will help to atone for the sins of his father and grandfather."

Alyssa was eager to dispel Philip's introspective mood before it took hold of him. "You must have atoned for your sins—and I for mine, for that matter—a long time ago, for our life here at Radcliffe has been blessed." She glanced again at Katherine and Edward and released a sigh. "Until today, that is."

Philip followed her gaze. "Kate will recover from this blow. She has a natural resilience. With God's help, she will make some worthy man happy, even if he be not Edward." His lips curved into a smile. "After all, despite all *our* adversity, we have been granted great happiness in the past ten years."

It was true. Since the death of Thomas, her husband and Philip's son, they had been happy. Alyssa did not speak her thoughts aloud. They rarely spoke of Thomas, except to the children. Even then, his name was mentioned as little as was possible.

"And Radcliffe, my dear home," continued Philip, "has been made infinitely more dear by the knowledge that, had it not been for my sweet Alyssa, it would have been forever lost to me and my descendants."

"You must remember that I did not produce Richard by myself. Your own son was his father."

For a moment, the planes of Philip's cheekbones grew sharper in the firelight. "I am not thinking only of young Richard, as you well know. But you are right. He is so unlike Thomas, that I sometimes find it difficult to remember that Thomas was his father." He made the sign of the cross. "May his soul rest in peace forever."

"Amen to that," Alyssa muttered. Although it was eleven years since Thomas had died, her blood still grew cold at the mere thought of her husband.

• • •

Lord Scrope's messenger tumbled from his horse. So cold were his feet that he almost fell to the ground when he stood upon them. The grooms in the stableyard at Richmond Castle were clustered around a charcoal brazier, striving to keep warm in the frigid weather. The orders he bore secured him a fresh horse within minutes, but this time, despite Lord Scrope's orders, he insisted upon being taken to the castle kitchen. There, he sat himself before the huge hearth, so close to the blazing fire that the brown lard dripping from the roasting pig spat out at him.

Between mouthfuls of tangy ale, warmed with a hot poker, he shared his sad news with the soldiers and servants. They all shook their heads and crossed themselves to hear such ill tidings, for everyone knew the sad yet triumphant tale of how Sir Philip had been attainted as a traitor to Queen Elizabeth, imprisoned in the Tower, and saved by the intervention of his daughter-in-law, Mistress Alyssa. And of how Radcliffe Hall had been bestowed upon the much-hated Earl of Sussex, and then saved by the birth of Sir Philip's grandson, Richard Radcliffe, the young Lord of Radcliffe Manor.

For ten long years, the inhabitants of Radcliffe had lived in peace. Now, alas, it appeared that their peace was at an end.

Leaning her hand on Philip's knees, Alyssa stood up, her joints stiff, and sat on the cushioned bench, to set a distance between them. "You have not told me yet exactly what Edward said to you to explain this sudden change of heart," she said.

They both turned to look at Katherine's pinched face. She had cried out her rage on Philip's breast and then had demanded that she be permitted to speak alone with Edward. But Edward himself had insisted that her mother and grandfather be present at their meeting.

Alyssa's heart ached at the sight of her daughter's tense body and tearstained face. The beauty of the morning had gone. Now it was distorted with misery and with the fury of the tirade she was addressing in a low voice to the white-faced and mainly silent Edward.

"Jesu," Alyssa whispered. "This will break her heart. She has loved Edward since she was a child."

"To me she is still but a child," Philip said.

"There you are wrong. Katherine is seventeen. Had it not been for Edward, she would long since have been wed, as you well know. It was only that . . ." Alyssa hesitated.

"That we wished her to marry the man she had set her heart upon, and who, we thought, loved her," Philip finished for her.

"Yes," Alyssa whispered, her thoughts dwelling on her own unhappy marriage.

Philip threw the shawl from his knees. "We were fools to have taken it for granted that they would wed."

"Why? Everyone thought that Kate and Edward would make a perfect match. You and Edward's father agreed upon it when they were mere children."

"So we did. But God decreed otherwise." Philip turned away to look into the fire.

"Is it another woman he loves?"

Philip gave her a strange, enigmatic smile and slowly nodded. "He loves another."

"Oh God, Philip, why did he not write of this to you first, so that you could have broken it to her gently? Not only has he rejected her; he has also humiliated her before her family and the servants. I cannot believe it of Edward. How will Kate bear it?"

"She must bear it," Philip said, his voice unusually harsh. "She has no choice but to bear it. And you must help her, Alyssa. You will find the right words to comfort her, to give her some of your strength."

Alyssa gave a wry smile. "I doubt it. She will not take this easily. Kate's nature is not a compliant one. Besides, it is to you, not me, that she always turns for comfort."

Philip frowned. "Perhaps she feels that you favor Joanna."

Alyssa twisted her hands together in her lap. "I wish it were so. It only seems thus because Joanna has such a compliant nature and she is still a child, of course. But as Kate has grown to womanhood, the rift between us has widened, not lessened." She shrugged. "God knows I would not have it so, but try as I might I cannot come near her nowadays. She deals with me with cold courtesy, no more. I swear she is closer to my sister Isobel than she is to me."

A smile flickered at the corners of Philip's mouth. "That in itself would gall you, no doubt."

Alyssa turned upon him. "You will accuse me of fanciful thoughts, no doubt, but I swear that Isobel is filling Kate's head with lies." She was appalled to see that her hands were shaking. In these placid years of middle age, her sister still had the power to rouse her to fury.

Philip leant forward to squeeze her hand. "Our beautiful Kate is too loyal to listen to any lies about her mother."

His assurance was no consolation to Alyssa. Philip lived in a warm cocoon, sheltered by those who loved him. He was untouched by the outside world, and appeared to think that nothing evil could touch anyone in Radcliffe, that somehow it was protected by some magic circle drawn around the manor's boundaries.

It was right that he should feel thus. He had had more than his share of suffering in the sixty-two years of his eventful life. It gave her great satisfaction to think that, during these last contented years, he had very seldom lapsed into those periods of melancholy which had so plagued him when he was a younger man.

She took up the shirt she had been embroidering in silver and sapphire silks for him and he took up his copy of Castiglione's *Il Cortegiano*, but Alyssa knew that his mind was not on his reading, for he turned only one page in an entire half hour. And after Katherine asked for permission to leave the parlor to "walk a little in the long gallery with Edward," the pages were not turned at all.

Yet it was Philip who eventually leaned over to place his hand on hers and say, "You are very pensive, my little one."

Alyssa was about to reply, when a shadow fell across the hearth. Hastily snatching her hand away, she turned to look up into her daughter's face.

It was evident that Katherine was struggling to rein in her emotions. "Edward is about to take his leave," she told her grandfather. "He awaits you in the hall." Her lips trembled. "Oh, Grandy, I cannot bear it. He—"

Philip sprang up to take her in his arms. "Hush, now, my darling. Your Grandy is here." He looked at Alyssa over Katherine's shoulder. "Go to Edward and tell him I shall be with him in a few moments," he bade her in a low voice.

Alyssa nodded and left the parlor. Philip would be better able than she to deal with her distraught daughter. She could not help feeling a pang of envy. Katherine was her firstborn child. Throughout Kate's childhood there had been a special bond between them, but it was there no longer and she greatly feared it would never return.

As she went into the hall, Alyssa was overtaken by a sense of uneasiness. Philip was hiding something from her, something concerning Edward, she was sure. She drew in a deep breath. If he was keeping some secret from her, then she would wheedle it out of Edward himself.

He was standing by the great oaken table in the hall, already cloaked and spurred. She had known Edward Carlton since he was a shy young lad, very much in the shadow of his three older brothers. Now that timid lad had grown into a handsome, self-assured man. "Edward will go far, whatever he chooses to do in his life," Philip had often said of him. He already had a burgeoning career at the bar in London and Philip was sure that it would not be long before some of Sir John Carlton's influential friends found his youngest son a position at Court.

Alyssa observed Edward now, the light from the hanging chandelier flickering on his barley-gold hair, and knew from the way he was dragging his riding gauntlets through his hands that he, too, was deeply disturbed by what had passed between him and Katherine.

"You are leaving so soon, Edward?"

He started, as if his thoughts had been a thousand miles away. "Forgive me, Mistress Radcliffe. I must return home. I barely had time to greet my parents or brothers before riding here." He made a pathetic attempt at a smile, but his face immediately returned to its former expression of tense melancholy.

"This is a bad business between you and Katherine," Alyssa told him. "Would it not have been kinder to Katherine and more civil to her family to have written to Sir Philip first, Edward?"

His cheeks flushed brick-red at her rebuke. "I deeply regret now that I did not, but somehow—" he began, but a sudden turmoil from the courtyard outside stopped him midsentence.

Alyssa had heard the sounds of a horse being ridden fast into the courtyard, but this was nothing unusual for Radcliffe, which was as famous for its breeding stables as for the beauty of Radcliffe Hall itself. It was the shouts and little cries of distress from outside that concerned her.

She was about to call for Tobias, when she saw that the steward was already running across the hall. "Stay here, madam. I will see to it," he said, holding up his hand to stop her from going outside.

Edward glanced at Alyssa. "I will go and see what's happening," he said, and strode across the hall and out the door.

"What is it? What is all the noise about?" Katherine ran swiftly down the stairs, her skirts swaying about her. Behind her came her grandfather, leaning heavily on the banister rail for support.

Joanna's plump face peered over the upstairs railing. "What in the name of heaven is happening?" she cried, and she, too, ran down the staircase, past her grandfather.

The nail-studded doors swung inward again.

Tobias entered first. Behind him came a horseman, his cloak and boots stiff with frost and dry mud.

Alyssa stood motionless, her hands crossed over her breast, as if she were trying to stop her pounding heart from leaping forth from it.

As Tobias approached, Alyssa could see that his entire face, even his lips, was the color of wood ash.

"This messenger is from Lord Scrope," the steward said. "He has ridden all the way from Carlisle."

Alyssa turned blindly towards the staircase. "Philip," she said, her voice rising.

But the messenger had already fallen to his knees before her. "It is bad news, Mistress," he said. He dragged a letter from inside his leather jerkin and thrust it at her.

Alyssa's fingers fumbled at the seal of hard wax. "I cannot open it," she murmured, and gave it into Katherine's hands. Again she sought for Philip, but he remained in the same position halfway down the wide staircase, his eyes fixed upon the messenger.

Her hands trembling, Katherine opened the letter. "Read it to us, I beg you," she whispered to Edward, who stood close beside her.

He took the paper from her. "It is addressed to Sir Philip," he said, turning to Philip.

"Read it," came the order from the figure on the stairs.

Smoothing out the paper, Edward began. "My dear friend. It is my very sad duty to inform you that . . . that . . ." Edward faltered and cast a look of appeal at Sir Philip.

"Continue," he said in a hoarse voice that sounded utterly unlike him.

Edward looked down at the paper again. "That your grandson, Richard Radcliffe, parted from this life this forenoon, the—"

Philip's inhuman cry blotted out Edward's voice.

Clutching her skirts, Alyssa rushed across the hall, but before she could reach the foot of the staircase Philip's body crumpled and fell, crashing down ten or more stairs, to land at her feet.

Chapter 2

Katherine Radcliffe would never forget that evening. Every detail of it remained etched in her memory, like acid upon metal: her grandfather's terrible cry, followed by the fearful crash of his body toppling down the stairs, then her mother's high-pitched scream. . . . Coming, as it did, so soon after Edward's rejection, the entire scene held the semblance of some horrifying nightmare, from which she prayed she would soon wake.

Everyone in the hall rushed to the foot of the stairs. Edward bent over her mother, who sat on the first step, cradling Philip against her breast, the blood from the great wound on his temple staining the bodice of her gown. Her eyes were dry, her mouth closed, but from some part of her came an eerie keening sound that turned Kate's stomach to ice water.

Edward straightened. "He is still alive," he said in a low voice to Tobias Ridley, "but the pulse is very weak. You must send immediately for the physician."

His words jarred the steward from his trance. "Yes, yes. Of course. I shall see to it immediately," he said, as if relieved to be given something to do.

How like Edward it was to turn first to another man, Katherine thought indignantly. Swallowing hard, she bent over her mother and grandfather. "Is there anything I can do?" she asked her mother.

Alyssa looked up, but her eyes showed no recognition of her daughter.

"Bring a cushion from the settle, Margery," Katherine ordered one of the women, "and for the love of heaven, Joanna, cease that noise." For Joanna was wailing and sobbing in the background, making it impossible for her to think clearly.

She took the tapestry seat cushion from Margery and placed it between her mother's back and the hard stair. Then she crouched down before her and touched her hand. "Edward says he is still alive, Mother. Tobias has sent for Dr. Tredwell."

This time her mother seemed to hear her. Her brown eyes moved from their fixed gaze upon Philip's marble-white face to meet Katherine's. They were the eyes of a stricken animal, the expression of mute appeal unbearable to look upon.

Katherine sprang up. "Someone fetch a hurdle so that we can carry Sir Philip to his chamber."

Edward took her elbow to draw her aside. Even now, she thrilled at his touch. *He will never touch you again*, a voice cried within her. "He should not be moved until the physician sees him," he warned her.

She turned to face him. "Oh, Edward." A sob caught in her throat.

"Have courage, Katherine." He clasped her hands tightly in his. "You are strong. They will need that strength now."

She shook her head. "I cannot be strong. How can I bear it? First you, then Grandy." She gave a little cry. "And Richard, my dearest little Dickon . . ." She buried her head against his breast to stifle the sobs that welled up from her throat.

His arms, those dear, strong arms were about her. Edward had kissed her but once in their entire lives, but those arms had enfolded her many times: to lift her when she twisted her ankle while she was running across the moor on Penhill, to comfort her when her favorite pony broke its neck after she had forced it to jump a high paling. . . . The thought of never again feeling Edward's arms about her was too appalling to consider.

I will win him back, she resolved. After all, he had assured her that he did not love another woman. His only explanation for not wishing to marry her now had been that he was being sent to Flanders on urgent diplomatic business.

I shall wait a dozen years for him if I have to, she resolved. *None but Edward shall be my husband.*

She flung back her head to look into his troubled gray eyes. "You are right. I must be strong. Thank you, my dear friend, for once again reminding me of my duty," she said with a rueful grimace. She rubbed her arm across her eyes, the silver braid on her sleeve scratching her forehead. "You'll be thinking me sadly lacking in backbone that I dissolve into the tears of a weak woman at a time when I should be most resolute."

"I could never think of you as a weak woman," Edward told her with a faint smile, but his eyes were still troubled, as if he could not understand the sudden change in her.

Fortified by her resolution, Katherine stepped back from him and went to her mother and grandfather. Joanna was with them now, fussing about like a bantam hen. Her mother hated to be fussed.

Katherine put her arm about her sister's waist to draw her aside. "Joanna, do you go and see to Grandy's bed. Have two warming pans set in it and make sure there are enough covers."

Joanna's eyes swam with tears. "Oh, Kate, do you think—"

Katherine pressed her fingers over Joanna's lips. "There is no time to think now," she said firmly. "We shall talk later, when we are in bed."

But, although she sent Joanna to her bed a few hours later, Katherine herself never went to her bed at all that night. When Dr. Tredwell arrived, he examined Philip and pronounced that he had suffered a severe heart seizure. "It is my opinion that he'll not survive past the night," he told her and Edward. "My concern is for Mistress Radcliffe now. I fear for her sanity. 'Tis a terrible matter to lose a child, and him her only son, at that. But she seems as much overset by Sir Philip's sickness, despite he's a man who's lived to almost his allotted span." He shook his grizzled head. "I've offered her a sleeping draught, but she refuses to take it, saying she must be there when Sir Philip awakes, but, in truth, I doubt he ever will."

Katherine kept her counsel and said nothing, but inwardly her heart hardened a little more against her mother.

When the physician left, she insisted that Joanna go to her bed, for she was swaying on her feet from fatigue. "I shall be up very soon," she assured her sister, kissing her tear-stained cheeks. "Meantime, I'll send Joan up to you for company."

Once the household was settled, with Tobias Ridley's habitual efficiency and Edward's assistance, there was little left for Katherine to do but wait. Waiting was the hardest part of all.

She had been able to weather much of the early part of the long night by dashing off messages to her mother's parents, Sir William and Lady Harcourt, and to her mother's sister, Isobel Colborne—although she doubted her mother would care to have Aunt Isobel near her at such a time. The two sisters were ever at odds with each other.

Katherine also sent word to her Great-Uncle Piers, the brother of Grandy's long-dead wife, Laura Metcalfe, and to Giles Challoner, her grandfather's dearest friend.

The task of writing to them had been a melancholy one, for she had to impart the news not only of the sudden death of her brother, the young Lord of Radcliffe, but also of the imminent death of Sir Philip.

When she could find no more to occupy her, Katherine wearily climbed the steps of the great oaken staircase that her father had had built a few years after her birth, and reluctantly went to share her mother's vigil at Grandy's bedside.

When she entered the bedchamber she saw, to her great surprise, that her grandfather's eyes were open and that he was speaking in a faint but earnest tone to her mother. Their hands lay tightly clasped upon the bearskin bed cover.

Now Philip's eyes were raised to meet Katherine's and, as she drew near to the bed, she saw in them an expression of both relief and appeal.

Her mother rose slowly from the stool by the bed, groaning softly as she straightened her knees. With a tilt of her head, she gestured to Katherine to stand a little apart. "Thank God you have come," she whispered. "He has been begging to speak to you these past several minutes, but I did not dare leave him, and Margery went to the kitchen for warm milk, so I could not send for you." Her forehead creased into a little frown. "He refuses to tell me what it is he wants from you."

Katherine could hear the resentment in her mother's voice.

"Make sure you do not tire him. He has very little strength left."

Katherine made no reply, but went to the bedside and took her grandfather's hand in hers. It was dry and hot to the touch, and felt as if it might crumble beneath her fingers, like parchment that has been burned in the fire.

"I am here, Grandy," she said simply.

His fingers caught hers in an urgent grip. "I . . . I must speak with you . . . alone." He looked past Katherine, at Alyssa.

"He wishes to speak to me alone," Katherine told her mother, not even trying to hide the small note of triumph in her voice.

Her mother's small chin lifted above her white neck ruff. Then she inclined her head slightly and left the chamber.

Philip's breath rasped in his chest. "I must have a priest, a Catholic priest." His hand clutched Katherine's convulsively. "I must be shriven."

Now Katherine understood her grandfather's desire for secrecy. Her mother was a staunch Protestant. Although it was unlikely that she would willingly deny him anything, he would not wish to compromise her beliefs—or her safety—by his demands for a Catholic priest to bestow the last rites upon him. Even at the end, she thought bitterly, he is placing *her* wishes before his own.

"But, Grandy, there are no Catholic priests hereabouts," she whispered, hating to disappoint him. "You know that."

His hand stirred frantically beneath hers. "Edward. Ask Edward."

She did not like to argue with him, but she failed to see how Edward could conjure up a priest when it was common knowledge that all the Catholic priests had been imprisoned or driven from the country.

"But is it safe to ask Edward?" she whispered.

Her heart turned as he smiled the rueful smile she knew so well. "I am about to go where none . . ." He paused for breath. ". . . none can harm me. Not even the Tudor despots. But yes, my darling *Lady Kaferine*, it is safe to ask Edward."

She blinked back tears at his use of her childhood pronunciation of her name.

He tried to raise himself up on his elbow, but could not find the strength. Katherine put her arm about him and he rested his head against her.

"But before you seek Edward, there is something I must tell you." Again he paused to catch his breath, but this time he began to cough and could not stop. For a few terrifying moments, Katherine thought he was going to die in her arms, but the coughing subsided and he lay, shivering violently, as if stricken with the ague.

The coughing had set his head wound bleeding again, the blood seeping through the plaster on his temple. "You must not speak any more," she told him. "I will fetch Mother and—"

"No." His voice rang out this time, effectively silencing her. "I have precious little time left. Do not gainsay me again." He struggled again to heave himself up and, this time, succeeded.

"Now that my beloved grandson—" He broke off, his eyes squeezed shut in his grief. Then they fluttered open again. "Now that Richard is dead, you, Katherine, are my heir."

Katherine gasped. She had not even considered this aspect of Richard's death.

"Alas, that through my own folly there is so little for you to inherit," he said.

"But, Grandy," she protested, "there is the entire estate of Radcliffe Manor."

He gave a deep sigh. "Your mother will explain. I cannot take the time to do so now. One thing I must tell you: When you were infants, unbeknownst to either of your parents, I had you and Joanna baptized in the true faith by a Catholic priest."

A shiver ran down Katherine's spine. It was not safe to be a Catholic nowadays. She wished her grandfather had not told her.

"Do not look so distressed. I was never one to force any particular faith or practice of it upon a person. Protestant or Catholic, it is for you to choose, my dear. I have had more than enough questions about my own faith throughout my life. But now that I am dying, I long to hear the old familiar Latin words of my youth. I feel in my heart that they will ease my passing."

"Oh, Grandy." Katherine bent her head.

She felt his hand stroking her hair. "Don't weep for me, child. I have lived a full life, and have been loved by . . ." He hesitated. "By my beloved wife, Laura, your grandmother, whom I shall meet on the other side, and by my three wonderful grandchildren."

He closed his eyes, the breath rasping in his chest like a saw cutting through wood-bark.

Again, Katherine was terrified that he would not open his eyes. "There was something else, Grandy?" she asked urgently.

He opened his eyes. "Yes, yes. Your faith you shall choose for yourself, but one obligation I will lay upon you. In the chest upon the sideboard there, you will find a packet wrapped in silver tissue. Fetch it here."

Katherine did as she was bidden and brought the packet to her grandfather. "Unwrap it," he ordered her.

She did so, to disclose a golden locket with filigreed engraving and a fine silver pin, headed with a translucent pearl.

"Do you remember these?" he asked her.

She shook her head.

"No, you would have been too young, I suppose. Queen Mary of Scotland gave me the pin on her wedding day, the day she married that popinjay, Darnley, the day that precipitated her downfall. The locket she gave me—"

"I remember now. I remember you telling me that she gave it to you on the day you left the Scottish Court."

He gave her a faint smile. "Aye, that's right. And do you remember the Queen herself, when she came to Bolton Castle?"

"Of course I do." How could she not, considering she had been reminded by him constantly of that time, more than twelve years ago, when Queen Mary had not only inhabited Bolton, but also visited Radcliffe Hall.

His hand tightened on hers. "You must never forget her. Never! Twelve years she has languished in English prisons. Twelve years. I failed to help her. The people of the North failed dismally in their attempt to free her. But there is still hope. I pass on to you the promise I made to her, but did not keep, that I would do all in my power to aid her in her quest to regain the Scottish throne and to take her rightful place as the heir to Elizabeth and the English crown."

He fell back against the pillows, exhausted.

"You must not speak any more," Katherine told him firmly. "I am going to fetch Mother."

He opened his eyes. "Not before you swear to me that you will do all you can to help Queen Mary."

She feared the unnatural light in his eyes. "I swear it."

"In God's name," he commanded her. "Swear it in God's name."

"I swear it in the name of God and His holy saints."

To her great relief, the strange light faded, leaving his eyes gentle and kindly, as before. "I thank you for it. Take the pin and locket. I give them into your safekeeping. Now fetch Edward to me."

"But Mother—"

"Edward first, and then, when I ask for her, your mother."

She was about to leave the room, but then turned and ran back to the bed. "I love you, Grandy," she whispered, laying her cheek against his. "I shall always love you."

"I know that, my dearest little one. You are a good girl, if a trifle headstrong at times." He raised his hand to lift her chin, so that their eyes met. "I have one more request, Kate."

"What is it?" But she knew already.

"That you be kind to your mother. She will be in desperate need of kindness when I am gone. The days ahead will be difficult ones for you all. Give me your word, Kate."

"I shall do my best," she told him, tight-lipped.

"That's my good girl. Now send Edward in to me."

Her mother was waiting outside the door. When it opened, she darted forward, but Katherine barred her entrance.

"He wishes to see Edward first, my lady Mother."

Alyssa's large eyes opened wider at this. "Edward? Why should he wish to see Edward?"

"That is his wish."

Her mother drew her slight figure up to its fullest height. "I shall see your grandfather first, to assure that he has not been overtaxed by your long time with him."

They were like hounds fighting over a bone. How ridiculous at such a time! Katherine caught her mother's arm. "I don't think there is much time," she told her. "It was his express wish that he see Edward first and then you."

Something in her expression must have conveyed itself to her mother's better sense, for she nodded slowly. "If it is his wish . . ." She brushed her forehead with her fingers, as if she could clear her mind thus, and gave Katherine a piteous smile. "I am not thinking very clearly at present."

Katherine put her arm about her shoulders. How small she was. She had never quite realized it before, perhaps because her mother had always been in absolute control of herself, her family and her household—until today.

"If you will but lie down for a few minutes, Mother, I give you my word that I shall fetch you as soon as Edward leaves grandfather. You must get some little rest."

"How can I rest," her mother said in a voice of quiet desperation, "when there is not only Philip to concern me, but also arrangements to be made for the burial of my little Richard?" Her face crumpled and she stood, swaying back and forth, her arms wrapped about her breast, and muttering, "Oh, my son, my son."

"I must fetch Edward, Mother. Here is Margery. She will put you to bed and make you a restorative."

"I will not take anything to sleep," Alyssa said fiercely. "I must stay awake."

"I said a *restorative*," Katherine told her impatiently, and gave her into Margery's care.

Despite Katherine's doubts that a priest could be found anywhere in the entire great County of York, let alone in remote Wensleydale, Edward left her grandfather's bedside, bidding her sit with him, and departed from the house without another word.

Just after the chamber clock in the hall had struck three, Edward gently shook her awake, as she dozed in a low nursing chair beside the bed, her head on Grandy's arm.

He beckoned her outside the bedchamber. "Where is your mother?" he asked.

"In her bed. She is asleep at last. I had Margery give her a very light sleeping draught."

Edward frowned. "Was that wise? She will wish to be with Sir Philip when—" He did not finish.

"When he dies?" Katherine's mouth twisted into a smile. "It seems you have my grandfather dead already, Master Carlton."

She looked past Edward at the man who stepped from behind him, his hood pulled across his face, and her eyes widened. "Oh, you found a—"

The stranger's raised hand silenced her. "It is best that we be discreet, Mistress Katherine."

Although he had spoken softly, the man's voice was as resonant as the old bell of Wensley Church. "Is there anyone else in the house, besides the immediate family and the servants?" he asked. As he lifted his head to speak to her, the hood fell back, revealing a face of singular beauty.

Awed by his face and mien, Katherine hesitated for a moment. Then she said, "My Great-Uncle Piers and his family and Giles Challoner and his wife have arrived," she said at last. "My Aunt Isobel sent word that she and my mother's family will come tomorrow morning."

The stranger and Edward exchanged glances. "Safe enough, I believe," said Edward. "So long as you are not seen, sir." He turned back to Katherine. "Where is Joanna?"

"She is either asleep or with my mother."

"Has she seen your grandfather yet?"

"Yes. She was with him for a quarter of an hour earlier, before she went to bed."

"Then it is not likely that she will ask to see him again until the entire family is sent for. Good." Edward made a reverential bow to the stranger. "Come, sir. Keep watch for us, Katherine. If anyone comes, *anyone*—even your mother—do not permit them to enter until you have warned us."

The priest turned to smile at Katherine. It was a smile of great tenderness, its radiance lighting his pale face as if it were a lamp shining from within. He laid his hand on her head. "God be with you, my child," he said.

The two men went into her grandfather's bedchamber and closed the door. Katherine was amazed. She had always considered Edward to be a Protestant, as were most of the younger generation, especially those who spent most of their time in the South. Yet here he was, not only able to find a Catholic priest for her grandfather, but treating the priest with great deference.

Surely she could not have been mistaken in Edward. She knew him too well. He must be doing this solely out of consideration for her grandfather. Yet even to consort with a Catholic priest was a felony and to procure one to administer the sacraments could mean imprisonment or even death.

Moreover, she sensed that this was no ordinary priest. Not only did he have a singularly beautiful voice, the voice of a gentleman, but he was a man of early middle age, and she knew that the few papist priests that had been left in Yorkshire, after the coming of the new church, had been graybeards and ill-educated, not vigorous and intelligent like this one.

Her heart pounding in her breast like a kettledrum, she stood guard outside the chamber door, starting at every noise that issued from below. And as she waited, her ears straining to hear what was being said inside the chamber, her sadly taxed brain pondered this new riddle.

Chapter 3

A great wind gusted about Philip, swirling the leaves, the plants, even the trees, as if they themselves were as light as the leaves. And he was at the very center of the vortex.

The wind was not unpleasant. It was warm and carried the hum of the reverberation of bells. Yet, when it lifted him and began to bear him, faster and faster, above his beloved moors, he struggled against it. "Not yet, not yet," he cried.

Then a voice called his name, *Philip, Philip*, and a light shone before him, at its core a vaporous, multihued form. And though the dazzling light blinded him, he knew the form was his beloved wife Laura.

"Not yet, my darling. Not quite yet. I must be shriven first."

The light throbbed and then faded. The wind slowed, like a humming top ending its spin, and he was still, the throbbing pain in his head returning in full force.

"Sir Philip," said a voice, urgently calling him.

He opened his eyes to focus them upon the anxious face that hovered above him. "Ah, Edward. Are you still here?"

"Yes, sir. I have brought you . . . a priest."

Philip closed his eyes and drew in a long breath, letting it out slowly in a long sigh. "God bless you, Edward. Now I may die in peace." He raised his head to look at the man who had stepped into the pool of candlelight.

"This is Father Campion, Sir Philip."

"Campion? Edmund Campion?" breathed Philip.

"The very same," said the priest, smiling.

"By all the saints," said Philip, fighting for breath, "what is the illustrious Father Campion doing here, in the remote dales of the North Riding?"

"I am here in the North for but a short time, to minister unto the needs of beleaguered Catholics. At present I am enjoying the hospitality of Mistress Bulmer at Marrick."

There was so much Philip would have liked to ask the great scholar, but the beating of wings filled his ears. "I have . . . but little time. I must confess. . . ."

Again, the radiant smile, and the priest reached into his cloak bag and put a stole about his neck. Motioning to Edward to stand a little way off, he took Philip's hands between his and prepared to hear his last confession.

When Philip had finished his halting confession, he feared from Father Campion's silence that his mortal sin was too heinous to receive absolution, that he would burn in everlasting hell for it. His face must have expressed the horror he felt, for the priest began the prayers of absolution, speaking in low tones so that Philip had to strain to hear him.

"My . . . penance?" Philip breathed, when Father Campion had finished.

"The sin was committed but once, you say?"

Philip nodded. "Once only."

"Then it is my belief that you have performed many penances since you committed this sin, Philip. Now you have confessed it, and through God's infinite mercy have brought about your own salvation."

Philip let forth a great sigh. Surprisingly, he felt no shame at sharing this long-kept secret with a stranger, only a vast sense of relief. The use of his given name drew him even closer to Edmund Campion. It was as if he had a dear friend, a brother with him at his passing. But still he was not completely at rest.

"The other . . . she—"

Father Campion frowned. "When was she born?" he asked.

The beating of wings grew louder. Philip shook his head, unable to concentrate. *Not yet*, he told the quivering flame that hovered above him. *Not yet, I beg you.*

"Was it before the end of King Henry's reign?" the priest asked urgently.

Philip strained to think, and then nodded.

"Then it will have been a Catholic priest who baptized her. Set your mind at rest, my friend. I will see to it."

Philip believed him. He sank back on the pillow. There was nothing more now that he could do. And as the sacramental eucharist melted upon his tongue, he committed his family into the hands of God. He was aware of Edmund Campion's cool, fragrant hands upon him, and then the priest was gone, leaving only the aura of his strong, confident faith behind him.

When his family entered the bedchamber, Philip lay quite still upon the bed, dwarfed by its ancient, rough-hewn tester and bedposts. To the surprise of all, he was smiling. He smiled upon his old friends, Piers and Giles, and upon his faithful steward and friend, Tobias Ridley, and his two weeping granddaughters. Then his eyes rested upon his son's widow and they filled with a radiant light.

Alyssa went to the bed and took his hand between hers. Philip struggled to speak, but nothing came. His chest labored in his efforts. A sharp spasm contorted his face for a moment. Then he held out his arms as if reaching for something far above him and shouted in a loud voice, "Now!"

The arms fell across his chest, which labored no more, and the light in his eyes dimmed . . . and was extinguished.

When Richard's body arrived four days later, they buried them both, the two Lords of Radcliffe, in the family vault in the Church of the Holy Trinity in Wensley.

To Katherine's relief Edward returned from a brief visit with his family to be with them on the day of the burial. She was not sure she could have borne it alone. For she *was* alone. Her mother had retreated into a world of her own, her drawn, white face a mask to hide her pain. And Joanna was little help, dissolving into tears at any given moment. Katherine's hand itched to slap her. There was time enough and more for tears when they at last got to their beds that night. For now, there were guests to entertain and arrangements to be made. And she, Katherine, was forced to do it all, with the help of Tobias . . . and Edward.

She turned now to watch Edward, the most handsome man in the hall, as he stood talking to Lord Scrope. *He will never leave me now*, she thought. Not now, when she was to become the mistress of Radcliffe Manor.

"Now that Richard is dead," her grandfather had told her on his deathbed, "you, Katherine, are my heir."

But what was the other thing he had said? Something about there being so little to inherit, through his own folly. It didn't make sense. The Manor of Radcliffe was a substantial estate, taking in not only Radcliffe Hall, its breeding stables and land, but also Farley Grange further up the dale.

She knew that her grandfather had been attainted for treason years ago and his land taken away and given to the mighty Earl of Sussex, but the Earl had given it back to her father, Thomas Radcliffe. And now that Richard was dead, God rest his dear soul . . . Katherine turned away so that she might wipe away the tears that sprang to her eyes. Then she blew her nose and stuffed her handkerchief back in her sleeve. Now that Richard was dead, *she* was the heir to Radcliffe.

"Katherine, my dear. You have been so busy about the place, that this is the first opportunity I have had to speak with you." Lord Henry Scrope, her grandfather's dear friend and Richard's guardian, smiled gently if a trifle nervously upon her. Poor man, he had had to cope with her mother's anguish since he had arrived. *Well*, thought Katherine, *he'll not have me weeping all over him*.

"My lord," she said, giving him a brilliant smile. "We shall be forever in your debt for all you have done for Richard . . ." Her face muscles hurt in her effort to retain the smile. ". . . and for us."

He took her hands between his. They were the hands of a soldier, a campaigner in the border wars, rough-skinned and hard. But Katherine also knew Lord Scrope to be kindness itself. Her mother had told her how Harry Scrope had remained her grandfather's friend, despite the fact that Sir Philip had taken part in the treasonous Rising of the North against Queen Elizabeth. He had even taken Richard as his ward, when Richard had become the Lord of Radcliffe upon their father's death.

His hands squeezed hers until they hurt. "I cannot tell you how sorry I am about young Dickon. I swear to God Himself, I did everything in my power to save him. My own physician attended him." His face working with emotion, he dropped her hands and turned his head from her.

"I know you did," Katherine said, touching his arm. "You were like a father to him, my lord. No one would doubt that he received the best of care."

Lord Scrope sniffed inelegantly and she liked him the more for it.

"Once the fever struck, it went through the castle like wildfire. Eleven died and many more were sick . . . and still are."

"And yet you have ridden all this way with Richard to bury him."

"I could not leave you and your mother alone at this time." His bushy eyebrows lowered in a half-smiling frown. "You know, you are a remarkable girl, my dear Kate. I know well how deeply you loved your brother and your grandfather and yet you have been a pillar of strength this day."

She drew herself up proudly. "As the mistress of Radcliffe Manor, I must learn to be in constant control of my emotions, my lord. I cannot allow my tenants and retainers to see me as a weak woman."

The smile faded, leaving only the frown. "Mistress of Radcliffe? Surely your mother has told you—"

"My mother has spoken hardly one word to me since the news of Richard's death reached us."

"But before that. When Richard was alive. Surely you knew." Lord Scrope's face, which had been pale before, now grew red and he looked about him as if desperately seeking someone to come to his aid.

"Knew what?" demanded Katherine, her exasperation overruling her good manners.

"I must speak with your mother," he muttered, turning from her.

"She is incapable of rational thought at present. Besides, it would be unkind to discuss anything of moment with her today. You may speak straightly with me, my lord."

"No, Katherine, I may not. You are still but a lass of sixteen—"

"I had my seventeenth birthday last month," Katherine reminded him hotly.

"Sixteen, seventeen. I will not be bullied by you into doing something I do not wish to do. At times, my dear Katherine, you remind me very much of your father."

She lifted her chin. "And he, of course, was reviled by all," she said bitterly.

"Thomas Radcliffe was a hotheaded young fool, but he had many good points. Alas, his early death did not give him the chance to prove himself."

"My mother hated him."

Lord Scrope heaved an exasperated sigh. "I am not here to bandy words with you about your late father, God rest his soul. I will leave you now to go speak with your mother."

Having given her a stiff little bow, he strode across the great hall, to make his way to her mother's side.

As Katherine watched them together, she saw her mother dart a shocked look across the hall at her. She also saw how her little hand took Lord Scrope's arm in a convulsive grip to hurry him away into the parlor.

Her stomach cramped. Something was being hidden from her. She had the feeling that the secret was about to be unfolded—and suddenly she did not wish to hear it.

Turning her back on the assembled guests, she hurried into the passageway behind the great oaken screen. The strain of the entire day, the realization that her beloved brother and Grandy lay in the cold, damp vault under the stones of Wensley Church, never more to laugh or play or make music with her, suddenly overwhelmed her.

She leaned her head against the rough stone wall and at last allowed herself to give way to her grief.

"So this is where you have hidden yourself."

Katherine scrubbed angrily at her eyes, as Edward came through the screen door, but she knew that she could not hide their swollen redness from him.

"Oh, my poor Kate."

It was only natural that he should hold out his arms to her, and even more natural that she should move inside them, to sob out all her loneliness and fears against his breast.

"I knew you would not desert me," she gulped, between sobs.

"My dear Kate."

She held up her face to him, shining with love, her lips moist and parted. His face came nearer, his head blotting out the guttering flames of the torches in the wall sconces. His mouth closed on hers and with eager hunger she responded, opening her mouth to his. This was the kiss of man and woman, not of childhood companions.

"My darling Edward," she murmured, when they paused to suck in air. "I knew you loved me. I knew it."

His arms grew slack as she spoke and, though she caught at his sleeves to hold him, he moved back from her, setting a space between them. The color had drained from his face, but for the two splashes of red on his cheekbones.

"I pray your forgiveness, Katherine. I have forgot myself." He looked positively sick, his body shaking. "Your grief . . ." He put out a hand to her and then snatched it away again, as if he feared that she might take it in hers.

"What in the name of heaven ails you?" cried Katherine. "In the name of God, Edward, you have but kissed me, not *mounted* me!"

"You do yourself shame to speak so crudely," he admonished her.

"Then stop acting like a fool. Admit you love me. I cannot

understand why you will not admit it." Her voice rose as she vented her frustration.

"Be still, Katherine. You are overwrought. Permit me to take you back to your mother."

She gritted her teeth. "Not until we have this out. First you tell me that you cannot marry me, but that you do not love another woman. Then you kiss me as if you love me in truth." She came closer to him and laid her hand upon the sleeve of his black silk doublet. "I challenge you to look into my eyes, Edward, and tell me that was merely a kiss between friends," she whispered.

This time he did not move away. "If I were to marry anyone, Katherine, it would be you," he said, in a voice of despair.

"There, I knew it." Katherine threw back her head to gaze at him triumphantly.

"But I cannot marry you, nor any other woman," he continued, as if she had not spoken.

She stamped her foot like a child. "Why? Why? I demand to know why."

"I cannot tell you." His voice was now as lacking in expression as his face. "Do not ask me. Let us go to your mother."

He took her arm in a firm grip, but she threw his hand off and ran to the door, flinging her arms wide to bar his way. "You shall not pass until you have given me an explanation," she told him.

He approached her warily, and took her wrists to draw her arms down, but she lashed out at him, striking him hard across the face.

"Devil take you, Kate," he said, goaded beyond endurance. "That is enough. You are behaving like a wildcat. I recognize that you have cause to be upset, but you have gone too far."

Tears filled her eyes. "I beg you to forgive me, Edward. You are right, I am overwrought." She placed her hands together in supplication. "I promise to be good, if only you will tell me why you are treating me so cruelly. You know I have always loved you. Our families spoke of our marriage when we were only infants." Her voice broke on a sob. "What have I done to have so turned you against me?"

"You must believe me when I tell you that you have done nothing. It is I who have changed."

"Then you do not love me anymore?"

He turned his face from her. "I love you, but I love God more," he murmured.

"But, Edward. You can love both God and me at the same time. It was God Himself who ordained marriage."

"Not for a priest."

He spoke so softly, his head still averted from her, that she was sure she had misheard him. "What did you say?"

He turned slowly to face her, his jaw resolute. "I said, 'Not for a priest.'"

For a priest, she repeated to herself. Then the enormity of what he had said penetrated her mind.

"You are going to be a priest?" she whispered.

He nodded slowly.

"A Catholic priest, a Roman priest, not a Protestant parson?"

Again he nodded, but this time he spoke. "Now you know why I did not wish to tell you. It was better that you did not know."

"But . . . I do not understand. I have never thought of you as a particularly religious person, let alone a . . . a Papist."

"It has happened very slowly. When I met . . ." He hesitated for a moment, and then continued. "When I met a particular man in London a short while ago I was convinced."

Suddenly she knew that the man of whom he spoke was the priest who had come to her grandfather the night of his death.

"And you are certain?"

He smiled. "Oh yes," he said with great conviction, "I am certain."

An icy shiver ran down her spine. "And you are going to the Continent to train—"

He pressed his fingers on her lips. "Hush. Do not ask any more questions. It is safer if you do not know."

"Surely you do not think that I would betray you!" she cried.

"It is your safety that concerns me. I care nothing for my own."

It was not his words but the look upon his face as he spoke them that convinced her at last, for his glowing expression was that of a man already resigned to his own martyrdom.

Chapter 4

Katherine was about to launch into all the arguments she could muster, but she was forestalled by the entry of Tobias.

"We wish to be left alone, Master Ridley," she told the steward coldly.

"That's as may be, Mistress Katherine, but your lady mother has sent me for you. Lord and Lady Scrope are about to take their leave." His stern expression reminded her of her duty on this, the day of her brother's and grandfather's funeral.

"You must go, Katherine," Edward said softly. It was evident that he was greatly relieved at the steward's intervention.

Casting Edward a last, despairing look, she swept past them both and entered the hall.

"Ah, Katherine, there you are." The long-faced Lady Scrope held out her gloved hands and drew her into an embrace. The strong scent she wore did not quite cover the smell of horse liniment. "We must take our leave of you. Harry hasn't even had time to see the children since his return." She patted Katherine's cheek and peered into her eyes. "Put your trust in God, dear lass. He will carry you through this terrible time."

Katherine nodded, trying to smile, despite the large lump in her throat. She held out her hands to Lord Scrope. "I thank you again, both of you, for all your kindness." She looked around, searching for her mother. "Has my mother bidden you farewell already?"

"She has retired to her chamber," said Lady Scrope. "I fear it has all been too much for her."

"Indeed it has, poor woman," said Lord Scrope. His kindly eyes were deeply troubled. "I believe Lady Colborne is with her at present."

Lady Scrope sniffed. "Much good that will do your mother! The last person she needs now is her sister. She asked me to tell you that she wishes you to go to her later, Katherine, when those guests who are not staying the night have left."

It was very much later, close to six o'clock that evening, when those who were not staying the night departed, accompanied by flaring torches to light the way in the cold darkness.

Katherine bade farewell to her mother's parents—Lady Harcourt having haughtily declared that she preferred to sleep in her own bed even if it did mean a bitter ride across the High Moor—and then turned from the doorway and shivered. She was weary beyond measure and longed for her bed and the oblivion she hoped sleep would bring.

"I am glad I don't have to ride home," Joanna said, giving her a wan smile. She, too, looked near to collapse with fatigue and her hazel eyes were swollen and dark-circled.

Katherine held out her arms and, in the shadow of the entranceway, the two sisters embraced. It was good to feel Joanna's warm, plump body against hers. That, at least, remained the same.

"Oh, Kate." Joanna's mouth quivered.

"Now, now. No weeping." Katherine gave her a little shake. "You have been the strong one today. I have watched you darting about the place, giving orders, being a support to Mother and our grandparents, making sure our guests were comfortable and well-fed. Whilst I have been as prickly as a bramble bush with everyone."

"Nonsense, dearest. Mother herself said how strong and reliable you were, not like me, a constantly flowing waterpipe."

"I am sure that Mother did not say that of you."

"No, but I say so," said Joanna with a wan smile. "Which reminds me, Aunt Isobel told me that Mother is asking for you. She is in her bedchamber, but not sleeping. She refuses to take a sleeping draught until she sees you."

Katherine's heart sank. She had no desire to face her mother when both of them were so weary and on edge. She was likely to lose her temper, and that she could not do, not today. "I shall go to her," she said, with a heavy sigh.

Joanna looked up into her sister's eyes. "Be kind to her, Kate," she begged. "This is not the day to be cold with her."

Katherine bit back a retort. Joanna was right, but, by Saint Peter, it would be hard to do when she felt as if her life and the world about her had shattered into a thousand pieces.

When she entered her mother's bedchamber, she found her aunt, Lady Isobel Colborne, and her daughter, Bess, there.

"There you are, Kate," her aunt cried in a bright voice, as if she were welcoming her to a dance.

Far taller than her younger sister, Isobel's black velvet gown, its bodice inlaid with pearls, set her fair beauty off to perfection. Katherine felt a pang of compassion when she saw how plain her mother looked beside her sister, her large, dark eyes great pools in her ashen face.

Bess turned to smile at her cousin. She was younger than Katherine by five years, but they were so alike they could have been twin sisters, for Bess was as dark as her mother was fair. And she certainly did not resemble her father, Lord Ingram Colborne, or her three brothers, all of whom were either fair or sandy-haired.

"Forgive me, Isobel, but I wish to speak with Katherine alone." Alyssa's voice sounded hollow, as if it were dredged up from a deep well.

"Of course, Sister." Isobel bent to peck at Alyssa's cheek. "Remember now what I told you. You must speak to Father about it as soon as possible, so that everything is set in order."

"Yes, Isobel," Alyssa said wearily. Her eyes followed her sister and niece as they went out. Then she turned to Katherine. "Sit down here, Kate," she said, patting the stool beside her chair.

As Katherine came nearer to her mother, she could see that her lips were raw where she had chewed upon them and her little hands, usually so still and soothing, fluttered about her neck and her severe black gown, like restless moths.

"What was Aunt Isobel saying?" Katherine asked, hoping to postpone whatever it was her mother wanted to talk to her about.

Her mother lifted her head and gave her the direct, unwavering look that always made Katherine feel uneasy. "We were talking of where we were going to live." Her mouth twisted into a wry little smile. "She wished to make it clear that we could not expect to move in to Colborne Place."

Katherine felt as if she had been turned to stone. "I don't understand," she whispered. "Why should we move to Colborne Place? Why should we live anywhere else but Radcliffe?"

Her mother rubbed her hand across her mouth, her tongue darting over her lips. "That is why I have sent for you, dearest." The hands grew even more agitated, picking at the jet beading on her bodice. "I thought you knew. But Lord Scrope said that—"

Katherine leaned forward to grip her mother's hands. "Radcliffe is ours, Mother," she said fiercely. "Now that Richard is dead, I am the heir. My father was the Lord of Radcliffe. I am his eldest living child. Therefore, Radcliffe is *mine*."

Her mother sighed and withdrew her hands from Katherine's to fold them in her lap. "Would to God it were so, Kate, but it is not. I should have explained before now, but I never thought there would be any need to, with Richard so healthy and—" She drew her breath in a dry sob and squeezed her eyes shut.

"Oh, Mother." Katherine leaned forward to embrace her, but inside she was seething with impatience. Yet, at the same time, she dreaded hearing what her mother had to say. She laid her hot cheek against her mother's cold one and then sat down on the stool again. "Tell me now," she said.

Her mother opened her eyes. "Radcliffe is entailed to male heirs only."

"It cannot be. Joisse Radcliffe, Grandy's grandmother, was the heiress to Radcliffe. That is why it is ours today. Grandy has often talked about her." Katherine lifted her head proudly. "He said that I was very like her."

Her mother's lips quivered into a little smile. "I know. He told me the same thing. But that was long before . . . before your grandfather was attainted for treason. He was stripped of all his lands and they were given to our kinsman, Thomas Radcliffe, the mighty Earl of Sussex."

Bewildered, Katherine shook her head. "Then how in the name of all the saints—"

Her mother held up her hand. "Hear me out, Katherine. No more interruptions, if you please. I am weary beyond belief and I cannot think if you keep interrupting me." Again, that direct look. "Your father served the Earl of Sussex and Queen Elizabeth most loyally during the northern rising." A look of flint entered her eyes. "To the point of arresting Sir Philip, his own father, and having him imprisoned. The Earl of Sussex rewarded his loyalty by returning to him the entire Radcliffe estate."

Katherine could not bear to sit quiet a moment longer. "Then it is still ours, as I told you."

"No, Katherine, it is not, for when the Earl of Sussex bestowed it upon your father, a new provision was made that the Radcliffe estate was from thenceforth to be entailed to heirs male only. When your father was killed, I was expecting a child. And that child, Richard, being male, became the Lord of Radcliffe. But you, my dearest," Alyssa said, with a sorrowful little smile, "are female. Therefore the estate reverts once more to the Earl of Sussex."

Katherine sprang up to pace about the chamber, her farthingaled skirts knocking against the furniture. "I cannot believe it. Why didn't you or Grandfather tell me all this before?"

Alyssa put a hand to her forehead. "I have told you already. Because we did not think there was any reason to do so."

Katherine ceased her pacing to face her mother. "The Earl of Sussex is immensely wealthy. After all, he is the Lord Chamberlain of England, one of the Queen's favorite councillors. What need has he of another estate in the most remote part of Yorkshire? If we ask him, would he not permit us to keep Radcliffe?"

Her mother's little smile was infuriating. It made Katherine feel like an infant in the nursery.

"No, my child. He would not. Sussex detested your grandfather. To have a kinsman, however distant, accounted a traitor was an acute embarrassment to the mighty Earl. It was a great disappointment for him when Philip was released from prison. It was an even greater disappointment when I brought forth a son, the male heir necessary for us to retain Radcliffe. No, Sussex will not take pity on us. It will give him great pleasure to turn us out of Radcliffe, and give it away to one of his retainers or, more like, sell it to the highest bidder."

Katherine confronted her mother, her hands clenched into fists. "He cannot. I will not permit it. Radcliffe is mine, ours. We shall refuse to leave it."

"Kate, Kate, my dearest Kate. Would you have us carried out the door thrown over some armed soldier's back, like sacks of grain?"

"I would have us fight, at least, for Radcliffe, for my inheritance, not walk out meekly like terrified mice."

Her mother's head drooped. "I cannot talk of this any more with you tonight. I am too exhausted. No," she said sharply, holding up her hand as Katherine opened her mouth to protest. "No more, I said. Leave me now and send Margery in to help me to bed."

Katherine stood in the center of the chamber, her body trembling. "I think the world is coming to an end. It is as if Doomsday has come upon us." Her hands opened and shut at her sides.

Her mother offered her no comfort, but turned her head away. "Leave me, I said." Her voice was harsh.

Katherine gave her a glowering look and left the chamber.

When Margery went in, Alyssa's face was buried in the velvet cushion. "There, there, my dearie." Alyssa felt the servant's hand upon her shoulder. "'Tis time tha went to thy bed. I've a good posset with some syrup of wild poppy here, that Dr. Tredwell prescribed for thee. Tha'll drink it down now, and then get to thy bed, and sleep. There's nothing like a good sleep to make thee feel better."

Alyssa could have laughed out loud. In less than one week, she had lost her home, her son, and Philip, the very light of her life. And one night's sleep could make her feel better? Nay, not one night nor one thousand nights.

"But afore tha drinks this, there's one says he must see thee tonight." Margery shifted her weight from one foot to the other.

"What in the name of heaven do you mean? Is it a member of the family, one of the servants?"

Margery shook her head.

Alyssa glared at her. "You must be out of your mind, then, to think that I would see some stranger tonight. I am surprised at you, Margery, for even mentioning it. Give me my drink and send the man packing. Or, if he insists, tell him to speak with Master Ridley." For she had suddenly thought that perhaps the man was an envoy from the Earl of Sussex. It would be just like that vulture to descend upon them on the day of Richard's and Philip's burial.

When she took the pewter cup from Margery, she found that her hands were shaking so hard she could barely hold it. Dear Christ, if only she could drain down ten such potions and slip away from this life. But that would mean eternal hellfire, never more to see Philip again. *Oh my darling, my darling, how can I go on living without you?* Now she knew the agony Philip must have felt when his wife, Laura, died.

The pain of her loss struck her like a violent blow in her breast. Gasping, she bent over, rocking back and forth, the liquid from the cup slopping onto her skirts.

Margery took the cup from her hands. "The man says that Sir Philip asked him to come to thee," she said softly.

Alyssa flung up her head to stare at her servant. "Sir Philip? How can you make mock of me thus, Margery, when you know full well that Sir Philip is dead?"

"Husha, husha, my dearie. This man saw Sir Philip afore he died, he says."

Alyssa's eyes widened. Maybe the man had a last message from Philip for her. Her hands clutched convulsively on the arms of the chair. She drew herself up. "You should have said so before. Have him sent in."

"There's nobbut me knows about him, mistress. He swore me to secrecy."

"Then fetch him in yourself, Margery. And be quick about it. Tell the man, whoever he is, that I can give him only five minutes of my time."

"Aye, mistress, I'll do that." Margery hurried away, leaving Alyssa to wrack her brain as to who this visitor sent by Philip might be. A friend from Scotland, perhaps? One of the exiles who fled to the Continent after the northern rebellion? Surely not, when it was twelve years since the Rising. Most of them were either dead by now, or living in poverty in foreign lands.

She heard soft footsteps outside the door and it opened. "This be the gentleman," Margery murmured, bobbing a curtsy as the black-cloaked and hooded figure passed her to enter the chamber.

"May we speak in private, Mistress Radcliffe?" Although the man spoke softly, there was no disguising the beauty of his voice. And when he put back his hood, she saw that his face was beautiful also. He reminded her of Philip as she had first known him.

She hesitated at his request, and then nodded at Margery. "Wait outside, if you please, Margery. And do not permit anyone to enter. You understand?"

"Aye, mistress." She bobbed a little curtsy to both of them and went out, quietly latching the door behind her.

"You have a message for me from . . . from Sir Philip?" she asked with a little frown.

"In a manner of speaking, yes." He looked about him. "Might I sit down? I have ridden a great distance and—"

Alyssa flushed. "Pray forgive me, sir. I am forgetting my manners. Be seated on the bench and warm yourself by the fire. May I send for some refreshment for you?"

He held up his hands, delicate as a woman's. "No, I beg you. I have very little time. Besides, it would be better if no one else knew that I am here."

"Will you at least tell me your name, sir?"

He gave her a tentative smile. "For your sake, I should prefer not to." She did not return the smile. "You surely cannot believe that someone sent to me by Sir Philip Radcliffe, whom I have buried this day, would be in danger from me, sir?"

"No, I do not think that. It is for your own safety that I withhold my name. As it is, my very presence here places you and your household in danger."

She knew then. A long sigh escaped her. "You are a priest, a Catholic priest."

He bowed his head. "I am."

"Someone sent for you to give Philip the last rites?"

He nodded.

"Oh, why didn't he tell me?" she cried. "Surely he could have trusted me."

"He did trust you. But, knowing the penalty for harboring a priest, he did not wish to place you in peril."

"Then why did he ask you to come to me now, after his death?"

"Because he was even more concerned for the mortal peril of your soul when your time for death comes."

A tide of warmth flooded Alyssa, where a moment before she had been cold. "So . . . he confessed all to you." Her eyes avoided his.

"He did."

"And he wished for me to confess to you as well."

"That was his wish."

"But I am not a Catholic, sir priest."

"I believe you were baptized as such."

Alyssa opened her mouth to hotly deny this, and then closed it again. The priest was right. Not only baptized a Catholic, but brought up as one in those days before Elizabeth came to the throne.

"I thought there were no priests left in England," she said, wishing to avoid the subject of her confession.

"We have come to change that."

"Ah. Then you must be one of the new missionary priests from the Continent."

"I am."

"Your coming will cause, has already caused, great disruption in our land," she said passionately. She and Philip had argued the point many times. "You seek to overthrow the Queen."

"Not so. We are strictly forbidden to deal in any respect with matters of state or policy in the realm. We come only to administer the sacraments, to preach the gospel to the poor, persecuted Catholics of our dear country who are denied the solace of the ancient faith of their ancestors."

She marveled at his restraint. He spoke in such ardent yet gentle tones that she could see how easy it would be to be swayed by him.

"Are you a Jesuit?" she asked.

He inclined his head. "I am an unworthy member of that blessed Society."

"Sir Philip read a copy of Father Campion's Brag to me."

The priest started a little at this. "I prefer to call it a 'Challenge' rather than a 'Brag.'" An almost mischievous smile tugged at his mouth.

"Never tell me that *you* are Edmund Campion!" Alyssa whispered.

"I do not wish to tell you that, Mistress Radcliffe. It is best that you do not know my name." He clasped his hands together. "Come, I have only a few minutes. Is it your wish to make your confession to me, or no?"

She smoothed her suddenly damp palms down her stiff skirts. "It is a very large sin," she whispered.

"But a sin that has been confessed to me already, and absolved."

She met his eyes. "Now I know why Philip was smiling on his deathbed. He was never at peace within himself in the matter of religion, nor of his . . . our sin."

"But he was at peace when he died?"

"Yes, Father Campion. Thanks to you, he was."

"Thanks to God, not me," he reminded her. "I am but His instrument. You, too, my daughter, can attain that sense of peace."

She hesitated. "Even though I am a Protestant and intend to remain so?"

"Even then." His lips twitched. "Although, I own that I wish I had more time to devote to talking with you on that subject, but, alas, I do not."

Alyssa drew in a deep breath and let it out slowly. "Very well. If it was Philip's wish, I shall confess to you."

As he drew the stole from his sleeve and put it about his neck, she went on her knees before him, placing her hands between his. "Bless me, Father, for I have sinned." The old words, newly remembered, came easily to her lips.

When she remembered that these delicate hands had held Philip's as he spoke his last words, she did not find it difficult to confess to him. It was as if Philip himself were communing with her.

When she had finished and he had pronounced absolution, he helped her to her feet. "I regret I cannot remain any longer," he told her. "As it is, I fear I have placed you and your family in peril by coming here."

"You must be sheltered by some family in the region. Surely they are in even greater peril."

"Ah, but they, being Catholic, take little account of the cost, when they have a priest to minister unto them. Catholics, being so laden down with fines and forfeits and deprivation of office and freedom, have little to lose. Your family, being Protestant, will lose far more if it be discovered you have had a priest here."

When she had led him to the door, Alyssa bent her knee and kissed his hand. "I am eternally grateful to you, Father Campion." She stood up and looked into his face. "You will take care, won't you? I fear greatly for your life."

"Then do not, for my life is worth nothing. This, our enterprise, is all. When we took it on, I and my brethren in Christ, we knew the cost. We knew well that imprisonment and torture and death lay at the end of the road. It was thus that the Catholic faith was planted, and thus that it will be restored."

Alyssa looked away from him for a moment, deeply moved. How she envied his unswerving, joyful faith. "You have not given me my penance," she said, suddenly remembering.

He smiled gently. "I will tell you what I told Sir Philip: that these past several years without sin have been your years of atonement. The constant memory of your sin and your regret that it was committed has been penance enough." He laid his hands on her bowed head. "*Pax vobiscum*, my daughter."

When at last she climbed into bed, Alyssa did feel more at peace than she had since the terrible day of Philip's death. And yet still she knew in her heart that her only regret for her sin was that it had caused Philip so much guilt throughout their otherwise contented years together.

Chapter 5

Captain Brendan Fitzgerald, of the Queen's army in Ireland, sat upon a damp sack of horse feed in his tent. He was trying to pen a letter by the dim light issuing from the horn-paned lantern, which hung from a meat hook stuck in the tent pole.

"God's blood!" he muttered, as yet another splash of rainwater fell onto his paper. "Colum, get in here! There's another whoreson hole in this tent."

His groom came in, with him the smell of wet horses and dung.

"For the love of God, Fitzgerald," muttered the other occupant of the tent, Lieutenant Jarvis, "can't you fix it yourself, to save that groom of yours having to come in? Pah." He waved his hand before his face, in a vain attempt to freshen the air.

Brendan grinned. "Is that a delicate way of telling me that my horse groom stinks?" he asked. "Of course he does. We all do. What would you be expecting, after an eleven-month campaign in the bogs and woods of Munster?"

"I certainly didn't expect it to rain without ceasing in the month of September."

Brendan moved his feet in the runnel of oozing mud on the floor of the tent. "Ah, but wait until December. This is a fine mist compared to the December rains."

"God's blood, how do you stand it, Fitzgerald? But then, I'm forgetting. You are an Irishman and know nothing else."

Brendan had grown accustomed to the superior attitude of the English officers. Several years in the Queen's army had schooled him—and his fellow Irish officers—to control his anger when confronted by English arrogance.

He glanced at Jarvis, who was beating his arms across his mud-splattered red coat in a vain attempt to get warm. "It would be wise of you to become something of an Irishman yourself, Jarvis. The rebels will have a fine time of it, to be sure, picking your red coat out on the hills with their muskets."

Jarvis surveyed Brendan's leather jerkin and frieze hose and the great mantle of wolf skins wrapped about him. "Would you have me dress like an Irish kerne?" he sneered.

"I would not, my friend. Be assured, you will find no kerne dressed as well as I."

From behind them, Brendan heard his groom snicker. "Have you the hole mended, Colum?" he barked, speaking in Irish.

"I have, sir. 'Twas but a small tear in the canvas." Colum backed out with every appearance of servitude, but when Brendan caught his servant's eye, he saw the look of contempt mixed with amusement there.

He settled the plank of wood that served as a desk on his lap again. "By the bye, Jarvis, you were wrong in thinking that I have never been anywhere but Ireland. As a youth, I spent two years in England."

Jarvis looked up from his task of drying his sword and polishing it. "Oh? I thought you were educated in Dublin."

"I was indeed. But I was also sent to England to improve my education . . . and for a little civilization."

Jarvis gave him a sharp look, but the bland expression on Brendan's face allayed his suspicions that Captain Fitzgerald was mocking him.

He was a strange man, thought Jarvis. After sharing a tent with Fitzgerald for four months he kept thinking he was beginning to understand him, but then the Irishman would say or do something that was totally incomprehensible, and he knew that Fitzgerald had eluded him once again.

There were many Irishmen who served with the English army

fighting against the rebels, but generally one knew exactly what their motives were: money, advancement, hatred of a particular clan or rebel. . . . But there was no knowing with Fitzgerald. He talked very little about his background, although his name bespoke his connection with the Geraldine clan, most of whose members were numbered amongst the rebels. Yet he had received a fine education, far superior to that of Jarvis himself, though he would never admit it. Now here he was, saying that he'd lived in England for two years. *There's no fathoming the man*, Jarvis thought, shaking his head.

The tent flap was flung back, letting in a gust of rain, and the new-appointed deputy of Munster, Captain Walter Ralegh came in, filling the tent with his height and vitality.

"God's wounds, what a night." He shook himself like a dog, casting drops of water on Brendan's paper.

Brendan sighed. "At this rate I shall never get this letter finished, to be sure."

"Writing to your sweetheart, Fitzgerald? Who is she, one of your kinsman Desmond's camp followers?" Ralegh clapped his hands to his sides, laughing at this sally against the captain. For Gerald Fitzgerald, the Earl of Desmond, was the leader of the Irish rebels.

Brendan's lips smiled. "Not so, Captain Ralegh. In point of fact, I am writing to the Earl of Sussex."

Ralegh threw back his head, greeting this return witticism with a roar of laughter that rang in Brendan's ears. "Just so, just so, the Earl of Sussex," he said, in his pronounced West Country accent. "I'll say this for you, Fitzgerald, you know how to give back what you get in full measure. Sussex, eh? You aim high, m'lad."

Still laughing, Ralegh hooked a stool from a corner of the tent and sat upon it. "Sit down, Jarvis, sit down," he told the lieutenant, who had risen upon his arrival. "No ceremony, if you please. We are at our leisure at present. If you can call sitting in a boggy wood in the County of Limerick leisure. Christ, what a godforsaken country!"

Brendan did not rise to the bait. In truth, Ireland *was* like a country that had been forsaken by God at present. And had been ever since Brendan had known it. As he chewed the end of his quill, half his mind listened to the conversation between Ralegh and Jarvis, the other half dwelled on the letter he was trying to write—and his reasons for writing it.

Fighting and murder and cattle-stealing had been part of the ways of Ireland since time began, he knew that from his mother. And though there had once been a time when the Christian church flourished in Ireland, that time certainly was not now. In their constant warfare against each other, the clans had indiscriminately destroyed church and castle. But the coming of the English under the Tudor monarchs had brought not the civilization they promised but death.

Five counties in Munster had been laid waste. Those people who had not been slaughtered, or hanged, perished from starvation. They lived in caves, devouring whatever scraps they could find. A little plot of watercress was a great feast to them. Some followed the army, who had precious little to eat themselves.

A few resorted to cannibalism to stay alive.

The sights Brendan had seen in the past two years were burned upon his memory. He was weary of famine and death and destruction. He wanted no more of it.

"Earlier this year, I wrote to Walsingham myself," Ralegh was telling Jarvis, "and said that unless the Queen sent a good Englishman to govern the province of Munster she could spend a hundred thousand pounds without any results. The war against the rebels has lasted two, three years and all we have to show for it is a thousand traitors more than there were at the start. And the new amnesty hasn't made one jot of difference." Ralegh spat into a pool of mud at his feet. "If I had my way I'd slaughter the lot of 'em."

Brendan's teeth clenched and then he forced himself to relax. "Ah, but then you would have no people to conquer, would you, my friend?"

"God's death, Fitzgerald, you know right well that our chief concern is that Spain or France could invade England from Ireland. Why, along the west coast it's easier to find an Irishman who speaks Spanish than one who speaks English. You know well the proverb: 'He that will in England win, let him in Ireland begin.' All the English seek is to bring peace, stop the clans from slaughtering one other, and govern the island with good laws. That, and bring the people back to Christianity. God's truth, man, half of them are not even baptized! I've even heard of men who boast of having three wives."

"Ralegh's right, you know, Fitzgerald," piped up Jarvis.

Brendan was tempted to pick the young Englishman up and throw him face-down in the mud. Only four months in the country and Jarvis was an expert. For that matter, Ralegh himself had been in the country a little less than a year, and yet here he was lording it over everyone. The man's high-vaulting ambition knew no limits.

Sensing that Ralegh was watching him, Brendan met his bright blue eyes and saw the glint of amusement there, this time not at his expense. Ralegh thumped Jarvis on the shoulder. "When you've been in this country fighting in the Queen's army for as long as Captain Fitzgerald has, m'lad, then you can offer your opinion. He may be only a few years older than you, but he has a lifetime of experience. Never forget it."

Brendan grinned at the red-faced Jarvis. "Do not be minding Captain Ralegh. We all think we are experts on this strange land of mine. The truth is that 'tis like a woman, unfathomable—and unconquerable."

"We shall see about that." Ralegh stood up to stretch and yawn. A sardonic smile crossed his handsome face. "I'll to my comfortable cot." He was about to open the tent flap, but then turned back. "I forgot to tell you. News has come that the papist priest Campion has been taken and lies in the Tower."

Brendan looked up. "Campion?"

"Aye, the Jesuit who challenged the Queen's councillors to a verbal duel in the matter of religion. He's been charged with treason."

"He'll be found guilty, of course," said Jarvis.

"Aye. Apparently he has already given out some names under torture."

Brendan closed his eyes for a moment.

"What's the matter, Captain? Are you weeping for the papist? No doubt you secretly sympathize with him, being a papist yourself."

"No, Captain, I am not a papist, as you well know. And, yes, Captain Ralegh, I am in sympathy with any man who is racked by the Queen's rackmaster. Besides, I knew Edmund Campion," he said, standing up. He was taller even than Ralegh, and had to bend his head to avoid it touching the top of the tent. "He taught me for a few months when I was a lad of thirteen. You may not know that Campion lived in Dublin eleven or so years ago. I was lodging with the Recorder of Dublin, James Stanihurst at the time, and Campion came from England to live with him also. For a while, Richard Stanihurst and I were taught by Campion there."

Ralegh's attention was caught. "Then that must have been when he wrote his history of Ireland."

"That is so. Have you read it?" Only on this one subject, literature, were the two captains on common ground.

"Aye, I have," replied Ralegh. "The Earl of Leicester kindly lent me his copy."

"Ah, yes. He was Campion's patron, was he not?"

"Best to forget that," Ralegh said gruffly.

"I believe that Campion had become a Catholic by the time he came to Ireland, but I do not remember any talk of his becoming a priest." Brendan shivered. "'Tis a pity to think of such a fine man being tortured."

Ralegh turned again to leave. "Well, so far he's given away very little, save a few names of the people he visited in Yorkshire."

"What will happen to them, I wonder?" asked Jarvis.

Ralegh shrugged. "That depends. If he only visited them, that is one thing. But if he said mass or administered the sacraments, that is another. For that they could be imprisoned or even tried for treason themselves."

Chapter 6

It was a month before Brendan received a reply to his letter and another month before he was released from the army and given a permit to go to England. He spent a few days in Dublin with his old friend, Richard Stanihurst, who had once been Edmund Campion's pupil at Oxford University. There, Brendan was able to scrub himself clean in hot baths and find some more suitable clothing before journeying to London.

On the day of his departure, news of Campion's trial arrived. "He will be found guilty, of course," Richard said, looking up from the letter. "Guilty of treason. That is what he is accused of. But I know how much he loves England and Queen Elizabeth. His guilt is solely that of being a Catholic priest."

They sat in silence for a while, mourning the downfall of their revered master.

"Four times they forced him to debate with England's leading theologians, and that after having been racked!" Richard told Brendan.

"And they refused him books or paper with which to prepare for the debates."

He looked down at his letter again. "Apparently, he told his accusers at the trial that if they condemned him they would also be condemning all their own ancestors and priests and kings, who were Catholic also."

Brendan gripped his friend's arm. "You must take care not to show your loyalty to Campion so plainly, lest 'tis thought you also follow his creed."

Richard's eyes gleamed. "I have half a mind to—"

"Beware, Dick. 'Tis a dangerous path to tread. Let us admire our teacher privately, but be ever mindful of his terrible fate. When will he be executed, that is, if he is found guilty?"

"Is there any doubt? Apparently, there will not be much delay after the verdict is given. Doubtless, you will have reached London by then. Will you go to his execution?"

Brendan shuddered. "Not I. 'Tis more than my fill I have had of killings. I prefer to remember Edmund Campion as I knew him, not with his beautiful face contorted in agony and his body mutilated and cut into four quarters."

Brendan arrived in London on the last day of November. It was raining, a steady downpour that brought a smile to Brendan's lips. "So, even in mighty London, it rains," he murmured to himself.

"Been raining these past two weeks, it 'as," said his boatman, as he rowed him downstream to Bermondsey. "Been good for business, though. The city roads is inches deep in mud, so everybody's taken to the river. 'Sides, the roads is clogged with people, all lined up to watch Father Campion pass on his way to Tyburn tomorrer."

Brendan's heart lurched. "So, he is to be executed tomorrow?"

"Aye, he is." The boatman paused, resting his oars, to peer more closely at Brendan. "Where've you been then, sir, that you don't know that? Everybody knows that."

Brendan gave him a faint smile. "I have come from the west."

"Ah, that explains it, then. I thought you sounded different, an' all."

When they reached the steps at the foot of the lane leading to the Earl of Sussex's great mansion in Bermondsey, Brendan was glad to escape the garrulous boatman's chatter.

The thought of Campion's coming ordeal sat heavy upon him. As one of the Earl's servants led him through the rain, Brendan gazed down at the muddied gravel path to avoid conversation.

Upon entering the house, he could not help smiling a very small smile, however, as he recalled Walter Ralegh's amazement upon learning that the Earl of Sussex had summoned Captain Fitzgerald to London.

"So you were writing to Sussex, in truth, then?" Ralegh had said, his surprise for once leaving him at a loss for words.

"I was. The Earl is my patron."

The look on Ralegh's face had been almost full compensation for his many jibes and sneers. Almost.

One of the house servants showed him into a private chamber. "His lordship will be with you shortly," he said, and left him alone.

Brendan looked about the small room. Despite its size, it was richly decorated, the walls paneled in rosewood, the ornate plaster ceiling painted in bright colors, the draperies hanging at the paned windows fashioned of crimson velvet.

Quite a contrast to his quarters for the past while, he thought wryly.

Seven years had passed since he had last seen the Earl. Since that time they had corresponded by letter only, and infrequently at that.

When the Earl of Sussex entered, Brendan's first thought when he rose from his deep obeisance was how sick and old he looked, far older than his fifty-five years. His tall figure was stooped like an ancient's, with hunched shoulders, and he was almost as emaciated as one of the starving people who dwelt in the hill caves in Munster.

"You are well, my lord?" he asked with some anxiety.

"Not as well as you, it would appear. You have grown several inches since last I saw you, Captain Fitzgerald."

"I was but a youth, then, my lord. And I would wish to remind you, sir, that I am no longer a captain," Brendan added firmly.

The Earl lowered himself into a chair by the fire. He stretched out his black-clad legs and lifted them onto a stool, wincing with pain as he did so. "Be seated," he barked, indicating the settle opposite him.

It was a command and Brendan obeyed.

"I am, as I told you in my letter, exceedingly displeased with you," Sussex told him. "Since I left Ireland, I have been your patron, overseen your education. I even brought you to England to—"

"To civilize me a little, my lord?" Brendan gave him a sweet smile.

The Earl's eyes narrowed. "Do not think to mock me, sirrah," he said in a voice of ice. "I have done far more than would be expected of me for a person of your position. And now you throw it back in my face and tell me that you refuse to serve in the Queen's army. You are an ungrateful dog!"

Brendan forced back the hot words that hovered on his lips. "So it must seem to you, my lord. But I beg you to understand my dilemma.

It is not that I flinch from duty. Not even from killing. But when I am become one of the instruments in the slow and dreadful slaughter of my own people, I can no longer stomach it."

He looked away from the dark, searching eyes and into the flames of the fire.

Sussex stirred impatiently. "It is what must be done to conquer the Irish, to bring them to God again, to—"

Brendan held up one hand. "Your pardon, my lord, but I have heard it all so many times before that I am heartily weary of it. What have you and the other governors of Ireland achieved in all these years? Nothing, absolutely nothing. Indeed, since you yourself left Ireland twenty years ago, matters there have grown steadily worse, not better."

Sussex put a hand up to his brow and rubbed it. "I begin to think we shall never solve the problem," he said softly, as if speaking to himself, "but we must, we must. Meanwhile, service in Ireland broke my health, as it has that of many other men. Since my return home to England, I have never been a truly well man."

He turned to survey Brendan with piercing eyes. "I was only thirty years old, not that much older than you, when I was appointed Lord Deputy. When I left the Court, I was a man of vigorous health, one of the best jousters." He held up one stiff-jointed hand. "Hard to believe now, eh? Only eight years later, I returned from Ireland, sick in body and spirit."

Brendan said nothing. He knew that Sussex spoke the truth. There had been many other men affected thus by Ireland. It was her way of wreaking vengeance upon them, he supposed.

"Would you have the same thing happen to me, my lord?" he asked eventually.

Sussex smiled his dry thin-lipped smile. "It would not happen to you. You are an Irishman, inured to the vagaries of its mists and rains and bogs."

"I fear that the time I spent inside the Pale and in England must have softened me somewhat, my lord." Brendan looked into the fire, staring at the leaping flames. "There have been many times when I wished to God I had been left uneducated," he said softly.

He waited for another explosion of "ungrateful dog!" but it did not come. They avoided each other's eyes, unspoken words hanging in the air.

Sussex fingered the chain of office on his chest, the golden Tudor roses glinting in the firelight. "Is it only the plight of the Irish people that troubles you?" he asked after a period of awkward silence.

"'Tis not only them," Brendan said with a heavy sigh. "It is as if . . . as if the country turns the soldiers themselves into savages. What I have seen makes me doubt the very existence of God."

"That is devil's talk, Brendan."

"And what I have seen is devil's work, my lord."

"Ah, you are speaking of the fort at Smerwick now."

"In truth, my lord, I am. To put six hundred men to the sword, when their officers have surrendered, is utter savagery, in my eyes."

"I would remind you that they were foreigners, not Irishmen. Italian and Spanish mercenaries."

"They were men, and had surrendered. Besides, there were women as well. Irish women. Some of them with child."

"Captain Ralegh was only following Lord Grey's orders, as you know. How could six hundred prisoners have been fed, with our army numbering only eight hundred and our soldiers themselves going hungry?"

"From a practical viewpoint you are right, of course, my lord. I told you that I am not the perfect soldier." Brendan gave him a bitter smile. "I am not like Captain Ralegh, for instance, who seems to gain immense pleasure from slaughtering his adversaries."

"Captain Ralegh is an able man. You would do very well to emulate him. He will go far."

"He will, indeed. Most particularly as he is kinsman to those who are close to Her Majesty." Brendan felt his face grow warm as he met the Earl's eyes. "He is, as you say, most able, my lord," he added hurriedly, "and well merits advancement. I hear that he wasted no time in getting himself comfortably settled at Court, now that he, too, has returned from Ireland."

Sussex lifted his feet, one by one, off the stool. It was obvious that the meeting was drawing to a close. "What is your intention, now that you have left the army? There is no place for *you* at Court, you realize."

There was no mistaking his meaning. Brendan stood up. "Even if there were, my lord, it would not be my wish," he said stiffly. "It is not in my nature to be a fawning courtier. I had hopes that, perhaps, I might purchase a small farm somewhere—"

"In Ireland?"

"Not in Ireland. It holds too many unhappy memories for me ever to be happy there again."

Besides, there was nothing to hold him in Ireland. None to mourn him if he never returned, neither mother nor sister nor brother. No one.

The Earl sat with his chin in his hand, staring into the fire for a while. "It might work," he murmured. He nodded his head several times, as if he were communing with the flaming logs, and then turned back to Brendan, who sat patiently waiting.

"I believe I may have the very place for you. It is not a farmstead, however, but a fine estate in Wensleydale."

"Where is that?"

"Pardon me. I forgot that you were not entirely conversant with the geography of England. Wensleydale is in the North Riding of Yorkshire."

"Ah, in Northern England. And this estate," Brendan asked hesitantly, "would it cost a great deal? I have saved most of my pay, there being little to spend it on in Limerick or even within the Pale, but I doubt that it would amount to—"

"It would be my gift to you," the Earl told him abruptly. "I am glad to be rid of it. Radcliffe Manor has caused me nothing but trouble."

"Radcliffe? But that is your name, my lord."

"Aye, it is. The Manor was owned by a distant kinsman of mine, but it has fallen into my hands again."

"Could you not be selling it for a fine price to someone?"

The Earl rose slowly to his feet, waving away Brendan's proffered arm. "Do you wish to have it or no? It is yours if you do, but I have no more time for quibbling with you. You have thrown away the chance you were given to gain advancement in the English army, despite the good reports I had of you. This is your last chance to set yourself up as a gentleman. Refuse it, and I wash my hands of you."

"In that case, I have no other choice but to accept your kind offer, my lord."

Something resembling a look of pleasure passed across the thin face. "Good. I thought you might, and have had my lawyer draw up the documents already."

Brendan did not try to hide his amusement. "Then I could have held my breath all this time, sir."

"You could, but I still hoped to persuade you to return to Ireland." Sussex picked up his walking stick. "There are two matters more before I turn you over to my man of business. One is your name. You will need to take the name of Radcliffe if you are to become the lord of Radcliffe Manor."

"I prefer to retain my own name, my lord." Brendan spoke very quietly.

"It is not a case of preference. It is an essential. That is the way things are done in England, to ensure a sense of continuity. As it is, you will have an uphill struggle to be accepted by the dalesfolk. They are a stubborn people."

I, too, can be stubborn, thought Brendan, but he knew that it was useless to argue with my lord of Sussex once he had made up his mind.

"The other matter I speak of is that of marriage. Evidently you have not formed any long-lasting attachments in Ireland, or you would not be so eager to leave it. A good marriage will be a great asset in your advancement. I had thought of a match between you and the eldest Radcliffe girl, Katherine."

Katherine Radcliffe. It had a pleasing ring to it. But a pleasant name did not necessarily mean a pleasant woman. Katherine Radcliffe could have a face like a goat.

"By your leave, my lord, I should prefer to be choosing my wife myself."

The Earl continued as if Brendan had not spoken. "Marriage with a member of the incumbent family would have made you more acceptable as the lord of Radcliffe. The people in the Yorkshire Dales are stiff-necked, as I discovered to my cost when I was President of the North. They are also tenacious in their adherence to the Catholic faith. Watch for that. It is an ever-present danger in the far north of England."

"Are these Radcliffes recusant Catholics then?"

"Not officially. They paid no recusancy fees to the Crown. But apparently Campion visited the house to administer the sacraments to Sir Philip Radcliffe on his deathbed and to Mistress Radcliffe, his daughter-in-law."

Brendan whistled. "Did Campion say so?"

"No. He said very little, despite the vile tortures he was subjected to. But he did admit to staying with a Mistress Bulmer at Marrick. It was easy to trace his travels from there. We have many loyal informants in the region. Campion made at least two visits to Radcliffe Manor."

"You said he had administered the last rites to . . . Sir Philip, was it?"

"Sir Philip Radcliffe, an attainted traitor who regained his freedom through that damned meddlesome gypsy, the Earl of Leicester."

"But he—that is, this Sir Philip—is now dead, I take it. Who in the family is left?"

"Two daughters and their mother. But you need not trouble your head over them now. The younger of the daughters, a girl of only fourteen, is living with relatives."

"And the other daughter—Katherine, you said her name was—and her mother?"

"They are imprisoned with Mistress Bulmer in the jail at York, awaiting their trial for harboring a Roman Catholic priest and receiving the sacraments at his hands. So you see, Master Radcliffe, the entire estate of Radcliffe Manor is now yours without any encumbrances whatsoever."

Chapter 7

The next day, the first of December, was gloomy, the sky leaden, the constant rain turning the roads and pathways to mud.

The Queen had retired to Richmond Palace two weeks earlier, to provide lavish entertainments for her most persistent suitor, the Duke of Alençon. She had left behind her, in London, a handful of her councillors—including the Earl of Sussex—to supervise the execution of Edmund Campion and the other Catholic priests who had been found guilty of treason.

My lord of Sussex left the house before daybreak. Brendan had been woken by the echo of slammed doors and then the crunch of footsteps on the wet gravel.

As he consulted that morning with the Earl's man of business, Brendan found it difficult to concentrate upon the papers before him, deeds and land titles. . . . Try as he might, he could not blot out the image of the priest who had been the most eminent scholar of his day being dragged through the mud on a hurdle.

When the great clock in the inner courtyard struck at the appointed hour of Campion's death, he excused himself and went outside, his cloak wrapped close about him, to pace on the stone-flagged terrace, which was awash with rainwater. He pulled the hood tight about his ears, lest the cheering of the crowd should echo down the river all the way from Tyburn.

"Almighty God, make the agony not last long for him," Brendan prayed. For he had seen several executions for treason in Ireland, and knew that the hangman was usually chosen for his skill at cutting down the prisoner at just the right moment, so that he might still be alive for the mutilation and disembowelment.

A flock of raucous starlings flew up from the eaves of the roof, startling him. He was surprised to find that he had been kneeling on the wet stones. He did not remember going down on his knees. It was rare that he prayed at all, never mind kneeling to do so. His cloak and hose were sodden, as if he had been there for far more than just a few minutes.

He rose and walked back through the courtyard. To his great surprise, he saw by the clock on the wall that close to three quarters of an hour had passed since he had gone outside. A sense of lightness flooded over him, as if a great burden had been lifted from his shoulders.

By now it would be done. Edmund Campion would be dead and at peace. Brendan had no doubt that, whether God were Protestant or Catholic, his old master would have been taken directly into His presence. No waiting in the antechambers of purgatory for Father Campion.

His spirits renewed, he returned to the business of learning about his new estate. Now that his mind was clear, however, he began to realize that this was no modest farming estate that the Earl was bestowing upon him. Radcliffe Manor consisted of a fine Hall with extensive grounds, a breeding stable renowned for its stock, a deer park and a smaller house with a sheep farm attached.

"I believe this smaller house, at Farley, would suit me very well," he told the Earl of Sussex the next morning.

The Earl had returned from Tyburn the previous afternoon, refusing to see anyone. Brendan had watched from the window of his cramped turret chamber, as the Earl was assisted from his boat at the landing steps. He had looked like a frail old man, leaning heavily on the arm of his servant, his thin body bent against the blowing rain.

As he watched him now, in his library, Brendan saw the sickly pallor of his austere face and wondered, not for the first time, exactly where my lord of Sussex's religious sympathies really did lie. But the hard eyes and grim lips gave away nothing.

The Earl leaned back in his chair, touching the tips of his long fingers together. "Why would you choose a mere farmstead when you are offered a fine estate?"

"Because I have had no training as a landowner. For that matter, I wonder if I would even be much of a farmer. The only life I know, apart from the two years I spent at Cambridge and the Inns of Court, is that of a soldier."

"Exactly so. Which is why I consider you a fool to be wishing to leave the Queen's army." Sussex did not try to hide his contempt.

"I will not serve in Ireland again."

Sussex sighed. "It is a great pity you are so stubborn. Your knowledge of Ireland, and of Munster in particular, would be invaluable in seeking out the rebels and in the resettlement of the province."

"Resettlement with Englishmen, you mean?"

"Of course, Englishmen. It is the only way to govern the country. As a loyal captain in Her Majesty's army, you yourself would receive a most generous portion of land."

Brendan smiled. "Land wrested from my own kinsmen," he said softly. "I thank you, my lord, for your offer, but I am thinking that perhaps, after all, I shall prosper better in your wild Yorkshire Dales. I shall take on Radcliffe Manor and its inhabitants, and conquer them peaceably."

The Earl shrugged his thin shoulders. "You have a hard task ahead of you. As I have told you, the people of the Yorkshire Dales do not take to strangers, particularly southerners."

"Ah, but then I am not a southerner, am I, my lord?" Brendan met the Earl's angry eyes with a smile.

He set off from London the next morning, accompanied only by Colum and one of the Earl's horse grooms who was to act as a guide until they met up with the party they were to join for the journey north.

The farther north they rode, the colder the weather became. The rain changed to sleet, and then to driving snow, so that they were able to travel only fifteen miles or so each day.

"At this rate we'll not be home by Christmas," grumbled the clothier from Wharfedale who had attached himself to Brendan during the journey.

Home. It had a strange ring to it, Brendan thought. What homes had he known? His mother's tiny chamber in the castle, where she had been banished to sit, endlessly sewing and spinning, deprived forever of the companionship of her sisters. The Stanihursts' comfortable house in Dublin. A shared dormitory at Cambridge. . . . These had been his homes. These, and the confines of a tent.

Was it likely that he would find a true home in this alien land amongst these harsh-voiced, suspicious northerners? Although he very much doubted it, by God, he would try. And if he failed, it would mean a return to soldiering or perhaps the life of an adventurer sailing on one of the enterprises to the New World that so occupied Walter Ralegh's mind.

Having traveled more than a week in progressively colder weather, he was beginning to think that Wensleydale and Radcliffe Manor were a mere figment of his patron's imagination, when their guide announced that they were approaching the town of Middleham. "Just a short ride across the moor to Radcliffe Hall," he assured Brendan.

Brendan was tempted to halt awhile at one of the inns in the cobbled market square. He was weary and his hands and feet were numb with the cold. But the thought of his goal being "just a short ride away" spurred him on up the rise, past the crumbling walls of what had evidently once been a mighty fortress.

As they rode over the treeless moor, the wind flung icy pellets of snow into their faces, its ferocity sapping their breath. In his entire life, Brendan had never been so cold.

He was debating within himself as to whether it might be better to turn his horse about to return to Middleham when their guide pointed to a steep bridlepath that led down the fellside. "Yon's the way to Radcliffe," he shouted above the howl of the wind. "Are they expecting thee, sir?"

Brendan nodded grimly. He had sent word ahead of his imminent arrival, but there was no sign of anyone riding to greet him.

Moreover, when he rode down the steep approach and reached the imposing iron gate in the high stone walls surrounding Radcliffe, he found it winched shut. *Perhaps I shall have to fight my way in*, he thought with a wry grimace.

He could hear Colum cursing in Irish behind him. Then the servant let forth a bloodcurdling yell that would have raised the very saints from their graves.

This brought the porter out. He rubbed his wrinkled hands together, his leathery face peering from beneath his hood, but he did not speak.

"I am your new master, Captain Fitz . . . Radcliffe." Brendan had hoped to be able to use his own name, but decided that he needed all the ammunition he could muster just to get himself inside the thick stone walls.

"Art tha now," said the porter, with a marked lack of enthusiasm. He turned and shuffled back into the gatehouse and, after considerable delay, they heard the screech of the wheel as the portal was winched slowly upwards.

As Brendan rode into the courtyard, he had the distinct impression that everyone had fled the place. It was utterly deserted. Although he could hear the snort and stamp of many horses, of their grooms and stable lads there was no sight.

His determination to be warm and friendly whatever his reception was being fast replaced by anger. "Holla there," he shouted, before Colum could emit his fearful yell again. If he did not make a strong impression at the start, he would never be able to prove himself to be the lord of this awesomely fine Hall.

He swung himself down from his horse and was about to stride across the yard and into the house when the front door swung open. A man of medium height, dressed all in black with a small white ruff, crisp at his neck, came out.

"Captain Radcliffe?" he enquired in a cold voice.

Brendan forced himself to smile. "That is right. You must be Master Ridley, the steward." He held out his hand, but it was ignored.

"Welcome to Radcliffe, sir," said the steward, the stiff little bow belying his words. "If you will follow me into the house, I shall have a groom attend to your mount."

"Colum shall take care of him."

The steward lifted his thin eyebrows, his eyes resting on the figure with long hair, dressed in a deerskin tunic. "I believe you would prefer to have one of our stable grooms care for your horse, sir."

Brendan's lips quivered. "Colum is my groom and will take care of my horse, if you would kindly direct him to the stables."

An oblique nod of the head acknowledged this order. Then the steward clapped his hands together sharply, twice, and there appeared, as if by magic, six or seven outside servants all eager to do their master's bidding . . . whosoever that master might be. It was very effective.

Brendan met the steward's clear gray eyes and his mouth slid into a wry little smile. *First mark to you, Master Ridley*, he thought, in reluctant admiration. He felt a stirring of exhilaration. If that was the way they wanted it, then so be it. The challenge had been thrown down. He would pick it up and, by Christ, he would win the engagement, however long it might take him to do so. But he would fight in his own way, not theirs.

When he stepped into the stone-flagged hall, he looked about him, his awed gaze taking in the fine linenfold paneling on the walls, the mullioned bay windows, the musicians' gallery and the two fireplaces, both filled with flaming logs.

"This is a magnificent hall," he said to the steward.

"It was built by the late Sir Philip Radcliffe's ancestor, and then improved by Sir Philip and his son, Thomas Radcliffe. But, of course, you will already know the history of the Radcliffe family, being a Radcliffe yourself, sir."

Another challenge.

"To own the truth, I am only distantly related to the Radcliffes. My true name is Brendan Fitzgerald. I was advised that I might be more acceptable as a Radcliffe."

His honesty seemed to surprise Master Ridley. "Sir Philip did the same. He was Philip Thomson before he took his grandmother's name, Radcliffe."

Brendan smiled. "Then I am following a far more worthy precedent, Master Ridley. What do you think? Should I keep to my true name or take on Radcliffe?"

Again, a look of surprise. "You are asking for my opinion, sir?"

"To be sure, I am. What better person to advise me than the faithful steward of Radcliffe."

A flush of anger mantled the angular face. "Doubtless you have heard of me from my lord of Sussex."

"From his man of business, to be exact." Brendan looked down into the steward's face. "'Twas not my intention to mock you, Master Ridley. I meant what I said. From what I have heard, your loyalty to your master went far beyond the usual bounds of stewardship. You shared both Sir Philip's exile in Scotland and his prison upon his return. I like to see such loyalty in a man."

"Loyalty cannot be bought."

"To be sure it cannot. It must be earned. And I tell you now, before we go any further in our dealings, Master Ridley, that I mean to do my best to earn not only your inestimable loyalty, but also that of all those who serve at Radcliffe."

Ridley did not even try to hide his scornful smile.

"You may smile, Master Ridley. To be sure, I cannot be blaming you for doing so, considering the circumstances. But I'd be willing to wager you that within one year I shall be accepted by everyone at Radcliffe as their master." Brendan's eyes fixed upon the steward's. "Of course, I shall need to enlist your aid in this."

"*My* aid?"

"But, of course, your aid. You are an educated man, a gentleman. You, especially, will understand that for Radcliffe to continue to flourish there must be harmony. And to achieve harmony, there must be loyalty and obedience to the lord of the manor. Would you be agreeing with me on that point?"

Ridley gave him a reluctant nod of the head. "But it depends upon what kind of man the lord of the manor is," he reminded Brendan.

"True. But with the male line extinct, a stranger had to be imported. At least I am a distant kinsman of the Radcliffes. Surely that is better than nothing."

The steward's thin lips trembled in what Brendan realized was a rare show of emotion. He looked down at the rush-strewn floor. "May I speak freely, sir?"

"You may not."

The steward lifted his head, his eyes widening in anger.

Brendan laughed and clapped him on the shoulder. "You many not until you have obeyed the laws of hospitality and offered me a glass of ale. My throat is parched after the long ride."

Ridley's slight body stiffened as if it had been starched along with his ruff. "I pray your pardon, sir. I had—"

"No more talk for now. Order the ale and take me to a fire where we may sit together and talk, whilst I thaw out. Holy Mother, 'tis cold up here in the North."

Brendan was led to a large parlor with a glowing fire, banked with peat. The smell reminded him of Ireland.

"Now, Master Ridley . . . what is your given name, by the bye?"

"Tobias, sir."

"I am not one for ceremony, I regret to tell you. Would it offend you greatly if I were to call you Tobias when we are in private together?"

The look of surprise was followed by the steward's oblique nod of agreement. In any other man, the little tilt of the head might have appeared obsequious, but in Tobias Ridley it was more like the gracious acknowledgment of a nobleman of high degree.

"Now, Tobias, you asked if you might speak freely. Bid the servant pour us two large cups of ale and then send him away, so that you may speak as freely as you please."

It was done in a moment, with Tobias evidently amazed at finding himself seated by the parlor hearth quaffing ale with the new Lord of Radcliffe.

Brendan took a good draft of the strong ale and then stretched his long legs across the fireplace, gently shifting the great body of the deerhound that lay before it. "Now, Tobias. Begin."

The steward sat on the edge of the stool, his legs tucked tightly beneath it. "I do not know where to begin, sir," he replied, gloomily staring into the pewter cup he held.

"Then let me begin for you, and you will tell me if I have read your mind. You and all the servants resent my coming here as master. I am a stranger to the ways of Yorkshire; not even an Englishman. Do I read you aright?"

Tobias nodded slowly.

"Ah, Tobias, you do not know the half of it. Not only am I a savage from the bogs of Ireland, but I also know next to nothing about being a landowner. Not even farming have I done." Brendan's eyes twinkled at Tobias over his cup, as he lifted it again to drink. "What do you think of that?"

"I think you have a great deal to learn, Master . . ." He hesitated.

"And that's another matter, Tobias. What should I be calling myself to make myself more acceptable, do you think?"

"You wish me to speak plainly?"

"Freely, plainly. For tonight, at least, nothing shall be hidden between us."

Tobias leaned forward, his elbow on his knee. "Then I think the name should be like loyalty."

Brendan understood him. "It should be earned?"

"Just so."

"Good. I like a man who speaks plainly. Remember that, Tobias, and we shall deal very well together. Then Master Fitzgerald it shall be, until I have earned the right to call myself Radcliffe."

The steward's legs uncurled themselves and stretched neatly towards the fire, but he did not speak.

Brendan sighed. "I do not need to be told that this is a house of sadness at present. I can sense it in the very stones. 'Twas not ever thus, I am sure."

Tobias Ridley shook his head. "For more than ten years it was the most contented house in the realm. Then disaster struck with first the death of young Master Richard and then of Sir Philip. And, as if that were not enough, the cruel taking of Mistress Alyssa and Katherine to prison."

Brendan was aware that he must tread with great delicacy if he was to maintain this tenuous truce. "Mistress Alyssa? She is . . ."

"Mistress Radcliffe, I should say. Mistress Katherine's mother."

"Mistress Katherine is the elder daughter, am I right?"

"Aye. And when I think of her and her mother shut away in that rat-infested prison for all these months when they have committed no crime, I . . ." Tobias turned away, his hands spasmodically opening and closing into fists.

"Was it Campion who denounced them?" Brendan asked gently.

Tobias turned back, his eyes wet. "That is the strange thing of it. Campion only gave the names of Mistress Bulmer and Dr. Vavasour in this region. No one knows who gave the names of our two ladies to Lord Huntingdon."

"The President of the North, you mean."

"Aye, and though I am a loyal Protestant, I say he is the most vindictive papist hater in the kingdom and would have them all strung up without a trial if he had his way."

"Perhaps it was Mistress Bulmer who gave away their names?"

"Not so, for she was in prison for other papist offences long before Campion gave her name under torture, God rest his soul."

"Amen to that." Brendan frowned. "'Tis very curious."

"What is even more curious is that Mistress Alyssa is a Protestant. Nay, you need not smile, sir, for I have often heard her and Sir Philip at odds over religion. What would she need a Catholic priest for?"

Brendan shook his head. "Perhaps she has an enemy."

"Mistress Alyssa? Nay, not her. A milder, sweeter, better-loved gentlewoman does not exist."

"Very strange. What has been done to try to secure their release?"

"Lord Scrope has done all that he is able to do, without making Queen Elizabeth suspicious of him. His wife is sister to the dead Duke of Norfolk, you see."

Brendan did see. It must be a precarious position for one of the most trusted of the Queen's servants, to be married to the sister of a man the Queen had executed for treason.

"Their friends and relatives send money for their comforts, but most of them are too scared for their own necks to do more than that."

"And the younger daughter? Where is she?"

"Mistress Joanna is with her grandparents, Sir William and Lady Harcourt at Harcourt Hall."

"I see."

A long pause ensued, broken only by the heavy snoring of the deerhound and the crackling of the logs in the fireplace.

"Tell me, Tobias. What like is Mistress Katherine?" Brendan asked, casually examining the mud on his riding boots.

Tobias hesitated, as if searching for the right words. "She is the most beautiful lass in the country," he said at last. "High-spirited as one of our fine fillies, but warm and kindly to all. She's tall for a lass, mind you, but then, you are more than six feet yourself, I would guess."

"I would remind you, Master Ridley, that we are speaking of Mistress Katherine," Brendan said severely. "What age is she?"

"Seventeen, going on eighteen."

"And she has no betrothed, no sweetheart?"

The steward's eyes flickered. "None."

Brendan frowned. "Surely that is strange; not to be betrothed by the age of seventeen." He cocked his head in a question at the steward.

"Sir Philip was considering the matter not long before he died. Have you no family, Master Fitzgerald?" Tobias asked hastily, as if he wished to change the subject.

Brendan grinned. "No wife, if that is what you mean by 'family,' Tobias."

"Nor any . . . attachments?"

Brendan laughed out loud at this. "Nor any attachments. A soldier has little time to form attachments."

Attachments. Encumbrances. "Radcliffe Manor is yours without any encumbrances," Sussex had said. But was it? Might it not be that the only way to become accepted as the true master at Radcliffe would be to wed Katherine Radcliffe? No doubt she would fall into his arms, ripe with gratitude for her release from prison and her return to her home as its mistress. If she was, indeed, as beautiful and spirited as the steward said, then that was not an entirely unpleasing prospect.

Brendan got up to fetch the ewer of ale from the sideboard, an action that greatly shocked the steward. He was even more shocked when his new master insisted on pouring ale for him, waving him back onto his stool as he did so.

Brendan bent to rub his booted foot on the hound's back, and then stood gazing into the fire.

"I deeply regret that I shall be staying but one night at Radcliffe," he announced, after enjoying the visible signs of Master Ridley's impatience for a while.

"Sir?"

"'Tis sorry I am that I did not think of it sooner, on my way north, for now I have to retrace my steps a hundred or so miles."

Hope lit the thin face before him. "York is not quite that far," Tobias said, gripping his cup very tightly.

"But then, to be sure, I did not have your assurance of Mistress Katherine's beauty to inspire me at the time, did I?"

Mater Ridley licked his lips.

"It is not that I do not trust you, you understand, Tobias. It is only that I must see for myself before I take the irrevocable step of trying to gain the release of the two Radcliffe ladies."

"Do you think you could do it, though, sir, when those with power like Lord Scrope and Lord Colborne have tried and failed?"

"Lord Colborne? Who is he?"

"The husband of Mistress Alyssa's sister, Lady Isobel Colborne. He is a member of the Council of the North."

Brendan whistled. "If I marry Mistress Katherine, it seems I would be marrying into illustrious company." He grinned. "Holy Saint Joseph. Is this me talking of marriage when I have run from the very thought of marriage since first I became a man!"

"But how can you secure their release from prison, Master Fitzgerald," Tobias asked again, "when others have tried and failed?"

"Ah, but you see, Tobias," said Brendan, setting his arm about the older man's shoulders. "They have so much to lose. I, being but a beggarly soldier of no name or fortune, have everything to gain." Feeling the man flinch from him, he quickly removed his arm.

"But you already have Radcliffe, sir."

"Do I, my friend, do I?" Brendan's voice was gentle. "Was that warm hospitable reception I received tonight a sign that I am master of Radcliffe?"

Tobias Ridley had the grace to redden.

"Now, now, Tobias, do not be smarting at what I say. You and the servants had every right to resent my coming. I give you fair warning, however, that I do not mean to earn your respect merely through wedding your Mistress Katherine. That is only part of it. 'Tis a great deal I must be learning before I can become master here. That will take time. Now, if you wish me to leave at daybreak tomorrow, I must to my bed. Give me a candle, if you please."

"I will light you to bed, sir."

As they mounted the great staircase, Brendan caught glimpses of several doors off the landing, but by now he was too weary to examine anything. Time enough for that when he made his triumphant return to Radcliffe Hall.

"I wish to send an urgent message by post to London, Master Ridley," he said briskly, when they reached the bedchamber door. "Can you arrange for it to go tonight?"

"Certainly, sir. Shall I wait for it now?"

"No. I shall place it outside my door. Send someone for it in a quarter of an hour exactly."

"As you do not have a valet, I shall send a servant to help you undress when you have completed your message."

Brendan was about to protest, but then remembering all the

intricacies of points and ruff strings decided to accept the offer. How much easier were his jerkin and frieze hose!

He turned to go inside the chamber, but Master Ridley still hovered on the doorstep, clearing his throat several times.

"Was there something else, Master Ridley?"

Ridley gave an abrupt nod and at last said, "Upon your arrival, you offered me your hand, sir. Would you do me the honor of doing so again?"

"Gladly." Brendan held out his hand and this time Master Ridley took it, although he looked a trifle pained as Brendan wrung his hand.

"You realize that I may not be successful in releasing them, do you not, Tobias?" Brendan said softly.

"Indeed, sir, I do," was the reply. "But at least all of us here at Radcliffe will know you have tried."

Chapter 8

Katherine turned on the hard pallet, and pulled the covers about her head, trying to stimulate some more heat. It was the cold that had woken her, that and her mother's soft groaning in her restless sleep.

For several minutes she lay, shivering, the thought of getting out from beneath the covers veritable torture to her. A shaft of pale light issued from the barred window high up on the stone wall, heralding the start of another bleak day.

Katherine threw back the bedclothes and swung her legs down. Hurriedly, she slid her feet into her wooden pattens to avoid standing on the filthy floor. She had begged for fresh straw, but had been told that she must "wallow in her papist filth."

Although their relatives and friends kept them supplied with food and clothing, nothing could compensate for the squalor, the intense cold that seeped into their bones, the lack of exercise, the stench. And now her mother was sick with the prison fever that had already killed several of the Catholic prisoners. What need to bring them to trial, when imprisonment would assuredly kill them in time?

She sat on the straw-filled mattress, despair washing over her, threatening to drown her. "Christ Jesu," she prayed, burying her face in her hands. "I am not of the stuff of martyrs. I am not a patient person. I cannot endure, like the others seem to be able to do. My faith is not as strong as theirs. Either grant me that patience or that faith, or release me, for if I have to bear this for much longer I shall lose my reason."

Katherine doubted that God would heed such a selfish prayer. It lacked the humility, the resignation necessary to reach the Almighty.

Her mother groaned again, more loudly, and Katherine went to her. "I am here," she whispered, placing her hand on her mother's forehead. Dear God, she was burning with the fever. She held the candle up so that she might see her face more clearly. Her mother's lips were cracked and bleeding, her teeth gritted together as her body was racked with violent shivering.

"Forgive me," she whispered to Katherine.

"Forgive you for what?" Katherine said. She held the wooden beaker of water to her mother's parched lips.

"For seeing the priest," Alyssa said, when she had drunk a little. "I should have sent him away, but it was what Philip wanted. It was his last wish." Her eyes filled with tears that ran down her face and into her tangled hair.

"Oh, Mother. Don't think about it anymore. I promise you we shall be home at Radcliffe before Christmas Day. Now, try to sleep."

It was a promise they both knew was impossible to fulfill. In the three months they had been there, only one of the Catholic prisoners had been released. Despite the protests of her maternal grandfather, Sir William Harcourt, to the Council of the North that neither his daughter nor granddaughter were Catholics, the unassailable fact of Edmund Campion's two visits was damning evidence.

"I'll sit with her, Mistress Katherine," said Margery, who had insisted on accompanying them to York when they were arrested. Katherine knew that it was only loyalty to her mother that kept her there.

She gave Margery a wan smile, and noticed for the first time how pinched and prematurely old the faithful servant's face had become over the past months. A spasm of guilt caught her as she recalled all those times she had snapped at Margery in her frustration. "No. You need your sleep, too." She caught her hand and squeezed it. "Why don't you go home to your son for Christmastide, Margery?" she said impulsively. "It is not right that you should be in this dreadful place when you could celebrate Christmas with your family."

"Nay, my hinny. Tha knows I'll not leave thy mother. 'Sides, thee and she might fall out if I weren't here to stand atween thee."

Katherine smiled shamefacedly. "Oh, Margery, pray forgive me," she cried, embracing the plump servant. "I only wish I could be patient, like Mother and the rest. But I cannot."

She strode across the cell and then turned, flinging out her arms. "When I think of even the meanest stable lad being able to ride across Melmerby Moor and up Penhill, I feel like screaming and beating my head against these wretched stone walls." She shivered, wrapping her arms tightly across her breast. "Oh God, Margery, what wouldn't I give now to be riding Silver Moon, to feel the wind blowing against me!"

"Tha can feel the wind blowing 'gainst thee without being out on the moor," said the ever-practical Margery caustically. "I've tried and tried to stuff these cracks in the walls, but whatever I do the wind whistles in."

Katherine bit back a retort. No one seemed to understand how she felt. God's wounds, she was only seventeen, bursting with life, and everyone was telling her to resign herself to God's will and endure. A chill swept over her as she remembered the Scottish Queen, imprisoned for thirteen years. She, too, had loved riding and hunting. Grandy had told her how he had provided horses for Queen Mary when she was kept at Bolton Castle.

She went to the barred window. Although it was too high for her to be able to see outside, she could hear the shouts and bustle from the busy streets of York. She leaned her head against the rough stone wall, shivering as the chill dampness pressed against her skin. Closing her eyes, she tried to conjure up the fresh smell of the forest at Jervaulx after a rainfall, the great vista of Wensleydale stretched before her, as she looked down upon it from high on Penhill, but, inexplicably, instead there swept into her mind the memory of a man's face. It had been a handsome face, with eyes of an unusual color, a dark blue, like the sky at midnight when there was a full moon.

She had caught only a glimpse of the man when he had visited the prison a few days before. At first her heart had leapt, thinking it could be Edward, for her dreams had been ever of Edward, coming to their rescue, catching her up in his arms. But after her initial reaction, she had seen that this man was far taller than Edward, so tall that he had had to stoop to enter their tiny chamber, and his coloring was dark not fair. He had doffed his hat, revealing curling black hair cut shorter than was the fashion, and made a bow to her and her mother. Although he had looked at them both intently, he had not spoken.

A visitor to the prison was nothing extraordinary, for people came every day to gawk and laugh at the prisoners for recreation. What was unusual, though, besides the man's height, was an air of intensity that fascinated Katherine. It was that, coupled with the fact that he had been accompanying the Earl of Huntingdon, the powerful President of the Northern Council, that made the man memorable.

Hearing voices and the scrape of the key in the lock, Katherine turned around. Time to break their fast, she thought, with no sense of relief. Indeed, her stomach rebelled at the mere thought of the watery gruel and stale bread that was their usual breakfast.

To her astonishment, it was not the turnkey who came in, but the Earl of Huntingdon and, beside him, the man who had just been occupying her thoughts. Instinctively, her hands went to her unbrushed hair and she blushed to think that she was still in her nightcap and the fur-edged nightrobe. Fortunately, it was made of heavy wool and covered her from neck to toe.

She drew herself up and surveyed them haughtily. "To what do we owe this unexpected and extremely early visitation?" she asked.

Her eyes widened with indignation when she saw the stranger smile, but before she could say more, another man stepped from behind him. Katherine gasped with delighted surprise. "Oh, Tobias," she cried, her hands outstretched to greet their steward.

He came forward to take her hands in his. It was then that she realized Tobias was also smiling. Her heart turned in her breast. She searched his eyes and saw in them the reassurance she sought. "Are we to be released?" she whispered.

He nodded, and then made a bow in the Earl's direction. "My lord of Huntingdon will explain."

Her mother raised herself up on her elbow. "Is that Tobias?" she asked in a weak voice. "Surely I must be dreaming."

Katherine darted to her side. "No, Mother, you are not dreaming. It is Tobias Ridley, our steward, come to take us home." For a moment ignoring the two other men, she took Tobias by the hand and drew him to her mother's bedside. "She is sick with the prison fever," she whispered. "I have been so worried about her." Tears filled her eyes, blurring her vision as she watched Tobias go on his knees beside the pallet.

She rubbed her eyes with her sleeve, and then turned to approach the Earl and his companion. "Forgive me, my lord," she said, sinking into a curtsy. "I am forgetting myself in my excitement." She looked into his cold eyes. "Is it indeed true? Are we to be released?"

"You are." He appeared to gain no pleasure in confirming the news of their release. "Her Majesty the Queen has graciously granted you and your mother, Mistress Alyssa Radcliffe, a pardon, upon the intervention of my lord of Sussex."

"The Earl of Sussex?" A wave of excitement swept over her. "Oh, my lord. Does this mean . . . can it be that my lord of Sussex has restored Radcliffe to us?"

"No, he has not," Huntingdon said coldly. "You see before you the new Lord of Radcliffe Manor, Captain Brendan Fitzgerald, late captain in Her Majesty's army in Ireland."

The stranger took off his hat and, smiling again, bowed to her. Katherine responded to neither the bow nor the smile.

She faced him, her expression stony. "You are the new owner of Radcliffe?" she asked, between tight lips.

"I am fortunate enough to have that pleasure, madam."

Captain Fitzgerald's voice was pleasant, the accent soft and lilting, but, however pleasant his voice or handsome his appearance, Katherine was determined to hate him. "What have you done to deserve Radcliffe?" she demanded. "You are not even a Yorkshireman."

"Madam," said Huntingdon, intervening before Captain Fitzgerald could reply, "I would have you know that it was at Captain Fitzgerald's instigation that my lord of Sussex espoused your case. But for him, you would have remained in prison."

"I would rather be in prison than be banished from Radcliffe for ever," Katherine cried.

"Katherine, you forget yourself," said her mother's voice.

Captain Fitzgerald held up his hand. "Let us cry pax for the moment." He bent his head in Katherine's direction. "Would you be agreeing with me, Mistress Radcliffe, that your lady mother should be removed to more comfortable lodgings and receive medical attention as soon as possible?"

His words, spoken quietly, brought her to her senses, filling her with shame. "Of course." Her hands twisted together at her waist. "I pray your pardon," she whispered. "I am indeed most grateful to you. It is just that . . ." She turned her head away.

"Say no more."

She felt his fingers brush hers, a touch as soft as a breath. She was intensely aware of his physical presence so near to her, the clean, fresh scent of him. It was as if he brought with him the smell of the wind and the moors, the smell of freedom. Yet what point was there in being free, if she could not return to her home?

"If you will permit me, my lord," Captain Fitzgerald said to the Earl,

"I think we should withdraw so that the ladies may dress and prepare for their departure."

Katherine swallowed down the bitter tears of disappointment. For one brief moment she had thought they would be returning to Radcliffe for Christmas. Instead it would be drafty Harcourt, with its shabby furnishings and mean fires. "We shall be ready in a few minutes," she told the three men in a firm voice. She would give neither Huntingdon nor this interloper the satisfaction of seeing her weep.

The men left, but Captain Fitzgerald turned in the doorway. "I must tell you, Mistress Radcliffe," he said, "that I was at Radcliffe only one night before I left for York, but I have since received many messages from your friends and, in particular, your mother's parents. Sir William Harcourt, your mother's father, was eager to come with us to York, so that he might accompany you on your journey back to Wensleydale, but I managed to persuade him to remain at home, the weather being so cold and the roadways icy."

"You seem to have quite a persuasive way with you, Captain Fitzgerald. First my lord of Sussex, then the Earl of Huntingdon . . . and my grandfather."

"You are forgetting Master Ridley in your list of my conquests, Mistress Radcliffe," he said, with a glimmer of a smile.

Her chin lifted. "No one conquers Tobias Ridley," she told him. "He is his own man."

But, later, when Captain Fitzgerald and Tobias returned to assist them, she saw to her astonishment that there was, indeed, some sort of strange alliance between Tobias and the Irishman. She was deeply hurt by it. Evidently she had been wrong in thinking that Tobias would be above the usual transference of a servant's loyalty to his new master.

Her mother sat on the pallet, her shoulders hunched under her cloak. She had lost so much weight she looked like a small child. "I shall try to walk," she said, her teeth chattering from the incessant shivering.

"You will be doing no such thing," said Captain Fitzgerald. Before she had time to protest, he bent and lifted her in his arms, as easily as if she were a pillow filled with thistledown. "Tuck the shawl about her head, Tobias," he told the steward. "The wind is keen."

Not so keen as the sharp pain in Katherine's heart as she saw Tobias, their faithful steward, jump to obey the command of his new master. And what gave Captain Brendan Fitzgerald the right to call the steward by his given name, as if they were old friends, she would like to know? Even her grandfather, respecting his steward's reticent nature, had usually called him "Master Ridley" in public. This man was assuredly no gentleman, she thought indignantly.

It was but a short journey from the prison to the lodgings in Petersgate that had been procured for them. Once her mother had been settled in the small but comfortably furnished bedchamber, the physician was sent for.

"Rest and nourishment should help to restore her," he told Katherine, when they repaired to the parlor after his examination.

"She will recover completely, won't she?" Katherine whispered, terrified by his expression.

"The fever has greatly weakened her constitution," he replied, shaking his head. "But if she is given this physic as I have directed your woman servant, she should rally very soon. Time will tell."

He left her there alone. God was cruel, she decided, or else He did not exist. First he had taken Edward from her—for although her love for Edward had never faltered, not one word had he written to her during their imprisonment—then had come the deaths of her brother and grandfather hard upon each other. Now, here was her mother, whom she both loved and hated, stricken down. The thought filled her with terror, for she felt somehow responsible.

Having seen the physician out, Captain Fitzgerald came back into the parlor. This was the first time they had been alone together. For a moment neither of them spoke. Then the man crossed the chamber in two or three strides, to throw another log on the small fire.

"Holy Mother of God, 'tis icy cold out there," he said, blowing on his hands and then holding them out to the fire. "Will you not be drawing nearer to the fire to warm yourself, Mistress Radcliffe?"

Despite her antagonism to him, Katherine did so. She sat on the bench, her spine very straight. She had the feeling that if she were to relax for one moment in this man's presence, she would be lost. *This is one person he will not be able to exercise his powers of persuasion upon*, she thought.

"Have you recently left Ireland, Captain Fitzgerald?" she asked in a cool voice, determined to take control before he did.

"I arrived in England only a few weeks ago," he told her. "And, by the bye, I prefer not to be called 'captain' now that I have left the army." He eyed the large box-chair beside the hearth. "With your permission?" he asked, tilting his head.

"But of course," Katherine replied.

He took off his sword, laid it down on the floor and sat down, all seemingly in one movement. She had noticed that, despite his great height, everything he did was performed with grace and an economy of movement.

He was quite unlike her idea of a soldier, all noise and bravado. In truth, she wished he were more of a soldier. Perhaps, then, she would have been less aware of him as a man. For something about him disturbed her greatly, and the feeling made her afraid and somehow excited at the same time.

She shivered.

"Are you still cold?" he asked, leaning forward so that he could have touched her had he but put out his hand.

"No, not at all," she replied, trying not to shrink back from him. "I am concerned for my mother, that is all. That, and the shock of our sudden release from prison, I suppose."

He seemed to be waiting for her to say more. When she did not, a spasm of what might have been disappointment crossed his handsome face. "I am assured that the physician is one of the best in York. The rest is in God's hands."

The silence again stretched between them. "I have much to thank you for, sir," Katherine said reluctantly, sensing that he had been waiting for her to thank him.

His expression brightened. "Not at all, not at all. When I reached Radcliffe and saw how matters were, I felt I must try to do something." He gave her a wry smile. "I am still trying to find my way about the ways of England, you know. Most especially the ways of the North, which is like another country altogether."

She allowed herself a small smile. "Of course it is. Have you never been to England before? You seem to be an educated man."

A strange expression flitted through his dark-blue eyes, but his voice was level when he answered. "I was at Cambridge University for one year and the Inns of Court for another. A thin veneer of civilization."

She shifted, his unwavering gaze making her uncomfortable. "And have you much property in Ireland, Master Fitzgerald?"

"I have none at all, Mistress Radcliffe. I have been a soldier of fortune, nothing more."

"And yet my lord of Sussex sees fit to bestow Radcliffe upon you, a stranger, not even an Englishman." The sudden rush of anger shook her entire body. "Why?"

He was very still, but the skin over his strong cheekbones grew white. "My lord of Sussex has been my patron since I was a youth in Ireland. Since he discovered I was distantly related to the Radcliffes, in truth. When the lordship of Radcliffe Manor reverted to him, he decided to bestow it upon me, as I had no land of my own."

"How truly generous of him to bestow *my* inheritance upon you, sir." Katherine was furious now, her eyes blazing at him.

"I would remind you, madam, that the inheritance is not yours." His voice was as cool as hers was hot. "In my few days in London, before I came here, I spent much time with the Earl of Sussex's man of business. He explained to me the history of Radcliffe Manor. It has not exactly been handed down from father to son, has it?"

His calm voice infuriated her even more. "My brother was my father's heir. Would you not call that being handed from father to son?"

"Ah, to be sure. But, then, your father did not receive it at the hands of *his* father, did he? No, he was attainted and Radcliffe forfeit to the Crown. Your father received it back through the patronage of the Earl of Sussex. And now it is I who am the recipient, at the same hands."

"But you are not a Radcliffe."

Master Fitzgerald shrugged. "A little part of me is."

"But not a Radcliffe of the Dales."

"Not yet, to be sure, but with your assistance I mean to become so."

The man was insufferable. "You may have gained our release from prison, sir, and for that I am grateful, but you shall never receive any assistance from me or any other member of my family to help you to become the true master of Radcliffe. That I swear in the name of God and all his saints."

"That is a great pity. 'Twill also be difficult for me, I'm thinking." Amusement quirked his lips.

Katherine sprang up, casting aside the woollen shawl about her knees. "God's wounds, I don't care how difficult it is for you. Do you really think that my family would be of assistance to you, when you are established as the master in our home, while we dwell in . . . in some hovel elsewhere?"

She burst into tears, which made her even more angry at him, that he should see her so utterly out of control.

He came to her. For a moment she thought he was about to put his arms about her, and her hands closed into fists. But his hands gripped her shoulders. He gave her a gentle shake, as if she were a child and then took her face in one large hand, his thumb close to her lips, forcing her to look up at him through wet eyelashes.

How dare he touch her! Apart from her relatives, no man but Edward had ever touched her with such intimacy, and she had known this man only a few hours.

"I have been unkind," he said softly. "I am quite forgetting the strain you have undergone. Pray forgive me. You will discover the one thing an Irishman can never resist is a good argument. I had no right at all to engage you in one, and you only a child."

This was beyond all endurance. "Why, you . . . you devil," she screamed at him. "I would have you know I am no child, sir. I am a woman. A fully grown woman. With a woman's loves and a woman's hates. And I hate you, Master Fitzgerald, more than I have ever hated anyone else in my life."

He grasped her wrists as she raised her clenched hands fists to strike him. "Why, yes, Mistress Radcliffe, I am very much aware that you are a woman," he said, ignoring her last words. "So much so, that I shall immediately do something to prove it."

Still gripping her wrists, he bent his dark head shutting out the light from the fire and the branch of candles. His body barely touched hers, but she was intensely aware of its heat. His mouth was firm and warm, the kiss gentle. Her own lips clamped shut to repel him, but as the kiss deepened, her eyelids fluttered closed and her mouth relaxed, softened beneath his.

Immediately, he withdrew and released her.

She did not know where to look. "You are a devil, indeed," she whispered, rubbing her wrists as if he had bruised them, which he had not. "And you are certainly no gentleman to take advantage of a lady who is without protection."

His slanted eyebrows raised. "A lady?" He grinned at her. "If I am no gentleman, then I am thinking we are well matched, Mistress Radcliffe."

She was trembling, but this time it was not from the cold, nor even from anger, although she deeply resented the kiss. She had vowed that no man but Edward would ever kiss her. Now this man had forced her to break that solemn vow.

"I think it is time you left here, sir," she told him, attempting to gather together the shreds of dignity. Even as she spoke, she was suddenly afraid. "You are lodging elsewhere, are you not?"

"I am." Frowning, he eyed her for a moment. "One thing you must know of me, Katherine, and that is I will never willingly give you cause to fear me. I have seen too much fear and terror in my short life to wish to see it in the eyes of those I love."

"Love?"

"That is what I said. Do you really believe I would have kissed an unprotected woman had my intentions not been honorable?"

Yes, she had believed that, but she did not say so.

He took her limp hand in his. "When the time is right, I shall speak to you and your family about marriage between us. But, for now, it will be sufficient that you know that, as soon as your mother is well enough to make the journey, I intend to take you home to Radcliffe.

And if you were to concentrate your energies upon nursing her instead of picking quarrels with me, she might even recover in time for us to be there to celebrate the day of Christ's nativity together."

Having rendered Katherine speechless, he swept her a deep bow, set his hat straight and strode from the parlor.

Chapter 9

For a long time, Katherine stood in the center of the parlor, seething. Grinning jackanapes! How dare a common soldier of no lineage touch her thus, kiss her against her will! She scrubbed her lips with the back of her hand to take away the taste of him.

It was evident that he had expected her to fall into his arms, mouthing her gratitude. Well, she would not do so. After all, in time someone would have gained their release. And as for marriage with him, she would sooner die first. Edward was the only man she would marry. She knew in her heart that Edward's love for her would prove stronger than his vocation. *One day soon he will return to England to claim me as his bride*, she told herself. When that time came she must be free for him.

Besides, even if there were no Edward, the last man on earth she would marry would be Master Brendan Fitzgerald. Marry a stranger, and a man from the bogs of Ireland at that? Never!

"Kate," her mother's voice called from the next chamber.

"I am coming," Katherine replied. She took a deep, steadying breath and crossed the little passageway.

Her mother lay on her back in the small truckle bed. Her eyes were still bright with fever, but when Katherine put her hand on her forehead she was relieved to find her much cooler.

"Why were you shouting?" she asked Katherine, with a slight frown.

"It was nothing to concern yourself with, Mother."

Katherine went to Margery, who was mixing one of her acrid-smelling concoctions in a pan over the fire. "Have you given her the physic the physician left?" she asked.

"Aye, I have, Mistress Kate. But she were right worried when she heard thee yelling."

Katherine glared at the servant. "I was not yelling. Besides," she hissed, "even if I was, I had just cause to do so."

"There is never just cause for a lady to raise her voice," said her mother's weak voice from the bed.

Katherine cursed inwardly. Even when she was sick, her mother was quick to rebuke her.

She went to stand at the bedside, her jaw tight with the effort to reign in her temper. "I leave it to you, madam my Mother, to decide whether or not I had just cause to rail at . . . at that wretch," she said.

Her mother struggled to lean up on one elbow. "Are you speaking of Captain Fitzgerald?" Her voice was sharp.

"He's not a captain anymore. Even when he was, it was in Ireland, so a captaincy means nothing."

Her mother sank back on her pillow. "Oh, Kate. Do not tell me that you have been having words with the man, after all his kindness to us."

"His kindness!" Katherine did not wish to upset her mother, but this was too much. "I would have you know, my lady Mother, that Master Fitzgerald is no gentleman. He . . . he forced himself upon me."

Alyssa shot up in bed. "What?"

"Well, that is . . . he kissed me against my will."

Margery pushed herself between Katherine and the bed, hands on her hips. "'Tis not kissing you I'll be doing, Mistress Kate, if tha dunna stop worriting thy mother. Tha've said enough for now."

"No, Margery. I shall be more worried unless I hear all." Alyssa patted the bed. "Come, Kate, sit down here beside me and tell me exactly what happened between you and Captain Fitzgerald."

Katherine did as she was told, reluctantly taking the hand that was held out to her. It was hot and dry against hers, like a sun-warmed autumn leaf. She squeezed it gently and then slowly slid her hand away.

"Start from the beginning," her mother bade her.

"There is little to tell," Katherine muttered, tracing the pattern of lilies and roses on the worn bedcover.

Alyssa sighed. "Then kindly tell me that little, so that I may rest easy."

"He made it very clear that he considered Radcliffe to be his—"

"As it is, I regret to say."

The tears in her mother's eyes made Katherine even more furious. "And he had the gall to tell me that he had learned all about Radcliffe Manor from my lord of Sussex's man of business, and brought up all the history about Grandy's attainder and Radcliffe being forfeit to the Crown." She paused for breath for a moment. "And he a stranger, and an Irishman at that. How dare he!"

Her mother sighed. "If I didn't know you, my dearest Kate, I would have been surprised to hear it of Master Fitzgerald, for he behaved with the greatest courtesy to me. I suspect that you goaded him into saying more than he should have done."

Katherine was outraged that her mother should take the stranger's part against her. "And the kissing; did I goad him into that, too?"

Her mother's lips quivered. "In a way, you probably did. You are never more beautiful than when your eyes flash and your cheeks color with anger, my darling Kate."

Katherine gritted her teeth. "Whatever the reason," she muttered, "he forced himself upon me and kissed me." She rubbed her hand across her mouth again at the memory.

Her mother frowned. "It was not courteous of him to do so, particularly when you were alone. Did he say why he had kissed you?"

"Yes. That is the most arrogant part of it all. Master Fitzgerald was pleased to inform me that he was going to marry me. Can you believe it?"

Her mother gasped. "Oh, Kate." To Katherine's utter amazement, her mother's pale face was suffused with sudden joy. "Oh, my dearest, why did you not say this from the start? I *knew* he was a gentleman from the moment he entered our cell," she said triumphantly.

Katherine was so astounded by her mother's reaction that she could not find words to respond.

"Oh, Mistress Kate," Margery said, from the other side of the bed, "'tis the best news us've had for many a long while."

Katherine sprang from the bed to face them both. "I think you've both gone mad," she informed them. "I would not marry the man if he was the last man on earth. And so I shall tell him the next time I see him." Their enthusiasm made her feel like some poor wild creature cornered by hunters.

Her mother closed her eyes for a moment. "I am too weak at present to argue with you, Katherine. Now that your grandfather is no longer—" She broke off, her mouth and chin trembling. "Now that he is not here to help you to see reason, I can only beg you to reconsider your attitude to Captain Fitzgerald. Think of all that his offer represents."

"I have thought of it already. To have to spend one day under the same roof as that man, with all his arrogance, is a hideous thought. To have to share his bed with him is totally abhorrent to me. No, Mother, whatever you do or say, I shall never marry him." Katherine's chin was up and her spine straight as a lance as she confronted her mother. "As I have told you many times before, I shall never marry anyone but Edward."

Alyssa put her hand to her forehead. "For the lord's sake, Katherine. You put me utterly out of patience. You know very well that Edward is no longer available to you as a husband."

Katherine flinched at her mother's cruel bluntness. "Then I shall remain unwed for my entire life," she said with a proud little smile. "But, mark me, one day Edward will return to me and I intend to keep myself free for him."

Alyssa turned her face away.

Margery patted her mistress's hand and gently wiped her face with a cloth dipped in rosewater. "Tha deserves a good thrashing," she told Katherine, glaring at her across the bed.

Concern for her mother made Katherine bite back a reply. *Oh God, why could it not have been Edward who came to our rescue?* she thought, swallowing down the tears forming in the back of her throat.

"I did not mean to agitate you, Mother," she whispered, bending over her.

Her mother turned to face her, summoning up a faint smile. "I know it. It is just that I am too weak now to find the right words to persuade you. You know very well that I would never force you into a marriage against your will."

As she herself had been, thought Katherine. She was well aware that the marriage between her mother and father had not been a happy one. Her Aunt Isobel had blamed her mother for that. But why should it concern Aunt Isobel so greatly after all these years, anyway? It was a puzzle Katherine hoped one day to solve, but for now the fact of her mother's unhappy marriage made her even more adamant.

"I am glad to hear it," she told her mother. "Besides, I could not bear to marry anyone other than a Yorkshireman."

"Captain Fitzgerald is related to the Radcliffe family," said her mother. "He told me so after he had carried me up here."

Katherine raised her dark eyebrows. "I was not aware of an Irish branch of Radcliffes."

"There are Radcliffes everywhere. No doubt it was on his mother's side. Perhaps they settled in Ireland a long time ago. But that is neither here nor there. The one important matter, which seems entirely to have escaped you, Kate, is that by marrying Brendan Fitzgerald you will be able to restore Radcliffe to our family. Your son will inherit the land of your father's and grandfather's forbears."

"I might not have a son," Katherine muttered sullenly.

"That is not the point, is it? For several years Grandy's grandmother, Joisse Radcliffe, sought to have Radcliffe restored to her. And then Grandy himself risked his very life to gain it back. Think of him, only eighteen—your age—utterly unschooled in the ways of the world, bravely bearding the great King Henry himself in his grand court, so that he might regain Radcliffe. And Thomas, your own father, would have done anything in this world to ensure that he and those of his blood would continue to be lords of Radcliffe Manor. Anything!"

Katherine was silent. Everything her mother said was true, she knew. She was terribly torn. She would be willing to swear in the name of Almighty God that her love for Radcliffe Manor was as powerful as Joisse Radcliffe's had been. Then she remembered the rest of her great-great-grandmother's story.

"But Joisse Radcliffe gave up Radcliffe Manor so that she might wed the man she loved," she said, a note of triumph in her voice. "It was Grandy who regained it for her."

This time it was her mother who was unable to respond. She turned her head sideways on the pillow, too weak to raise it, so that she might look at Katherine. The sigh she gave was one of intense weariness and resignation.

Then she rallied. "You are right, Katherine, it was. But, although I do not wish to give you further pain, I would remind you again that Edward is not here and has not written one word to you during our imprisonment."

Katherine's chin went up. "Perhaps he does not know we have been in prison."

"Lady Carlton knows and she writes regularly to him." Her mother's eyes closed. Tears squeezed from her closed eyelids. "I had so hoped to spend Christmas at Radcliffe," she whispered, "with all the memories of the happy times I spent there with those I loved." Her face crumpled as if she were in great pain.

Katherine scrambled onto the bed, dragging at her skirts, so that she might kneel on it. "Don't cry, Mully," she whispered, the old childhood name coming unbidden to her lips. "Please don't." She gathered her mother's small body into her arms and rocked her against her breast, their roles strangely reversed.

Her mother had been so brave, so strong throughout their imprisonment. Now weakness and the despair that came from knowing that she was not, after all, to know the joy of homecoming overcame her and she sobbed out her grief against Katherine, her tears dampening the bodice of her daughter's black fustian gown.

"Let me take her, Mistress Kate," said Margery.

Katherine shook her head, her mouth working. She stroked her mother's tangled hair, smoothing it back from her face. Her skin was still soft, but the imprisonment had aged her. There were fine lines etched between her eyebrows, and her nut-brown hair had lost its richness.

Katherine had never really looked at her mother's face before. She had taken it for granted. It had always been there. Calm, sometimes severe, occasionally joyful. Her mother rarely laughed out loud, but she smiled frequently. That quiet smile of contentment. Now Katherine had it in her power to restore some small part of that contentment. Or she could condemn her mother to spending the rest of her life away from the place that housed her happiest memories.

It would serve her right, said a voice from deep within her. *To banish her forever from Radcliffe would be just punishment for her sin.* But the thought of holding such power over her own mother terrified Katherine. Better to leave her punishment to God.

Her mother lay spent now, the wrenching sobs quieted. For a moment Katherine thought she might be sleeping, but when she looked down she saw that her mother's eyes were wide open and filled with supplication.

Gently, Katherine eased her back on the pillows. "I am going to send again for Master Fitzgerald," she told her mother. "I shall ask him if he would be prepared to wait for an answer regarding our marriage. That way, if you are well enough to travel, we could at least return to Radcliffe for Christmas."

Her mother's trembling smile and the squeeze of her hand was Katherine's reward.

It was a compromise. She had not given in completely. To do so would have meant abandoning all hope of marrying Edward. This way she would have time to write to him, to beg him to reconsider. Surely when he heard that she was being forced to wed a stranger he would hurry back to her. It would mean losing Radcliffe, of course, but at least her mother would have regained her health by that time and would be better able to settle elsewhere.

Katherine forced away the thought that she, too, would have to leave Radcliffe. She would face that when the time came. Besides, she could live anywhere—even in a cave—with Edward by her side.

Chapter 10

The rumble of cartwheels over the cobblestones awoke Katherine the next morning, although the sound was strangely muted.

She knelt on her bed, breathing upon the window pane and rubbing at the rime of frost so that she could see out. The street below was covered with a fresh fall of snow. The street was so narrow and the top-heavy houses so close that she could see into the room of the house opposite. Having lived all her life in a large manor house, she was momentarily fascinated by the sight of the nightcapped woman moving in and out of her vision in the flickering light of the candle that stood on some table or chest behind her.

Although Katherine had slept little during the night, her mother had slept well. When she had tiptoed to her bedside earlier that morning, her breathing had been soundless and her pulse quiet. Praise God, her fever had abated.

But Katherine's fever of impatience had not. If only she could have spoken to Master Fitzgerald last night, directly after the conversation with her mother, but when he had arrogantly swept from the house, he had left without telling her his whereabouts in York. Now she must wait until he deigned to appear again. Alas, waiting was not her strong suit.

The cold draft whistling through the gap between the window and its frame brought her back to reality. Hurriedly, she took up the earthenware water jug. But when she went to pour some water into the basin, she found that it, too, was ice-covered and she had to break the ice with the handle of her hairbrush.

Shivering, she dashed some of the icy water on her face, scrubbing it dry with her shift as there was no towel. She dragged on her gown, cursing softly that she had to appear before the new Lord of Radcliffe in the same creased gown of black fustian.

Once she was dressed, she opened her door and went out into the passageway. "Margery," she said in a loud whisper outside her mother's door.

There was no answer.

Katherine lifted the latch and opened the door. Margery was sound asleep in the chair beside her mother's bed, her head resting on the bed, pillowed in her arms.

Despite her impatience, Katherine could not waken her. The poor woman had had little sleep in the past few nights.

Drawing the door to, she stood in the passageway, wondering how in the world she was going to get her dress laced up, when she heard the clatter and clang of pans from below. There was also, she suddenly realized, the tantalizing smell of new-baked bread. Mistress Sedgwick, the hostess of the lodgings, was evidently up and about.

She hurried back into her chamber to drag the hairbrush through the tangled hair that fell almost to her waist, and threw her cloak about her to cover the open back of her gown. Then she trod quietly down the narrow stairway.

The door to the kitchen was closed, but she could hear a woman's voice talking and laughing; Mistress Sedgwick's by the sound of it, for the woman had a voice as large and robust as herself. Then she heard the sound of someone whistling "Greensleeves," the tune that was on everyone's lips since the song sheets had been published the previous year.

Katherine paused, wondering who was with Mistress Sedgwick. One of the kitchen maids most likely. It was early yet for any other guests to be up. She knocked upon the paneled door and then thrust it open. The kitchen was wreathed in steam and, as she stepped inside, a welcome rush of heat enveloped her.

"Come in, mistress, come in," boomed the landlady. She was standing at the end of the long table, up to her elbows in flour, kneading a great mound of dough.

Katherine came in gladly, relieved to be warm again.

"Good morrow to you, Mistress Radcliffe."

Katherine started at the sound of the masculine voice. The tall figure of Brendan Fitzgerald rose from the seat in the inglenook.

"Good morrow, sir," she replied, drawing her cloak more tightly about her.

Devil take the man—and Margery, for having been asleep when she was in need of her.

"Have you eaten yet?" he asked.

She shook her head, wondering all the while how she could retreat from the kitchen.

"There's warm ale and fresh bread. Nay, nay, Mistress Sedgwick, you keep on with your baking," he told the landlady, who had started to wipe the flour from her muscular arms. "I can serve Mistress Radcliffe. You look cold," he said to Katherine. "Sit you down by the fire here."

Before she knew it, she found herself seated before the fire, with a mug of warm ale redolent with nutmeg in her hand and a dish of thick-sliced bread spread with butter on her lap.

So disarming was the soft voice that one obeyed his orders before realizing that they were, in truth, orders. Katherine's spine tightened. She must guard against that in the future. But, for now, it suited her plan to have him think her a weak female, in need of his protection.

"Did you sleep well?" he asked.

"Yes, sir, I thank you," she said, looking up at him.

She had forgotten how very tall he was. His head barely missed the beams in the smoke-blackened ceiling.

"I trust your mother is feeling better."

"Very much so. The fever has left her." In her genuine relief, Katherine smiled up at him. "We have a great deal to thank you for, sir."

He shook his head. "Not at all, not at all." He stood, looking openly at her, a slight smile about his lips.

It was growing warm by the fire. She was also uncomfortably aware of her flushed cheeks and tumbled hair. She set down the tankard of ale and stood up.

"Are you too warm? Give me your cloak."

Before she could stop him, the cloak was lifted from her shoulders. She made a last grab at it, her fingers sticky with butter, but she was too late. A tide of red swept up her bare neck and into her already flushed face.

"Give me back my cloak, sir, if you please," she said through tight lips.

She saw from the dancing amusement in his eyes that he had seen the laces dangling about her waist and the gaping sides of her gown.

"Ah, the problem common to all ladies," he said. "Vanity, vanity. Now if you were like your maidservant," he continued, going to hang her cloak on a hook behind the kitchen door, "you would have laces at the front, so that you could do them up yourself. Or like Mistress Sedgwick, no laces at all."

Katherine stood in the center of the kitchen, fuming. The man was not only insufferably arrogant, he was also an interminable chatterer.

"Now," he said, returning to stand before her, "if you will but turn about, I shall soon have you set to rights."

"Thank you, sir." Katherine's voice was icier than the water in her jug had been. "My servant shall see to it. Please give me my cloak." She heard Mistress Sedgwick's deep chuckle and turned to give her a baleful glance.

"If tha'll wait one moment, mistress," said the woman hastily, "I'll have my hands clean and do it for thee."

Brendan Fitzgerald came even closer. "Now you would not be having the poor woman leave her breadmaking, would you," he said, his lips quirking, "when I could have you laced up and all decent in the veriest twinkling?"

Katherine gritted her teeth. She was about to make the man some scathing response to put him in his place, when the thought flashed into her mind that it would not hurt to have him believe she was attracted to him. That way, perhaps, he would be more likely to agree to her proposition.

"I thank you, sir," she whispered, blushing and hanging her head like a silly, simpering wench.

"Come closer to the light so that I may see what I am doing," he told her.

She moved into the pool of light from the lamp on the table and turned her bare back to him, bracing herself against the moment when he first touched her.

"Pardon me," he said as he lifted her hair from her back, parting it into two tresses. His fingers were warm against her skin, so warm she felt they were burning feathery paths across her back. Deftly, he drew the laces through their eyelets.

"Is that too tight?" he asked, when he was almost finished.

She shook her head, not trusting herself to speak. She knew that the tingling she felt in her breasts was not caused by over-tight lacing. She had never before been quite so aware of herself as a woman. The feeling was distinctly unsettling.

"I thank you, Master Radcliffe," she said when he tied the final knot. She looked up at him with what she hoped was a suitably bashful smile.

He made her a stiff military bow. "Your servant to command, madam. Will you finish your breakfast now?"

Katherine cast a look at Mistress Sedgwick, who was obviously enjoying this early morning entertainment. "What I should really like to do, sir, is to walk outside for a little. I have been cooped up for so long in that filthy prison that a walk in the fresh air would seem like heaven."

She told no lie. But her motivation was as much to get him on his own as to breathe in the brisk winter air.

"The snow is heavy underfoot, you know," he warned her.

She smiled. "We dalesfolk are not afraid of a little snow, Master Fitzgerald. We have snow in abundance in the Dales, as you will soon discover."

He shivered. "Holy Mother, and here was I thinking this was unusually severe weather. In all my life, I do not recall being so cold as I was when I awoke this morning."

"Come, sir," she said. "A brisk walk on a cold Yorkshire morning will do you a power of good." She took his arm. "I wish to speak *alone* with you," she whispered, with a little frown in Mistress Sedgwick's direction.

"I am greatly honored," he said, giving her another of his military bows, but there was nothing formal in the laughter in his eyes.

Katherine deliberately turned her back on him to tie up her hood-strings, not wishing him to see her anger. The man's assurance was insufferable.

"There now," she said sweetly, turning back to him, "I am ready for our walk."

"Are you certain you will be warm enough?"

"Of course. Come, Master Fitzgerald. Never tell me you are fearful of a little snow."

He opened the kitchen door for her. "Not with you beside me, Mistress Radcliffe."

She swept past him and marched down the passage ahead of him, but he was there to open the heavy outer door. She hesitated for a moment before stepping out into the busy street. The months of imprisonment had made her unused to people. Besides, even Middleham Moor on

Fair Day was not as busy as this. People poured past her, laughing and chattering, their feet turning the pristine snow to mud.

They both stood together on the threshold, eyeing the snow that drifted down, sparkling for a brief second on clothing or hair before it melted.

"Are you sure you would not prefer to talk with me in the parlor where there's a fire?" asked Master Fitzgerald.

"Quite sure. What I have to say to you is private. Besides, as I told you, I have a great longing to walk outside." Katherine shivered. "You cannot understand what it is like to live day and night in the one small room."

He took her gloved hand in his. "You must not think of it," he said gently. "It is all in the past."

She made no protest when he drew her hand through his arm. In truth, it felt good to be pressed close to his side as they began to walk along the crowded street. For once, it suited her to be cosseted, for her footsteps on the slippery cobblestones were a little uncertain and she was lightheaded from the noise and pressure of people about her.

She was about to speak to him when the great bells of the minster began tolling for Matins, making it impossible for him to hear her, although he bent his head down so that their faces were close. They both burst into spontaneous laughter, which ceased abruptly as their eyes met. Katherine held her breath, wondering if he was about to kiss her again, but all he did was wheel her about and guide her down a side street, saying, "If we are to converse, we must find a quiet place to do it."

They walked down Deangate and eventually came to Goodramgate, where the crowds had thinned out considerably. Snowflakes drifted down, settling on her companion's cap, making its peacock feather droop. Although Katherine's feet were beginning to freeze, she felt a strange compatibility with the man whose arm she held. The snow seemed to distance the other people from them, so that she and he were cocooned, isolated from the world, yet safe within it.

She stopped walking to turn to him.

"Are you cold?" he asked anxiously. "Shall we find an inn where we can warm ourselves."

"Not yet. What I have to say to you will not take long. Then we shall find somewhere to get warm before we walk back."

He looked down a small lane. "Wait one moment," he said, and started off at a run, before she could stop him. He had caught sight of a chestnut vendor at the corner of the lane.

Katherine hurried after him, attracted by the sight of the glowing coals of the brazier. As he purchased a bag of piping hot chestnuts, their shells almost black from their roasting, she warmed her hands before the brazier, pleased as a young child to hear the hiss of the snowflakes on the coals and the popping as the shells split.

"Rest here awhile whilst tha eats the nuts," said the vendor. They did not need a second bidding, but sat close together on the empty ale cask the ancient offered them.

While Brendan opened the chestnuts and shook a little of the salt in the twist of paper upon them, Katherine began to speak.

"I regret that I have not given you proper thanks for all your kindness, Master Fitzgerald," she said in a low voice.

He waved his hand in protest, offering her three peeled chestnuts on his open palm. She tried to pick them up, but her gloved fingers could not grip them. So he fed them to her, one by one, his fingers brushing her lips as he did so. And when he gave her the last chestnut, his fingers lingered against her mouth so that her tongue licked against them inadvertently as she darted it out to lick the salt from her lips.

A slow smile spread across his face as, very deliberately, he licked the selfsame fingers her tongue had touched. She felt a strangely pleasurable quickening in the pit of her stomach as she watched him.

"Delicious," he said.

Katherine sat up, her spine very straight. "Master Fitzgerald, I must return to my mother. Pray allow me to finish what I wish to say to you without further interruption, if you please."

He bowed his head to her. "I beg your pardon. Pray, continue."

"When you spoke to me last night, I was still bemused by the sudden release from prison. I did not quite comprehend all you said to me. Am I right in thinking that you wish to marry me?"

"You are."

She raised her eyes to his face. "And would you wish to marry me right away?" she whispered, hoping that the cold would have made her cheeks sufficiently pink to appear as if she were blushing. "You see, sir," she added hesitantly, "I do not know you at all."

"After this morning, I believe you might agree that we have got off to a fine start."

"Oh, yes. But . . . marriage is such a great matter. You see, I am only seventeen, Master Fitzgerald." For once, she did not add, as she usually did when telling her age, that she would be eighteen in January.

"There are many women married at a much earlier age than that, Mistress Radcliffe."

"Yes, but I . . . I had not been thinking of marriage yet, you see. My grandfather kept me apart from men." Again she raised her dark eyes to his. "I must own I am a little fearful of even the thought of marriage, particularly with a stranger from another country."

Brendan's arm drew her against his side. "I told you before that I shall never give you cause to fear me, my dear Katherine."

Katherine stiffened momentarily. How dare he use her given name! He hastily drew his arm away. "Forgive me," he murmured. "I must learn to become more the gentleman and less the soldier with you, I can see."

Flatter the man, flatter him, Kate Radcliffe, and you will get your way with him, she told herself. She met his troubled eyes. "You have been the kindest gentleman I know to me and my mother. Not only have you rescued us from prison—which is more than even my uncle, Lord Colborne, or my grandfather's dearest friend, Lord Scrope, could do—you have also, by offering to marry me, made it possible for me to remain in my own home. I shall be eternally grateful to you for that. All I ask for is just a little time to get to know you before our marriage is formally announced. Would you grant me that?" She placed her hand on his sleeve in a little gesture of supplication.

He grasped her hand tightly between his. "How could I not grant you anything you desire? For my part, however, I have no doubts at all."

He was hooked already, as securely hooked as one of the bream from the River Ure, dangling at the end of her line. "And I may stay at Radcliffe with my family meanwhile?"

"Of course you may. It is your home and soon to be *our* home. Think of that." His eyes gleamed. "I have never before had my very own home."

For a moment, Katherine felt a qualm of guilt, but it did not last.

His hands tightened on hers. "But promise me it will not be overlong before we are wed, my dear Katherine."

"I promise that I shall not wait long to give you my answer, Master Fitzgerald."

Long enough only to await a reply from Edward. She knew from Edward's mother that it would be another year, at least, before Edward took his final vows. He surely would not stand by and see her forced into a marriage with another man, and a foreigner at that.

Chapter 11

When she heard that they were to return to Radcliffe, Alyssa was eager to leave York that very day. It took the combined efforts of Katherine and Margery to keep her in bed.

"We must return in time for Christmas," she insisted, almost hysterically. The thought of seeing Radcliffe after all these months of imprisonment flamed in her mind, setting it afire with hope and longing.

As always, it was Tobias Ridley who brought his calm reason to the situation. The following morning, Alyssa sent for him as soon as she had woken, before daybreak. She insisted on dressing and ordered Margery to help her to the little parlor. There, she sat beside the fire, wrapped in several shawls, waiting for Tobias to come.

When, at last, the latch lifted and Tobias was shown in, she turned eagerly to greet him, her hand extended. "What a welcome sight you are, Tobias!" she said, her eyes glowing.

He did not take her hand, but made his usual formal little bow, the two small spots of color on his cheekbones an acknowledgment of the warmth of her greeting.

"You may leave us, Margery," she told the servant, who bobbed a curtsey and left the room. "Sit down, Tobias," Alyssa said, waving her hand at the bench beside her.

He inclined his head and sat down, neatly smoothing the skirt of his short, black gown over his knees when he had done so. "You appear to be much improved in health, Mistress Radcliffe," he told her. "I am glad to see it."

"I am greatly improved in health, Tobias, and have sent for you to arrange for our immediate return home."

He regarded her with one of his grave expressions. "Is that wise, when you have been sick with a high fever? It is still snowing and there is a cold wind blowing today. To travel in this weather would be foolhardy, I believe."

She leant forward, her hands clasped tightly. "Oh, Tobias," she said in a low voice, "I must go home. Only you can know what I have been feeling these past months. All my memories of Richard and Philip are there, at Radcliffe."

She turned away from him, her mouth trembling.

Tobias stiffened. His face registered dismay as he watched the heaving shoulders. He wondered for a moment if he should call for Margery or Mistress Kate. But he did not. She was right. Only he could truly realize what she must have suffered in these months since the deaths of Philip and her son.

He stretched out a tentative hand and let it rest lightly on hers. How small her hands were beneath his. Before he could draw his away, she had clutched at it convulsively and turned to him with a tearful smile.

"Dear, dear Tobias. How would we manage without you?"

"It is my belief you would manage very well." The small smile brightened his pale, austere face. Slowly, he disengaged his hand from hers. It was not seemly that she should clasp the hand of the steward of her household.

"We have shared so much, Tobias, you and I. But more than anything we share our mutual love for Sir Philip. You see," she said, giving him one of her direct looks, "I am not ashamed to admit it to you. I shall never forget how you went into exile in Scotland with him, how you shared imprisonment with him, nursing him back to health." Her eyes filled with tears. "But for you, Tobias Ridley, we would never have had him with us for those ten years. The happiest years of my life," she whispered.

His hands tightened into fists as he thought of the years before that, of her deep unhappiness with Thomas Radcliffe. "Sir Philip was my master," Tobias said abruptly. "It was my duty to serve him."

"Oh, Tobias," Alyssa said with a sigh, "can you not put away the mask of a servant just for now? I am in great need of your advice and I wish to talk to you as a friend, not my steward. After all, Philip used to think of you as a younger brother."

Tobias rubbed hard at his neat beard. "That was different," he muttered. "That was in the perilous days of the Rising. The only way I could persuade Sir Philip to accept me as his companion in his flight to Scotland was to resign as his steward. 'Very well, Tobias,' said he. 'From henceforth you are my brother and my friend.'" He blinked rapidly.

Alyssa's smile was one of great tenderness. "And from henceforth you were both brother and friend to him, the most loyal friend a man could have. Now, for the moment, I ask you to forget that you are the Steward of Radcliffe and become my friend."

His gray eyes met hers. "That would not be right," he told her.

His rebuke made her feel like a twelve-year-old child again. "Oh, for the love of heaven, Tobias, have you forgotten that you are the son of a gentleman, better educated than most of those who lord it over you? I need your advice and would remind you that I am no longer the mistress of Radcliffe. You also seem to have forgotten that Radcliffe belongs to Captain Fitzgerald now."

"Is it possible that I would forget such a thing?" he said, stung into anger.

"It is about Captain Fitzgerald that I wish to speak to you. What is your opinion of him?"

Tobias considered his answer. "I do not know what to make of him," he said at last, with a slight frown. "Throughout our journey to York, he spoke little of his life in Ireland."

"Did he talk of his parentage, of his father at all?"

"Not one whit. On that subject, he was silent. I did not think it my place to ask him."

"No, of course not. But he must be a gentleman, surely, to have the mighty Earl of Sussex as his patron." An involuntary shiver ran over Alyssa as she spoke the Earl's name. Although more than ten years had passed since their last meeting, at her husband's funeral, she would never forget the Earl of Sussex's coldness and his suspicion of her and Philip.

"It would seem so. Master Fitzgerald—he prefers that to 'Captain,' by the bye—"

"I must try to remember that. Katherine is forever warning me about it."

"He has received a good education in both Ireland and this country; a year at Cambridge University and he read Law at the Inns of Court."

Alyssa shook her head. "One has to wonder why a man of his good looks and seeming ability would wish to retire to out-of-the-way Yorkshire."

"That is true."

"A captain in Her Majesty's army at the early age of—what is he, twenty-four, twenty-five years, would you say, Tobias?"

"I would think so, yes."

"Strange that a young man who is the protégé of the Lord Chamberlain would prefer life in the remote Dales to service in his own country. Indeed, Sussex might have found him some office at Court. After all, Thomas was also under his patronage and *he* did extremely well in his service. The Earl can be generous to those he likes," she admitted.

"All this is true," said Tobias.

"But it is also beside the point. Whether we like it or not, Fitzgerald is now the Lord of Radcliffe. And he has proposed marriage to Katherine. Although I cannot like the informal manner in which he has spoken to her on the subject, I cannot fault him too heavily for it. After all, it is not often that a man releases his future wife and mother-in-law from prison."

Tobias allowed a small smile to escape him.

"What surprises me," continued Alyssa, "is that he should make such a hasty decision to wed Kate."

Tobias adjusted the already neat, crisp ruffs at his wrists. "I suspect that it was not as hasty as it seemed."

Alyssa leaned over to peer up at his face. "Why you sly fox, Tobias. Was it you who put the idea into his head?"

Tobias's eyes widened. "I? Why I am merely the steward at Radcliffe. How could I do such a thing as to make suggestions as to a wife for its new landlord? Mistress Kate is very fair to look upon. It would be difficult for any unattached gentleman to resist her."

"And you have already ascertained that Capt—Master Fitzgerald is without any attachments."

Master Ridley raised his eyebrows. "But of course, madam. That surely goes without saying."

Alyssa pursed her lips together to keep from smiling. "And it would be a great advantage for him to marry the daughter of the house of which he is to become the master."

"Precisely what I told him," said Tobias, falling into her trap.

"Sly fox," she mouthed at her steward, but he pretended not to see.

He gave her a stern look, but this time she refused to be subdued by him. "No, you need not frown at me like that, Tobias Ridley. You cannot frighten me anymore, you know. I would remind you that I am no longer the shy young maiden fresh from the schoolroom that I was when I first came to Radcliffe as Thomas's bride." She stared into the fire. "Oh Lord, what a long time ago that seems; almost twenty years. I am a middle-aged woman now, thirty-six years old, past my prime, I fear."

Tobias made protesting noises in his throat, but did not commit his thoughts to words.

"And you, Tobias, must be—"

"An old man."

"Nonsense," she said with a laugh, refusing to be silenced by him. "You were at least five years younger than Philip, which makes you, what, fifty-five now?"

Tobias looked down his aquiline nose at her. "I believe you summoned me here to ask for my advice, madam, not to engage in a discussion about our respective ages."

Alyssa grimaced. "You are quite right to rebuke me. Forgive me, Tobias, I am in a giddy, light-headed mood. A mixture of relief at being released from prison, I would suppose, and excitement at the thought of going home." She laid her hand on his stiff silk sleeve. "I beg your pardon, dear friend, I did not mean to tease you."

She could feel the muscles in his arm tense and she quickly drew her hand away, remembering that he did not like to be touched.

"What I wish to ask you," she said, folding her hands quietly in her lap, "is whether you think that Brendan Fitzgerald will be a good husband for Katherine. We must be careful that, in our desire to keep Radcliffe in the family, we do not force Kate into a marriage that would be abhorrent to her. Will he treat her with kindness, do you think?"

"If you will pardon me for saying so, madam, I am not certain that kindness is what Mistress Katherine needs in a husband. It is a firm hand she needs."

Alyssa nodded. "You are right, as always," she said with a sigh. "But I would wish to see him deal kindly with her also."

Tobias frowned and appeared to be consulting the turves of glowing peat in the fireplace. Then he spoke. "I have spent several days in Master Fitzgerald's company now. It is my opinion that he would be a good husband for her. Barnaby tells me that he has a fine way with horses."

"And that is the greatest compliment a Yorkshireman can give a man, of course," Alyssa said, smiling.

"But will you be able to persuade her to marry him, that is the question, is it not?"

"She still insists that she loves Edward Carlton, despite the fact that he never answered one of the letters she wrote to him from prison. It broke my heart to hear her ask the jailer each morning if there were any letters for her. Surely it would not have hurt him to write her some note of consolation? Particularly when it was because of a priest's visit that we were incarcerated."

"I doubt he would be permitted to do so." As soon as the words were out, Tobias muttered a curse under his breath.

"You need not concern yourself, Tobias. Katherine told me Edward's secret when we were in prison. It is hard to keep secrets to oneself in such close confinement. In truth, I had not realized that *you* knew."

"Servants' gossip," Tobias said curtly.

"Ah, yes. While we are talking of Catholic priests, do you think it was Father Campion who divulged our names?"

His jaw tightened. "In truth I cannot say, madam. 'Tis said he gave only the names of those the authorities already knew, such as Mistress Bulmer and Dr. Vavasour."

"I would like to think that he did not give us away," she said. "Have you heard . . . was the torture very severe?"

"They racked him several times, I believe, and there were other . . . other methods used, also," he said reluctantly.

"Dear Christ," she whispered. "He was such a kindly man and gave Philip great solace in his dying. We live in a cruel world, Tobias."

He did not meet her eyes, knowing instinctively that they were filled with tears.

"Oh God, to think that that might be Edward's fate, also," she said. "He will never come back to Katherine, will he?"

"If he were ever to give up his training as a priest, he would have done it by now, to return to help you and Mistress Kate when you were in prison. No, I fear Master Carlton's love for the papist church is far greater than his love for Mistress Kate."

"Do not sound so bitter, Tobias. He could not help it, I am sure."

"Nay, but he could have behaved as a gentleman should and informed Sir Philip much earlier of his change of heart."

"It still would have made no difference to Kate, you know. She is as tenacious as her father was. She is utterly convinced Edward will return to her one day."

Tobias turned upon her, his usually passive nature suddenly transported to action. "Then we must rid her of that notion, once and for all, Mistress Alyssa, or she will never agree to marry this Irishman and Radcliffe will be lost to all of you."

Alyssa nodded slowly. "Once we are back at Radcliffe, I shall write to Edward's mother. Between us we shall find a way of convincing Katherine, I am sure. Which brings me back to what I was saying when you first arrived. I wish you to make arrangements for our journey home immediately. And, before you make protest again, I must assure you that I am perfectly well enough to travel. Christmas is only five days away and I am determined to celebrate it at Radcliffe."

The thought came into Tobias's mind that it was not only from her father that Kate had inherited her determination. "Very well, madam. I believe that Master Fitzgerald has already made enquiries with regard to a horse litter—"

"No litter, I pray you. I loathe the things. Their wretched swaying makes me sick to my stomach, as you well know, Tobias. No, I shall ride pillion behind you or Master Fitzgerald. Have you money for the hiring and the provisions for the journey, by the bye?"

"I have." Tobias clapped his hand to the leather purse strapped to his belt. "Your father gave me money for your needs before we left, although Master Fitzgerald insisted on paying for our expenses on the journey to York."

"How kind of him! You know, I liked the man the first time I saw him entering the prison beside that cold-fish Earl of Huntingdon. He may be somewhat ignorant of our ways here, but he has an air of quiet confidence about him that I find attractive."

Tobias murmured something beneath his breath.

Alyssa smiled. "Evidently, you are not in agreement with me on that score. But I shall not waste time in arguing the point with you. I refuse to permit you to dampen my spirits today." Although she was still seated, she spread her arms wide, so that one large shawl fell from her shoulders. "We are free, Kate and I, and going home to Radcliffe."

He stood up and made a solemn bow. "That is indeed a cause for great rejoicing, madam."

Her smile faded as she met his eyes. "You know, Tobias, I shall always wonder who it was who betrayed us."

"Most likely it was Campion. Do not think any more about it."

"I shall try not to, but one thing I do know is that all the present troubles in our kingdom are caused by one person, and that is the Scottish Queen. Even in her prison she spins her web, drawing in innocent flies. I swear that men like Edward and Campion would not be risking their lives in the Catholic cause were she not busy hatching schemes with France and Spain against England."

"Forget her. She is no longer any concern of yours."

Alyssa's eyes blazed. "How can you tell me to forget her? Were it not for Mary, Queen of Scots, Philip would still be alive today. His health was broken by his exile and imprisonment. Were it not for Queen Mary, Philip would not have been attainted and Radcliffe would belong to us, not to a total stranger."

Tobias murmured agreement. He refrained from pointing out that were it not for Queen Mary and the uprising in the North, Alyssa's husband Thomas Radcliffe most likely would still be alive and causing her much grief.

"Queen Mary is safe in Sheffield Castle, securely guarded," he reminded her. "Queen Elizabeth will never release her. Mary cannot harm any member of the Radcliffe family."

"I suppose you are right, as always," Alyssa said, sighing heavily.

Queen Mary could not harm her, Tobias thought grimly, after he had taken his leave of his mistress, but there remained someone who could and had already done so.

There had been many present at Radcliffe on the nights of both Sir Philip's death and of his funeral, when Edmund Campion had made his fateful visits. Tobias vowed he would not be at rest until he found out who it was who had denounced Alyssa and Katherine Radcliffe to the authorities.

Chapter 12

The journey from York took three days—three days of biting wind and impassable snowdrifts that had to be skirted, and nights spent at crowded inns. But the ever-pressing fear that they would not reach Radcliffe by Christmas kept the women going, despite the men's protests.

By the time they reached the small town of Middleham, high on the southern slope of Wensleydale, both Alyssa and Katherine were so weary they could barely speak. Alyssa's bones were causing her such pain, she wondered if she would ever be able to walk again.

"Will you not come inside to warm yourself, Mistress Radcliffe?" Brendan asked her, when they stopped at the Black Swan Inn to rest the horses before their short ride across Middleham Moor.

"Thank you, Master Fitzgerald, but I think it best that I not dismount, lest I not be able to walk across the yard." She gave him a faint smile.

"That is easily remedied," he said, and before she could protest he had lifted her down from the pillion and carried her into the snug parlor of the inn.

He was rewarded with a warm smile from Katherine. Jesu, the girl was fair. *Dame Fortune is indeed smiling upon you, Brendan lad*, he told himself, watching the color flood back into Katherine's face as she warmed herself before the fire. Although he had never relished the idea of being tied to one woman, the thought of this beauty sharing his bed, his life, could speedily reconcile him to marriage.

Be easy now, lad, he admonished himself, addressing the stirring in his loins that resulted from his thoughts. *She's not yours yet*. Their year of mourning would be up in February, which brought them to Lent. They would have to wait until May to be married. Five long months. Ah well, he would spend the time in getting to know his retainers and his land, as well as his betrothed. The prospect was not an entirely unpleasant one.

Brendan might not have been quite so sure of himself had he been able to read Katherine's thoughts. She, too, was considering the future, as she bent over the fire, enjoying the warmth that had begun to permeate her frozen body.

May would be the earliest they could marry, she was thinking. That would give her more than sufficient time to send word to Edward through his mother. No doubt her letters from prison had been misdirected and that was why he had not responded to them. As soon as the festivities were over, she would ride over to Swaledale and give her letter to Edward directly into his mother's hands. Long before May, Edward would have returned to Yorkshire to claim her as his bride.

Meanwhile, she must continue to play this game of Marry Me with the gullible Irishman, so that she and her family would not be thrown out of Radcliffe. When Edward returned, he would provide her and her family with a home.

But it will not be Radcliffe, cried an inner voice.

Katherine stood up abruptly. "I think we should get on before the light goes," she announced.

"I am in agreement with you," said Brendan. "I sent word ahead from Masham—"

Katherine laughed at his pronunciation.

"Holy Mother," he said, smiling good-naturedly. "I shall never be able to get my tongue around your strange-sounding Yorkshire names. As I was saying, Mistress Radcliffe," he continued, with a mock frown, "at Master Ridley's prompting, I have sent word to Sir William and Lady Harcourt and to your aunt and her husband, Lord Colborne—"

"And to Great-Uncle Piers, I trust."

"Would you be having me send messages to the entire neighborhood?"

"Yes, indeed I would, Master Fitzgerald," cried Katherine, her eyes glowing with excitement. "That way everyone will be there at Radcliffe to greet us." She spun around, to stand before him, cheeks flushed, her velvet cap awry. "How will we ever be able to thank you enough, sir?" she cried, impulsively grasping his hand.

"'Tis not kind to ask such a question when we are not alone," he said, half laughing at her, but Katherine saw, deep in his eyes, something that stilled her exuberance and caused her heart to contract.

She drew her hand away and turned from him, the shadow of fear upon her. Although she was still inexperienced in the ways of men, she had realized in that single moment that to trifle with this man might be dangerous.

They had intended to ride across Middleham Moor and approach Radcliffe from above, but they were advised by the innkeeper that the snow was so deep up on the heights of the high moor that they might become bogged down in a drift. So they were forced to take the long way around and ride along the southern bank of the River Ure, which was frozen into silence.

By the time they reached the foot of the sloping fell, dusk had drawn in upon them. But when Katherine looked up, she saw the vast north windows of her home ablaze with light to welcome them, and her heart lifted at the sight. She glanced at her mother and then quickly looked away again when she saw the glint of tears on her cheeks.

She knew instinctively that the tears were not wholly joyful ones.

"'Tis a fine sight from a distance, Radcliffe Hall," said Brendan, drawing his horse in beside Katherine's.

She ignored him, continuing to drink in the sight of the gabled walls, the ornate chimneys against the rosy dark sky. She could not bear to think that this man, this incomer from Ireland, with only one servant to his name—and that servant a savage garbed in animal skins—was the lord of *her* home, of *her* manor.

He rode on beside her up the steep rise, relaxed in the saddle, the reins gathered in one gloved hand. She had taken note of his horsemanship on the journey and grudgingly admired it. His was not the elegant style of her grandfather, of course. No one could ride with Grandy's grace. But there was no doubting the Irishman's ability, casual though it seemed.

"Are you glad to be coming home?" he asked her in his soft voice, as they approached the outer limestone wall surrounding Radcliffe Hall.

She turned to look at him, her chin raised. "Of course I am," was her sharp reply. If he was expecting further tokens of gratitude from her, he would be disappointed. She refused to be continually thanking him for having had them released from prison, for graciously permitting them to return to their own home. The home was hers by right, anyway.

"Then I am content," he said, leaving her taut with anger, for his very tone seemed to suggest that, but for him, she would still be languishing in prison without a hope of ever seeing Radcliffe again.

The fact that this was so made it even harder to bear.

The sudden onslaught of joyous shouts and frenzied barking of dogs as they rounded the snow-covered bowling green and terraced garden and arrived in the forecourt completely erased Master Fitzgerald from her mind.

"Here's my darling great-niece, more beautiful than ever, I see!" That was her grandmother's brother, Great-Uncle Piers Metcalfe, his face raddled from overindulgence in sack, but as good-natured as ever.

Well-loved faces and forms crowded in upon her: gruff Sir William Harcourt, her mother's father, tears flowing unashamedly down his chapped cheeks; his wife, with her wind-tossed veils, her usual cool composure blown away as she tearfully embraced first her daughter, then her granddaughter; and Joanna, darling, darling little Joanna, sobbing out her joy and delight as if her heart would crack.

"You will all be frozen into ice blocks if you stand out here a moment longer." The cool, clear voice cut through all the cries and exclamations.

Katherine turned to the doorway, where her mother's sister, Aunt Isobel, stood, with her husband, the dour Lord Colborne, behind her. She watched as her mother disengaged herself from Grandsire Harcourt's warm embrace and extended her arms towards her sister.

"I bid you welcome to your home," Isobel said, but she made no move from the doorway and waited for Alyssa to come to her to embrace her. Her welcome to Katherine was far warmer. "My dearest niece," she said, her lips pressed to Katherine's cheeks. "You are most welcome. Come inside quickly, or you will perish with the cold."

How did Aunt Isobel always manage to look so beautiful, whatever the circumstances? Here was everyone else windblown and red-nosed from the cold, disheveled from embraces and jostling, and she stood there, her fair beauty unblemished, the intricate whorls of silver thread on her velvet overgown gleaming in the torchlight. Beside her, Katherine always felt like some blowsy village hoyden. Yet, despite her cool beauty, Aunt Isobel had always been kind to her; frequently more kind than her own mother.

They all thronged into the great hall, which was ablaze with the light that shone from the iron chandeliers and the wall sconces. The huge stone fireplace had been piled high with apple logs that emitted their fragrance as they crackled and spat, their flames also lighting the hall and issuing the warmest of welcomes.

Every possible corner and object had been festooned with festive greenery. Bay and laurel, holly and trailing ivy bedecked the paintings on the walls. The great shield and sword from the battle of Agincourt gleamed beneath its drapery of laurel branches, and from the central iron chandelier hung a great kissing ball of holly and mistletoe, the red and white berries and shiny green leaves glistening in the candlelight.

They had even assembled the waits to entertain them, so that the strains of "Wassail, Wassail" mingled with the sound of everyone talking at once and not caring if they were not heard.

Uncle Piers did not need a second bidding to bring on the wassail bowl, which was already on the table, the wreaths of steam issuing from it reflected in the mirror-bright polished surface.

"I give you a toast," Piers cried, holding up his brimming silver tankard. "To the joyous return of Alyssa and Katherine Radcliffe to their rightful home."

"Alyssa and Katherine, God bless 'em!" Goblets and tankards and silver cups were filled and raised, and then sipped or drained, depending upon the drinker.

As Katherine paused in her lively conversation with Joanna to sip her drink, breathing in the spicy fumes of cinnamon and mace, she caught sight of the tall figure standing separate in the screen entrance, the current of air from outside swaying the heavy curtain that almost shrouded him.

Her heart gave a little lurch of dismay.

"I pray you all, be silent for a moment!" she heard a voice call out. It was only when the voice shouted again, with authority, "Silence!" that she recognized it as her own.

The noise died to a murmur, and then stilled completely. Everyone's face turned to her, expectantly.

"In all our joy at being together again on this blessed eve of Christ's Nativity we have quite forgotten one person," she began, her body trembling with the knowledge that she, one of the youngest there, was addressing them all with an air of superior authority. She did not care. Someone must say it.

She raised her cup. "My beloved friends and members of my family and loyal servants of Radcliffe, I ask you to join me in drinking a toast to the person without whom we would not be here: the new Lord of Radcliffe, Master Brendan Fitzgerald!"

For a moment, no one responded to her request. Bewildered faces looked about them, seeking for the subject of their toast. But Katherine had already started across the hall and stood, smiling, before Brendan.

"You should not have done that," he murmured, but his eyes were suspiciously bright.

In answer, she took his hand, from which he had hurriedly stripped his riding gauntlet, and drew him into the center of the hall. "May I present to you all Master Brendan Fitzgerald, our gallant rescuer." She raised her cup and saluted him with it, before turning to the assembly. "I pray you, join me in a toast to Master Fitzgerald."

This time there was no sign of hesitancy. A chorus of voices pronounced his name as his health was drunk.

Brendan smiled down at her, his hands still clasped in hers.

"A kiss, a kiss," cried Piers. "The man deserves at least a kiss for all his pains."

Katherine immediately regretted her impulsive gesture of kindness, but, realizing that it would seem churlish in her to refuse, particularly as they were standing directly beneath the kissing ball, she lifted her face for her second kiss from Brendan Fitzgerald.

After all, she told herself as he bent his dark head towards her, I am supposed to be betrothed to the man.

The kiss was most decorous; on the lips, but light and brief. She knew a fleeting moment of disappointment as his hands slid down her arms and then released her.

Avoiding his eyes, she turned from him, glad to see that people were milling about him now, eager to speak with him, welcoming him.

"That was nicely done, my dear Kate," said her mother, who was resting in a pillowed chair by the fire. "You put me to shame. I should have presented Brendan immediately upon our entrance into the house."

Katherine's shoulders tensed. Now her mother was calling him by his given name. It was becoming more and more difficult to extricate herself from Master Fitzgerald's clutches.

"He looked so forlorn, standing there by himself. I would have done the same for anyone."

"Of course you would." Her mother reached out her hand to Katherine, who kissed it and then immediately turned away, seeking for someone to give her an excuse to leave her.

"I am very weary, Kate," Alyssa said in a faint voice. "This has all been rather overwhelming for me."

Katherine looked down at her mother and saw that her face was ghostly white. "Are you feeling unwell again?"

"Not really unwell, my dear Kate. It is only that . . . that . . ." Her countenance seemed to waver before Katherine's eyes, the lips quivering, eyelids blinking rapidly. "The memories are crowding in," she whispered. "I would prefer to be alone before they completely overcome me."

Before Katherine had time to send for Margery, she found Tobias at her side.

"Do you wish to retire, Mistress Radcliffe?" he asked.

"If you please, Master Ridley," was the whispered reply.

"I shall carry you—"

"No, Master Ridley, you shall not. You are not so large a man that you can manage even me, slight as I am, up that large flight of stairs. Fetch Master Fitzgerald, if you please. He is young and strong."

Master Fitzgerald was duly fetched and said that he would be honored to carry the mistress of Radcliffe upstairs, if she was willing to place her trust in him.

Before she had time to say yea or nay in reply, he had lifted her in his arms and carried her up the stairs.

"Yes, Master Fitzgerald," Alyssa said, when they reached the door to her bedchamber, "I am inclined to place my trust in you."

"'Tis a little late you are in saying it, then," he said, grinning down at her.

"Yes, you are right," she replied, when he had set her on her feet. "And I was also more than a little late in presenting you to our assembled friends and members of our family below. For that, I must beg your pardon, Master Fitzgerald."

He turned his head away, pretending to survey the beautiful chamber, with its carved paneled walls and rich furnishings. "I do not expect people here to welcome me," he said in a muffled voice, addressing the far wall. "I am well aware that I have a hard task ahead of me. I told Master Ridley that I shall work hard to earn the trust of all at Radcliffe, and I mean to do so, with God's help, however long it takes me."

"I believe you, sir. Now, here is my tiring woman. Forgive me, but I must go to my bed." Alyssa laid her hand on his arm. "We will speak of your marriage with Katherine tomorrow, with my father. One word of advice before you go, Brendan. Be patient with Katherine. She has been cosseted by us all, particularly by her grandfather."

"Maybe so, but I shall not soon forget her kindness to me this evening," he said.

"Katherine has a kind heart, but I warn you, she is also hot tempered."

"I give you my word that I shall be gentle in my wooing."

Remembering Tobias's words that it was firmness not kindness Katherine needed in a man, Alyssa foresaw a rough time ahead for Brendan Fitzgerald. Despite his self-confidence, he was young and seemed inexperienced in the ways of the world—and of women. The one thing she must do for him as soon as possible was remove the obstacle of Edward Carlton from his path.

But once she had been undressed and tucked into bed by Margery, with a hot stone wrapped in flannel at her feet, Alyssa's mind was filled with other thoughts besides those of Brendan and Kate. She dismissed Margery reluctantly, at the same time both longing and dreading to be left alone with the thoughts and memories that flooded in on her, now that she was beneath Radcliffe's roof once more.

She had been taken from Radcliffe in September, when all the work of harvest and stillroom had been filling her time. Before that, the numbness of her loss had not really completely worn off.

When she had ridden into the courtyard this evening, her heart had leapt with joy. She had thought at first that it was a natural reaction to the sight of her home. But then, a moment later, her heart had plummeted, leaving a feeling of chill darkness that no amount of welcoming could dispel. And she knew that the leap of joy had been for Philip. Whenever she had ridden in from visiting her old home, Harcourt Hall, or even after just a few hours at the market or hawking on the moors, he had always left his work to rush out to greet her.

He would never do so again.

She must make the best of the many years that probably stretched before her, but she knew that without Richard—the boy who had been their pride and hope—and Philip, her one true love, from henceforth her life would be empty and meaningless.

"The one thing I can do for you both, my darlings, is to ensure that Radcliffe remains in this family and with its descendants," she whispered into the darkness.

She made that pact with them and God on her knees before climbing back into bed again and falling into an uneasy, dream-ridden sleep.

Part 2
1582-1583

Chapter 13

The celebration of Katherine's eighteenth birthday in January came and went. Then the lambing season was upon them. Yet Katherine still had not received any reply to the long letter she had given to Lady Carlton to send to Edward.

When February began to draw to a close, she thought she would burst with impatience after being cooped up for so long, with not even the solace of hawking or coursing hares to help pass the time and release some of her pent-up energy.

Her mother and the women sat in the solar spinning and plying their needles, seemingly content to work while listening to Joanna play to them on the recorder or lute.

Meanwhile, despite the difficulties of the severe winter and heavy snows, Master Fitzgerald was riding about the manor with Tobias and their bailiff, Applegarth, becoming acquainted with Radcliffe's retainers and tenants.

As she sat in the warm solar, with the pale morning sun shining in the windows, Katherine wished with all her heart that she could be out there with the men.

When she heard the clatter of their horses' hooves in the courtyard, she threw down the sheet she had been hemming for her wedding chest. Springing up from her stool, she rushed from the solar, ignoring her mother's sharp, "Katherine!" which was repeated on a louder note as she sped downstairs.

Grabbing an old cloak and a pair of pattens from the press by the kitchen entrance, she hurriedly put them on, and then wrestled with the heavy iron latch of the side door. Hearing her cursing, one of the indoor servants ran to her aid. In a matter of moments, she was outside, hurrying across the kitchen yard and into the stable area.

Her heart beat furiously. This is where I belong, she thought exultantly, her breath gusting before her in the frosty air. Outside. Not sitting in a stuffy solar, sewing, with nothing but women's chatter about such boring matters as Ann Harper's latest baby and the weaver's visit next week to entertain her.

Exhilarated, she watched as the men dismounted and the grooms led away their horses. Brendan was still mounted, she noticed. Despite her antagonism to the man, she had to admit he was extremely good to look upon. His black hair, which he wore longer now, was blown about his face.

"Good morrow to you, fair Kate," he cried, and slid from his horse with that ease she both deplored and admired.

He strode across the yard to her, his right arm wrapped around something he bore within the confines of his cloak. With odious familiarity, he clapped his left arm about her, drew her to him, and kissed her full on the lips.

His mouth was cold and he smelled of peat and horses. Instinctively, her hand went up to the collar of his cloak as if she would keep him there. His kiss deepened and his arm tightened about her, pulling her close against his lithe body. Her lips softened and parted beneath his, and she felt his tongue moist against her mouth.

The wriggling of something against her breast made her pull away. "What in heaven's name have you got there?" she demanded.

He threw back his head and laughed. "The poor creature is jealous of all the attention you are getting from me." The grooms laughed as he opened his cloak to reveal a tiny lamb, shivering in the crook of his arm.

"Oh, the poor little thing," cried Katherine.

"Its mother died in a drift up on the moor. Colum is going to adopt it," he said, grinning at his groom. "But first we must take it into the kitchen and see if we can get some milk into the poor creature."

He looked down at her, his smile fading. "By Saint Patrick, Kate, you are a gladsome sight to see on a morning," he said softly, his eyes glowing with an intensity that disturbed her. "'Twas good of you to rush out to greet me, as you did." He took her chin in one hand. "And to welcome me with a kiss that would put fire into a man even colder than I was." He bent his head as if he were about to kiss her again, but she ducked away and walked towards the entrance.

"I would have you know, Master Fitzgerald," she said, her tone full of scorn, "that betrothed or not, a gentleman does not publicly kiss a lady before the servants, particularly in a stableyard."

"Ah well, and there was I, believing what I've been told, that Englishwomen are renowned for their kissing, even to bussing strange gentlemen who are visiting their homes. And I am surely not a stranger, am I, dear Kate?"

Katherine stopped and swung around to give him one of her haughtiest looks. "No, you are not a stranger, but neither are you a gentleman, sir. And I wish you would not call me Kate. That name is reserved for members of my family and my closest friends."

"Ah, but Kate, sweet Kate, in but two months I shall be the closest of your friends, shall I not?" His hand lifted to press against the side of her throat, and she felt her pulse there leap in response to his touch. He slid his hand under the weight of her hair to the back of her neck, drawing her face close to his for another kiss.

What in the devil's name was the matter with her, she wondered, that she should be repelled and yet at the same time so strangely attracted by this man? Perhaps his weird long-haired groom, Colum, was his familiar, concocting spells to bewitch her. She had heard them speak together in a strange language, which Brendan had assured her was the Irish tongue. But, for all she knew, it could be the language of sorcery.

As his mouth touched hers, she crossed her fingers behind her back, and this time made sure that she did not respond in any way to the kiss.

He pulled away from her and shrugged his shoulders. "I must not be a glutton," he said, and bowed her into the house.

Although Katherine was determined to set a distance between them, she could not resist going into the kitchen with him, to see what he would do with the lamb, which was bleating piteously.

The kitchen servants were busy preparing for dinner, but they ceased their chopping and basting and pastry-making to observe this strange new master of theirs.

First he set the little creature on the floor, but its black-hosed legs were so feeble it would have toppled over had he not scooped it up again.

Katherine sighed impatiently. "Give it to me," she said, tying an apron about her. She sat down upon a three-legged stool by the hearth and took the lamb from Brendan.

One of the servants had anticipated her by warming some milk in a small copper pan suspended in the trivet. "Hold the pan for me, if you please, Master Fitzgerald," Katherine bade him.

"Your servant to command, my lady." He knelt before her in the rushes, taking the pan from the trivet. "Dear saints in heaven, 'tis hot," he exclaimed, almost dropping it.

Grinning, the kitchen maid offered him a heavy cloth with which to hold it.

Holding the squirming lamb under her left arm, Katherine dipped her middle finger into the warm milk and gave it to the lamb to suck. At first, it butted against her hand, but soon its natural instincts took over, and it began to suck on her finger, its jaws surprisingly strong.

Brendan moved closer, so that she could dip her finger more quickly into the pan and drip less milk on the way to the lamb's mouth. His kneeling body was pressed against her legs. He seemed transfixed by the regular movement of her hand, milk dripping from it, back and forth. She avoided his eyes, but became aware both of his gaze upon the swell of her breasts above the bodice of her gown and of his heightened breathing.

After a while, the lamb's jaws loosened and it snuffled and grunted and wheezed, like an old man sated with his bread and milk, and then fell asleep on Katherine's lap.

As her left hand clutched the fleecy curls on the lamb's back, Brendan set down the pan and reached out for her other hand. "I long for the day when I can see you feed our firstborn child," he said very softly.

The moment throbbed between them, vibrating throughout Katherine's body. Then she stood up and thrust the lamb at the kitchen maid. "Feed it thus every hour, Mary, and make certain the milk is not too hot, lest you burn its mouth."

Before Brendan had time to do more than scramble to his feet, she swept from the kitchen.

How dare he! she fumed. How dare he talk to her of "our firstborn child," and look at her with open lust in his eyes.

Her mother intercepted her at the head of the stairs. "I wish to talk with you, Katherine."

"I pray you, Mother, give me a little time to myself. It would be best if you wait. I am feeling extremely vexed at present."

The last thing she needed now was one of her mother's sermons on propriety and the correct conduct for a lady.

Her mother's small figure seemed to contract. "I, too, am vexed, Katherine," she said frostily. "To run from the chamber like some wild moor pony without a by-your-leave is hardly the manner in which the future mistress of Radcliffe should behave, is it? What have I told you before about setting a good example to the servants?"

Katherine heaved an exasperated sigh, but she gave her mother the requisite curtsy and a brusque "I pray your pardon, my lady Mother," before going into the solar.

Inwardly, however, she seethed at her mother's hypocrisy. How could she, of all people, speak of good conduct and setting an example to the servants? she thought, as she leaned against the oriel window to look out over the snowy fells. She gritted her teeth, wondering how long it would be before her resentment boiled over, like that hot milk in the kitchen pan.

During their shared imprisonment she had grown closer to her mother, but their return to Radcliffe had resurrected all the old suspicions.

She had thought that it might be easier to forget with Grandy no longer there, but everywhere she went: his music room where his golden lute lay in its case; the parlor, with his favorite velvet-cushioned chair drawn up to the fire, empty; his bedchamber, with the great, carved bed—particularly there—reminded her of him. And, alas, her mother's presence only served to defile those memories, spoiling Radcliffe for her.

But far worse than anything was the not knowing. Oh, she had no doubt that her suspicions were correct. She had had the evidence of her own eyes and ears to attest to the truth of them. What she did not know was the extent of her mother's heinous sin.

Since she had first suspected her, she had forced away the knowledge, appalled by it. In truth, the thought of having her suspicions confirmed was more horrible than any nightmare could be. But now she burned with the desire to have it settled once and for all. Only then, perhaps, could she be at peace with herself and the world.

"You look chilled, Kate. Will you not come and sit by the fire?" Joanna's sweet voice broke into her thoughts.

Katherine smiled at her sister and came to sit on the bench before the fire. There was only one person whom she could ask, she thought, as she took up the sheet she had been sewing earlier. That person was Aunt Isobel. Only she, Katherine sensed, would tell the ungarlanded truth about her mother's past.

As she watched her mother's white-capped head and the neat fingers plying the needle in one of her exquisite works of needlepoint, Katherine determined to arrange a visit to her aunt as soon as possible, so that she might put to her the questions she had been dreading to ask for more than three years.

"Aunt Isobel has invited me to ride over to Colborne Place to choose some silverware for my wedding gift," she told Alyssa one morning the following week. "I thought that as the weather has improved I might go there tomorrow, with your permission."

Her mother frowned. "Are you certain that your aunt invited you? She did not mention it to me when I saw her at Harcourt Hall last week."

"It was then that she spoke of it to me. Doubtless she forgot to tell you. May I go, Mother? Tobias said that the roads and bridlepaths are clear all the way to Masham and Tanfield now."

Her mother hesitated for a moment, although her fingers continued sorting the embroidery silks in her lap. It was evident that she was undergoing some inner conflict. "Very well," she said at last, with a sigh of resignation. "You may visit your aunt, so long as you do not wish me to accompany you."

"Of course not." Katherine smiled at her, feeling like a player on a stage hiding behind a smiling mask.

"Will you take Joanna with you? She is looking pale from the long winter confinement."

"If you please, my lady Mother, I should prefer not to. Aunt Isobel expressly said that it was to be a visit by myself. Of course I shall take Grace with me."

"And your horse groom, mind."

"And my horse groom."

She tried not to flinch when her mother drew down her head to kiss her cheek. "You are being such a good girl over this wedding with Brendan. I knew that, once you came home, it would be your choice to remain at Radcliffe."

Katherine looked down at her. "It is all pretence, Mother. I keep telling you, Edward will return for me. I shall not be marrying Master Fitzgerald."

Ignoring the look of dismay on her mother's face, Katherine picked up her skirts and ran to her chamber determined that her mother would not see the rush of tears to her eyes.

A groom was sent to Colborne Place with a message for Lady Colborne. Aunt Isobel returned word that it would give her great pleasure to have her niece visit her, particularly as Bess had been sick with the ague and a bad cough and would greatly welcome a visit from her favorite cousin.

This did not sound like the intimate conversation Katherine wished to have with her aunt, but she would have to see if some opportunity presented itself. Besides, when the next morning came, she began to have second thoughts about broaching such an appalling subject with her aunt. Perhaps she would be so horrified she would go directly to her sister and inform her that Katherine suspected her of what, in the eyes of God, at least, amounted to the terrible sin of incest.

The prospect make Katherine feel extremely sick.

She was so delighted to be able to ride out, however, that her gloom was quickly dispelled by the sight of dainty snowdrops circling the feet of trees and the sounds of bleating lambs from the fellsides. Spring was in the air.

Colborne Place was a far larger house than Radcliffe Hall. The central great hall was more than two centuries old and successive generations of Colbornes had added to it, so that the house lacked Radcliffe's perfect symmetry.

Its long gallery, though grander by far than Radcliffe's, did not have the large windows and magnificent view of Katherine's home, for Colborne was built in the low-lying valley of the lower stretch of the Ure, not high on the fellside of Wensleydale as Radcliffe was.

No, thought Katherine, as she was led upstairs to her aunt's solar by the stiff-faced steward, *I would not exchange Radcliffe for this place.*

Nor, she thought later, after she had dined on roast turbot and mutton with carmeline sauce with her aunt and uncle, did she envy her Aunt Isobel. Lord Colborne was not merely discourteous; he was offensive. He stuffed his food into his mouth and belched openly, without using his napkin. And when he deigned to address his family, he roared at them, spraying food from his mouth over the table.

As for Katherine, he spoke only a few words to her, and these consisted of coarse remarks about how she filled her gowns very nicely nowadays, his protruding eyes stripping her of her clothing as he spoke. She had never been quite so uncomfortable with anyone before and felt heartily sorry for her aunt and cousin Bess. Although her male cousins were as boorish as their father, they still seemed to go in fear of him.

It was fortunate for them all that Lord Colborne, being a member of the powerful Council of the North, usually spent most of his time in York.

Katherine was not certain if she should be glad or sorry when, after dinner, her aunt told Bess to go and rest in her chamber for a while. "Your eyelids look heavy and you are pale," she told her daughter, when she opened her mouth to whine a protest. "You do not wish to lose your beauty from lack of rest, do you now?"

Vain little Bess tossed her dark curls and looked anxious. Having been assured that she and her favorite cousin would have more time together later, she flounced away to her chamber, nose in the air, every bit as haughty as her mother.

Lady Colborne's proud smile followed her. She could barely tolerate her three sons, all of them sandy-haired and stockily built like their father, but she openly adored and cosseted her little Bess. There were times when Katherine's hand itched to slap her young cousin, but now that she was older she realized that Aunt Isobel was much to blame for the girl's vanity and selfishness.

"She does look a little wan, does she not?" said Aunt Isobel, when Bess had left. "But, in truth, I sent her for a rest so that I might have some comfortable conversation alone with my favorite niece, now that she is a full-grown woman of eighteen." The perfectly shaped mouth smiled warmly upon Katherine. "And a very beautiful woman, at that."

Blushing, Katherine curtsyed to her aunt and murmured her thanks. Coming as it did from Aunt Isobel, whose golden beauty still surpassed that of most women in the great County of York, the compliment meant far more to her than any of her own mother's avowals that her daughter was the most beautiful in the land.

"Come, let us walk in the long gallery and get some exercise," said her aunt. "And you shall tell me all the gossip from Radcliffe. I wish particularly to know all about Master Fitzgerald."

When they reached the gallery, Aunt Isobel wrapped her arm about Katherine's waist. "Now, tell me how you like your betrothed."

Katherine fell silent, not knowing how to answer this.

"Am I correct in thinking that you are not happy with the thought of marrying this Irishman?" Aunt Isobel asked, her voice gentle.

This kind understanding was too much for Katherine. She turned in her aunt's arm and wailed, "Oh, Aunt Isobel, I cannot tell you how unhappy I am." Laying her head against her aunt's breast, she burst into tears.

"My poor, dear child. Come, sit down here." She guided the sobbing Katherine to the hearth and made her sit on the bench before the fire. "Tell me all about it."

"I only pretended to agree to marry him so that we could come home to Radcliffe. But now that Edward hasn't replied to my letter, my mother has said I must marry him, that otherwise we shall all be turned from Radcliffe and that Edward will never reply to my letter anyway. And I know he will, he will." Katherine let out a long wail and buried her head in her aunt's lap, rocking back and forth in her anguish.

Her aunt drew her into her arms, pressing her head against her fragrant bodice, which emitted waves of jasmine scent. "Edward," she repeated. "You mean Edward Carlton?"

Sniffing, Katherine nodded.

"So you still love Edward."

Katherine sat up abruptly. "I shall love him forever. And I know that he still loves me, despite his wish to be a priest."

Her aunt became very still and then she pursed her lips. "Ah, so that is where Edward Carlton has disappeared to," she said softly. "He has gone to be a Catholic priest."

"I should not have told you," Katherine said, suddenly dismayed.

"Surely you do not think I would divulge your confidence?" her aunt said, an expression of hurt in her blue eyes. "Besides, I had guessed at it already."

Katherine sighed with relief. "Oh, Aunt Isobel, it is so good to be able to tell you everything. I have written to Edward again, begging him to return to England to rescue me from this marriage, but it is now more than two months since I wrote and still I have had no reply from him. And my mother will force me into marriage with Brendan, I know it, and I hate him." She turned upon her aunt, her eyes blazing. "But I hate my mother even more. She is unkind and . . . and evil."

Her aunt's expression was greatly pained. "Oh, my dearest Katherine, you must not say such terrible things about your own mother."

"It is true. I could tell you such monstrous things about her that—" She could not continue, but sat, her fingers plucking incessantly at the fur edging on her overgown. "She did not love my father," she said eventually.

Aunt Isobel's face grew smooth as marble. "No, she did not. That, alas, is true. And Thomas Radcliffe was a man of many good qualities."

"I knew it. Although I do not remember him, I knew it. Yet she will never speak to me of him. She denies me even the pleasure of knowing about my own father."

"You may speak to me about him whenever you wish, dear niece," said her aunt with a strange little smile. "You must not forget that I, too, knew Thomas Radcliffe. Our two families had been linked since we were children."

Her aunt's kindness gave Katherine the courage she needed. "I think she loved my grandfather," she whispered, her eyes upon her own restless fingers.

Aunt Isobel's body stiffened. "But of course she loved him," she said lightly. "Everyone loved Sir Philip."

"No, no, you do not understand, Aunt Isobel. I believe that she . . . that they . . . that she and my grandfather were lovers."

"Good God, child, what are you saying?" Her aunt's vivid blue eyes registered shock and horror.

But her aunt's tone rang hollow in Katherine's ears. She was convinced that Aunt Isobel, in truth, was not amazed by what she had told her. "I have seen her come from his chamber late at night."

Her aunt did not meet her eyes. "She could have been nursing him when he was unwell."

"There were other things. Occasionally, when they thought I was not looking, they held hands and looked at each other as lovers do."

Her aunt was silent.

"I tell you, Aunt Isobel, my mother is evil. I believe she seduced my grandfather, bewitched him with spells when he was too old and weak to withstand them."

Her aunt stirred uneasily, rubbing her long-fingered hands together. "That is a monstrous accusation to make about your own mother, Katherine, the woman who gave you birth; my own sister, I would remind you."

"But you have not denied it," Katherine cried. "You know it is true, don't you?"

Her aunt's eyes locked with hers. "Have you talked of this to her, to your mother?"

"Of course not, how could I?"

"Take my advice, dear niece. If you value your own comfort, your security, never, never even hint at your suspicions to your mother."

Katherine's blood chilled. "Then I am right," she whispered.

Her aunt rose with a rustle of heavy silk. "We must leave the subject. It is not a wholesome one. Perhaps one day, when you are a little older and less vulnerable, we shall return to it. My advice for you now is to try to put it out of your mind, or you will never be at peace with your mother." Her white forehead crinkled into a thoughtful frown. "Perhaps it might be best, for the contentment of you both, if you separated yourself from her when you are wed. She should not live with you at Radcliffe."

"Yes, yes, you are right," Katherine said, her head spinning. "But I am not going to be wed."

"My dearest niece, my intended meaning was when you are married to Edward, of course. I am certain that you will hear from him very soon." Isobel wound her arm about Katherine's waist to help her up from the bench. "Now let us forget all this unpleasantness and enjoy the remainder of the afternoon in contemplating your wedding gift for when you marry your Edward."

Chapter 14

March brought the scurry of winds across the Dales and flocks of golden plover sweeping over the moor, which still bore pockets of snow in its hollows.

On the seventh of March, Katherine was proved right. The long-awaited letter from Edward at last arrived. It was borne to Radcliffe Hall by Sir John Carlton himself. "I feared that, if I sent it with one of my men, it might be intercepted," he explained in a low voice to Alyssa, when Tobias had shown him into the solar.

He handed her the letter.

Alyssa had risen to greet him. "It is addressed to me, I see, not to Katherine."

Sir John leaned upon his stick with both hands. "His vows do not permit him to correspond with any person outside his own family. He had to ask for special dispensation to be able to address a letter to you, Mistress Radcliffe."

Still holding the letter, Alyssa crossed her hands at her waist. "I pray your pardon and that of Lady Carlton, Sir John. Katherine's is a very stubborn nature." She gave him an unwavering look. "She still loves Edward greatly and refuses to believe that he is unshakable in his decision."

Sir John nodded brusquely at the letter. "That should convince her. I leave it with you. Your servant, Mistress Radcliffe." He turned on his heel and was halfway to the door when he turned again. "I pray your pardon, Alyssa. We wished for this marriage as much as you and Sir Philip did. They were perfectly suited." Although Alyssa had not moved, she could see even from a distance that his jaw was trembling. "He was our favorite son."

"It is God's will," Alyssa said.

He made her a sketchy bow. "No need to come down," he told her and was gone before she could respond.

So, Edward's reply had come at last. She welcomed it, but dreaded imparting the news to her daughter. Even the fact that it was not addressed to her would enrage Katherine. To salve the wound a little, Alyssa decided she would not read it. She would hand it to Katherine with the seal unbroken.

She waited a long time, listening to the halting footsteps on the stair, as Tobias escorted Sir John downstairs. The poor man had aged ten years since Edward's departure. She went out onto the landing and leant over the railing to watch as Tobias helped Sir John into his cloak.

She went back into the solar and nervously walked about, adjusting a picture on the wall, straightening a cushion, clicking her tongue to the linnets in their golden cage . . . before picking up the letter again. Then she drew in a long breath, released it and called for Tobias. Best get this over with as quickly as possible.

As she had guessed, Tobias was already waiting outside the door, and came in immediately.

"Would you fetch Katherine to me, if you please, Tobias?"

His all-seeing eyes took in the letter in her hands, but he said nothing.

"Aye, Tobias, 'tis a letter from Edward. Be prepared for fireworks."

"I'll fetch Mistress Katherine myself," was all he said.

Katherine had been outside, in the breeding stables, but she must have seen Sir John ride out, for she collided with Tobias as he left the solar.

"Your lady mother wishes to see you."

She rushed into the solar, bringing with her the smell of the stables.

Alyssa saw that her skirts were creased and mud-stained, but she stifled the rebuke that sprang to her lips. This was definitely not the time to be upbraiding her daughter about her appearance.

"Why was Sir John here?" Katherine demanded, her cheeks flushing scarlet. "I shouted to him, but he rode out without even acknowledging me."

Poor Sir John, thought Alyssa. His courage must have failed him. She could understand that. She, herself, was feeling exhausted at the mere thought of the coming confrontation.

There was no way in which to soften the blow. "He brought this letter with him." She held it out to Katherine.

The hectic color faded instantly from her daughter's cheeks. Her eyes fixed upon the letter, as if it contained a scorpion, ready to strike. "Is it from Edward?" she said at last, her hands gripped together so tightly beneath her chin that the knuckles whitened.

Alyssa nodded.

Katherine approached her mother and took the letter from her. "But . . . it is addressed to you," she said, her tone puzzled.

Alyssa inclined her head. She maintained her air of seeming calm, despite the hurried beating of her heart.

"But at least Edward has written," Katherine said. "I told you he would write, but you wouldn't believe me." Her fingers tore at the seal, allowing the hardened wax to fall in fragments upon the floor. Then she ripped open the paper.

As far as Alyssa could see, it consisted of only one sheet, written in Edward's neat hand. As Katherine's eyes devoured it, Alyssa remained in the one position, not daring to move even a muscle.

The creaking of a wagon and sounds of men's voices, shouting to each other, filtered in through the open window, alleviating the fearful silence.

Katherine did not look up from the paper, although Alyssa knew she must have read it by now. She stared at it and then slowly crumpled it into a tight ball in her right hand. "Edward is not returning to Yorkshire," she told her mother. "He has gone to Rome. He has at least one more year of training before he takes his final vows."

Alyssa was amazed at Katherine's calm. "My dearest Kate," she said, her heart aching for her. She moved a step closer to her, barely breathing, lest a sound might disrupt this unexpected reaction to Edward's final rejection.

"Edward is not coming home," Katherine said. "He says in this letter," her fingers tightened about it, "that he cannot comprehend why you would have permitted me to write letters to him, when you evidently knew the circumstances of his departure from England."

She reeled off the words, as if they were burned upon her memory. Her eyes were fixed on some object on the wall far above her mother's head.

Alyssa grew very cold. "Come, sweetheart, sit you down and we shall talk about it," she suggested in a soothing voice.

She held out her arms to Katherine, and when she made no move, made an attempt to embrace her.

Katherine thrust her away and, without warning, attacked her with flailing fists, striking her upon the head, the breast. At the same time, wild screams issued from her mouth, filling the solar, spilling out of it into the entire house, inhuman screams like that of a demented creature.

Tobias burst into the chamber. "Mistress Katherine, stop this," he shouted, striving to catch at her to stop her assault on her mother.

Alyssa tried to ward off the blows, but her heart was smitten far harder by the vituperation that spewed from Katherine's mouth as she lashed out at her.

"It is all your fault, you witch! You're a harlot and a witch! You put a curse on Edward. No doubt you wanted him for yourself. God damn you to hell, you . . . you vile, disgusting strumpet!"

Now Joanna rushed in and tried to catch at her sister's arms, but she, too, was struck and fled from the room, crying out that Kate had gone mad.

"Get back to your posts!" The sudden command reverberated throughout the house.

Crouched in a corner of the solar, where she had instinctively retreated, her hands covering her head in an attempt to protect herself, Alyssa wondered who in the name of heaven had shouted. Then the solar door was flung wide and she looked up through the hair that had fallen about her face, to see Brendan Fitzgerald, like some black avenging Vulcan in the doorway. "What in the name of Jesus is going on here?" he roared.

Before anyone could reply, he strode across the chamber to haul Katherine away from her mother, grasping her wrists from behind and wrapping his arms about her, so that she could not move.

"Easy now, my darling Caitlin, easy," he said softly, as if he were addressing a crazed horse.

Katherine continued to scream, but as he turned her within his grasp, so that she faced him, the screams changed to a guttural wailing.

For some reason, the sound reminded Alyssa of the terrible plague that had struck the district almost twenty years before. And then she realized, with a cold sick horror, that Katherine's cries reminded her of the wailing of Philip's wife, Laura, when she first knew she had been stricken by the dread disease.

Tobias came to her and helped her up. "Are you hurt?" His gray eyes were wide with anxiety.

Alyssa staggered as she stood up. She grasped his arm. "No, no. Mere bruises, I am sure." Her mouth quivered. "Oh, Tobias."

He placed an arm awkwardly about her, so that she might lean against him. Katherine was sobbing now, her back to Alyssa and Tobias. His expression grim, Brendan made a brusque nod in the direction of the door, indicating that they should leave.

"But . . . I should stay with her," Alyssa whispered, as Tobias guided her to the door.

"Best not." Tobias gently pushed her out the door and pulled it shut behind them.

As the door closed, Brendan felt a sense of relief. He had heard the appalling things Katherine had said to her mother and knew there was no chance of calming her if Alyssa remained in the room.

He had yet to discover what had caused this extraordinary outburst, but for now his entire mind was concentrated on soothing the distraught girl in his arms. As she sobbed great, gusting sobs that shook her entire body, she murmured incoherently, the sounds buried against his chest.

Supporting her with one arm, he rubbed his hand up and down her back, up and down, stroking the tangled hair, the tense neck beneath it. "Easy now, my lovely, easy, my beauty. Brendan's here. He won't let anything harm you. Easy."

He repeated the words, over and over, as if they were some incantation that would restore her reason. She was shivering, but he did not dare move closer to the fire, for fear the spell would be broken and she would return to reality too quickly.

Dear God, how soft her body was, how pliable against his. As he repeated the same words and continued stroking her back, he became intensely aware of the reaction of his body to the closeness of hers.

During the past two months it had grown increasingly difficult to maintain the light, bantering tone and mien of a distant wooer, for despite the fact that Katherine was, at times, a termagant who had for too long been given her own way by her doting family, he had fallen deep in love with her.

He, Brendan Fitzgerald, who had never attached himself to any woman for more than a few weeks, had succumbed to the charms of this acid-tongued beauty who was his betrothed. She was like some wild creature, at times bad-tempered and waspish, but he greatly admired her free spirit.

Now it caused him great pain to see her so distressed, but no doubt it was some small matter that had become exaggerated in her mind, and she would soon be smiling again. One thing he had learned was that Katherine Radcliffe's nature was naturally warm and sunny. He was certain that this squall would soon be over.

He realized suddenly that she had ceased sobbing. Loosening his hold a little, he stroked the tumbled hair from her face. "Better now?"

Slowly, she raised her head from his chest and looked up at him. His heart turned in his breast. The expression in the dark eyes under the swollen, red lids was stricken, hopeless. And he knew then that whatever it was that had caused her anguish was not over, might never be over, and a thrill of fear ran through him.

"You are cold. Shall we move closer to the fire?"

She shook her head and slowly, very slowly, moved from him, not actually pushing him from her but separating herself; first her head from his chest, then her breast and waist, all receding from him, and leaving him feeling cold himself.

"Take me to my chamber, I pray you," she whispered. She was barely able to stand.

"I shall have a fire lit there first," he told her.

She shook her head, but he was adamant. "You must be warm," he said firmly. "A fire in your grate and a warming pan in your bed. It will take only a moment to do."

He sat her down on the bench before the fire and then went to the door to give his orders to the servant outside. He could see Alyssa and Tobias hovering by the door of the long gallery, but ignored their questioning faces. Katherine's welfare must come first. Then, and only then, would he find out the reason for her frenzy.

When he came back into the solar, he sat down beside her on the bench. She had not moved an inch. Her hands remained limp in her lap, palms upward. He could see the imprints of her nails in them.

He gathered her hands in his. "Your chamber will be ready for you shortly. May I pour you some wine?"

She shook her head.

"Come," he coaxed. "A little claret or sack would do you good."

Her dark eyes met his. "Let me be," she said.

He pressed her no further.

"Where is my mother?" she asked, after a silence broken only by the sound of her ragged breathing.

"Resting in her chamber," he said lightly.

"I should go to her." Her eyes filled with tears. "I never struck my mother before." She stared into the fire, trying to blink the tears away.

Jesu, let me say the right thing to her, prayed Brendan. "She will forgive you. She knows how upset you were."

She nodded. "Yes, you are right. She will forgive me."

Brendan was greatly relieved. He had said the right thing, it seemed. But he did not understand the peculiar emphasis Katherine had laid on her last words.

A tap came at the door. "That will be Grace, come to help you to your chamber."

She gripped his arm, her fingers digging through his doublet sleeve. "Don't let Joanna come near me, I beg you. Do not let *anyone* but Grace near me."

"I give you my word, no one shall come near you but Grace."

He helped her up. She was like an invalid, frail and trembling. He hated to see her thus. She was always so strong, so full of vitality.

Katherine's maidservant, Grace, waited outside the door for her. "Shall I help you to your chamber?" Brendan asked Katherine.

"No, Grace will be enough." A ghost of a smile flickered on her tear-streaked face. "You have been very kind."

He might have been a stranger who had just assisted her across the roadway. God damn whatever or whoever had caused this terrible change in her. God curse his or her eyes!

He saw Tobias approaching. "Not yet, Ridley," he barked. "I shall send for you when I am ready. Until then keep everyone out, including Mistress Radcliffe."

He slammed the solar door to and went to the sideboard to pour himself a large measure of wine. As he turned, he caught sight of the crumpled ball of paper on the ground. He had noticed it before, but thought nothing of it. It looked like a letter that someone had written and then tossed aside.

He bent to pick it up. It was indeed a letter, and one that had been sent. Pieces of waxen seal still adhered to it. He set it down on the sideboard and began smoothing it out. This was not an easy task, for the paper had been crumpled so tightly that it was creased in a hundred places.

Could this be the cause of Katherine's impassioned outburst?

The paper was addressed to "Mistress Alyssa Radcliffe of Radcliffe Hall." Brendan turned it over. It was written in a strong, neat hand. A masculine hand, he thought. He should not be reading this. It was a private letter, addressed to Mistress Radcliffe.

He glanced first at the signature. Edward Carlton. Aha, so that was why Sir John Carlton had paid a brief visit to Radcliffe without even speaking to him. Although he was growing inured to the uncivil manner in which the local landowners treated him—as if he, as Lord of Radcliffe, did not exist—it had occurred to him that it was uncommonly churlish of Sir John not even to pass the time of day with the new owner of the house he was visiting.

Perhaps this letter held the explanation of both Sir John's and Katherine's strange behavior.

Not able to see the writing clearly, because of the creases, he augmented the sunlight that streamed in through the large window by lighting a candle with a spill from the fire and moving the candlestick close to the paper.

> *Dear Mistress Radcliffe: It has not been easy for me to gain permission to write to you. The rule is that I may correspond only twice a year with close members of my family.*

Brendan frowned. Strange. Could this Edward Carlton—who was probably one of Sir John's four sons—be writing to Mistress Radcliffe from prison?

> *My mother has sent to me several letters penned by your daughter, Katherine. I believe you are acquainted with the true circumstances of my departure from England last year, and therefore I find it difficult to comprehend why you have permitted Katherine to continue to write pleading letters to me. I was, naturally, exceedingly distressed to hear of your recent imprisonment. Although I did not reply to your daughter's letters, I did write to my father, asking him to do everything in his power to gain your release. I have no reason to think that he did not do so, even if he was not successful in this mission. It was with extreme relief that I learned of your release. I ask now that you convey the following message to your daughter. I have at least one more year of training in Rome before I take my final vows. Katherine must not write to me again at any time or for any reason. She must erase the past and*

everything that was between us from her mind. In truth it would be best if from henceforth she considered me as one dead. Forgive me if this sounds harsh, but her letters have caused me great embarrassment and concern. They must not continue.

The letter was signed,

Ever your humble servant, Edward Carlton.

Chapter 15

Brendan remained gazing at the crumpled page until the words blurred before his eyes. Then he read it twice more, to commit it to memory.

He was shaken by a mixture of emotions: pity for the girl who had read this cold dismissal of her evident love for the writer; angry contempt for the writer himself, this Edward Carlton who would throw Katherine aside in favor of sterile priesthood. . . . But most of all Brendan was furious with the entire Radcliffe family and their steward for having duped him.

He had been led to believe that Katherine was an innocent maid, her skittishness with him a manifestation of her lack of knowledge of men. Now he knew that she had given her heart to another man long before he had come to Yorkshire. It explained much that had puzzled him about her.

Picking up the letter, he strode to the door and flung it wide. "Ridley!" he roared in a voice that his troop would have recognized as one to which they should come running at the double.

Not being one of his soldiers, Tobias Ridley crossed the landing at his usual moderate pace. "Sir?" he said, his eyebrows raised in enquiry, when he reached the solar door.

"Ask Mistress Radcliffe to come here."

The steward's lips tightened. "I shall ask if Mistress Radcliffe is able to see you, sir."

"Let us have no more game-playing here, Master Ridley. Fetch Mistress Radcliffe to me immediately."

Tobias hesitated for a moment.

"Do not be forcing me to remind you who is the master here, Ridley," Brendan said very softly.

Tobias blinked rapidly. Taking one step back, he made a small, neat bow and walked back to the gallery, his pace still moderate.

Brendan had to smile a little. Despite his anger, he could not help admiring the steward's composure under heavy fire. The man would have made an excellent officer.

A delay of several minutes ensued. More strategy on Ridley's part, no doubt, although Brendan was beginning to realize that Mistress Radcliffe was also a force to be reckoned with in this encounter. Her gentle, soft-spoken exterior hid a steely strength, he suspected.

Today she would discover that they were alike in that particular.

When Alyssa came into the room, Brendan knew a moment of pity. Although her hands were clasped composedly before her, her left eye was swollen shut and she walked with great care, as if she were afraid of falling. Tobias hovered behind her, ready to assist her.

"Pray be seated, Mistress Radcliffe," Brendan told her and himself placed her in the main chair by the fire. Her hand was very cold and trembled in his, as if she were an old woman, not a still vigorous woman of less than forty.

"You may go now, Ridley," he told the steward.

"With your permission, Master Fitzgerald, I think it best for Mistress Radcliffe if I remain."

"You do not have my permission. Kindly leave us."

A nerve jumped in the steward's cheek and his teeth clenched in anger. Brendan realized the man was in a damnable position.

"I shall treat her gently, I assure you, though neither she nor you deserve it. Now go."

"Leave us, Tobias," said Alyssa's voice from the fireplace.

Without even a nod of the head, the steward retreated.

Having made sure that the door was latched fast, Brendan sat down on the settle across from Alyssa.

"I must beg your pardon for sitting in your solar in my dirt," he said, gesturing to the mud on his boots and his clothing. "When I heard the commotion, I did not think to remove my boots."

"It is no matter," she said dully. "Besides, it is your solar, not mine, Master Fitzgerald."

"I will not debate that point with you at present. We have far more pressing matters than solars to discuss." He leaned forward to hand her the letter. "Forgive me, but I found it necessary to read this. Although it is addressed to you, I think you would agree that its contents affect me considerably."

Her only response was an almost imperceptible movement of her head.

"You have not been honest with me, Mistress Radcliffe. And I've a notion that 'tis not usually in your nature to be dishonest."

She lifted her chin. "To my knowledge, Master Fitzgerald, I have neither lied to you nor deceived you in any way."

"Ah, madam, there are so many ways of deception, are there not? Yours and your family's and steward's was the sin of omission. You all omitted to tell me that the maid I was to marry loved another man. 'Be gentle with her, Master Fitzgerald,' said you to me, 'she is young and unknowledgable in the ways of men. She'll come around in time.'" His hand tightened on the letter. "And all the time I was wooing her, playing the young gallant with her, she was writing to this . . . this Edward Carlton. A man who thought so little of her that he has gone to Rome to be a papist priest."

His anger stirred in him, so that he could no longer remain seated, but got up to pace about the chamber.

"She has written to Edward but once since your coming," Alyssa told him.

Brendan rounded upon her. "No doubt begging her lover to come and rescue her from marriage with a vile Irishman."

Alyssa said nothing, so that he knew he was right.

"And this," waving the letter, "this letter was his answer to her appeal."

He stood over her, towering above her, but her gaze remained fixed upon her lap.

"You alone are to blame for this, Mistress Radcliffe. You chose to force your daughter into a marriage that was abhorrent to her rather than to lose Radcliffe. You—and your steward, no doubt, who values his position and thought I might put some Irish adherent in his place—gulled me nicely into thinking Katherine's affections were mine for the winning. I do not blame her, you realize. It is yourself I blame, you and Tobias, who entrapped me with talk of Katherine's beauty when first I came to Radcliffe. Between the pair of you, I have been made to look a gullible fool."

He swung away to stare out the window at the greening valley. "How everyone in the dale must be laughing. The thickheaded Irishman caught by the wily Radcliffes. No wonder Katherine called you those vile names."

Behind him, Alyssa sprang to her feet. "Enough! How dare you speak thus to me, sir. You think because I am a woman that you can attack me, without even permitting me to make answer to your accusations. By God, Master Fitzgerald, if Sir Philip were here you would not be speaking thus to me."

He turned to face her, the blood rushing into his face. "But he is not, is he? And that is the crux of the matter. I am the new Lord of Radcliffe and because I wished to make the changeover an easy one for all, I have not asserted my authority as I should have done from the start."

His anger receded as he looked at the swollen face, the restless little hands picking at the black gown. "But you are right, Mistress Radcliffe. I have not heard your side of the story. Pray be seated." He gave her a glimmer of a smile. "'Tis a terrible temper I have when I am roused."

She did not respond to the smile, but she did sit down again. "When you accuse me of forcing Katherine into a marriage against her wishes, you do me a great injustice, Master Fitzgerald," she said in a low voice. "For I was forced into such a marriage myself. Do you truly think I would do the same thing to my daughter?"

Brendan leaned his back against the wall. "Perhaps. To save Radcliffe for your daughter and your descendants you might."

Her head snapped up, her eyes flaring, but then the fire died, and Brendan knew that he had made a hit.

"Katherine and Edward Carlton had been promised in marriage since she was an infant," she said. "No formal contract. Philip said they must wait until they were old enough to decide for themselves. He did not wish to see happen to Katherine what happened to me, you see. He felt he was responsible for the unhappiness of many because he had forced his own son, Thomas, into marriage with me against his will."

For a moment, both eyes were closed and her face contorted as she relived unhappy memories. Then she looked up at Brendan. "It was on that terrible day last February, the day that ended with the arrival of the news of my son's death and with Philip's collapse, that Edward announced to us and to Katherine that he could not marry her. Later, on the day of Philip's funeral, Katherine discovered that he was going to take holy orders, to become a Catholic priest."

"But this . . . this urge to join the priesthood cannot have come upon him suddenly, surely? Could he not have let her down more gently?"

Alyssa smiled wryly. "Edward knew Katherine very well. He knew that she would try to argue him out of it, as she did, in truth, that very night."

"How could he do such a thing to her?"

Alyssa shrugged. "His love for the Roman Church was greater than his love for Katherine. That is it in a nutshell, Master Fitzgerald. But it nearly broke her heart. And then the deaths of her brother and her beloved grandfather . . . I thought she would go mad."

"If I had Edward Carlton here at this moment, I swear I would wring his neck."

She smiled again, a tremulous smile. "I had much the same feeling at the time, particularly as it was Edward who brought Edmund Campion to our house."

"Are you telling me that Carlton was also responsible for your imprisonment?"

"Not directly, of course. We do not know who betrayed us. To give Edward his due, it was not his fault. Sir Philip was begging for a priest to give him the last rites. Edward knew that Father Campion was in the district and brought him here to minister to Philip."

Alyssa's lips clamped together in a vain attempt to force back the tears. "Not only do I not blame Edward, I bless him for it. Because of him, Philip died happy. Father Campion was a very special person."

"He was, indeed," Brendan said softly.

She looked surprised. "Did you know him?"

"I did. He was my tutor for a short while in Dublin when I was a youth."

"How very strange. But you are not a Catholic, are you?"

"No," he said shortly. "Despite my family name, from the age of eight I was raised as a Protestant. At that time, though, Edmund Campion was not entirely open about his conversion. Indeed, the Earl of Leicester was still his patron."

"Leicester?" A strange look came into her eyes. "I met him once, at Hampton Court."

"Did you, indeed." He was not at all interested in my lord of Leicester. "But we are digressing. We were speaking of your plan to force Katherine into marriage with me in order that you might keep Radcliffe."

"It was not my mother's plan, it was mine."

The voice startled both of them. Brendan turned, to see Katherine standing in the doorway. She was still dressed in her mud-stained

135

clothes. "You must not blame my mother," she said, coming forward into the chamber. "It was my plan to agree to marriage between us, so that you would bring us back to Radcliffe."

Brendan's jaw tightened. So she, too, had deceived him. "And what was your intention thereafter? To have me murdered?" He saw now that he had indeed been a gullible fool, blinded by her beauty and his growing love for her.

Katherine gave him a bitter little smile. "That would not have worked, would it? Radcliffe still would not have been ours. To own the truth, I did not know what would happen. I placed all my reliance in Edward. I would not listen to my mother when she told me Edward would never return to England; not for me, at least. Edward will save me . . . and Radcliffe, I thought." Again, the bitter smile. "You must think me a foolish child, Master Fitzgerald."

They faced each other across the room, both forgetting the presence of Alyssa.

Brendan shook his head. "To say truly, I believe it is God who has been enjoying playing with us both."

Silence fell heavy between them, as they both thought their own dark thoughts and bade farewell to their dreams.

It was Alyssa who spoke at last. "What is your wish, Master Fitzgerald? Must we leave Radcliffe immediately or may we have a little time to gather our personal belongings together?"

Brendan looked at her as if she had spoken in a foreign tongue.

"I shall go over the inventory with you," Alyssa continued, "so that you may be assured we shall not take anything that is not ours."

"And where will you go, Mistress Radcliffe?"

"I assure you we are not destitute, sir," she said, with a proud lift of her head. "I have my parents' home, Harcourt Hall, and my sister, Lady Colborne—"

"You loathe Aunt Isobel," cried Katherine.

"There is also Horton Grange, a small property in Coverdale that was part of my dowry. That will not be yours, sir. The three of us, together with two or three servants, could manage very well there."

Brendan imagined how difficult it would be to live in such confinement after spending so many years in the spaciousness of Radcliffe Hall.

"Mistress Radcliffe, I have a notion to speak with your daughter alone. Would you grant me permission to do so?"

She looked from one to the other. "Only if Katherine is agreeable to it."

Katherine nodded. She had not looked once at her mother since she came in. Now she turned to her and winced when she saw her swollen face.

"Very well." Alyssa stood up, not able to stifle a groan as she did so. Brendan went to her aid, and helped her from the solar. He knew from the sudden scurry on the landing and in the hall below, that the entire household had been waiting, straining their ears to hear what was happening.

"Tobias!"

"Sir?" The steward stepped from the shadows of the passageway.

"Escort Mistress Radcliffe to her chamber and have the physician sent for, to attend to her. I insist," he told Alyssa, who was protesting vehemently.

She clutched his arm. "I beg you, sir, do not shame Katherine further by sending for Dr. Tredwell," she whispered. "My women can attend to all my needs."

He took her hand in his. "I wished only to make you comfortable," he said. "It was not my intention to shame her." His mouth twisted in a grimace. "To make your daughter happy was always my one desire."

"I know it." She gave him a sad smile. "Life can be very cruel, can it not?"

She limped away, leaning on Tobias Ridley's arm, leaving Brendan feeling desperately sorry for the things he had said to her.

When he returned to the solar, he found Katherine rereading the letter. She hurriedly pushed it under the settle cushion as he came in.

"Shall I leave you for a while longer?" he asked.

"No. We must speak now." The face turned to his was gaunt. No one would call her beautiful now.

He sat down in the chair and leant forward. "I wanted us to be alone, so that you might speak your mind freely, without referring to your mother or her wishes."

She made no reply. Indeed, her face was wiped clean of expression, reminding Brendan of the faces he had seen on soldiers after battle.

"If you had your wish, what would you choose to do?" As soon as he spoke the words, he regretted them, seeing the sudden sweep of emotion across her countenance.

"Would you live with your grandparents," he asked hurriedly, not waiting for her answer to his first question, "or with your aunt? Although it is not my intention to turn you and your family from Radcliffe immediately," he said gently, "I must marry and raise a family here. It would be better for all of us if you were to establish yourselves elsewhere as soon as possible, I am thinking."

"You no longer wish to marry me, then?" Her words seemed to come from a great distance.

Brendan was amazed. "I . . . I thought marriage between us was out of the question."

She raised her eyes to his. "I do understand that you would no longer wish to marry me, after . . ." She waved her hands, unable to find the right words to complete her sentence, and looked away. "Only, it seems so cruel that my entire family must suffer the loss of their home because of my folly."

He stared at her. "Katherine, look at me." She did so. "Are you telling me that if I were willing you would still be prepared to marry me?"

She nodded once.

"And this is not because you fear your mother's wrath?"

She smiled for the first time. "She has more cause to fear mine, I regret to say. If I hate my mother, it is not because I fear her."

The calm manner in which she spoke of hating her mother disturbed him, but the rift between mother and daughter was not his concern at present.

"It would be a marriage such as any other; no better, no worse than most, I suppose," she continued. "We both would benefit from such a union. I would retain the home and property that I inherited from my ancestors. You would gain the continuity and the good will that attends the Radcliffes of Wensleydale."

She might have been speaking of the merging of two merchant companies, so cool was her tone.

"And you would be willing to accept marriage on such a basis?" he asked.

"Why, Master Fitzgerald, you surely do not believe that most marriages are not based thus? Yes, I would be willing. And you need not worry that I should withhold your conjugal rights, or some such thing," she told him without flinching from his gaze. "I know what is expected of me as a wife."

My body you shall have, but not my heart. She might as well have spoken the words, for they hung between them, as if written in the ether.

Brendan took her hand in his. It lay there, cold and lifeless. He wanted to sweep her into his arms, breathe life back into her. He would even have preferred the mad, passionate creature who had beaten her mother to this empty shell. But, still, his heart leapt at the thought of taking her as his bride. He would wed her and then woo her so well that she would soon forget her damned Edward.

He squeezed her hand. "I give you my word, Katherine, that if you marry me I shall make you a good and faithful husband." He brought his face very close to hers. "If you marry me, I shall never wittingly give you cause to regret your decision."

"Then, Master Fitzgerald, I shall marry you."

She did not flinch from his kiss—nor did she respond to it.

Chapter 16

For as long as she could remember, May had always been Katherine's favorite month. The sound of the cuckoo calling on the wing, the sight of the jewel-green meadows and the River Ure shyly sparkling beneath a blue sky had set her spirits dancing, so that she felt at one with the lambs that gamboled on the fellsides, the kestrel soaring over the moorland heights.

But this May was different. This May she was to be married to a man for whom she cared nothing one way or the other. She neither liked nor disliked Brendan Fitzgerald. In common with many women before her, she was marrying for necessity, not for love.

"At least you are able to remain in your own home," her mother reminded her with an edge to her voice, as she helped Katherine dress on the morning of her wedding.

Katherine gritted her teeth. Better not to say anything than to have an argument with her mother before all her friends.

"Now the gown, now the gown," Joanna cried, clapping her hands with excitement.

The gown was lifted from its wrapping, its silver threads shimmering in the sunlight that streamed in through the casement windows.

"Lift up thine arms, Mistress Kate," said Margery.

Katherine lifted her arms, the jasmine scent they had added to her bathwater wafting from her hair and body. She felt the coolness of silk on her bare arms as eager hands drew the gown down over the Spanish farthingale that swung about her, anchored with ribbons tied at her waist.

"See how beautiful you look." Joanna held up the mirror of polished steel so that Katherine might see herself.

Not wishing to spoil her sister's pleasure, Katherine glanced into the mirror. The gown was indeed beautiful. Fashioned of cloth-of-silver interwoven with blue silk, it had a close-fitting bodice and slashed sleeves lavishly decorated with pearls. The ruff at her neck was gleaming white, but almost as white was the face above it, her eyes like dark pools.

She turned away.

"She will need some carmine for her cheeks," said Aunt Isobel, who had been surveying the dressing from the far side of the chamber.

Katherine gave her a grateful smile.

Her aunt came to her and patted her cheek. "'Tis a rare bride who enjoys her own wedding day," she said with a smile of sympathy. "Would you like me to do your hair for you?"

"Oh, Aunt Isobel," breathed Katherine, "would you?" She felt rather than saw her mother's hurt expression. Her mother had been talking eagerly to her last night about how she planned to fashion her hair. But Aunt Isobel, who traveled frequently to York and occasionally even to London, would know so much more about the current hairstyles.

The bridemaids, who were already dressed in their finery, gathered round to watch Lady Colborne's long white fingers with their large-gemmed rings creating curls and tendrils and waves with great dexterity—and the aid of the curling tongs heated in the brazier.

When she was at last ready, her aunt bade her look at herself again. This time Katherine was more satisfied with her appearance and smiled at her reflection. Her cheeks were a healthy pink. Her hair was a masterpiece, the usually unruly curls formed into tendrils and elegant rolls about her face. It hung loose down her back, its waves tamed by Joanna's vigorous brushing.

"Now for my old wedding headdress," her mother said and reached up to place the caul of golden mesh studded with pearls on Katherine's head.

Katherine hadn't the heart to tell her that the gold clashed with her cloth-of-silver gown.

"Thank the Lord the gold has not tarnished after all these years," her mother said as she pinned the caul into place. Their eyes met. "You are the most beautiful bride I have ever seen," Alyssa told her daughter.

Instinctively, Katherine embraced her mother, hugging her close against her body. For this moment, at least, she was the mother she had loved and turned to throughout her childhood and she felt in desperate need of her comfort.

"You will be ruining her hair, Alyssa," said Isobel's voice from behind them. The moment shattered into a thousand pieces, and disappeared, like dust, into the atmosphere.

"Now let me put on the garters," cried Joanna, the blue silk ribbons clutched in her hand.

Katherine lifted her skirts, and stretched out her leg, displaying the hose of rose-pink silk clocked with silver.

Giggling, Joanna tied on the garters, one above each knee.

"Are they too tight?" she asked anxiously.

Katherine swung first one leg and then the other. "Exactly right. I don't want them to fall off."

Now it was Joanna's turn to be embraced. "No, no, sweetheart. No tears," Katherine told her sister in a stern voice. "After all, it is not as if I were leaving home, is it?"

Joanna's plump face brightened at this reminder. "I wonder how Brendan will look today." Brendan had stayed overnight with the Challoners.

Unlike her sister, Joanna had not taken long to fall headlong in love with her future brother-in-law, blushing scarlet when he complimented her on a new gown, ever ready to play a game of tables or bowls with him.

If only it were Joanna, not me, marrying Brendan Fitzgerald today, thought Katherine. After all, Joanna would be fifteen in July. Many girls were married at fifteen.

She suddenly felt faint and her stomach tightened into a knot, as the thought came into her mind that, if she had married at fifteen, she would now be Edward's wife. He would be by her side, not in some cold seminary committing himself to a life of celibacy and denial, a life that could be cut short by the cruelest of deaths if ever he set foot on English ground again.

"Are you feeling unwell, Kate?"

Her mother's anxious enquiry brought her back to her senses.

Katherine put her hand to her temple. "No, no. Just a little light-headed, that is all."

"I understand, my love." Her mother squeezed her hand. "We will be out in the air very soon. The ride down to the church will help you to feel better. It is a glorious day."

Katherine felt like screaming. She wanted neither her mother's sympathy nor her assurance that the ride or the air would make her feel better. Did she not realize that all Katherine wanted was for time to halt, never to move again?

But time moved inexorably on so that, in a seeming dream, Katherine was mounted pillion behind their head groom, Barnaby, on Silver Jennet, one of Radcliffe's finest brood mares. Margery and Grace made sure that her gown was covered by her taffeta cloak, so that the dirt thrown up by the mare's hooves would not soil it.

The wedding party moved off, accompanied by cheers and shouts from those servants who had to remain behind to finish the preparations for the wedding feast.

Down the steep bridlepath Katherine rode, flanked by her grandfather, Sir William Harcourt, on one side and her illustrious uncle-in-law, Lord Colborne, on the other. Behind her streamed her many relatives, Metcalfes and Harcourts, and friends she had known since her childhood, many of whom had spent the night in the row of guest apartments that were built against the eastern wall of Radcliffe Hall.

Yet, despite being surrounded by this great crowd of people who knew and loved her, Katherine had never in her entire life felt quite so alone.

When they clattered over the ancient bridge and rode up the slight rise to the Church of the Holy Trinity, she saw that most of the inhabitants of Wensley had turned out to wish her well.

Katherine raised her hand in acknowledgement of their shouts, but she could not hear what they were saying. All her senses seemed to be enveloped in a curtain of heavy velvet, dulling her hearing, blurring her sight, depriving her of feeling.

But when at last all the wedding guests were seated and she descended the two steps into the ancient church, the joyous sound of the portative organ and the men's voices lifted in an anthem crashed in on her, sweeping away the velvet cover, leaving her a quivering mass of sensation.

As she moved down the aisle with the burly rector, Parson Bennett, at her side, she looked to both sides of her, smiling all the while, playing her part to perfection.

But her first glimpse of her bridegroom was almost her undoing, for he was an utter stranger in his magnificence. Gone was the colorless, serviceable clothing, almost as plain as that of a servant. He was dressed all in crimson and gold, his doublet slashed to reveal the gold damask beneath. With his great height and dark coloring, he looked like a prince, not like a poverty-stricken Irishman of doubtful parentage.

She felt a stab of fear.

Then he smiled at her, his teeth white and his eyes vivid blue, and she saw in his admiring expression that he thought her beautiful beyond compare. And when he drew closer to her and took her hand in his, she realized that not only his hand but his entire body was trembling, and he became plain Brendan Fitzgerald again.

She responded correctly to all the vows. It was he who stumbled and mixed his words. But when the rector pronounced them man and wife, her head swam again, as it had done in her bedchamber.

She realized then that she had been nursing a hope that the church doors might crash open, that Edward would come striding down the aisle, forbidding the marriage to continue. Now it was too late.

For a moment, the stone walls and pillars with their faded colors spun about her. She staggered and was terrified that she would fall, but Brendan's arm was strong about her. "Almost done," he whispered. "Lean on me."

Although she was grateful for his support, she shrank from his touch. His imposing height, his strength, his very essence, all reminded her of the intimacies to come. The thought made her stomach churn.

When they had taken communion and the final prayers were said over them, the rector bade Brendan kiss his wife. He needed no second prompting, but to the delight of everyone watching took her in his arms and kissed her soundly.

You are mine, the kiss said, *and I shall do with you whatsoever I will.*

To the accompaniment of pealing bells and the laughter and chatter of the assembly, they walked down the aisle and out into the churchyard. There they stood, blinking in the sunlight, to receive the good wishes of their guests and a shower of bride-cake crumbs.

Katherine was sure that her face would crack from the constant effort to maintain a smile.

Out of courtesy, the bridegroom was being treated as if he were a Yorkshireman, not an incomer from the misty bogs of faraway Ireland. It would not last, of course, but for today the men came to him to shake his hand and the women to kiss him.

As Katherine stood to one side, her eyes met Brendan's over the head of Mistress Fanshawe, a monstrous woman with three chins, who was embracing him with great fervor. Despite herself, Katherine could not help smiling at Brendan's grimace and silent appeal to her to come to his aid.

"Why, Mistress Fanshawe," she said, "what a beautiful gown."

In truth, it was a hideous gown of bright tawny satin that went ill with the woman's bright-red wig.

"Ah, here is your new bride. You have caught us out, Mistress Fitzgerald," she said archly.

Mistress Fitzgerald. It sounded strange in Katherine's ears. A name that was utterly alien in England.

"Thought you were going to take the name Radcliffe," Lord Colborne said in a belligerent tone to Brendan.

The comment had been made in Lord Colborne's usual loud voice that demanded to be heard. The hum of conversation and laughter died into silence, which was broken only by the incessant bleating of sheep on the fellsides and a sudden bray of laughter from someone in the crowd.

"One day I shall, my lord," replied Brendan in a pleasant tone, turning to him.

"Should do so now. Don't like a member of my wife's family being called by the same name as those damned scurvy rebels in Ireland."

Katherine could feel the tension in Brendan's body. She glanced up at him and was surprised to see that his face, though a little pale, still bore a faint smile. They were a strange contrast, the squat, sandy-haired Yorkshireman and the tall, handsome Irishman. The thought suddenly came to her that, had she not known, she would have taken Brendan to be the nobleman.

She thought Brendan would never reply, so long did the silence last. She was about to break it herself with some light remark, when at last he spoke.

"When first I came to Yorkshire, five months ago, I made a vow to a gentleman whom I greatly respect that I would not take the name of Radcliffe until I had earned it. I shall not break that vow for any man, be he a member of my wife's family or no."

Though he spoke in his usual soft accent, Brendan's voice carried through the churchyard and beyond.

"Well said, lad," a voice cried daringly from outside the low church walls. A thin scatter of clapping greeted this approbation, but most remained silent, fearing to offend Lord Colborne, who was not renowned for his benevolence.

145

"Enough of this clacking," said Sir William, to Katherine's great relief. "Gather up thy bride, lad, and let's get to the eating and drinking."

There seeming to be general agreement on this suggestion, the company mounted their horses in the lane beyond the churchyard. Brendan sprang onto his great black gelding, which was his own, not one of the Radcliffe stable, and Katherine was put up behind him. *Like his chattel*, she thought darkly, wishing she could ride her own horse.

With their bridesmaids and men about them, they led the way back to Radcliffe, where the wedding feast was to be held, despite Sir William's wishes to the contrary.

"Kate should be wed from Harcourt Hall," he had complained to Alyssa when she told him. "Never heard the like, to have the bridegroom taking the bride back to his home for the wedding feast."

"It was Master Fitzgerald's wish that we treat Radcliffe as if it were still ours for the week of the wedding," Alyssa had told her father. "He felt that it would make Katherine easier in her mind."

"Harebrained, that's what he is. Easy to see he dotes on our Kate, poor fellow. She's got him twisted around her little finger already."

Alyssa was not quite so sure about that. Master Fitzgerald was a difficult man to fathom. Just when you began to think that he was far too pleasant for his own good, his eyes would take on a steely glint and his mouth snap shut like an animal trap, which boded ill for whoever had displeased him.

She kept her counsel, but secretly she thought that Brendan Fitzgerald would surprise the insular inhabitants of the Dales one day. She also had the feeling that Tobias was of her mind. So well did she know her steward by now, she could guess what he was thinking from just a flicker of emotion across his guarded countenance.

As she rode up the familiar bridlepath, her thoughts turned to the one person above all who should have been at this celebration of her daughter's wedding. *I miss you, my darling*, she told him. *My life is empty without you.*

Life with Philip at Radcliffe had been eternally bittersweet. So near to each other and yet so far. But it was the pact they had made. Better to remain together as father and daughter, than to live apart. It had not been easy to maintain a life of celibacy together, particularly for Alyssa, who was so much younger. Besides, to have learned such pleasure once at his hands, only to be denied it for the rest of her life, caused her endless torment.

She looked at her beautiful daughter, riding behind her handsome bridegroom, and wondered what lay ahead for them both. The mandatory horoscopes had promised them health and happiness, long life and many children, of course, but Alyssa knew from her own experience that the first love of a young girl could last a very long time; sometimes an eternity.

Pray heaven it would not prove so for Katherine.

Chapter 17

The long day was drawing to a close. They had danced and sang and watched jugglers and fire-eaters and dancing dogs. The head table on the dais was littered with the remains of the feast: bones from capon and beef on gilt dishes; melting jellies and creams; the crumbling remnants of a pastry subtlety which had been in the form of a beautiful church when it had been carried in an hour before.

Katherine felt if she ate one more bite of food she would explode—and if she danced one more step her legs would drop off. She was bone weary and melting with the heat. Her beautiful wedding gown was sticking to her body and both big toes were poking through holes in her silken hose. A trickle of sweat ran down her back as she sat, listening to Brendan playing his pipe.

He stood in the center of the hall, the small pipe incongruous in his strong hands, but the music he drew from it was so pure and sweet that everyone paused to listen to it. It was strange music, filled with sadness and longing, and Brendan's expression matched it.

How little she knew about this man who was about to bed her, thought Katherine. Her heart beat a hurried tattoo at the thought she had been trying to force from her mind all day. But the time was almost upon her and could no longer be put aside.

Would he be kind, she wondered, or would his ill-concealed attraction to her make him like the eager stallions in the stable stud, their first encounter brief, hot, even violent, with little preparation for it? On the other hand, perhaps that would be preferable to something that took a long time.

Her mother had tried to talk to her about the wedding night, but she had brushed her aside with a brusque "I know all about it."

Now she wished she had listened to her and not to Dame Joan and Margery, who had dwelt salaciously on the monstrous size of a man's organ and what pain it caused.

"Dreaming?" said Brendan's voice, close to her ear. "I hope 'twas of me."

Katherine started, heat spreading up her neck to her face.

"Why, sweetheart, you are blushing," he teased. "You *were* dreaming of me, then."

She looked up at him. "Yes, I was." She bared her teeth in a smile, but her eyes dared him to say more.

He heeded their message. "We are being asked to lead the last dance. 'Tis one of those hectic galliards which leave me standing flummoxed, as you say in Yorkshire. I give you fair warning, dear wife, I expect you to support your husband in this endeavor."

He was overly modest about his dancing, but it was easy to see that, although he knew most of the steps, he lacked experience. "'Twas little chance we had of dancing in the sodden bogs of Ireland," he had told her earlier, with that glint in his eye which always made her wonder if he were being serious or not. At times, during the past weeks, she thought she had seen anger behind his seeming good humor, but then he would laugh or make some quip and the look would disappear.

Having made her an exaggerated bow, he led her down from the dais to the head of the dance. The fiddler struck up a chord, to be joined by the recorders and viols and lutes from the musician's gallery, and they were into the thick of it, everything else forgotten in the hectic pace and intricate steps of the dance.

When they came to the end, Brendan lifted her in his arms and twirled her about, pressing her body to his. He did not release her when he had set her down, but held her there, pinned to him, and kissed her. It was a rough, raw kiss that delighted the crowd. She could feel the heat of his body, sense the urgency of his desire for her, and she was afraid.

She pushed feebly against his grasp, but he would not yield, merely laughing down at her. Panic swept her as she realized how strong he was, capable of doing as he pleased with her against her will. Wide-eyed with fear, she struggled against him and he released her.

She stepped back from him, shaking her head, her breathing shallow and fast.

She heard snickers of laughter and someone made a crude jest that set up a burst of laughter from the men who were dicing in a corner of the hall.

Brendan held out one hand. "Come, Kate, do not be afraid of me. 'Twas all in jest." Then, when she did not respond, "Let us return to the dais. You are being foolish."

There was no doubting his anger. The dark eyebrows drew in over the strong nose. The last thing she wanted was a scene before everyone in the hall. "I pray your pardon. It . . . it is the heat and I am very weary." She gave him a wan smile to placate him.

His good nature was restored instantly. "To be sure you are. It is as hot as hell in here. Let us go outside in the garden for a moment to restore your spirits."

Before she had time to say yea or nay, he drew her hand through his arm, pausing only to tell Tobias where they were going, and walked across the hall and out onto the stone-flagged terrace.

Katherine realized that she had been safer by far amidst the crowds in the great hall than out here, where the evening breezes stirred the leaves and the scent of the early blooming syringa and lilies of the valley hung sweetly in the air. The dale stretched out before them, much of it hidden by the trees that covered the fellside, but she could see the lights of Wensley twinkling through the foliage.

A gust of wind blew against her, cooling her skin. Unthinking, she slid her hands under her heavy hair and lifted it, to allow the breeze to play upon her neck.

"Sweet Jesu, but you are beautiful," Brendan said, his tone as reverent as a churchman's.

She looked up at him, her arms still raised, aware of the tightening of her breasts against the taut fabric of her gown. He drew nearer and gently placed both hands on her breasts.

She drew her breath in sharply, but otherwise did not move. From somewhere in the woods below a nightingale began to sing, its throbbing note piercing the air. Now Brendan's hands were moving very slightly, exerting no pressure, his thumbs brushing back and forth across her nipples.

Katherine heard his intake of breath as her nipples rose to his touch, hardening against it. She let her hair fall, so that its silken weight covered his hands. The pleasurable feelings his touch evoked intensified, radiating downwards, into the very pit of her stomach, and beyond.

Her fear forgotten, she put her arms about his waist, feeling the soft leather of his belt and the hilt of his ornamental dagger in its sheath.

Groaning her name deep in his throat, as if he were in pain, Brendan's right hand tightened on her breast, his left arm sliding to her back to clamp her body against his. This time his kiss was not one of the gentle kisses he had occasionally given her. His mouth opened upon hers as if he sought to devour her.

Katherine's teeth clenched. Her body became rigid as a board and she slid her arms from his waist, to push against him with all her strength, seeking to separate herself from him.

He released her, stepping back to stare at her. In the light from the lanterns on the terrace, she saw that his pupils were dilated. "What is it, what is the matter?" he demanded.

"I do not like to . . . to be mauled." Her look was defiant.

"Christ!"

He turned angrily to pace across the terrace and stood, his back to her, watching the night wind shivering the trees below them. It looked as if a May storm was brewing. The air was sultry and held a suggestion of rain.

He made a brisk turn and came back to her. "Come, let us go in. We should not be deserting our guests."

She did not like to see him this way, his expression grim. It augured ill for the remainder of the night. She laid a tentative hand on his sleeve. "Do not be angry with me," she said, with a little smile.

For the first time in her memory, he did not respond to her smile, but stood looking at her until she, herself, was angered at his silence.

"You might say something, instead of just standing there, glaring at me."

"I might, indeed. I have already said that we should return to our guests."

"Not before you tell me what you are thinking," Katherine demanded.

"If I do, you will not like it. Therefore, let well alone."

She had never known him to be so exasperating. Her treacherous body was still tingling from his arousal, at odds with her for having put an end to its pleasuring. What kind of common whore was she, to gain pleasure from another man's touch, when she had vowed to love only Edward?

"Tell me," she screamed at Brendan, in a voice as raucous as that of the peacocks that strutted about on the new-scythed lawn.

He took a step forward, his eyes glittering. "Very well, madam. If you insist. I was thinking that if I were another man, you would not blow hot and cold. You would not make *him* feel like some Goth bent on rapine every time he touched you."

His breath came fast as he waited for her to reply. When she did not, he laughed mirthlessly. "And wasn't I right to say that you would not wish to hear what I was thinking?"

He was right, of course. To hear her exact feelings expressed by him had shocked her greatly, but she would not give him the satisfaction of telling him so. She looked at him coldly. "You are my husband now, sir. By the laws of God and the state you may do with me as you will. But you will never, never be master of my thoughts."

He took a hasty step towards her and, for a moment, she thought he would strike her. She lifted her chin, defying him to do so, but the clenched hand loosened and fell to his side.

A low rumble of thunder sounded in the distance. "Come, madam, let us resume our false, smiling faces again and return to our guests." He held out his arm. After a moment of hesitation, Katherine placed her hand upon it and he led her back into the house.

Catcalls and whistles greeted them as they entered the hall. "Couldn't wait, eh?" cried one wit.

Brendan grinned, but Katherine remained stony-faced beside him, wishing with all her heart that it was a week from hence and this was all over.

Her mother came to them.

"We crave your pardon for having left the house," said Brendan to her. "Kate was feeling the heat and we went outside for a little air."

"It is very warm. I think we shall have a storm." Alyssa's eyes were on her daughter's face. "I am come to tell you it is time for the . . . the bridal bedding, Kate." She rested her hand on Katherine's arm. "I would speak with you alone for a moment, dearest."

But Katherine had enough of private conversations. She wanted none of her mother's "I understand how you must feel" or "By tomorrow it will be over." It would never be over. The bedding was only a part of it. She was wed for life to a man she neither loved nor respected. A man who, through a quirk of fate, held in his power all that remained for her now: Radcliffe.

And for the sake of Radcliffe, she would submit to this man tonight and any other night until she provided an heir for Radcliffe. After that . . .

"Your pardon, my lady Mother, but this is neither the time nor place to be holding a private conversation. I see Joanna and the other bridemaids waiting for me." She made her mother a curtsy and went to join her sister and the giggling bridemaids, to be escorted upstairs to the bridal chamber.

As she was being undressed and put into the large bed, it was Aunt Isobel who gave her both solace and practical information. "Rub this into your private parts beforehand," she whispered, pressing a vial of ointment into Katherine's hands, "and do not fight him. That only makes your body tense and the pain greater. Set your mind on other matters while he is at his work. One consolation, when they are young and eager, like your new husband, it does not last long."

"My thanks, dear aunt." Katherine slipped the vial under her pillow.

Aunt Isobel took her face between her perfumed hands. "You are my favorite niece, Katherine. I wish with all my heart that it were your bedding with Edward Carlton I was attending tonight, not with an Irish soldier who has no idea whatsoever how to behave with a lady. No doubt all his amorous encounters until now have been with camp followers."

Katherine shivered involuntarily at the thought, but now it was too late even to think, for, to the accompaniment of a pipe and tabor and raucous singing, Brendan was being led into the bridal chamber by the men.

To her horror, she saw that he was dressed in a long mantle of wolf skins, making him look, in truth, like one of the very Goths he had mentioned. *I will not be afraid*, she told herself, *I will not let him master me*.

She sat up in the bed, glad that she had insisted on wearing her wedding nightgown of white silk that her mother had stitched. It was far easier to appear haughty and self-confident in this ridiculous situation if one was clothed, rather than naked, beneath the bedcovers.

It was her uncle, Piers Metcalfe, who made a move to remove Brendan's mantle. "Nay, sir," said Brendan. "I'll undress myself when the time comes, not before."

This was something different. It was usual to see the bride and groom in bed together before the posset was given them.

"That's spoiling our sport," growled Sir William. "'Tis the custom hereabouts to undress the bridegroom and set him in the bride's bed."

Katherine could see that her grandfather had, as usual, overindulged in the wine and ale, as had many of the men who voiced their discontent. Please God, don't let them anger Brendan, she prayed. She had visions of them stripping the alien wolf-skin mantle from him and bodily throwing him down on the bed.

Her mother intervened. "No doubt Brendan has his own customs, Father," she said in her soft voice, "and we should respect them." She turned to Brendan, who stood immobile beside the bed. "One custom I know you will not deny me and that is to take some of the wedding posset I prepared for you and Katherine myself."

His bow was gracious. "I will do so with pleasure."

Alyssa went to the sideboard and poured some of the steaming hot posset into two silver-gilt loving cups. She presented one to Brendan. "I wish you health and good fortune and happiness, my new son. May the love of God and of your wife attend you all your days."

She took the other cup to Katherine. "To you, my beloved firstborn daughter, I wish the same as I wished your husband. May God bless you with many children to fill our beloved Radcliffe. And may your ancestors add their prayers to mine to bring blessings on the house of the Radcliffes of Wensleydale."

Blinking away tears, she kissed Katherine and then, on tiptoe, Brendan.

Katherine drank a little of the strongly spiced posset, breathing in its fumes.

"My wife and I thank all of you for your good wishes," said Brendan, summoning up a smile. "I salute the gracious and loving spirit of my new mother, who has given me a warm welcome into her home and family." He held up his cup and bowed to Alyssa. "And Master Ridley, who has been both a patient instructor in the ways of husbandry to this poor student, and a good friend." Again he bowed, this time to Tobias, who stood in the background, looking as if he wished he could make himself instantly invisible.

"Now, we must bid you all goodnight. My beautiful bride and I have much to say to each other."

This sally was greeted with laughter and good humor was restored. Having at last been persuaded to leave by Tobias and Alyssa, the guests retreated slowly, with much ribaldry and shaking of loud rattles to dispel evil spirits from the bridal chamber.

At last the door closed. Brendan immediately strode across the herb-strewn floor to turn the key in the latch.

Although, in a way, Katherine had been relieved to see them all go, a feeling of panic swept over her as she realized that she was locked in with this stranger from across the sea, who was dressed like a barbarian.

She sat up straight in the bed, her back pressed against the ornate paneling, her teeth chattering. All her resolution to stand up to this man, to treat him with all the hauteur befitting the rightful heir to Radcliffe vanished.

He returned to stand beside the bed. "Are you cold?"

Katherine nodded, her teeth audibly chattering now.

"The storm has brought cold air with it. You will soon be warm."

She shrank back, not from the actual words, but from their implication.

He let out a long sigh. "Oh, Katherine, for the love of God, do not be continually thinking ill of me. I meant that I will put more logs on the fire." He picked up her goblet from the table. "Take some more of this. It will warm you." She drank it down obediently. Anything to avoid his wrath, tonight at least. He sat down on the bed.

Although the mantle was barbaric, the clean smell of him, overlaid with a musky scent, and the elegant cut of his hair spoke of a man of the civilized world. He took the goblet from her hand, set it down on the floor, and then raised her hand to kiss it. It trembled in his.

"I hate to see you fearful of me," he said softly.

Her chin lifted. "I am not. It is only that I am weary and . . . and this is the bed in which my grandfather died."

His smile was gentle. "That is the way it is with beds, sweetheart. We are born in them, we die in them, we make love in them."

Instead of reassuring her, his words chilled Katherine. It was probably in this bed that her mother . . . She shivered violently. "I feel sick," she whispered. It was the truth. Her stomach was rebelling from the constant tension mixed with too much rich food and wine. Now it was spinning, and her head with it. But he would think it was just another one of her ploys, of course.

He bent over her to place a hand on her brow. "You have no fever."

"Brendan, I am not dissembling. I do feel sick. But I am sure it will soon pass."

His answer was to lean over, this time to pick up the pillows from the bed.

"What are you doing?"

He made no answer, but took the armful of down-filled pillows and placed them on the floor by the fire. Then he threw three more logs on the fire, sending red sparks up the broad chimney, banking the sides with peat, to keep in the warmth. He returned to the bed for the bearskin bedcover and laid it, too, on the floor in front of the hearth.

"Where is your nightrobe?"

"On top of the chest, I think."

He went to the chest and took up her new nightrobe of jewel-red cut velvet. "Is this it?"

She nodded.

He brought it to her and flung back the bedclothes. "Put it on," he said, holding it out for her.

Wonderingly, she did so, too miserable to disobey his orders.

As soon as she had put the nightrobe on, he lifted her in his arms and bore her to the fireplace, laying her down on the bed he had made there. It was like a warm nest.

From outside came the rumble of thunder.

To her surprise, he sat down in the X-shaped chair that had been her grandfather's favorite, and took up a small harp, which she had never seen before.

"Rest," he told her. "And I will play to you."

She let her head lie against a pillow, but kept her eyes fixed upon him.

He strummed the stings of the instrument, tuning them a little, and then began to sing in the Irish language, one of the sad, plaintive melodies that spoke of loss and sadness. Yet, despite its melancholy, the music was soothing and his voice warm and musical. She felt the tension in her neck ease away.

After a while, he came to sit beside her on one of the pillows. "Does your belly still ache?"

"Only a little now."

He stretched out beside her. "Turn on your back."

By now she was in a dream state, her mind numb. She turned on her back, trying not to let her muscles tighten again as the fear of what he was about to do assailed her once more.

"Easy, my darling, easy." She felt his hand flat on her belly, circling slowly, starting in the center, and then extending.

She closed her eyes, allowing herself to stretch languourously under his sensuous stroking. The pain in her belly eased, to be replaced by another type of ache that his comforting made worse, not better.

The thunder increased, rumbling down the dale, echoing across the fells.

"Is that better?" he asked eventually, lifting his hand from her body.

"Yes." She opened her eyes to find his face very close. "Thank you." How could she ask him not to stop? How could she tell him that she needed him to continue, that his touch had set up a growing ache within her that only he could assuage?

To her dismay, he stood up. "I thought I might read to you."

Read to her! Was the man out of his mind? She had been deeply afraid that he would force himself upon her as soon as the door had closed behind their guests and family. Now she was beginning to wonder if he intended to consummate their marriage at all. Not that she wished for it; she still dreaded what was to come. Her only wish was that he would continue with the touching, the stroking. Now he was going to read to her. The men of Ireland were strange beings, indeed.

Still clad in his mantle, he came to sit beside her before the fire again. "Malory's *Morte d'Arthur*." He held up the book, which was bound in red vellum. "Do you like it?"

"It is one of my favorite books. Is that my grandfather's?"

"No, it is mine."

She was thinking that she still had much to learn about this husband of hers, when he began to read: "And thus it passed on from Candlemas until after Easter that the month of May was come, when every lusty heart beginneth to blossom and to bring forth fruit. For like as herbs and trees bring forth fruit and flourish in May, in likewise every lusty heart that is in any way a lover springeth and flourisheth in lusty deeds."

As he read on, the words filtered to her mind, spreading their sensuous message throughout her body. It was May now. Outside, a storm was building. Inside, the bedchamber had suddenly become too hot.

"Are you not too warm?" she asked him suddenly, her eyes half-closed. "Your mantle must be very heavy."

He stopped reading, lifting his eyes from the book to her. "I will take it off later," he told her. As he began reading again, Katherine removed her nightrobe.

"I do not understand," she said, after he had read a few more lines.

"What is it you do not understand?"

She hesitated. "Why you are reading a book to me?"

He looked bewildered. "I thought you said you liked *Morte d'Arthur*."

"I do. But . . ." How could she explain, when she did not know herself what it was she wanted?

"Would you like a little plain claret wine or a few grapes, perhaps? I do not think either would hurt you."

She shook her head.

"Has the pain returned?"

She opened her eyes wide. "Yes, yes, it has."

"You should have told me so before. Would you like me to rub it again?"

She nodded, the waves of desire already spreading at the very thought of him touching her.

He set the book down and began again his gentle motion, only this time his fingers extended farther, brushing her breasts at times—when he would murmur an apology—or even, once or twice, pressing the mound that lay between her thighs.

The aching was building, building, now concentrated in that one part of her, the throbbing center of her being. She stretched out her legs and wantonly spread her thighs a little, longing for his touch to linger *there*.

A small moan escaped her.

"What is it, my darling?"

"Please, Brendan, please touch me." She was his slave, or he was hers. She wasn't sure which it was, nor did she care.

He moved his hands down, to draw up her nightgown about her waist, and then further, above her breasts. She could hear his hurried breathing, feel his breath against her hot skin, but she cared nothing for this. His hands were on her breasts and then running down her waist and flanks. Still, he did not touch the melting core of her.

Now she sensed he too was in pain, his labored breathing betraying him. Perhaps if she were to kiss him, it would help to ease him. She encircled his head with her hand, his hair springy beneath her fingers, and drew it down.

Yes, he was in pain, for he groaned as she kissed him. This time, it was she who pressed her tongue against his lips, wishing he would open his mouth to hers. She was all open to him now, mouth and breasts and thighs open to him. But he was still closed to her.

She sought to open his cloak, but he stayed her. "Not yet, sweet love."

She wanted to cry out, to scream, so demanding was the throbbing between her legs.

Touch me, you fool, she wanted to scream. But he, not realizing her great need, kept touching her breasts and stroking her belly, his fingers barely brushing the very edge of the triangle of curling hair.

She could not bear it one moment longer. She took his hand in hers and drew it down. Ah, now at last he understood. His fingers brought her to the edge of ecstasy—and then retreated again.

"You must not be so hasty, my dearest wife," he whispered, when she gasped out her need. His hands fumbled unsteadily at the clasps on his mantle. When they were open, she helped him to cast it off. He lifted her onto it; the bristling fur was strangely pleasurable against her bare back.

"I wish to make you truly my wife on the only part of Ireland I can still call mine," he told her.

She knew a moment of fear, but the clamoring demands of her body overrode the fear. He looked down at her, his eyes bright with the fever of desire, the firelight casting a ruddy light over his naked body.

Still he did not bring his body close to hers, but began again his caresses in the secret moist folds of her. When he knew she could wait no longer, he set a pillow beneath her hips. At the very moment of her fulfillment, he entered her, so that her waves of ecstasy mingled with the sudden pain of his penetration.

Tears sprang to her eyes as he moved as slowly as he could within her. He was drowning in her tears and in the pleasure her sweet body was giving him. "Do not weep, my darling," he gasped. "It is almost over."

With the last thrust, he crushed her to him, covering her mouth with his, to stifle his cry of relief and ecstasy.

And outside, the clouds burst open and poured forth the long-awaited rain on the fertile land.

Later that night, Brendan awoke with a start, wondering where he was. The sound of teeming rain, the bluster of wind and roll of thunder made him think he was back in Munster again, sheltered from the rainstorm blowing in from the ocean by only the canvas walls of his tent.

Almost immediately he realized that it was bed curtains, not canvas, that surrounded him, and that he was in Radcliffe Hall on his wedding night, lying on the bed to which he had borne his bride after their marriage had been consummated.

Smiling in the darkness, he reached out his hand—to find that the other side of the bed was empty. And now that his eyes had adjusted to the darkness, he saw that the bed curtain on that side was slightly open.

He climbed across the bed and swung his legs over the side, wincing as the curtain rings rattled very slightly. When he reached the end of the bed, he saw her in the seat of the bay window, her figure illuminated by a flash of lightning.

She was not seated upon the cushions, but kneeling, with her head flung back, looking out at the storm, her arms lifted and spread against the unshuttered window, like Saint Andrew in his martyrdom.

Every so often, she emitted a long sobbing sigh, as if she had been weeping for a long time and was exhausted from it.

It was the most desolate sound Brendan had ever heard.

He stood there for a long time, fearing to move, his feet pricked by the sprigs of rosemary and lavender strewn upon the floor.

Then he crept back to the bed, to lie between the cold wedding sheets, listening open-eyed to the rain pattering against the windows, the moaning of the wind in the chimneys.

Chapter 18

The hope that had been kindled in Brendan's breast on his wedding night faded and died during the following months. It was not that Katherine denied him his marital rights, but never again did she abandon herself to him as she had on that first night. She lay on their bed, more beautiful than ever with her creamy skin and high, firm breasts, a sacrifice on the cold altar of wifely duty.

If she had ranted at him, as the old Kate would have done, he could have borne it more easily, but her cold indifference drove him to a frenzy. Whenever he laid with her, she made him feel as if he were committing an act of violation.

Never again did he hear her weep after they had lain together, but frequently, after she had fallen asleep, he would lie awake, staring at the carved tester above him and tears would come unbidden to his eyes.

"Do you wish me to move to another chamber?" he asked her one morning, as he watched her move silently about the bedchamber.

She raised her head, her expression genuinely surprised. "Why?"

"I thought you might prefer to sleep alone."

"I made a choice not to do so when I agreed to marry you."

Brendan's smile was bitter. "That is true. But as you seem to gain so little pleasure from sharing my bed, I thought you might prefer to have you own."

He knew from the sudden light in her eyes that this would be her preference, but her words denied it. "We have been wed several months now and I am still . . ." she hesitated, her hands moving across her stomach, "still barren."

"You have heard no complaint from me on the matter. Besides," Brendan added, his voice more gentle now, "a few months is nothing."

She muttered something beneath her breath, which he could not hear. Then she raised her dark eyes to his. "I wish to have a child, a male heir for Radcliffe. To achieve that, we must lie together as often as we can."

Now he understood. He was merely a stallion, useful only for breeding purposes—and even then he was not considered by the Radcliffes of Wensleydale to be of sufficiently good stock. He thought of the never-mentioned Thomsons of Leaze Mill, Sir Philip Radcliffe's milling cousins, and of Sir Philip's grandfather, Tom Thomson, once the horsemaster at Jervaulx Abbey, and smiled grimly to himself. What irony!

"Very well, madam," he said with a stiff military bow, "I am at your service."

And so they continued to sleep together, moving apart to the far sides of the bed after they had coupled, the space between them eloquent of the distance that separated them in their daily lives together.

For the few months before the wedding, Brendan had lived in a fool's paradise, his manner more that of a love-stricken youth seeking to engage the affection of his beloved than of a man in his mid-twenties, experienced in the arts of love and war.

During that time, he had thought little of the outside world, of Ireland and Ralegh, of Edmund Campion and the Earl of Sussex. But now that the first flush of passion was over—although, alas, his love for Katherine was now deeper than ever—his thoughts had begun to return to the world beyond the remote and narrow sphere of the Yorkshire Dales.

Although the North Riding of Yorkshire was physically remote, news from the South and from Scotland reached its inhabitants surprisingly fast. Unfortunately, most of that news was not good.

The Spanish were in the ascendancy. There were rumors of a plot to turn the young King of Scotland—and the inhabitants of that country, which was so close to Yorkshire—to Catholicism, so that a combined Scottish and Spanish army could invade England from the north. This news was particularly fearsome to northerners. The thought of a great army rampaging through their land was a terrifying one. The Scots were one thing, they were the traditional enemy, particularly the border clans, but the Spaniards were both feared and loathed throughout the land.

"Ralegh did the right thing, slaughtering those Spanish troops in Ireland," Lord Colborne told Brendan, when they were discussing the latest rumors. He spoke about the Smerwick massacre as if he knew every detail of what had happened.

Brendan, who had seen at firsthand the results of the order to kill all prisoners, was silent. Smerwick had been one of his main reasons for leaving the Queen's army, for leaving Ireland itself, in truth.

He had left Ireland to find peace, security, a home, but he was beginning to realize that he belonged to neither Ireland nor Yorkshire. In truth, he belonged nowhere. All he had done was replace one sort of loneliness with another.

The news from Ireland was even worse than he expected. Five counties had been laid waste and only the traitors, his own kinsmen the Fitzgeralds, under the leadership of the Earl of Desmond, seemed to have survived the devastation. The ineptitude of the Governor, Lord Grey, was openly discussed even here, in the North, where little was known about Ireland.

And as he sat and listened at these discussions, saying little, thinking much, Brendan's heart ached for his once beautiful country. He felt like a traitor for having deserted her when she most in need of men who loved her.

But the main talk at Colborne Place or Bolton Castle, when the powerful Lord Scrope was in residence, or in the smaller manor houses in the district, was of the increasing fear of another Catholic rising on behalf of Mary, Queen of Scots, a rising that would most likely be backed by the mighty armies of both Spain and France.

Protestant England was almost completely surrounded by hostile Catholic countries and so, with the fear of invasion from one or the other, the strong feeling against even the mildest manifestation of the Catholic faith increased. Seven priests had been hung, drawn and quartered in the month of May alone. The recusancy fine for not attending the parish church on Sundays had been increased to a crippling twenty pounds a month for each person in a household.

"You had best take great care," Lord Scrope warned Brendan gruffly, when he visited Radcliffe Hall in August to discuss the purchase of a pair of fine coursers from the Radcliffe stable.

Brendan had liked Henry Scrope immediately upon their very first meeting. Subsequent encounters had given him no cause to change that first impression. The most powerful of the Yorkshire lords, Warden of the Middle March and once host to Mary, Queen of Scots when she had been imprisoned in Bolton Castle, Lord Scrope appeared also to be a man of scrupulous honesty. He was a close friend of the Radcliffe family and his warning to Brendan came as such.

"The Radcliffes have been under suspicion ever since Sir Philip's involvement in the northern rising thirteen years ago," said Lord Scrope in an undertone as they walked away from the stables to the orchard, its fruit trees laden with fruit. "In truth, my lord of Sussex would doubtless have found some way of repossessing Radcliffe Manor had I not taken on the wardship of young Richard Radcliffe."

His face suddenly turned brick-red as he remembered Brendan's position. "That is not to say—"

Brendan smiled. "Have no fear, my lord. From the little I know of my noble patron, I would heartily agree with you." His smile faded. "I also know very well how my presence at Radcliffe is resented by the local people, not only because I am an incomer and Irish-born, but also because of the ill-feeling here against my lord of Sussex."

"Quite so. And that is even more reason why you must take great care. As an Irishman, you, too, are suspected of being sympathetic to the Catholic cause. Alyssa and Katherine were imprisoned for harboring Father Campion, perhaps taking the sacrament from him. To anyone with even the least suspicious nature, Radcliffe would seem to be a veritable hotbed of Catholics."

Brendan met his enquiring eyes directly. "I assure you it is not."

"Good. I am glad to hear it. I still cannot fathom who it was who betrayed Alyssa and Katherine. To my knowledge—and I and Lady Scrope have known her for many years—Alyssa Radcliffe has no sympathy for the Catholic cause." His bushy gray eyebrows drew in over his nose. "It is Katherine who troubles me. She is not still writing to Edward Carlton, is she?"

Brendan stiffened. "You tread on dangerous ground there, sir."

"Aye, you have the right to bristle at me," Lord Scrope said hastily, "but, believe me, I have both her interest and yours at heart when I ask a question of such a personal nature."

Brendan's anger faded. "To my knowledge she is not. And having seen the letter he wrote to Mistress Radcliffe last February, I doubt that

Carlton will engage in any correspondence with a member of my household again."

"I am especially glad to hear that. I care deeply for the Radcliffe family, Fitzgerald. Sir Philip was a particular friend of both my father and me. Now that your kindness has enabled his family to return to their ancestral home, I am anxious to ensure that nothing untoward occurs to disturb them again."

"I assure you that is my wish also, my lord."

"Good, good." As they walked back to the stableyard, he took Brendan's arm. "Remember, my lad, to be ever on your guard, particularly for Katherine. She is a hotheaded lass, always has been. Takes after her father there. Likes to go her own way. And nowadays there are eyes everywhere. One cannot trust even members of one's household or family. Take warning. Remove anything that might hint at a Roman tendency. Breviaries, prayer beads . . . Even if it's only a small wooden cross, burn it!"

He hurriedly released Brendan's arm, as Lady Scrope and Katherine came into the stableyard. "Ah, here are our ladies, Fitzgerald," he said in a loud voice. "So you recommend that I take the bay gelding as well, do you?"

The conversation was now fixed solely on the various merits of the horses Lord Scrope had tentatively chosen, his wife being as knowledgeable about horseflesh as he.

Lord Scrope and his lady left Wensleydale at the end of August, he to his position as Governor of Carlisle Castle, she to her post in the Queen's household at Court, but Lord Scrope's warnings remained with Brendan.

Fearful of any harm that could come to Katherine, he secretly began to search the house for anything that might be construed as papist by a foe—or even a friend. The thought of having Katherine wrested from him and imprisoned again, or worse, terrified him. There were several women of rank in prisons throughout Yorkshire at this very moment. Stories of young girls being stripped naked and thrown in amongst prostitutes, merely for saying an Ave Maria on their rosary beads, were rife.

He must be vigilant at all times to save Katherine from such a fate.

Using the excuse to Tobias that he wished to check the inventory and discover exactly what it was that he owned, Brendan began with the cellars and the attics. In the latter, he discovered a beautiful gilt crucifix, about two feet long, studded with rubies and pearls.

Reluctant to destroy such a treasure, he decided to take Alyssa into his confidence. Lord Scrope had assured him that she had no Catholic sympathies. It would be far easier to search the house if he enlisted her aid. But he sensed that it might be best to do so when Katherine was away from home.

And so, one day in late September, when Joanna and Katherine had ridden to Coverdale to visit their grandparents, he told Alyssa of Lord Scrope's warning.

"He is right, of course," she said calmly. "I should have thought of it myself. After all that has happened in the past year, we must be especially vigilant."

"I did not like to look further than the cellars and attics without a member of the family with me. After all, much of the contents of the house must belong to you, Mistress Radcliffe."

"Some," she agreed. "Linen and hangings and such. Not a great deal, though. When I came to Radcliffe Hall as Thomas's bride, it already had the most comfortable furnishings imaginable. There was little I could add. Have you found anything that might prove dangerous?"

"One thing. A large gilded crucifix. It was at the bottom of a chest, wrapped in old curtains."

"It must be the cross that used to be above the altar in the chapel. Where did you put it?"

"It is in the music chamber at present, beneath a stack of music manuscripts."

"Let us go there directly, then." She led the way up the broad staircase to the music chamber.

Sir Philip Radcliffe's presence was everywhere in this house. In the long gallery, where his portrait hung on the east wall, the farseeing blue eyes in the ascetic face watching them all. In his large collection of valuable books—a positive treasure trove to Brendan, who had seen only one collection to equal it and that had been in the Earl of Sussex's library. Strange that a mere knight in a remote part of Yorkshire should have amassed such an admirable collection.

But, most of all, Brendan sensed Sir Philip's presence here, in the small chamber devoted to the playing—and writing, Tobias had informed him—of music.

It was sparsely furnished: three stools and a plain wooden chair, two chests filled with music manuscripts and books. The rosewood spinet, decorated with gilt and enamel, dominated the little room. Beside it stood Sir Philip's closed lute case. The chamber had the musty air of disuse.

"I wonder what he would have thought of me."

"I beg your pardon?" said Alyssa.

Brendan smiled. "Forgive me, Mistress Radcliffe. I was thinking aloud. I was wondering what Sir Philip Radcliffe would have thought of a foreigner becoming Lord of Radcliffe Manor."

She surveyed him for quite a considerable time, until he grew uncomfortable. Then she said, with a little smile, "I believe that Sir Philip would have liked you, Master Fitzgerald. You must remember that he, too, was considered unacceptable at first by the local gentry. Despite his ancestry, he was not raised as a gentleman. His father was a stable groom, his mother a miller's daughter."

Brendan was amazed that she would talk to him of such matters. "But at least he was a Yorkshireman, a dalesman."

"Nevertheless, it was not an easy task for him to earn the respect of the local landowners."

"But he succeeded."

"Indeed, he did. Even after his involvement in that damnable Rising and his imprisonment in the Tower, he was respected."

"I should take him for my example, then."

"You are a very different man. A soldier. A man of action. Philip preferred his books and his music to the hurly-burly of warfare and politics." She opened the lute case and ran her fingers over the strings of the lute, a faraway look in her eyes.

"They why, if you will pardon me for asking, did he become involved in the uprising?"

She turned upon him, her nut-brown eyes flaring. "He joined it because of one person only, the Scottish queen. She bewitched him, as she did many men who stepped inside her magic circle. He sought to rescue her from imprisonment; that is why he joined the Rising that stripped him of his good name, his estates, and, in the end, shortened his life by many years."

Brendan was taken aback. He had not thought his calm, quiet mother-in-law to be capable of such passion.

Alyssa's breath came quickly. "And still she is weaving her magic webs, casting her spells, not that far away from us, in Sheffield Castle. I tell you, Brendan, England will not be safe until Mary, Queen of Scots is dead." Her eyes were narrowed in something approaching hatred. "Once she is gone, the Catholics will have lost their reason for opposing Queen Elizabeth, and the country will at last be at peace."

Knowing what he did of the might of the Spanish empire, Brendan doubted that the death of the Scottish Queen would alter their determination to invade England, but he saw no point in saying so.

"Meanwhile," he reminded her gently, "that gives us very good reason to ensure that Radcliffe contains nothing that might label its inhabitants as adherents of the Catholic faith. I have heard that the Northern Council is already sending out pursuivants to search houses they suspect."

She looked at him blankly, as if his words had drawn her back from another world. "Quite right, we must make our own search immediately. I pray your pardon, Brendan," she said, with a tremulous smile. "I fear that when I veer onto the subject of the Scottish Queen, passion overrules reason."

When he showed her the cross, she confirmed that it was, indeed, the crucifix that had once hung in the chapel. "To think that this has been in the Radcliffe family for two hundred years or more," she said, her fingers tracing the carved figure of Christ. "I cannot bear the thought of burning it. Philip would never forgive me."

"It cannot remain in the house," he said gently, seeing her distress. "If we do not destroy it, we must find a hiding place that would never be connected to Radcliffe Hall."

Her face brightened. "Yes, yes. With all the caves and disused lead mines hereabouts that should not be difficult."

"Can you think of anything else incriminating that might be in the house?"

"I will go through all Sir Philip's possessions. He deeply resented having to dispose of his religious books and pictures. I had great difficulty in persuading him that he jeopardized not only himself but all members of the family by keeping them. I know for certain that he did keep his grandfather's old wooden rosary beads." She looked up at Brendan, tears in her eyes. "I should have buried them with him."

He laid his hand on hers. "This is not easy for you, I know, but it is for the best, to be sure."

"You are right. We cannot risk our family's life for the sake of a few beads and pictures, can we?"

Brendan's heart warmed at the implied inclusion of himself in the family.

Alyssa sniffed, sought for her white linen handkerchief in her black skirts, and then said briskly, "We shall tell Tobias what we are doing. It would not surprise me if he carried in his head a list of every item we own. I shall undertake to search all the bedchambers myself. I know I have nothing questionable, but Katherine may have." Her eyes met Brendan's. "Perhaps something her grandfather gave her," she hurriedly explained.

"I pray you, feel free also to search among my belongings, lest I have something of my mother's that I have forgot."

"Your mother was a Catholic, then?"

"Most of Ireland's inhabitants were," he said lightly, "until the English came."

"And your father, too?"

Brendan stiffened. "Like many, my father was born and baptized a Catholic. Afterwards, who knows? There are many who publicly practice a religion which privately they refute. All I know is that I was educated as a Protestant."

Alyssa frowned. "Pray forgive me if I appear to be prying, but I thought that your father, being a Fitzgerald, would have remained a Catholic?"

Brendan shrugged. "'Tis not a subject we ever discussed." He turned away and picked up the cross. "Now, madam my Mother, we must to work before Kate and Joanna return."

Alyssa said no more. Brendan rarely talked of his family and, if the subject arose, it was ever his way to turn the conversation quickly to something else, as he had just done.

Seeing from the window of the parlor that the shadows across the courtyard were beginning to lengthen, she hurried to the main bedchamber, anxious to search through Katherine's belongings before her daughter returned from Harcourt Hall.

As always, when she saw the great carved bed where Philip had breathed his last, she felt as if a hand had squeezed her heart. She had learned to live with the pain of her loss, and even grown inured to the day-to-day reminders of him that existed everywhere in the house, but the sight of this bed was always her undoing.

Be at peace, my darling, she told him. *With your guidance and Brendan's good sense we shall manage well.*

She often spoke to him thus, usually in her mind. At times, though, she addressed him aloud; in bed at night, or during those infrequent times when she was able to escape, alone, to gallop her mare across Middleham High Moor and up to the windswept moor above Coverdale that held such potent memories.

She turned from her contemplation of the bed, smiling to herself. Within the staid matron nearing two score years in age dwelt the maid who had loved Sir Philip, a man older even than her father, since she was twelve.

"To work, Alyssa, to work," she admonished herself, her voice as sharp as her own mother's.

She began with the chest filled with finely wrought linens that had been Kate's hope chest for her wedding.

Nothing there but bed linen and embroidered cushion covers and tableware.

She turned to the large silver casket that had been one of her gifts to her daughter on her wedding day. The casket had three layers of velvet-lined drawers and appeared to contain nothing but Kate's jewels. One by one, Alyssa opened the different-sized drawers to examine rings and beads, bracelets and earrings, all of which were familiar to her.

When she came to the last drawer, the long one at the bottom, it stuck halfway. Sliding her fingers to the very back of the drawer to release it, she encountered there a tiny package wrapped in a piece of silver tissue.

A shiver of distaste ran over her. She hated to be prying into her daughter's privacy. After all, it could be something Edward had given her a long time ago.

It could also mean the difference between life and death to her beloved daughter, she told herself, as she drew out the package and began to unwrap it.

"What the devil are you doing with my casket, Mother?"

At the sound of Katherine's voice, Alyssa's hand convulsed on the package. She slowly turned, her face flushed with guilt, to face her daughter, who was standing in the doorway.

Chapter 19

Katherine was about to repeat the question when her mother turned around slowly to face her. She was holding something in her hand. "I didn't hear you ride in," she said, with a nervous smile. "How fares everyone at Harcourt Hall? Is your grandmother recovered from her fall last week? I should have gone with you, but—"

"I asked you what you were doing searching through my casket, Mother." Katherine slammed the door closed behind her and advanced into the chamber. "I cannot believe that you would wait until I am gone out, so that you might act as a spy upon me." She felt bloated and sick with the rage that filled her.

"Do not use that tone of voice to me, Katherine. I am your mother and deserving of your respect."

"Respect!" Katherine spat the word out. "I owe you no respect, madam my Mother." She stripped off her riding gloves and flung them on the chest at the foot of the bed. "Kindly give me whatever it is you have removed from my casket." She held out her hand.

"Not unless you undertake to show me what it is," returned her mother, now equally imperious.

"Give me a reason why I should do so."

"Because it is my wish, Katherine, and I am your mother."

The two pairs of brown eyes clashed; Katherine's almost black with fury, Alyssa's fraught with concern.

"That is not a good enough reason, and you know it," Katherine said. "I am forced to remind you that you are no longer mistress of Radcliffe, Mother. I am. You therefore have no right even to enter this chamber without my permission."

"Now you are going too far," her mother said, eyes narrowing. "You are insolent, Katherine."

Katherine's face flushed with triumph. "Insolent I may be, but you cannot deny that I am right, can you?"

Her mother's anger ebbed away, leaving her face pale as skimmed milk. "No, I cannot deny that you are now the mistress of Radcliffe."

The admission lessened Katherine's sense of triumph. Her mother's body sagged, as if she were suddenly desperately weary, making her appear even smaller than usual.

Sweet Jesu, why must life be so complicated? Katherine wished she could be more like Joanna, so accepting of life, of people, without question. If only Aunt Isobel had not been at Harcourt Hall today. If only she had not asked her aunt to tell her more about the past, about her mother and father and Grandy.

If only she had not come home, her mind reeling with what Aunt Isobel had hinted at, to find her mother searching her bedchamber.

"It was your husband's wish," said Alyssa.

"My husband's wish that you search through my belongings? Oh, I am well aware that some sort of affection has sprung up between the two of you in the past months, but surely he could have come to me first. Or have you been busy sowing seeds of distrust about me in his mind?"

Alyssa sighed heavily. "It is futile to continue this conversation, Katherine. Before he returned to Carlisle, Lord Scrope warned Brendan that the Council is planning to search the houses of all those who are suspected of having Roman Catholic sympathies. He said it would be wise to destroy or remove anything that could be even remotely connected with the Roman Church: crosses or missals or beads. Brendan found the chapel cross stowed away in the attic above the solar. I had forgotten all about it. There may be other things hidden about the house that we have forgotten."

A strange smile flickered across Katherine's face. "Are you saying that you suspect me of being a secret papist?"

"Of course not. I am saying that, unwittingly, we all probably have something that might be considered suspicious by a hostile pursuivant. For instance, I had quite forgotten about those wooden beads that once belonged to your great-great-grandfather. Now, perhaps, you will understand why I was looking in here."

"You should have asked me, not gone furtively behind my back."

"Yes, I suppose I should, but we . . . we seem to be so at odds nowadays that I thought it wiser to do it while you were out." Alyssa unfurled her hand, displaying the half-open package under her open palm. "What is in here?"

"It is something Grandy gave me on his deathbed."

Alyssa flinched. "Forgive me, Kate. I did not know," she said in a low voice.

But, despite her mother's flush of shame, Katherine knew that her mother was consumed with curiosity. "I will show you," she said. "So that you may set your mind to rest."

She snatched the package from her mother's hand and set it on the carved chest beside her brushes and combs. Then she opened it, carefully smoothing out the piece of silk inside the tissue. "Doubtless you remember both of these," she said. She held up, first, a golden locket on a faded blue silk ribbon, its cover delicately etched and enameled, and then a pearl-headed silver pin. "It was Grandy's wish that I have them. Mary, Queen of the Scots gave them to him, as I think you know. He valued them highly and bade me keep them always and treasure them, as he had."

She did not tell her mother what else her grandfather had said when he had given her the pin and locket, but as she ran her fingers over the two delicate objects, his words sprang to her mind again. *You must never forget her. I pass on to you the promise I made, but failed to keep, that I would help her take her rightful place as heir to Elizabeth and the throne of England.*

She had failed even more dismally than her grandfather, for until now she had quite forgotten the vow she had made to him on his deathbed.

Katherine looked up from her contemplation of the locket and pin, and was surprised to see her mother's mouth tight-lipped, her eyes blazing with anger.

"That woman haunts us yet. You cannot keep that locket. It contains her portrait. If it were discovered here you could be accused of being one of her supporters, a traitor to Queen Elizabeth."

Alyssa's hand reached out for the locket.

"No, Mother." Katherine's voice stayed the movement. "Do not touch it. That locket is mine, given into my care by my grandfather."

"It cannot remain in this house."

"I believe that is my decision to make, not yours. Now kindly leave my chamber, if you please, my lady Mother, so that I may change from my riding clothes."

Her mother held out her hands in a gesture of appeal. "Oh, Kate, do not risk your future, your life, for the sake of that . . . that sorceress. Too many men and women have died in her cause already. Others, like our kinsman, the Earl of Westmoreland, live in poverty and exile because of her. Would you risk your life, and that of your family, for the sake of the portrait of the woman who stole away your grandfather's heritage, shortened his life?"

But Katherine turned her back on her and rang her brass bell loudly to summon Grace to help her change. She removed her riding hat, drawing forth the pins from her hair with trembling hands.

Shaking her head in silent defeat, Alyssa walked slowly from the room.

No doubt her mother would now go to Brendan with complaints about her, thought Katherine. Let her. Behind that sweet, mealy-mouthed exterior her mother was a whore of Babylon, a Jezebel! Respect her? Katherine despised her. She could not bear the thought of living under the same roof with her a moment longer.

She was about to find a safe hiding place for the locket and pin when the door opened. "Grace, help me off with my riding boots, if you please. They are all mud. And take—"

"That can wait."

It was Brendan who had entered the chamber, not her tiring woman.

"What have you been saying to your mother to have her rush past me in tears?" he demanded.

Katherine put up her chin. "I found her rummaging in my jewel casket."

"With my permission. She must have told you that, to be sure."

"She did, but that did not make it any more acceptable. You had no right to tell her to search my things."

He shook his head. "Caitlin, my darling," he said softly, "when will you be realizing that I do have the right to give orders in my own house? And I am telling you now that I will not have you upsetting your mother so."

She went to him, heedless of her muddy boots and cloak, and laid her hands upon his chest. He stood very still, barely breathing, as she looked up into his face.

"Brendan, I know you care for my mother. I am sure it is most commendable in you to do so. But you do not seem to realize how . . . how difficult it is for me to have her here, living beside me."

She swung away from him, pacing to the window and back again. "She makes me feel as if I am still a child of ten or so. I am stifled by her. She watches everything I do and seeks to correct my every move. I swear I cannot bear it one moment longer. I must be mistress in my own household."

"And what do you wish me to do about it?" Brendan asked. She could not tell from his expression what he was thinking of her for speaking thus of her mother.

She clasped her hands together earnestly. "I would have you speak to her, suggest that she move back to Harcourt Hall with my grandparents, particularly now that my grandmother is unwell."

A little smile tilted his mouth. "But it is my understanding that your mother does not have too amicable a relationship with *her* mother. An inherited trait, is it?"

"It is not a laughing matter, I assure you." Katherine swallowed hard. "It is my belief that our marriage may be suffering because of the antipathy I feel for my mother."

His smile twisted. "Amn't I right in thinking, dear heart, that our marriage is suffering because of the antipathy you feel for me, not for your mother?"

Her breast rose and fell fast beneath her hands. "I truly believe that if you grant me this one request, we might deal better together, Brendan."

"So I am to gain from tossing your mother from her home, is that it?"

"She would be more content also. It does not make her happy to have me scratching at her all the time."

He grasped her arms, his fingers biting into them. "And had you thought of another alternative, my dear wife? That you try to be kinder to your mother, the woman who gave birth to you?"

Be kind to your mother, her grandfather had said on his deathbed. Her second reminder this day that she had not heeded his wishes.

Tears welled up in her eyes. "Oh, Brendan, if only you knew why I feel as I do," she whispered.

His touch grew gentle, his fingers now running up and down her forearms. "Could you not try to tell me why?"

If only she could. But it was unthinkable. Only one other person knew and that was how it would remain. She pulled back from him, shaking her head vehemently. "No."

"Then I am unable to help you, my lady wife," he said coldly. "I would remind you that you are fortunate to have a mother who loves you and thinks only of your well-being, as yours does. You are but eighteen years old and doubtless still have much to learn about the management of a household. As far as I am concerned, your mother is the mistress of Radcliffe until you prove yourself of sufficient maturity to take her place. Which, I might add, you are far from doing at present."

He strode to the door and turned briskly, his hand on the latch. "Let me hear no more talk of turning your mother from Radcliffe," he warned her. "And you will do her bidding with regard to the things she found in your casket."

For a long time after he had gone from the room, Katherine stared at the door. She felt numb, trapped by this alliance between her mother and husband. There was no way of escaping either of them. In the daytime she must contend with her mother, at night with her husband.

Oh God, dear God in heaven, she prayed, *please give me a child*. A child would bring her the household's respect.

A child would keep Brendan from her bed.

But her prayers went unanswered. Another long, icy winter passed and she was still barren. She began to think that she would never become pregnant and, when spring came, even went to the extreme of asking her mother for remedies for infertility.

"You have not been wed a year yet," her mother told her gently, as they worked together in the closet near the kitchen where the physics and ointments were made and stored. "It takes time. Do you enjoy lying with Brendan?" she asked, her eyes on the dried comfrey roots she was grinding to a fine powder with a pestle.

Katherine's entire body grew rigid. She shook her head. This was a subject she refused to discuss with her mother, of all people. She moved away to write a label for the jar her mother had filled with hyssop ointment.

"Perhaps that is the source of the problem," her mother said, pursuing the matter like a terrier with a rat. "Is Brendan kind to you in bed?"

Katherine bit her lower lip, wishing with all her heart that she had never approached her mother on the subject. "He is very kind," she muttered.

"I thought he would be. Then it is only a matter of time, dearest. Meanwhile, I will make up a decoction of catmint for you." She came to Katherine and slid an arm about her waist. "And if you will but relax and try to enjoy Brendan's lovemaking more, the baby will surely come."

The sound of a knock on the door and Tobias Ridley's voice from the doorway was a merciful release. "Do you know where Master Fitzgerald is, mistress?" He had a tactful way of calling them both "mistress" as if they were equals in his mind, which greatly pleased Katherine.

"The last time I saw him, he was in the breeding stable with Barnaby," Katherine told him.

Alyssa looked up from her work. "Is something the matter, Tobias?" she asked, frowning.

"I am not certain, but there is a messenger come by post from London. He wears the livery of the Earl of Sussex and says he carries a message of great urgency for Master Fitzgerald."

Katherine exchanged glances with her mother. All kinds of forebodings ran through her mind: The order for their release from prison had been rescinded. Radcliffe was to be taken away from Brendan and bestowed upon someone else. Brendan had been accounted a traitor for his connection with the Fitzgerald rebels in Ireland.

The last seeming to be the most likely, she clutched Tobias's arm. "I will come with you to fetch him. I wish to be with him if it is bad news."

"The messenger is taking some much-needed refreshment in the kitchen," the steward told her. "He has ridden thirty miles today, he tells me. If you will wait in the parlor, Mistress Katherine, I will send John for Master Fitzgerald and ask him to join you and the messenger there."

A short while later, Brendan came to the door of the parlor. "I am still in my stable dirt," he said apologetically. His anxious expression reflected the concern Katherine was feeling.

"Never mind that. This is my lord of Sussex's man." She gave a nod in the direction of the liveried servant who stood by the doorway. "He says it is a matter of great urgency."

The messenger stepped forward. "Master Fitzgerald?"

"I am he."

The man bowed. "My lord of Sussex asked me to be sure to put this into your hands alone, sir." He drew forth a letter bearing a heavy seal from his leather pouch.

Katherine's heartbeat quickened as she watched Brendan take his dagger from his belt to break the seal. She could see that his hands trembled as he unfolded the letter.

After what seemed to her more like an hour, but was most likely only a minute or so, Brendan turned to the man again. "You know the contents of this letter?"

"I do, sir."

"Will he survive until I come, do you think?" A little nerve jumped in Brendan's cheek.

"It is to be hoped he will, sir."

Brendan nodded, his eyes fixed upon the letter. "It is, to be sure."

"Is it bad news, Brendan?" asked Katherine.

He turned to give her a frowning look, as if he had forgotten she was there. "My lord of Sussex is very sick. His physicians do not expect him to last much longer than a few weeks."

Katherine let out a great sigh of relief. "Oh, is that all?"

Brendan rounded upon her, his eyes widening in anger. "I would remind you, madam wife, that my lord of Sussex is not only my patron, but also the reason why you and your mother are not languishing in prison at this moment."

Katherine bridled at this reprimand before the Earl's servant, but the expression on Brendan's face stopped her mouth.

He turned again to the messenger. "You must take some rest before making the return journey. I shall have my steward find a bed for you. Catch some sleep whilst I write my reply."

Brendan did not utter another word to Katherine until Tobias had led the man away. Then he turned upon her, more angry that she had ever seen him.

"Oh, is that all?" he said, mimicking her hasty words. "No doubt the messenger will carry your kind words directly back to his master."

Katherine's chin lifted. "Forgive me, but I did not realize that you bore such a strong affection for the man."

"The man, as you call him, is the mighty Earl of Sussex, Lord Chamberlain of England, and the Queen's most trusted councillor."

"I most humbly beg your pardon, sir." She made him a deep mocking curtsy.

"He is also my patron, the man responsible for . . . for my education and preferment."

Seeing how shaken he was by the news and by her subsequent lack of tact, Katherine's mood softened. "Forgive me," she said softly. "I truly did not realize you held him in such esteem."

"You also should hold him in esteem. He gave Radcliffe to me, and therefore, restored it to you. Not only that, but he was a distant kinsman of your family and also your father's patron, was he not?"

"Yes." She gave a faint smile. "Indeed, they were namesakes, he and my father, both named Thomas Radcliffe. Is that not strange?"

Brendan drew in a sharp breath. "Passing strange," he murmured, and to her amazement, crossed himself.

"Never tell me you are a papist, sir husband," she said mockingly.

He darted an embarrassed glance at her. "An old habit left over from my infancy." He looked again at the letter. "My lord of Sussex wishes to see me before he dies," he said. "It is also his wish that I bring my wife with me."

"Me?" she said, amazed. "Why in the name of all the saints would he wish to see me?"

"He remembers you as a small child, he says. And wishes to meet again the daughter of Thomas Radcliffe, one of his most trusted adherents, who is now the wife of his erstwhile ward."

Excitement swept over Katherine. "Am I to go to London with you, then?" she asked, her eyes gleaming.

"You are. We must leave at dawn tomorrow."

"So soon?" Katherine's voice rose in dismay. "I shall never be ready in time."

"You must be. There is no time to waste."

"London! Oh, Brendan, I never thought that I would see London in my entire life." Her delight faded. "But what about clothes? I have nothing new to wear. And all the fashions are bound to have changed since my wedding gowns were made."

He looked at her with utter incomprehension. "We are going to a man's deathbed, Kate, not to a coronation."

"Do you think we shall go to Court while we are in London?" she cried, clapping her hands together. "Shall we see the Queen, do you think? Oh, but I have nothing suitable to wear for Court."

He grasped her by the upper arms and brought his face very close to hers. "I do not care if you appear before Her Majesty stark naked, madam wife. God's wounds! Will you never cease acting like a cosseted child?"

She shrank from this uncommon spleen in him. "I was merely excited at the thought of my first time in London," she said in a small voice. "And concerned that I might not have suitable clothes."

"From what I have read in this letter, the only clothing you need take to London will be your mourning weeds." His eyelids hid his eyes for a moment. "I pray to God we will not arrive too late."

Chapter 20

Katherine had never seen Brendan in this strange mood before. He became a man of action, barking out orders for the arrangements for the journey, conferring with his steward and bailiff, but the usual smiling countenance and easy nature were entirely absent.

He did not sleep that night, but sat up with Tobias and Barnaby and Applegarth discussing the imminent births in the stable, the hay harvesting, the lamb-selling—all of which would have to be done this year without Brendan's presence.

Katherine, herself, slept little. She had been up until well after midnight sorting gowns and caps and gloves and jewels—and overseeing their packing into her traveling coffers.

"Be sure to bring your wedding gown . . . and the green that's my favorite," Brendan told her, when he marched into the bedchamber to choose his own clothing.

Katherine was about to remind him caustically that he had chided her earlier for thinking of best gowns, when he flung at her over his shoulder, "But do not be forgetting to pack your black mourning gowns as well," before striding from the room again.

Long before dawn, the household was bustling, with servants scurrying to and fro, carrying out the boxes to be strapped on the packhorses, filling their panniers with goods and victuals for the long journey. Colum and Katherine's groom were to ride with them. John Briggs, Brendan's valet, inherited from Sir Philip, would also accompany them, but Grace was to be left behind.

"We'll hire a woman for you at each stopping point," Brendan told Katherine. "One woman is enough on the journey. Any more would slow us down."

"I'll have you know, sir, that I can keep pace with any man," was Katherine's angry response.

"I know that well, dearest Kate." He gave her a fleeting smile that died upon his lips almost immediately.

Once they had made their farewells, sad on Alyssa's part, joyful on Katherine's, they rode off through the outer courtyard and the open gate. The fluffy, rose-tinted clouds that fringed the sky towards Middleham promised another warm May morning, although appearances could be deceptive in the changeable climate of the Dales.

But Brendan was not observing the sky. As soon as they had ridden up the fell from Radcliffe and made the turn southward, all his energy seemed to drain from him. Silent and stone-faced, he rode beside Katherine. When she spoke to him, he looked at her as if she were speaking across a vast chasm of both time and distance before giving her a brusque response.

Throughout the long day and the ensuing evening at the inn on the outskirts of York, Brendan's strange melancholy persisted, dampening Katherine's excitement at the prospect of seeing the great metropolis of London, the very hub of the kingdom.

At The Golden Fleece they met with a small company who was also riding to London, a rich gold merchant and his son and their servants. By the time they had supped together, it had been decided to join forces.

"Safety in numbers," said the lean merchant, who was understandably anxious for the valuable merchandise he was bearing south. "Only last week, I heard that a silversmith and his wife were robbed of all their valuables and left on the roadway, stripped naked as newborn babes."

"Would you have agreed to his suggestion so eagerly had there been any women in his party?" Katherine asked Brendan in a teasing voice later, as she was undressing in the small, low-ceilinged chamber above the parlor.

Brendan looked up from the coffer he was opening. "I would not. Nor would I had the man been your usual merchant, fat as a tub of pork lard. It is our good fortune that he is as eager as us to reach London, and will therefore push his horses to do so."

He approached her, holding out her nightrobe. "Are you vexed with me for saying we could not bring Grace with us?"

She looked up at him, ready to list all the difficulties of being without a maidservant, but, seeing the deep sadness still in his eyes, she changed her mind. "Not at all," she said, with a toss of her head. "I am quite well able to take care of myself." She took the nightrobe from him. "But there is one thing I cannot do," she added, presenting her back to him.

It was not until she heard his sharp intake of breath that remembrance of that other time in another inn in York flooded over her. It was passing strange that she should feel that same frisson of excitement now, when she had been married to this man and shared his bed for a year. But nothing about this journey was usual. Added to her excitement about visiting London was a feeling of freedom, as if she had left all the shackles of fear and suspicion behind her in Radcliffe.

Much as she loved her home, she knew that she welcomed this change and vowed to make the best of it.

She felt his fingers against her back, loosening the lacing of her bodice.

"Should I draw the lacing out completely?" he asked. She could hear the slight tremor in his voice.

"Yes, you will have to, and untie my kirtle as well, so that I can step out of it."

Slowly, he pulled the lacing free, his fingers brushing her bare back above her shift. Instead of tensing herself against his touch, she allowed her body to relax so that she was almost leaning against him as he worked at the gown.

As he cursed softly beneath his breath, she laughed. "If I were to ask you now for a servant, would you deny me?"

She heard his low chuckle, the first since the letter from Sussex had arrived. "I would not, my dearest Caitlin."

His use of the Irish version of her name usually riled her, but for the first time she loved the sound of it. Spoken with the soft lilt in his voice it sounded like a caress.

"There," he said. "All done."

"You will need to help me further," she told him, her back still turned to him. She held out her arms, so that he might pull the sleeves from them.

His hands slid across her back, drawing the bodice from it, and she tugged down the sleeves. She could feel his breath hot on her shoulders, hear his heightened breathing.

The bodice was hanging loose at her waist now. Without withdrawing from him, she untied the kirtle, pulled it down over her hips and then stepped out of it. Dressed only in her shift of finest lawn, she still stood with her back to him.

Quite deliberately, she leaned back against him, pressing her buttocks against his thighs, her shoulders against his chest.

"Oh, Kate," he groaned. He pulled her closer against him, his arms crossing in front of her, hands moving on her breasts, his face buried in her hair. His hands moved down to her hips, circling her buttocks, and then forward to slide between her thighs, only the thin fabric between him and her clamoring need.

"Will you?" he asked, as he always asked.

"Yes, oh God, yes."

He lifted her and carried her to the strange bed, not even bothering to draw back the tapestry cover.

For the first time in their marriage, Katherine thought of his needs, his pleasure. "Does this please you?" she asked him shyly. "And this?"

It seemed that everything she did pleased him, so much so that he could not wait for her, and poured his seed into her in great gasping spasms, leaving her stranded, fraught with disappointment.

He did not use his hands to satisfy her, however, but bade her be patient for a short while. "If my mistress will but tarry a little for her humble servant, he will be pleased to serve her again," were his words. "This time to her liking."

He was true to his word. Never before had she welcomed him into her body with such eagerness. He stroked her slowly, maddeningly slowly, and then she caught the quickening of the beat and moved in unison with him, building to the peak, the summit of pleasure. She opened her eyes and looked into his, wanting to watch his expression when the moment came.

But when it did, everything in her vision went black, as if it were only within her innermost self that lights and sounds exploded in a million fragments. She was aware only of the eddying waves of pleasure slowly receding and then of his body, panting on hers, his sweat soaking the shift that lay in a roll about her waist.

There was dampness on her face also and she knew from the sobs that racked his body that it came from Brendan's tears.

Her arms tightened about him. "There, my dear, there," she crooned. Easing his weight off her, she lay beside him, her arms about him, until he fell into a sound sleep.

Although, next day, Brendan retreated into his shell of silence again, there were times when she caught him looking sideways at her, an expression of wonderment on his face. She smiled to herself to see it.

But that night, when they rested at the inn at Doncaster, he asked her if she loved him now, and although she longed to be able to say the words, she could not bring herself to do so. How easy it would be to say, "I love you, Brendan," but she could not.

When she saw his face, like a brightly lit window suddenly covered by a dark curtain, she hated herself.

"I have a great liking for you," she said, hoping to appease him thus, but she knew it would never be enough for him.

He gave her a wry smile. "That is better than nothing, to be sure."

That night, and every night thereafter on the journey, she did not abandon herself to him when he lay with her, lest he gain the false impression that because he gave her pleasure, she loved him.

Surely it must be sinful to derive such carnal delight from an act with a man one did not love, she thought, and flushed with shame in the darkness to think she had become such a brazen wanton. "Breeding will out!" she whispered to herself, squeezing her eyes shut to hold back the tears that pricked them.

Six days later, they paused on Highgate Hill to look down at the smoke-wreathed roofs of London. Katherine was amazed to see that the city spread out, east and west, as far as she could see. As they rode down, drawing ever nearer to the city, a babble of sound rose in one steady stream to assail her ears.

They parted from the gold merchant and his company at Eastcheap and then began to ride over London Bridge.

Katherine had never before seen such a bridge. It was terrifyingly narrow, with shops and chapels built upon it; even, to her amazement, a great timber mansion, four stories high. They rode through the center of the house and shops, pushing their way through the crowds of shoppers and vendors and sightseers, their noise echoing inside Katherine's head.

It was a great relief to ride through the great stone gate on the south side of the Thames and leave the bustle of the bridge behind. They rode along the river bank, past a ramshackle inn and some mean tenements. The stench was so overpowering that Katherine's head swam. She covered her nose and mouth with her hand, willing her stomach not to heave.

For the past day or so she had been suffering with nausea from the heat and fatigue and had felt increasingly unwell as they neared London. Now she wondered how much longer she would be able to ride before she puked up the parsnip fritters and brawn pie she had eaten for breakfast that morning.

"Have we much further to go?" she gasped.

"We are almost there." Brendan leant towards her to hand her a clove-stuffed orange he had purchased from a vendor on the bridge.

Giving him a grateful smile, Katherine held it to her nose to breathe in the spicy fumes.

She was about to ask Brendan how in the name of heaven the Queen's Lord Chamberlain could live in such a place when they turned down a narrow lane. When they had ridden not much more than half a mile, she was amazed to see that the lane led to a pleasant place of woods and pasture.

"This was Bermondsey Abbey until the dissolution," Brendan explained.

Only a small part of the abbey remained. In its place had been built a great mansion of timber and stone, with a vast wall of red brick.

When they rode up to the gatehouse and under the stone arches to the gate itself, Brendan gave the porter his name.

The man peered at him beneath grizzled eyebrows. "Wait 'ere one moment, sir."

"Am I not expected?" asked Brendan, his voice sharp.

"In a manner of speaking, you are, sir. But then, in a manner of speaking, you are not."

Katherine saw the consternation on Brendan's face. "Is something the matter, do you think?" She was weary beyond belief and the thought of not gaining access to the Earl of Sussex's home after this long journey made her voice rise in panic.

"Pray God we are not too late," Brendan muttered. The phrase had been the main theme of their journey, spurring them on. "Is my lord of—" he began, but the porter had shuffled away into his tiny apartment in the thickness of the wall.

The next thing they knew, a lad of about eight shot from the porter's door and raced across the cobblestoned courtyard, disappearing into a side door in the main building.

As they waited, Brendan's face grew paler and paler. Eventually he dismounted from his restless horse and marched to the door of the porter's cramped quarters. "I demand an explanation for being kept here. Is my lord of Sussex still alive?"

The man came out. "'E is, sir, the Lord be thanked, but failing fast. I've sent for 'is lordship's secretary."

The man sucked on a piece of his beard when he spoke, making his speech even more incomprehensible to Katherine. London speech was an ugly nasal sound, with a descending whine at the end of the sentences.

"Ah, 'ere's Master Wingate to see you, sir."

Brendan turned to greet the Earl's thin-legged secretary. "How is he, Master Wingate?"

The man took his outstretched hand and then hurriedly released it. "I pray your pardon, Captain Fitzgerald, for having kept you waiting, but—"

Brendan interrupted him to present him to Katherine. It occurred to her, although she did not know the man, of course, that the secretary appeared singularly agitated.

"Your servant, Mistress Fitzgerald," he said, with a small bow. He immediately turned from her to Brendan again. "We had hoped to have you here before the family came," he said in a voice so low that Katherine could barely catch his words. "But my lord of Sussex's health has suddenly worsened. The entire family has been summoned to his bedside."

He moved from foot to foot, as if his square-toed shoes pinched him.

Brendan's eyes narrowed. "Are you telling me, Wingate, that they do not know I have been summoned here? That Lady Frances knows nothing about the letter you sent me?"

The secretary looked as if he were about to burst into tears. "Exactly so, sir."

"Sweet Christ in heaven!"

Katherine felt a sinking in the pit of her stomach. Something was terribly wrong, and she had not the slightest idea what it could be. She might as well be in a foreign land surrounded by people speaking in a foreign tongue.

She signaled to her groom to hold her horse and swiftly dismounted. "What is the matter?" she demanded.

The secretary looked abashed, as if he had utterly forgotten her presence. He cast a look of appeal at Brendan, who took Katherine's arm and drew her aside. "There is a crisis in the Earl's health, Kate, and all the family have gathered here to be with him."

"So? Why should you not be here also? He is, after all, your patron."

He sighed. "That is so. He is." He turned again to Master Wingate. "What is to be done?" he asked him.

"I dare not turn you from here. My lord would never forgive me. He has been asking for you every day. 'Has the boy come yet?' he keeps asking me. 'Do you think he will come today?' It is almost as if he is waiting for you to . . . to . . ." He turned away, to blow his nose loudly in his silver-edged handkerchief.

Brendan's jaw trembled. "There is no way for me to slip in privately, perhaps at night?" he asked.

The secretary shook his head. "None at all. There are members of both families—Radcliffe and Sidney—with him at all times. The physician has told them that he could last a week, or even longer, but it could also be only a day or so. All he can say is that the time is nigh, whether that time is long or short. His brother, Sir Henry Radcliffe, has ridden all the way from Portsmouth to be with him."

Brendan squared his shoulders. "Then there is naught to be done but to brave them all and see him."

"It will not be easy." Master Wingate's pale eyes flickered over Katherine.

"It has never been easy, Wingate." Brendan's voice was fraught with a strange bitterness. "But I will not have him die without seeing me, merely because I am too much the coward to face his wife and family. It was his wish that I come, that is enough for me."

Katherine placed herself before Brendan. "If you do not tell me instantly what is the matter here, I shall scream!"

"It is nothing very much, my dear Kate. Only that . . . that Lady Frances and her family will not be greatly pleased to see me."

Katherine blanched. "Do you mean to tell me that we have come all this way and will not be welcome?"

A small tense smiled lingered on Brendan's lips. "That is it in a nutshell, sweetheart."

"But why?"

"Enough questions. Remount your horse," he ordered her, as if she were a soldier in his battalion, and his eyes, when they looked at her, were as cold as winter.

A shiver ran over Katherine, but, sensing that he was in desperate need of her support, she made no further protest. Mounting her horse, she followed him and Master Wingate through the gateway and into the inner courtyard.

As the gate clanged to behind her, she felt like the robber woman they had passed at the south end of London Bridge, imprisoned in a cage with no means of escape.

Chapter 21

When they had dismounted, their grooms were directed to the stables and Master Wingate led Katherine and Brendan through the carved stone entranceway, up the broad staircase to the great presence chamber.

Katherine became aware of eyes boring into her, the eyes of both servants and visitors. She had not expected to inspire such interest. When her cloak was taken from her, she was extremely glad that Brendan had insisted that she wear her cloth-of-silver wedding gown today.

Hidden for a moment in the doorway by Brendan and the secretary, she patted her hair into place beneath her taffeta hat with the pleated crown and then stepped forward into the crowd of people gathered in the chamber.

They swiftly crossed the tiled floor, affording Katherine only a brief glimpse of the elegantly dressed people assembled there. She was not certain if it was heightened imagination caused by her extreme nervousness, but she thought she heard her name whispered and a laugh following it.

What was definitely not her imagination was the hush that fell upon the crowd as she and Brendan walked through, and the sudden babble that followed their exit through the far door.

The door closed behind them. They were in a small antechamber built into a corner of the house. There, Master Wingate left them, promising that he would return.

Katherine immediately rounded upon Brendan, who was staring out the tiny casement window with its distant view of the river. "For the love of God, Brendan, tell me what is going on here. I feel as if we were two lepers escaped from a lazar house."

But before he could reply, the door opened again and Master Wingate crooked his finger to summon them into the adjacent chamber.

She knew instantly from the hushed atmosphere and the dimmed candlelight that this was the Earl of Sussex's bedchamber. The great oaken bed with its rich hangings of crimson silk was set upon the dais against the long wall of the chamber. The bed curtains were drawn back halfway.

Brendan stepped forward and immediately the eye of every person there was turned upon him. Taller than any man there, magnificent in his sapphire-blue doublet and silk-lined cape, in Katherine's eyes he dominated the chamber. There was a proud tilt to his head as he surveyed them all. Every muscle in his body spelled defiance. "To the devil with you all," he seemed to be saying.

A man in rich apparel approached them. Apart from Brendan, he was the tallest man in the room, but twice Brendan's age, with thinning, gray-streaked hair.

Katherine poised herself for his greeting to them. When he spoke, it was as if a pail of icy water had been dashed into her face.

"How dare you show your face here!" The words were addressed in a low voice to Brendan. "You must be out of your mind to come here at such a time." The man's rage was palpable.

"I come at my lord of Sussex's bidding, Sir Henry." Brendan held himself as stiff as if he were under royal inspection. He drew the Earl's letter from inside his doublet and, holding it between two fingers, handed it to the man.

Sir Henry Radcliffe perused the letter and then, without another word, turned on his heel, and took it to the woman with the austere face who was standing at the foot of the bed, her hand on the carved bedpost. She beckoned to a woman servant, who brought her a candle in a gilt holder for light to read it by.

When she had finished, she looked towards them, her face and mien proud and unbending. Then she nodded once and, tossing the letter onto a table, crossed the chamber to speak to them.

"Well, sir," she said, addressing Brendan, "it is a great while since we last met."

"A very great while, my lady," said Brendan, when he had lifted his head from his deep obeisance to her. "I was but sixteen at the time. On my way to Cambridge University."

"Just so." Her cold blue eyes raked Katherine, who hurriedly made her a deep curtsy. "And this is your wife, Katherine Radcliffe, of whom my husband has spoken?"

"It is, my lady."

"I remember your father, Thomas Radcliffe, well, madam," said Lady Frances. "He served my lord with great loyalty and valor. *He* was a gentleman."

The emphasis on the first word was all too obvious. Katherine glanced at Brendan, but his eyes were fixed on the bed. She could tell from the slight flush about his jaw, however, that he had heard and understood the inference.

The Countess crossed one heavily beringed hand over the other at her waist. "I am surprised to see Thomas Radcliffe's daughter here in such awkward, nay, such embarrassing circumstances."

"I have come here at my husband's request," replied Katherine, indignant at the Countess's veiled insults.

"Ah, yes. Your husband." The Countess smiled. "It might have been more . . . politic, shall we say, for you to disobey your husband's bidding this once."

Brendan drew his eyes from the bed. "I would remind you, my lady, that it was *your* husband's wish that I bring my wife here. You will have seen that from the letter."

The Countess drew herself up. "My lord of Sussex was not a well man when he dictated that letter. You might have saved yourself a long journey, sir, had you remembered that. Or did you think that by coming here, and bringing your wife with you as well, the two of you might gain even more bounty from him in the hour of his weakness?"

Katherine was breathless with apprehension as she saw how the blood drained from Brendan's face. Before he could say something he might later regret, she broke in. "My husband has thought of nothing but the health of my lord of Sussex throughout our long journey. Not a night has passed that we haven't knelt in a church to pray for his beloved patron."

"Is that what he calls him, his patron?" The Countess's laughter brayed out, shocking in this place of approaching death. The approach of Sir Henry Radcliffe stopped her from saying more.

"My brother will see you both now," he told them. "Do not stay long with him. He is very weak. And, I warn you, he must not be excited in any way."

"You have my word on it, sir. Come, Katherine." His head held as high as any prince's might be, Brendan led Katherine to the bedside.

Her mind was reeling. The chamber was filled with ill-feeling, indignation, rage—all directed at Brendan, at her and Brendan. Her brain seethed, wondering what in heaven's name Brendan had done to incur such enmity in his patron's family. The answer lay here, she was sure, here in this bed, in this emaciated man, whose facial bones looked as if they might burst through the almost transparent yellow-tinged skin.

The Queen's councillor was not yet sixty, Katherine knew, yet he looked like an ancient of four score years or more. He might have been a skeleton already, had it not been for the fierce, dark eyes that fixed upon them both like a hawk eyeing its prey.

"You came at last," he said in a hoarse voice. "I thought you would never come." He was forced to pause for breath at every second word.

"We came as soon as we could, my lord. It is a long ride from Wensleydale."

Brendan stood, as awkward now with the Earl's eyes devouring him as he had been princely before the rest of the company. "May I present my wife, my lord?" Brendan said at last, seeking to break the silence.

"Ah, yes." The Earl bared his teeth in a ghastly semblance of a smile. "Raise me up so that I may see her."

Brendan put his arm about the frail figure, and lifted him higher against the pillows.

"So you are Thomas Radcliffe's daughter."

"I am, my lord, and proud to be so," replied Katherine.

"Well said, child, well said. He was a man of great loyalty. Hotheaded, but valiant. His early death was a tragedy. Murder, it was, you know."

Katherine stiffened. "So I have heard, my lord."

"Some say it was his father, that traitor, Sir Philip," the sick man muttered. "Others said it could even have been his own wife that arranged his killing. We shall never know now."

Katherine was horrified that the matter she thought secret between her and her aunt should be common knowledge.

Brendan shook his head at her, as if to suggest that the Earl was wandering in his mind, but she knew better.

"Approach me, Katherine Radcliffe," said the Earl.

She did so, repulsed by the skull-like visage and the fetid odor of ill-health that lay upon him.

He shook her hand in his bony fingers. "She is very beautiful, Brendan. Did I not choose a fair bride for you?"

"You did, my lord."

"And a Radcliffe, at that. Very fitting." He released Katherine's hand. "I wish to speak with you alone now," he told Brendan fretfully. "With no one else to hear."

"I will leave," Katherine said, relieved to be able to retreat from the enclosed enclave of the bed that made her think of a burial vault. "I wish you good health, my lord."

The Earl grimaced. "Better to wish me the merciful release of death, my child. Will you kiss me, Mistress Katherine?"

The very thought of doing so was repugnant to her, but she bent to kiss his withered cheek. His stale breath fanned her face. "Care for him, I beg you, Katherine," he said in a harsh whisper. "Make him content."

"I give you my word I shall do so," she promised, willing to promise anything so that she might escape the confines of this bed.

"And bear him many children so that Radcliffes will continue to flourish in Radcliffe Hall and throughout Yorkshire."

"With God's help, I will, my lord."

Only then did he release her. "Go now, and leave me alone with Brendan."

Throughout this exchange Brendan had stood on the first step of the bed dais, watching the two of them together. Sensing Katherine's dismay and bewilderment, he wondered if he had done the right thing in bringing her with him. He watched her retreat to the far end of the chamber, standing alone, and then turned back to the Earl.

"Draw the curtains to," came the order.

"Is that wise, my lord? As it is, I am—"

"Do as you are bid."

Remembering Sir Henry's warning that he must not be excited, Brendan obeyed him, drawing the curtains, cutting off both sight and sound of those who waited in the chamber.

"Sit down on the bed. I cannot strain my neck to look at you."

Brendan sat on the edge of the bed, careful to avoid the legs that stretched down beside him.

"My thanks to you for coming."

Brendan was about to murmur some platitude about duty or service, but changed it to a heartfelt, "I thank you for asking me to come, my lord."

"In the circumstances, many would have ignored my letter."

This time Brendan made no reply.

A long pause ensued, in which the Earl looked at Brendan and Brendan looked down at the bed cover. Their meetings had always been awkward, but never before as awkward as this, the most important meeting between them.

"The Queen has promised me land in Ireland, near Cork. It will be yours."

"My lord," protested Brendan, "you have already given me more than enough. I do not—"

"Save your breath. It is already done. Somers and Wingate know all about it."

Brendan murmured his thanks, his heart too full to say more.

"All this," the Earl waved his hand, "all my estates here and in Essex go to my brother, Henry, as my heir. Do not envy him, Brendan. They are heavily encumbered with debts. Serving the Queen faithfully for almost thirty years has drained my coffers entirely, I fear. There will be little left for my brother." His hand brushed across Brendan's. "Even less for my only son."

The words hung in the air as their eyes met.

"You have given me all I need," murmured Brendan.

The Earl's chest labored for breath. "I should have acknowledged you, brought you to Court. After all, I had no other son."

"Do not distress yourself thus, my lord. You could not have acknowledged me. You had Lady Frances to think of."

The Earl's lips twitched ruefully. "She was my excuse. But it was damnable pride that held me back. I was the virtuous Sussex, ever strong, the model of rectitude. A fine contrast to that damned gypsy, Leicester. Lord, how he would laugh if he knew that I had a bastard son!"

"He shall not learn it from me."

"No, by God, you never spoke of it. Yet most men in your position would have done so."

"My mother—" began Brendan.

"Do not speak of her." The Earl's voice was harsh. "I did all I could for her."

Brendan was silent. He had been eight when they separated him from her. Several years later, he was told that she was dead. He knew nothing more—and would never know, it seemed.

"Ireland has been the very death of me, but in return it has given me a son to be proud of." The Earl's eyes closed, and then opened again. "I must rest. Yet I do not wish you to go."

"It is best that I do, I think," Brendan said gently.

"Perhaps it is." After a long pause, "You are content at Radcliffe Manor?"

"I am, truly content."

"They have accepted you as their lord, those stiff-necked dalesfolk?"

"Indeed they have," lied Brendan for the second time.

"Good, good." His voice was growing weaker. "You must take my name, at least. No more 'Fitzgerald.' From this day forward you are Brendan Radcliffe. That is an order from a dying man, Master Radcliffe, one you cannot disobey."

"Yes, my lord."

"Will you call me . . . it, this one time?"

Brendan was puzzled for a moment, and then, seeing the expression, like a hunger, in the Earl's eyes, he knew what it was he wanted.

"I pray you, Father, bestow a blessing upon your son." He swallowed hard, but nothing could hold back the tears that had been suppressed for so long. And he saw that his father was in the same plight.

"May God pour his blessings on my son and upon his children, and his children's children, blood of my blood, seed of my seed."

Brendan clasped the frail hand in his and bent his head to kiss it. The fingers touched his cheek and then his hair.

"Now go," his father said violently, as if he spoke in anger. "And, whatever happens, do not return."

Brendan took one last look at him and then, dashing back the curtain, stumbled from the dais.

Chapter 22

All this while, Katherine had stood in a corner of the large presence chamber, utterly ignored but for the sly glances and whispers cast in her direction. She had never in her life been treated with such discourtesy and marveled that two of the highest families in the land, the Radcliffes and Sidneys, should behave in such a manner to a visitor. If these were London ways, she deplored them.

She was bone-weary from the long ride and parched with thirst, yet not even a glass of wine or a biscuit had she been offered. She leaned her aching back against the paneled wall, anger at Brendan building inside her.

"And what, might I ask, is such a beautiful flower doing all by herself in a corner?"

The voice startled her. She looked up, to meet vivid blue eyes that shone appreciatively at her. Their owner was almost as tall as Brendan, but of a broader build, with rich-brown hair and beard, both of which were curled. He was dressed in a magnificent doublet of red and black slashed with gold that outdazzled everyone else in the chamber.

"I am waiting for my husband," Katherine replied

The man groaned. "Ah me, I am quite cast down. The beauty has a husband. Moreover, the husband attends her."

She could not help smiling at his banter, but was unsure how to reply to it.

"Ah lady, do not smile thus. Your beauty will crack my heart into a million pieces." Then, seeing her consternation, he presented himself. "Walter Ralegh, at your service, beauteous lady." He spoke with a strange accent, a broad drawling of his vowels.

"Oh. So you are Master Ralegh." Brendan had spoken to her of Walter Ralegh, Queen Elizabeth's new favorite, but his disparaging description had not prepared her for the aggressive charm, nor the good looks, of the man.

"You speak as if you have heard of me, mistress of the fiery eyes." There was a tinge of mockery in his voice, and she realized that there were probably few people in London who had not heard of the notorious Walter Ralegh.

"I know of you, sir," she said shyly. "My husband has spoken of you to me."

"Then I must know him, I suppose." He appeared bored at the very mention of a husband who knew him. "Who is he?"

"Brendan Fitzgerald. I believe you met in—"

"Fitzgerald!" Ralegh roared, quite oblivious to the disapproving glances being cast at him. "Is the Irish captain here? By God, I should like to see him."

His wish was granted almost immediately, for Katherine saw Brendan come into the presence chamber, accompanied by a small man dressed in black, whose hand gripped Brandan's arm, as if he were guiding a blind man.

"Are you sick?" Katherine asked Brendan when he reached her, for she could see that his eyes were glazed, as if he were, indeed, blind.

"Well met, Fitzgerald," said Ralegh, clapping him on the shoulder, but Brendan looked blankly at him, as if he were an utter stranger.

"Never say you have forgotten your old comrade in arms, Captain Ralegh, sir."

Brendan seemed to gather himself together. He drew in a deep, ragged breath and let it out again. "Your pardon, Ralegh. I had not expected . . ." His voice trailed away.

"What in the name of heaven is the matter with you?" whispered Katherine, his strange conduct shaming her.

The little man in the black silk gown gave Katherine a disapproving frown. "Master Radcliffe is not himself at present," he said.

"Master Radcliffe?" She and Ralegh said, in unison.

"It is my lord of Sussex's wish that Master Fitzgerald be known as 'Radcliffe' from henceforth."

"I should like to know what right my lord of Sussex has to dictate a change in name for my husband," said Katherine, filled with indignation.

They were now the center of attraction in the presence chamber. Surrounded as they were by Ralegh's entourage and with Katherine's voice rising from their midst, every eye was drawn to them.

The man, whom Katherine took to be the Earl's steward, drew his small stature to its fullest height. "As the appointed lord of Radcliffe Manor, your husband—"

But Brendan would not permit him to finish. His face drained of all color, he gripped Katherine by her wrists. "My lord of Sussex has every right," he said, glaring down at her. "As my father he has every right to dictate my name." He flung her from him, so that she might have fallen had Master Ralegh not caught hold of her.

"Your father! Brendan, what do you mean?"

But he was already striding from the chamber, leaving everyone staring after him.

"I must go with him," Katherine said distractedly, close to tears.

"May I suggest that you leave him alone for the moment to gather his thoughts?" Ralegh said. "Why not take a little refreshment first? Then Master Latymer here shall take you to him."

"No, I thank you." Katherine lifted her head, simulating a pride she was far from feeling. "My place is with my husband. Please take me to him now, Master Latymer."

The steward pursed his lips. "If that is what you wish, Mistress Radcliffe, although I think it might be best if you were to heed Master Ralegh and—"

"It is my wish."

"Very well." The steward turned to Master Ralegh. "Your pardon, Master Ralegh. I shall return immediately to discuss with you the arrangements for Her Majesty's imminent visit to my lord."

After questioning the servants stationed throughout the mansion, they discovered that Brendan had gone outside to the knot garden. Once he had sent for Katherine's cloak, Master Latymer seemed relieved to be able to place her in charge of a page, who led her down a flight of steps and across a paved terrace to the knot garden.

"Leave me," Katherine told the page, when she saw Brendan's tall figure pacing the graveled paths between the beds of sweet-scented musk roses edged with foot-high hedges of dark-green box and golden privet.

Her senses were filled with the fragrances emanating from the flowers, but her rage blotted out every pleasant thought, the meaning of Brendan's words now having fully penetrated her mind.

His father! The Earl of Sussex was Brendan's father.

Brendan watched her as she approached him along the pathway. As she drew near, he held out his hands, his lips forming a smile. "Have you forgiven me my anger, my darling Kate? It is good of you to come to comfort me."

Katherine dashed his hands away. "Comfort you? Do not expect to receive comfort from me."

The smile died instantly. "Ah, it appears I was mistaken."

"Mistaken, indeed." Tears of fury filled her eyes. "How could you do it to me, Brendan? How could you expose me to such . . . such humiliation? All those people staring and whispering and laughing! The Countess sneering down her long nose at me. And no wonder, poor woman. Imagine how she must have felt, to have her husband's bastard come boldly to her home, with all her family about her, shaming her before them all!"

He stood motionless, arms straight by his sides, the dark blue of his eyes turned almost to black.

"I said before that you were no gentleman," she cried. "Little did I realize how right I was, that you were a bastard. And now you choose not only to flaunt your bastardy before the Earl's family, but also to drag me there with you to see you do it." She drew in a sobbing breath. "Oh, Brendan, how could you have caused me such humiliation and disappointment—and on my first visit to London, too! You knew how excited I was about coming here. Yet I had to wait until I arrive, weary and thirsty and hungry, to learn that the man I have married is a bastard."

"At least I am the bastard of an earl," he said, with a wry smile.

"How can you smile at such a time? What difference does it make if you are the bastard of an earl or a peasant?"

"A great deal of difference," said a voice from behind them.

Wrapped up in themselves, neither of them had heard or seen Walter Ralegh approach.

Not caring that he was a man of influence at Court or the Queen's favorite, Katherine turned upon him. "I am having a private conversation with my husband, sir, and do not wish to be disturbed."

Ralegh looked not one whit disturbed by this haughty rebuke. "I envy you, Fitz . . . ah, that is, Radcliffe. There's nothing I admire more than a woman with fire in her." He smiled at Katherine's indignation. "Your pardon, Mistress Radcliffe, but it occurred to me that you and your husband might not have obtained lodgings for the night. That is my sole reason for leaving my important discussion with Latymer regarding Her Majesty's proposed visit here. Have you a lodging?" he asked, directing his question to Brendan.

"I had hoped that we would stay here," replied Brendan with a shrug and a wry grimace. "When I obeyed the Earl's wish that I come immediately to London, I had not expected to find Lady Frances and the Sidneys here upon my arrival."

"No, indeed, I should imagine not."

Katherine was even more infuriated to see that the two men appeared to understand each other very well. The look of mutual understanding they exchanged made her feel like a country wench, with no knowledge at all of the grand world of the nobility.

"What did you mean, Master Ralegh, when you said it made a great deal of difference being the bastard of an earl?" she demanded.

"Katherine, that's enough on the subject." Brendan's tone told her that it would be best not to persist. "Captain Ralegh asked us about our lodging for the night. And my reply is that I do not know where we shall rest."

"Oh, Brendan," wailed Katherine, suddenly forgetting everything else, "I am so weary and thirsty. I long to wash and take my riding boots off. I swear, I feel as if I have lived in the damnable things since we left home."

Ralegh smiled delightedly. "And I swear that you will be like a fresh breeze of moorland air in the stifling, perfumed atmosphere of the Court, Mistress Radcliffe."

Katherine stiffened, not certain if she had been given an insult or a compliment.

"I assure you, Captain Ralegh, we shall not be going to Court," Brendan said brusquely.

"We shall see," said Ralegh. "Meanwhile, I have a solution for the problem of your lodging. You shall stay with me."

"We could not possibly be imposing ourselves upon you."

"No imposition whatsoever. I have an abundance of apartments at my disposal in Durham House, on the Strand." He cocked his head at Brendan, the bright blue eyes twinkling. "My fortunes have changed a little since we were in Ireland together, Captain."

"So I have heard, Captain."

Although Katherine could see that Brendan was reluctant to accept Master Ralegh's offer, the thought of traipsing about London all day looking for suitable lodgings made her bold. "I think we should accept Master Ralegh's kind offer," she said, bestowing a brilliant smile upon him. "That is, if he has sufficient room to house us."

"More than sufficient," the Queen's favorite said, giving her a flourishing bow. "It would be an honor to share my humble home with my old comrade and his fair wife."

Brendan gave Ralegh a strained smile. "It appears I am outnumbered. I thank you, sir, for your kind offer of hospitality. We shall not be with you long, I assure you."

They traveled to Durham House by river on Master Ralegh's private barge, their grooms, horses and bags having been taken care of by one of Ralegh's servants.

Durham House, which, Ralegh told them, had for a long time been the London residence of the Bishop of Durham, was far from being humble. Like a great castle on the river bank, its turreted walls rose sheer out of the river.

The steps from the river mooring went directly into the house itself. Katherine shivered. The walls were slimy wet to the touch and the air was dank. But the main chambers, when they reached them, were richly furnished and comfortable.

When the door closed behind Ralegh's steward, who had brought them ale and wine to drink, Brendan surveyed the bedchamber they had been given. "Methinks Master Ralegh has indeed come a long way since I saw him last in Ireland," he said with an edge to his voice.

"It is churlish of you not to acknowledge his kindness to us, at least," said Katherine, as she drew the pins from her hat and stripped off her gloves. "Who knows where we would have slept tonight had he not offered us his hospitality."

Brendan walked across the room, to look out the window at the busy river. All Katherine could see was his profile. It was as if his face was suddenly new to her. In the fine-cut nose, the dark, slanting eyebrows, she now caught a glimpse of his father. But the harsh lines of the Earl's face were gentled in Brendan's by the curving mouth, the springy dark hair.

He turned, to find her observing him. "You were right, Kate," he said, with a heavy sigh. "I should never have brought you to London with me."

He sank onto the window seat, leaning his head back against the central frame of the casement. "When I received his letter, I could think of nothing else but that my father had at last expressed a desire to see me and that he wished me to bring my new bride with me." He shook his head slowly. "What a fool I was to think that I could walk into the Earl of Sussex's house without any member of his family seeing me, or caring that I was there."

"I take it that the Countess knew about you before today."

"They all knew about me. The Countess and every member of her proud family, the Sidneys, and the Earl's brother, Sir Henry. Had my father been as ruthless as many thought him to be, he would have ignored the fact that I existed, left me with my mother in Munster, unschooled, uncivilized . . . and, perhaps, more content."

There was that wry, deprecating smile again, twisting his mouth as if he had eaten one of the sour crabapples from the orchard at Radcliffe.

Katherine went to sit upon the stool by the empty hearth, but said nothing. Her breathing was light, shallow, as if the slightest noise might disturb this sudden self-revelation of her husband's. Brendan had never before spoken of himself or his former life to her. She wanted to hear more.

He looked down at his hands, hanging between his knees. "My mother was a Fitzgerald, a young kinswoman of the Earl of Desmond. My father was the Governor of Ireland, still a comparatively young man, handsome, tall, intelligent. His wife was far away. The rigors of the campaign in Munster were physically and emotionally draining. He found solace for a few nights in my mother's company. Only a few nights."

He did not look up. Nor did he continue his story.

At last, after a while, Katherine said very softly. "Was she married? Your mother, I mean."

"No. She was a maid of sixteen. Very beautiful. My father dishonored her."

Katherine was shocked. "Do you mean he took her against her will."

"Not at all," Brendan said, his voice harsh. "She fell passionately in love with him and offered herself to him. 'Twas she told me that, I remember. Being but a lad, I thought it like a romance from a French book or from one of the tales of the knights of King Arthur." He smiled. "And though she was cast off by her family and shunned by them and the two of us were hidden away in a remote Fitzgerald castle, she never ceased to love the mighty English Earl, nor to tell me how chivalrous he was, despite him being an Englishman. She, it was, who eventually smuggled out a letter to him, telling him he had a fine son, eight years old, and that it was her desire to have that son raised to be a gentleman like his father."

His eyes squeezed shut and he heaved a sigh. "She knew that in writing that letter 'twas likely she would lose me. And so she did. I was plucked from her side, kicking and screaming, and taken to Dublin, where I received my schooling in how to become an English gentleman. Which included being soundly beaten if ever I dared to speak a word of the Irish language."

He addressed the polished oak floor, speaking to himself, as if he were in one of the old confessionals, with the one listener hidden behind a curtain. Then he fell silent.

"Did you ever see your mother again?" Katherine asked eventually.

"I did not. I never knew what happened to her. Then, when I was sixteen and at Cambridge, I received word that she had died. All those years shut away in a room not much larger than a cell, like a prisoner. God in heaven!"

He sprang up, to pace across the floor, and then swung about to face Katherine. "Yet when I asked him about her today, he would not speak of her, saying he had done all he could for her. Dear Christ, surely he could have taken her from that place and made her life more easy. There was I, living the life of comparative luxury within the Pale and in England, with my mother half-starved and imprisoned in a chamber that was so damp that snails crawled on the walls."

He turned from her, to stare blindly out the window. "But, more than anything, what galls me, Kate, like salt in an open wound, is that I did nothing about it." He clenched his jaw, to hide its trembling.

She went to him then, wrapping her arms about him and laying her head against his chest. "What could you, a mere lad, have done?" she said, turning her face up to him.

"Something, I should have done. Something other than forgetting her."

"But you never did forget her, did you?"

He looked down at her, meeting her eyes for the first time. "I suppose I did not. But I am racked with guilt whenever I think of her."

"You must not be. When first she lay with your father, she knew the likely result of what she did. If he truly did not force her, she acted of her own free will." A thought came into her mind and she gave him a radiant smile, her arms tightening about him. "Had you asked her years later if she regretted it, I swear your mother's answer would have been, 'No. Not one jot.' For a short time, she was able to be with the man she loved. She would not have chosen to exchange that for any amount of comfortable living thereafter."

His arms tightened about her. "Do you truly think so?"

"Certainly, I do," Katherine said fervently. "And your coming, a living symbol of that love, must have been an added blessing."

He grinned down at her. "I would remind you, dearest Kate, that that is not what you said earlier today, when you learned I was a bastard."

She flushed. "Of course not. I was thinking solely of myself then, as you well know."

"Nevertheless, you were right. To have exposed you to that humiliation at Bermondsey was inexcusable. Only, you see," he said wistfully, "'twas my last chance to see my father and speak with him. Unlike you, my darling, I had no home, no loving family surrounding me in my growing years."

Katherine stepped back, a sudden coldness enveloping her. "You are forgetting, my dear husband, that my father died when I was only six years old. You heard what the Earl said." Her voice dropped to a whisper. "My father was murdered. Perhaps by my mother. I would rather be an orphan than have that knowledge perpetually on my mind."

"What arrant nonsense! Who could ever think of your mother arranging your father's death? A more kindly, sweet woman does not exist."

"Then why would the Earl say so?"

"He is a sick man. His mind was wandering."

"But, Brendan, it is what my Aunt Isobel told me, also."

Brendan gave her an incredulous look. "Lady Colborne told you that your mother arranged for your father's death?" He frowned, and then shook his head. "I cannot believe she said that of her own sister."

"Well, she did." Katherine faced him, nausea rising into her throat. She must tell him now, or she would never again have the courage to broach the subject. "She also confirmed what I had long suspected, that my mother and grandfather were lovers."

This time there was no hesitation on Brendan's part. "I cannot believe it," he said flatly.

"You must believe it," she said passionately. "For it is so, and I have known it for a long time. Now, perhaps you will understand why I feel the way I do about my mother."

It was a day for confessions on both sides. And though talking of it made her heart pound and her stomach churn, Katherine felt a great sense of relief at being able to share this, her daily nightmare, with Brendan.

"If I had to choose between them," he said, "I tell you it would be your mother's word I would believe over your aunt's."

"I would it were so." Katherine's teeth were chattering despite the warm breeze that blew in the open window. She was racked with the sick shaking that always overtook her when she thought of her secret knowledge of her mother.

Brendan put his arms about her and lifted her against him. Then he swung her up, to carry her to the curtained bed. Although both were still clad in their cloaks and boots, he set her down on the bed and lay down beside her, gathering her into his arms.

"My poor darling," he whispered against her hair. "To think you have carried such a burden in your heart for so long. Thank God you have told me at last." He stroked back the dark tendrils of hair from her face and pressed his cheek to hers. "Now that we have shared our darkest secrets, it will all be different between us, you will see. As soon as we are able, we shall shake the dust of London from our feet and start back to Yorkshire."

A darkness fell upon Katherine at the thought of going home to Radcliffe again. Despite her earlier anger and disappointment, she felt safer here with Brendan in the strangeness of London.

"Do not look so downcast, sweetheart," Brendan said. "I swear on Christ's holy name that, as soon as we return to Radcliffe, we shall seek out the truth of your father's death together. Then we shall all be able to live in harmony and contentment at Radcliffe."

She looked at him in wonder. "You would think of my concerns today, of all days? You make me feel ashamed of myself, Brendan Fitzgerald. Or, I should say Brendan Radcliffe, should I not?"

He leaned up on one elbow, twisting a strand of her hair around his finger. "Will you mind being Mistress Radcliffe again, just in London, of course?"

"No, I shall not mind. But do not change the subject, sir husband. I wish to thank you for caring for me, for—"

He looked deep into her eyes. "You know well it is not just caring, Kate." He hesitated, as if he wished to say more, but had decided against it. "My one wish is to see you content," he said, his voice lighter than before. "Content with me, and with your mother, at Radcliffe."

"With you, perhaps," she said, meaning it for the present. "With my mother, I doubt it."

He took her face between the palms of his hands. "I have lost a mother and am about to lose the father I have only just found. I cannot regain your father for you, but I can help you regain your mother, and mean to do so."

His optimism was contagious. "Oh, Brendan, you make me feel all things are possible." She swung her legs over the edge of the bed. "But now that we are here in London, could we not stay just one or two days before we leave for home again? After all, who knows when we shall return."

"It would be my preference to leave London first thing in the morning, but I have to see my father's man of business before I leave. So you shall have your wish. I shall escort you on a tour of the great town before we depart. But, first, I suggest we go forth to procure some food before we both starve."

Chapter 23

Although it irked Brendan to be forced to accept Ralegh's hospitality, he had to allow that his erstwhile companion-in-arms was generous in the extreme. He had given them two of his finest apartments and, when they ventured out into the upper landing, it was to find a retinue of servants prepared to wait upon them, with offers of refreshment, assistance in changing their clothing, and escorts to take them to wheresoever they chose to go in London.

It was evident that Ralegh, for whatever reason, had chosen to treat him with as much pomp as he would a prince from a foreign land. It was also evident that the fairly humble—in estate, if not in personality—son of a country squire from Devon had risen to great heights in the less than two years since Brendan had served with him in Ireland.

He had heard many rumors of the swift ascendancy of the arrogant Walter Ralegh, but nothing could have prepared him for this: a private barge with the boatmen all clad in Ralegh's livery; a mansion—nay, a veritable palace—by the river, manned by an army of servants; clothing on Ralegh's back that looked as if it was worth more than the entire Radcliffe estate.

To be the reigning favorite of the Virgin Queen was, it seemed, to be all-powerful. Yet Brendan sensed that the old restlessness still stirred within Ralegh, only now it was tamped down like powder in a cannon, ready to explode at any moment. What had happened to all Ralegh's dreams of exploring the New World, of discovering Utopia?

Perhaps he would find that out later, for Ralegh had sent word from Greenwich, where he had returned to Her Majesty to discuss her coming visit to her ailing Lord Chamberlain, that he wished Brendan to join him and a few companions for a light supper when he returned from Court.

As I maintain a bachelor establishment, Ralegh's message, written in his own flourishing hand, concluded, *it would give me the greatest pleasure if Mistress Radcliffe were to do me the great honor of presiding at our table.*

Katherine's eyes danced with excitement when she had finished reading the message, which had been brought to them while they were eating the splendid dinner that had been set out for them. "To think that I am to be the only woman at the table with the Queen's favorite! What should I wear, Brendan? I swear Master Ralegh is so grandly dressed that anything I have will not be good enough."

"My darling Kate, you will never in a million years be dressed as well as Ralegh, for he has to dress to match a Queen, remember. Wear your green damask and the emerald ring your grandfather left you. And your mother's pearls." Brendan smiled across the table at her. "Besides, to me, you are superior to any queen, whatever you wear."

"Hush." Katherine looked quickly about the great dining hall, where they were dining in solitary state. "One of the servants might hear you."

Brendan shrugged. "What of it. I cannot be chastised for telling the truth."

By the time they had finished dining, there was little time left for exploring the sights of London. Having been assured by Brendan that he would be happy to escort her the next morning, once he had finished his meeting with Master Wingate, Katherine decided to spend what was left of the day supervising the unpacking of her clothes and the preparation of her costume for dining with Master Ralegh and his friends.

Brendan was wondering how he would pass the remainder of the afternoon, when he received another missive, this time from Bermondsey. "It appears that Master Wingate will be too busy with Her Majesty's visit tomorrow to be able to meet with me," he told Katherine. "Instead, he wishes to attend me here this afternoon, as soon as possible."

"That decides it, then. I shall unpack and settle in here, whilst you have your meeting."

Brendan frowned. "Do not be settling in too comfortably. I have no intention of remaining in London. Indeed, we could leave tomorrow, now that I shall be able to complete my business with Wingate today."

Katherine's eyes widened with dismay. "You could not do that to me, Brendan. You gave me your word that we should spend at least a day seeing London."

Brendan grimaced. "Your pardon, my love. So I did. Very well, then. We shall depart on Thursday," he said, with reluctance. Something, he did not know what, was urging him to leave London as soon as possible.

"Oh, thank the Lord for that," said Katherine. "You scared me for a moment. But even Thursday gives us little time to see the city."

"I pray your pardon, but I am eager to return to Radcliffe."

Katherine looked away. "I wish we could stay here forever," she whispered.

"We cannot," he said gently. "You must not be fearful, Kate. We have no secrets from each other now, remember? Something tells me that our life at Radcliffe will be quite different, once we have sorted out this mystery of your father's death."

She nodded, but did not appear convinced by his confidence in the future.

"I must change and then go down to meet Wingate. What will you do for the rest of the afternoon?"

"I am feeling suddenly weary and my belly aches," she said, rubbing it. "I fear I must have eaten too many mussels. When I was downstairs I caught sight of a fine garden to the west of the house. Once I have prepared my dress for tonight, I think I shall walk or sit there for a while. If I am not here when you return, come and seek me there, in the garden."

The meeting with Master Wingate did not last long. He was patently anxious to return to Bermondsey to help with the preparations for the Queen's visit the next day.

The gist of what he had to relate to Brendan was that the Earl would be giving him a large parcel of land in Ireland. It would be Fitzgerald land, of course, which would be confiscated by the English Crown once the rebels were caught and peace was established. Although part of it had been laid waste and deforested, there was much that was good growing land.

"It is too much," Brendan murmured. "He has already given me Radcliffe, which is more than enough."

"You need not farm the land in Ireland yourself. Rent it out once the English settlements are made."

"And become an absentee landlord, as Ormonde has been? That has been part of the ruination of Ireland: The lords who were ordered to remain at the English court, leaving their lands to others to manage."

Master Wingate shrugged, signifying that this was not his concern. "One more matter before I leave you, Master Radcliffe. My lord of Sussex has expressed the desire that when he dies you attend his funeral."

An iron hand clutched at Brendan's heart. "But he particularly desired me not to see him again. I took that to mean that I might return to Radcliffe immediately."

"He does not wish to see you again. Nevertheless, he does wish you to attend his funeral, which will take place at Boreham."

Boreham. The great Radcliffe family estate in Essex. Brendan felt like a badger caught in a steel trap. "And does Lady Frances know this?"

"She does. And has accepted his lordship's wishes in the matter."

Brendan could imagine how reluctant her acceptance had been. The thought of having to face the entire Radcliffe and Sidney family again was a daunting one. One thing was certain, he would attend the funeral alone. Katherine would not be subjected again to the humiliation she had undergone today.

When he sought her in the garden by the river, he did not tell her about the Earl's wish. Indeed, he was in two minds as to whether or not he would obey it. The pall of fear that had hung over him since the morning continued to loom, making him uneasy. The desire to fly London grew more intense, building like an unreasonable panic inside him. It was not like him to be a prey to sick, unnamed fears. This, in itself, increased his uneasiness throughout the rest of the day.

There were only three other men at Ralegh's dining table that evening. Brendan was surprised. He had expected a horde of courtiers and sycophants. It was not long before he realized that he and Katherine had joined an exclusive inner circle of Ralegh's friends.

At first he could not see the connection between the old man with the flowing white beard and black skullcap, the young man with the sparse beard and penetrating dark eyes, and the tall, black-bearded even younger man—he looked as if he were barely into his twenties—whose dark eyes darted from Brendan to Katherine and back again, as if he were attempting to fit them into a larger picture in his mind.

Even the introductions did not help him to establish any connection between the extremely diverse men.

"My friends," said Ralegh. "I have had the good fortune today to renew an acquaintance with Captain . . . ah, that is, Master Brendan Radcliffe, who served with me in Ireland two years ago. I have had the even greater good fortune to meet his beautiful wife, Mistress Katherine Radcliffe, who is gracing us with her presence this evening. So be on your best behavior, sirs." He raised his eyebrows at Katherine. "I give you fair warning, madam, we rarely have a member of the fair sex to dine with us here, so you must forgive us if our conduct is not as courteous as it should be."

She curtseyed to the men, smiling at them all. "Gentlemen, I am honored that you have invited me to dine with you and ask that you do not feel in any way constrained by my presence."

It was nicely said. Brendan gave her a little glance of pride, marveling at her poise in such strange company.

Ralegh turned to his friends, indicating each with a flourish of his hand as he presented them. "Dr. John Dee, Her Majesty's astrologer, of whom you have doubtless heard. He it is who has prepared the charts for my brother Humphrey Gilbert's second enterprise to the New World, which is to depart from Plymouth in less than two weeks time. You must ask him to tell you about his theory that your namesake, Saint Brendan himself reached the New World centuries ago."

The old man in his long black gown, relieved only by the white ruff and long white beard, bowed to Brendan, and he returned the bow.

"Lord Henry Percy," Ralegh said, indicating the tall young man.

"My lord." Brendan's bow was far deeper this time, in recognition of the eldest son of the Earl of Northumberland. He wondered even more at Ralegh's strange collection of friends. To his knowledge Ralegh was a staunch Protestant, yet young Percy's father was locked up in the Tower at this very moment, for his involvement in Catholic plots to free Mary, Queen of Scots. And his uncle, the seventh earl, had been executed for leading the Northern Rising in which Katherine's grandfather had been attainted.

"And, lastly, Master Thomas Hariot. This small body hides a great mind, Radcliffe. Master Hariot is preparing the maps and charts for the mariners who will explore the New World. He will also be aboard my new vessel, the *Bark Ralegh*, when she sets out on her second voyage, so that he may see at firsthand the remote and hitherto unexplored territories north of Florida."

Katherine curtsyed again to the three men, looking rather bemused, but Brendan was beginning now to understand. Many a night in their tents or over rough tables in even rougher castles in Ireland, Walter Ralegh had expounded his theories on exploring the New World, his eyes glowing with excitement.

These three men also shared that excitement. Indeed, the atmosphere in the richly furnished dining chamber was pulsating with unspoken words, unshared ideas eager to be spoken and shared. The feeling was contagious. Brendan felt in himself a profound eagerness to hear what each man had to say.

When he was seated beside Lord Percy, he smiled down the table at Katherine, seeking to set her at her ease, but she was in conversation with the elderly Dr. Dee and, it seemed from the way the old man was bending eagerly towards her, already captivating him.

Brendan felt a rush of pride. He had seen the younger men's admiring looks at his wife. She basked in their evident appreciation, so that in her emerald gown with the milk-white pearls at her slender throat, her grandfather's large emerald ring on her finger, she looked more beautiful than he had ever seen her. And this beauty was his alone.

He felt the stirring of desire and wished he could sweep her up and carry her away to the chamber above the busy river. *Later*, he told himself with a secret smile, sure that with this new mood of openness between them, she would welcome his lovemaking.

He rather envied Katherine's assurance as she spoke to the Queen's astrologer, for he was feeling far from assured in this company. But, although at first he was content to eat and listen, he soon found himself drawn into the conversation. And when it turned to Ireland, he was encouraged by astute questioning to share his ideas about the best way to solve the Irish problem.

The four men were as good listeners as they were speakers, and Brendan loved to talk, so that the meal itself dragged on to almost midnight. And then, just as Brendan was beginning to think that he and Katherine could retire, Ralegh dashed his hopes.

"Mistress Radcliffe, if you would excuse us," he said. He snapped his fingers at the servant behind his chair, who came forward bearing a silver-gilt canister and a case, which, when opened, displayed several clay pipes. "We would like to blow a cloud and, as the hour is late, we are sure you would choose to retire to your chamber."

Brendan stood up, but was waved back. "No, no, not you, Radcliffe. The night is yet young. My steward will escort Mistress Radcliffe to her chamber and ensure that she has everything she needs."

Ignoring Ralegh's assurances, Brendan went to Katherine. "Do you wish me to come with you?"

"Certainly not," she told him, lifting her head so that her slender throat gleamed like alabaster in the candlelight. "I bid you good night, husband and gentlemen."

Brendan knew her too well not to sense that she was disappointed, but whether her disappointment was for her banishment from the general company or that he did not come with her to bed, he could not guess.

By the time the men took their leave, Brendan was weary beyond measure, and his throat was burning from the powerful tobacco Ralegh had forced upon him to smoke. To Brendan it was an obnoxious habit, but one that Ralegh was forever pressing his friends to enjoy. As always, with Ralegh, he would not accept no for an answer.

It had been a long and emotionally wearing day. No doubt Katherine was asleep by now. Besides, Brendan was not sure he still had the energy to make love to her. All he desired now, in truth, was the escape of a long sleep.

When the three men had left, Ralegh sat down at the table again and pushed the decanter of ruby-red claret across to Brendan. "Help yourself."

Brendan protested that he must retire or he would fall asleep in his chair.

"Nonsense, the night is young," said Ralegh, as uncaring as ever for other people's feelings or wishes. "Just one last glass. I wish to speak with you alone for a short while."

As Ralegh's guest, it would have gone against all the laws of hospitality for Brendan to refuse his host's request. Reluctantly, he accepted the offer of more wine, although he suspected they both had drunk more than enough for the night already.

Ralegh leaned back in his chair, surveying him with an amused smile on his lips. "So, my friend, what did you think of my companions?"

"I found their conversation extremely stimulating."

"Did you now? I thought you might. I think you would agree with me that they are all out-of-the-ordinary men."

"Undoubtedly." Brendan's suspicion that there was something Ralegh wanted of him increased.

"You, yourself, are not a man in the common mould, Captain Fitzgerald." Ralegh waved an impatient hand. "Your pardon, but I cannot get used to 'Radcliffe.'"

Brendan shrugged. "No matter. It was not my choice to use the name, I would remind you."

"Most men would have made much of it."

"Would they? If they were bastards?"

"Ah, but, as I told your wife, it is one thing to be the bastard of an ordinary man, but quite another to be the bastard of the Earl of Sussex, one of the most important men in the realm."

"I see no difference. A bastard is a bastard."

"Now that you have your father's acknowledgement, you could be anything you chose to be, rise to any heights."

"I am what I have chosen to be. I have a fine estate and a beautiful wife. What more could a man want?"

"God's blood, Brendan! Is that all you desire, an estate and a wife? In Christ's name, where's your ambition, your desire to set down your name in history?" Ralegh crashed his fist down on the table in his disgust.

"I regret your disappointment in me," Brendan said, smiling. "You cannot expect everyone to have your lofty ambition, Captain."

"I do not expect it of ordinary men." Ralegh leaned forward to stub his finger in the air at Brendan. "But, yes, you do disappoint me, for I believe you to be capable of greatness. It is a fearsome waste for you to be hidden away in the wilds of Yorkshire, especially when you have your freedom to do anything you wish."

"As you do not."

Ralegh's swarthy face glowered at Brendan, the eyes widening and then the piercing blue almost hidden by the heavy lids. Although Brendan knew the man's unpredictable nature, the change in his mood was remarkable. He wondered how many people at Court had been terrified by such a look, knowing what power this man held in his hands. The Queen's Oracle, someone had called him.

But Brendan, not being a courtier and having nothing to fear from Walter Ralegh, merely lifted his glass to drink more of Ralegh's fine claret and saluted his host with the empty glass, before setting it down again.

The gesture snapped Ralegh from his anger. "You have hit it on the head exactly, my friend," he said, leaning across the table to pour more wine into Brendan's glass. "I am like a wild bird trapped in a gilded cage." He fixed Brendan with a piercing regard. "I recall that you were never a man to tell tales, Fitzgerald. I believe I can be certain that what I say here will not be repeated."

Brendan merely inclined his head in reply. The thought of hearing Ralegh's confidences made him uneasy, but it was possibly more prudent to remain than to suggest that it was time they both retired to their beds.

"It is *I* who should have been captain of the *Bark Ralegh*." The blue eyes flashed. "*I* should have accompanied my brother on this expedition to the New World. But she forbade me to go! After I had spent more than two thousand pounds on equipping my own ship and made her the finest vessel sailing the seas today, *she* said she could not bear the thought of possibly losing me.

"Christ!" Unable to remain seated, Ralegh thrust back his chair to pace back and forth beside the table. "She keeps me clipped beside her like one of her mewling lapdogs. She picks at my brains like a raven. 'What think you of this, Walter? What should be done about that, Walter?' Everything I do is second-hand. At my instigation, that fleet is to sail to Newfoundland in a week or so's time and establish a new colony there. But shall I sail with it? Oh, no, I shall not. I, who long to explore all those tantalizing new lands, am kept permanently anchored in the safe harbor of the Queen's perfumed Court."

To emphasize his disgust, he spat into the dried herbs that were strewn on the oaken floor, and then leaned on the back of his chair to glare across at Brendan. "And you, who are free as that wild bird we spoke of, sit there and say nothing."

"You have not given me the opportunity to do so," Brendan pointed out.

Ralegh sighed heavily. "You are right. I have harangued you unmercifully. Not the conduct worthy of a good host, I regret to say. Do you recall Michael Butler?" he asked suddenly, his brain darting like lightning to another subject. He dragged out the heavy chair to sit down again and poured himself more wine.

"Butler? Are you meaning the Earl of Ormonde's young kinsman, Lieutenant Butler, who served with us in Ireland?"

"Aye, that's the man. He's now Captain Butler. I've made him the captain of *Bark Ralegh* in my stead."

"Good God, the lad cannot be much more than twenty!"

"Aye, but he's a good man, despite he's an Irishman. A man with driving ambition and, what is more important, a desire to venture into the unknown."

"Which I have not, you are implying?"

"Had it not been for Michael Butler, I would have put your lack of ambition down to the fact that you are Irish, but so is he. Come, Brendan, what do you say?" Ralegh's excitement was like a fever, one that Brendan sincerely hoped was not contagious.

"What do I say to what?" he asked, with a smile of amusement mixed with consternation.

"If I cannot sail the seas and chart new lands and settle them myself, I can at least choose the right men to do so for me. As you learned tonight, Ireland is to be settled with Englishmen, once Fitzgerald—I beg your pardon—once the Earl of Desmond is caught and executed. My brother, Gilbert, has the Letters Patent to colonize the New World north of Florida. We need good men to establish the settlements in the Americas. And captains for the ships that sail there. You could have your pick, Fitzgerald. Just tell me what you choose and it shall be yours."

So stunned was Brendan by Ralegh's offer that his brain seemed turned to sludge, and he found it impossible to form a coherent reply. "I . . . I do not know what to say."

Ralegh's head jerked back in a hearty laugh. "I have ambushed you, have I not?" He seemed delighted at Brendan's bewilderment. "I did not intend to overwhelm you, but I had to broach the subject tonight."

"Because I am leaving London soon, you mean?"

Ralegh smiled. "Nay, my good friend, because you are to appear at Court tomorrow evening, when Her Majesty has returned from her visit to your father at Bermondsey."

Brendan stiffened. "I believe I told you before, Ralegh, that it is not my intention to go to Court."

"Not even when the Queen herself desires you to do so?"

Brendan's hands clenched on the table. "Her Majesty knows nothing of me."

"On the contrary, Her Majesty knows everything about you," Ralegh said, very softly.

Brendan froze, cold anger solidifying inside him. "You told the Queen about me?"

"I did."

"About my . . . my parentage?"

A satisfied smile, and a nod, were his reply.

"In the name of God, Ralegh, why?"

Again the blue eyes narrowed, but this time not in anger. "I have already told you. If I cannot venture forth from my gilded cage myself to make history, at least I shall be the one to choose who will."

Smiling, Ralegh leaned back in his chair, the candlelight gleaming on his curling hair and beard, on the great pearl shivering in his ear.

To Brendan, Ralegh's smile appeared more terrible by far than any expression of anger might have done.

Chapter 24

As she and Brendan walked down the long corridor that led to the royal presence chamber, Katherine's seeming assurance hid a terror that she might trip on the edge of the Turkish carpet and fall flat on her face, her farthingale tip-tilted, to her everlasting shame.

Her face burned at the very thought, the heat spreading through her body, so that she felt she would faint. Her fingers gripped Brendan's hand and when he glanced down at her she gave him a tense little smile.

He looked magnificent in his wedding suit of crimson and gold, far more handsome than any of the other courtiers, even Master Ralegh, and he moved at her side with a firm grace that should have reassured her. But despite his calm appearance, Katherine knew that Brendan, too, was uneasy at the thought of this coming audience with the Queen.

He had come to bed very late last night—or, rather, early in the morning. She had been asleep. He had not woken her deliberately, but the shivering that racked his body and the uncontrollable chattering of his teeth drew her from her deep sleep into semiconsciousness.

He lay on his back, staring wide-eyed at the moonlit chamber, the shivering so violent it made the bed shudder.

Katherine knew well these horrors of the night. Her own sister had often had to take her in her arms to calm them. And so, without asking him what was troubling him, she instinctively gathered Brendan into her arms, stroking his hair, kissing his face, murmuring soothing words . . . until the shivering slowly died away.

And, because she knew it would ease him, she had given him her body and sheltered his, and they had become one in a tender, sweet lovemaking that had been unlike any other time between them.

But when the morning came she knew, from the haunted look in his eyes, that the darkness had returned.

During the entire morning of sightseeing, Brendan had been like a man walking and talking in his sleep, going through the motions of showing her St. Paul's and the Tower, with its menagerie of wild animals.

Although he put on a great show of sharing her enthusiasm when they watched the lions prowling in their cages and the monkeys swinging from their wooden bars, Katherine knew that his mind was far away. Yet something stopped her from asking him what was the matter. Most likely it was the coming death of his father that weighed heavily upon him. Still, it was strange that he seemed unable to share his emotions with her. After all, on their first night in London, he had spoken quite openly of his feelings about his father.

In the antechambers of Whitehall Palace, the voices of the great gathering of people had been strident, almost hysterical. But as she and Brendan entered the Queen's presence chamber, the atmosphere changed. An air of reverence muted the voices and laughter of the courtiers, and the music of lute and viol was subdued, as if everyone and everything in this magnificent chamber with its soaring roof were swathed in silks and velvets.

As an usher led them down the center of the chamber, Katherine was reminded of their wedding day, almost exactly a year ago. She gave Brendan a sideways glance, suddenly realizing how much her perception of her husband had changed since then.

On the day of her wedding, she had seen Brendan as a stranger from Ireland, a necessary evil to gain Radcliffe for herself and her family. Now, he was someone she relied on, turned to in times of trouble, fought with, laughed with, made music with. The man who thought of her pleasure before his in their lovemaking. A strange, at times unfathomable, man, who seemed lost in a faraway, mystical world when he played the melancholy tunes of his country on his pipe. An earl's bastard, who was modest but never humble. A man who was at the same time infinitely gentle and infinitely strong.

A wealth of feeling washed over Katherine like a tidal wave. She turned her face eagerly to his, the hitherto unspoken words hovering on her lips . . . to find, to her dismay, that they were but a few feet from Queen Elizabeth, who sat above them in a thronelike chair on the crimson-carpeted dais, and that Brendan was preparing to kneel before Her Royal Majesty.

With more speed than grace, Katherine knelt beside him on the floor, careful to spread her silken skirts over the Spanish farthingale.

She did not raise her head until she heard Ralegh's deep voice presenting them to the Queen. Then she looked up, to find that Her Majesty's eyes were upon Brendan. "You may rise, Master Radcliffe, Mistress Radcliffe, and approach us." She smiled, her lips only partially open to avoid a full display of yellowing, chipped teeth.

Katherine had heard much of the beauty of the Queen. If she had once been beautiful, she was no longer, although she painted her face heavily in a semblance of beauty.

This was a woman of almost fifty who had not accepted her age gracefully, but flaunted her body by wearing her bodice cut very low, almost to her nipples. Yet something there was about her that spoke of courage and fortitude, mingled with feminine coquetry, that made men adore her. She was the flame of England and the men who served her unstintingly the moths around that flame, willing to be scorched if only they could approach her.

"Well, Master Radcliffe," said the Queen, when they drew nearer to kneel before her on one of the dais steps. "We have heard much of you from Master Ralegh. Why have you not attended us at Court ere now?"

"I was not invited to do so, Your Majesty."

Brendan's bluntness seemed to delight her. "That has not stopped others from doing so," she cried, and laughed loudly at her own jest. After a discreet pause, her courtiers joined in the laughter. "Ralegh tells me you were a captain in our service in Ireland."

"I was, Your Majesty."

"Why did you resign your post?" she demanded, her voice sharpening. "There is still much work to be done in our troubled realm across the sea, particularly in Munster. The traitor Desmond is not yet captured. We are greatly in need of loyal and able men in Ireland."

Katherine could see Brendan's hesitation and held her breath for him. Please God, let him say the right thing, she prayed.

"I left Ireland because I felt it was time to marry and beget a family."

The Queen's bright eyes fixed upon Katherine for the first time.

"You have chosen a bonny wife, Master Radcliffe. But why is she here and not at home with the children you have begotten upon her?"

Katherine's face flamed with anger. She opened her mouth as if she would give answer to the Queen, but Master Ralegh's almost imperceptible little shake of the head stopped her.

"Master Radcliffe and his bride were only recently wed, Your Majesty," he said, his voice smoothing the awkwardness. "I believe this is Mistress Radcliffe's first visit to London."

"Ah, yes. You are from Yorkshire, of course." The nostrils of the long nose seemed to flare a little. Yorkshire was not a favorite county of the Tudor monarchs. Its people were too proud, too independent. It was in Yorkshire and the North that the only rebellion in the Queen's long reign had taken place.

"I am." Katherine held her head proudly. "My father was Thomas Radcliffe of Wensleydale, who, before his untimely death, faithfully served Your Majesty and my lord of Sussex."

"Thomas Radcliffe, eh?" This time the Queen smiled more warmly upon Katherine. "Draw nearer, both of you." She turned to one of her ladies-in-waiting. "Mary, bring a cushion for Mistress Radcliffe that she may be seated whilst we talk."

Katherine was relieved to get off her knees, for the floor was hard and the queasiness that had overtaken her recently was stirring in her belly again. She sat upon the gold-tasseled cushion on one of the steps, spreading her skirts about her. "I thank you," she said softly, giving the rather plain-faced lady-in-waiting a grateful smile.

The attendant responded with a sweet smile that transformed her face for a moment and then returned meekly to her post behind the Queen's chair. The honor of being chosen as one of the Queen's attendants would be fraught with many dangers, Katherine imagined.

They were now isolated in a little island of privacy on the dais at the end of the chamber: the Queen with her three women attendants and Ralegh, Katherine and Brendan, the cloth of state bearing the royal arms—lions passant with the French fleurs-de-lis—hanging behind them.

The Queen leant forward, displaying even more bosom than before, so that Katherine felt shame for her. But Her Majesty, being royal, was without shame it seemed. "It is passing strange that the daughter of Thomas Radcliffe should have wed the son of another Thomas Radcliffe."

Katherine felt Brendan stiffen beside her, but he did not speak.

Queen Elizabeth held out her hand. "Master Radcliffe, as one of our loyal captains in Ireland *and* the only son of our dear friend and councillor, my lord of Sussex, you are doubly welcome."

Brendan hesitated for a moment and then took the Queen's hand and kissed it. "Gracious Majesty, you do me great honor," he murmured.

To Katherine's amazement, the Queen's eyes filled with tears. "I do not know how we shall manage without him. He has been the most loyal and steadfast member of our council. His service in Ireland and the North has ruined his health, shortened his life." Her voice sank. "Had I recalled him to Court sooner, he might have lived another ten years. I am to blame for his early demise."

Her ladies looked appalled. Ralegh was about to speak, but Brendan spoke first, his lilting voice gentle but firm. "My lord of Sussex has lived to serve his queen. In the few times we have spoken, I know that service to Your Majesty was at the very center of his life. If he dies knowing that he has served you faithfully and well, he will die content, Your Majesty."

A slow smile spread across the painted face and this time she did not try to hide her teeth. "We thank you for those kind words, Master Radcliffe. You are a worthy son of a worthy father."

Brendan blinked. "You do me too much honor, Your Majesty," he murmured. "In the circumstances—"

"We shall not speak of circumstances, Master Radcliffe. We bring you here to speak of your future."

Again, Katherine felt Brendan's body tense beside her. She wondered what the Queen had in mind for him. Some special honor, perhaps, befitting a son of her trusted councillor? Albeit a bastard son. But it seemed she was not overconcerned about Brendan's illegitimate status. Walter Ralegh had been right. To be the bastard son of an earl *was* a different matter. Perhaps Queen Elizabeth felt sympathy for Brendan, having herself frequently been denounced as the bastard daughter of King Henry.

Katherine felt a thrill of excitement. Could it be a knighthood Her Majesty intended? Surely she could not be thinking of knighting Brendan so soon? 'Lady Katherine Radcliffe.' It sounded well. Her heart thumped in her breast as she waited for the Queen to speak again.

"We have great plans for you, Master Radcliffe," said the Queen, leaning forward with her chin on her long-fingered hand in a conspiratorial fashion. "Your ears should have been afire all day, for your name has been spoken many times today, most particularly by my lord of Sussex and Master Ralegh. You have two ardent admirers there."

Brendan ran his tongue over his lips, as if they were dry, and there were tiny beads of sweat on his brow. He made an attempt at a smile, but Katherine could see that he was deeply troubled and fear stirred within her.

The nausea that had been troubling her made her feel faint again, the hum of low-pitched voices coming and going in waves.

"Yes, Master Radcliffe, I have been discussing your future with several people today. Master Ralegh is of a mind to send you off as captain on one of our ships to explore and colonize the New World. What think you of that?"

"I have never thought of myself as a sailor, Your Majesty," Brendan replied.

"What!" cried the Queen. "With your Irish namesake, Saint Brendan, the most famous navigator ever known? Would you not wish to embark on a voyage to search for the Land of Heart's Desire for your queen, Brendan Radcliffe?"

He gave her a stiff little smile. "Whatever Your Majesty wishes," he murmured.

Katherine's head swam and her heartbeat quickened. She did not like the way this audience with the Queen was going. She began to wish they had never left Radcliffe.

"My lord of Sussex was not quite so adventuresome on your behalf," continued Queen Elizabeth. "He found himself unable to concur with Ralegh's plans for you or with mine."

"What did my lord wish for me?" asked Brendan, as if it hurt him to speak.

"Alas, my dear Sussex chose an old man's life for you, the life of a landlord on his small estate in the remote part of the Queen's realm, the North Riding of Yorkshire. A life cut off from Court and service to your queen."

"And could I not serve my queen in Yorkshire?" Brendan asked lightly. "Perhaps Your Majesty is more in need of loyal subjects there, where the inhabitants are cut off from the sunlight of your royal presence."

"I think not," the Queen said curtly. "As we have said, that is the life for a man who is old and tired of public service. Not for one who is vigorous and imbued with many God-given talents."

The Queen leant forward, her eyes raking Brendan. "Nay, good Master Radcliffe. As a man who knows Ireland and the Irish language you are invaluable to us. I have lately appointed Master Ralegh as commander of a large company of fighting men in Ireland, but," she said, allowing her gaze to dwell tenderly upon Ralegh for a moment, "we are in need of his good counsel here for a while. It is necessary, therefore, to send sound deputies in his stead. Our intention, Master

Radcliffe, is to appoint you one of those deputies in Munster, so that we may flush out the treacherous Fitzgeralds and their leader, the so-called Earl of Desmond."

The blow had fallen. As Katherine gave Brendan a stricken look, she knew that this was what he had been dreading all day. *Why did you not tell me?* she wanted to scream at him.

"Well, Master Radcliffe. What think you of this?" The Queen's voice was sharp, for the reception of her pronouncement had not been as enthusiastic as she had expected. "You will receive generous reimbursement for your commission, we assure you," she said caustically.

A line of red scored Brendan's cheekbones. "I assure Your Majesty that I was not thinking of monetary reward."

"You surprise me, Master Radcliffe," the Queen said drily. "What were you thinking of, then?"

"I was thinking of my new estate in Yorkshire, and of my new wife, who is as yet without child," Brendan replied.

"You are an honest man at least." She turned to Ralegh, whose keen eyes jumped from Brendan to Katherine. "What would be your reply to your friend's concern about his estate and his barren wife, Walter?"

Ralegh set his hands on his hips, his smile like a challenge thrown down at Brendan's feet. "My reply to my friend would be that he is a young man and should have a young man's desires to see the world, and to serve his queen in so doing. As to his estate, it prospered without him before. With good, well-chosen servants it can continue to do so." His lips curled into a smile. "And Mistress Radcliffe would most ably manage the Manor of Radcliffe, I should imagine."

"And what of Mistress Radcliffe's barren state?" demanded the Queen.

Disregarding all formalities, Brendan sprang to his feet. "My wife's state, barren or otherwise, is not to be discussed here. Most especially not by you, Ralegh!"

Aware that Brendan's raised voice had caused two members of the Queen's guard to close in on them, Katherine pulled on Brendan's sleeve, but he shook her off and stood, glowering at Ralegh, his chest heaving.

"My dear friend, I pray your pardon," Ralegh said, laughing. "Had I but realized how uxorious you were, I would have ensured that you had more time with your beautiful wife before we suggested this commission for you. Perhaps Her Majesty might be persuaded to postpone your commission for a few weeks so that you might have more time to alter Mistress Radcliffe's barren state."

"Damn you, Ralegh," Brendan said between his teeth. His hand fumbled at his empty velvet sheath for his sword, but it had been left behind in the antechamber.

"You forget yourself, Master Radcliffe." The Queen's voice cut through the tension between the two men, effectively silencing them both.

Katherine felt the room begin to swirl slowly about her. "I believe Mistress Radcliffe is not well," said the voice of the kindly lady-in-waiting.

"See to her, Lady Mary," barked the Queen's voice, coming to Katherine through a mist.

Sinking down on the cushion, she felt the kind hands moistening her forehead with a wet napkin, loosening her neck ruff. Beside her, Brendan was still on his feet.

"This commission, Your Majesty. Is it an offer Your Majesty is making, or a command.?"

"A command, Master Radcliffe. Your queen's command."

The swirling grew faster and Katherine sank into a violently spinning vortex, down, down into blackness.

Chapter 25

The fainting spell must have lasted only a very short while, for when Katherine regained consciousness it was to hear the Queen's shrill voice saying, "Take her away, for mercy's sake. If there's anything I cannot abide, it is swooning women."

In that moment of utter humiliation, Katherine turned her face up to the Queen. "I have . . . never swooned in my life before," she gasped.

Brendan was leaning over her, his face anxious. Katherine took his arm and, leaning heavily upon it, rose to stand before Queen Elizabeth. Although the bright torches and hangings and faces were a blur before her eyes, she made an attempt at a curtsy. "I pray Her Majesty's permission to withdraw from her presence," she murmured, praying also that she would not puke before she left the royal presence.

"It is granted," snapped the Queen. "One of our ladies will attend you. We wish to speak further with your husband."

A feeling akin to hatred stirred within Katherine. Gripping Brendan's arm, she met the Queen's scornful eyes without flinching. "I should like my husband to escort me back to Durham House," she told the Queen. "Then, he may return to Your Majesty."

It was an act of defiance, but she no longer cared. She looked away from the Queen, to catch Ralegh's amused expression—and hated him as well. She and Brendan were like two puppets entertaining their masters. In a flash of insight she understood her grandfather's hatred of the Court and determination to stay away from it, even before his attainder.

And she was also beginning to understand his lifelong hatred of the Tudor monarchs, which had been handed down to him by *his* grandfather.

"Very well," said the Queen, with a shrug of her shoulders. "But it is our hope, Mistress Radcliffe, that you will not stand in your husband's way. We trust you will not wish to tie him perpetually to your apron strings to wallow in rural domesticity in far-off Wensleydale." She made the place sound as if it were some contemptible hole in the ground, not the finest dale in Yorkshire, at the same time lifting the plucked and painted auburn eyebrows at her ladies, all of whom dutifully laughed.

Katherine lifted her chin. "I shall never stand in my husband's way, Your Majesty. He may do as he pleases for all I care. But just for now, I should like him to accompany me." Her voice trembled. She was afraid that if she did not leave immediately she might start weeping, which would give the Queen even more cause to ridicule her, for if she could not abide swooning women, no doubt she loathed weeping women even more.

Brendan bowed low. "If Your Majesty permits—"

"Perhaps Mistress Radcliffe would permit me to escort her to Durham House," a voice from behind them intervened.

"Ah, Robin," said the Queen, with a great sigh as if she were infinitely bored by the entire situation. "I do not care who escorts Mistress Radcliffe, so long as she is removed before she pukes all over my carpet."

For Katherine had begun to sway and did indeed feel as if she was about to vomit in the royal presence.

Before any more could be said, Brendan caught her up. She protested feebly, but Brendan ignored her and strode away from the dais. The thought of being borne down the long corridor in this humiliating fashion, with all the people thronged there watching, appalled Katherine, but by now she felt so ill she no longer had the strength to speak.

"This way," said the same voice, in some urgency. "There is a door behind the dais directly out to the Queen's private garden. The air will revive her."

Willing herself not to be sick, Katherine buried her swimming head against Brendan's chest, the gold braid on his doublet pressing against her cheek.

Once outside the chamber, Katherine insisted on being set down and, after a descent down a short flight of stairs, they were outside. "Here you are, sweetheart," said Brendan, guiding her by the arm, for she was walking blindly. "Sit down here, by this pond."

Katherine felt clipped grass and hard ground beneath her hands. She found herself seated upon a turf seat beside a lily pond, the pink-tipped white lilies translucent in the twilight. A breeze fanned her cheek and immediately she began to feel a little better.

Now, at last, the tears came. "Oh, Brendan." She bent her head to hide her face from the stranger who stood beside her husband.

Brendan put his arms about her. Unlike other husbands, he had never hesitated to show public affection for her, before friend or stranger. "Never fear, my darling," he whispered. "We shall soon be gone from this place."

"You should return immediately to Her Majesty or she will be even more displeased," the richly dressed courtier warned him.

Brendan hesitated. "I do not like to leave my wife alone—" He halted, not knowing quite how to put it.

"Alone with me?" The man's teeth flashed white in his corpulent, but still handsome, face. "Never fear, Master Radcliffe. We shall not be alone. My page and guard attend me in the shadows there." He nodded over his shoulder. "But, of course, you do not know who I am, being newly come to Court." The words were spoken in a somewhat wry tone.

"I believe I do, my lord. You are the Earl of Leicester."

"I am."

"That makes me wonder even more at your kindness, for you evidently know who I am. And no doubt," Brendan added, his voice bitter, "Master Ralegh has spoken at large about my parentage."

"He has. Master Ralegh was delighted to expound upon the fact that the saintly lord of Sussex was as human as the rest of us, after all."

"Damn his eyes," Brendan said through clenched teeth. "Which is why I wonder that you have shown my wife and me such courtesy. It is general knowledge that you and my . . . the Earl of Sussex are not friends."

"Let us say that my lord of Sussex and I have learned to tolerate each other, being conjoined these many years by our common goal to devote ourselves to Her Majesty's service. Indeed, I shall sadly miss crossing swords with Sussex. Life at Court and in Council will not be the same without him. I hear he has not long to live."

"That is so, my lord. Any day now, the physician says."

"I must own that I was curious to see if this suddenly sprung-up natural son of my old foe was like him in any way. In features you may be. Sussex, too, was a handsome man in his youth. But in character—"

"Not at all, I fear, my lord," Brendan said firmly.

Leicester laughed. "Do not be apologizing for that to me, of all people. Another Sussex pontificating at Court would be too much for me. But my interest was not solely in you, Master Radcliffe. I also wished to meet your wife."

He turned to Katherine, who was looking from one to the other of them, hearing the words but not really taking in their meaning. "You may not realize, Mistress Radcliffe, that I became acquainted with your mother when she visited London many years ago."

Katherine was amazed. "My mother. Are you certain, my lord, that it was my mother?"

"You are the daughter of Alyssa Radcliffe, are you not?"

"I am."

"So I was led to understand. You also remind me of her. You have a certain disconcerting way of looking directly at people I remember she had."

"And still has, my lord, as I know to my cost." Katherine smiled at the man who, it was said, had long been loved by Queen Elizabeth. Indeed, many said he was the only man who had managed to bed her. But he had never gained his greatest desire, which was to wed her. And so, eventually, he had married another woman and, after a long time, been forgiven by the Queen for it and permitted to return to the Court. He was past middle age now, his figure running to fat, the bearded face mottled with red, as if he indulged too much in wine, but there was no doubting that he was still a handsome man for all that.

"You must return immediately," he said again to Brendan, "or you will lose all your chances of placating Her Majesty with your Irish tongue, and end up with nothing for all your pains."

"I have asked for nothing. I wish nothing from Her Majesty," Brendan said bitterly. "It is Master Ralegh who has done the asking for me, damn him."

"Ah, now I begin to understand. You have been press-ganged. You do not share our Walter's voracious appetite for adventuring across uncharted seas, then?"

"I do not. Nor, to own the truth, do I wish to return to Ireland, my lord."

"Not many men do, I hear, after service there."

"I have an added burden in Ireland," Brendan murmured.

"Ah, yes. One word of warning to you on that subject. The mere whisper of the names Fitzgerald or Desmond sets everyone at Court atremble. Nothing enrages Her Majesty more, apart from mention of the Queen of Scots, perhaps. My advice is that you avoid at all cost reminding Queen Elizabeth of that other side of your family, lest you lose not only your freedom to do as you please, but also your fine estate in Yorkshire."

Katherine tensed as she saw the two men's eyes meet in the dusk and the look of sudden fear in Brendan's.

"For that reason, most especially, Master Radcliffe, I would advise you to hie yourself back to the Queen's presence and swear to devote yourself to her service for as long as Her Majesty pleases."

It was well past midnight before Brendan crept into the bedchamber, closing the door softly behind him to avoid waking Katherine. She was not asleep in bed, however, but sitting in the window, gazing down at the boats and barges being rowed up and down the river, the light from their lanterns bobbing like fireflies in the darkness.

"You are still awake?" Brendan's eyes peered at her in the dim light. Most of the candles had long since guttered out and only the one by the bedside still flickered, its light barely reaching the bay window.

"Yes. I have been sorting out my clothes and packing them with John's help."

"What! At this time of night? Why were you packing? We do not have to leave London immediately, you know."

"You may not be. I shall."

He crossed the floor in three strides to kneel before her. "Come now, Kate, it has been a terrible day, I know, but it will all not seem so bad once you have slept."

She drew her hands away from his. "Bar one other, it has been the worst day in my life. I have been humiliated, held up to ridicule, and then banished to my bed like an infant, whilst Her Majesty discusses your future with you. I was treated as if I had no interest whatsoever in where you go or what you do."

"Of course you have, sweetheart. All my thoughts tonight have been for you, not for myself."

"I doubt that very much." Katherine's tone was scathing.

He stood up. "What would you have me do? Defy the Queen of England and walk from the Court? You heard what Leicester said. Had I but breathed my true name, she would have had me clapped in irons and thrown into prison, so furious is she about the Fitzgerald rebellion."

He ripped off his gold-tasseled gloves and shied them, one by one, across the room. Katherine had rarely seen him so angry.

"I would remind you, madam wife, that I, too, have been humiliated tonight," he cried, clapping his chest. "Not only humiliated, but I have been given a great blow. As if that were not enough, you behave in a manner quite unlike yourself, swooning and weeping at the Queen's feet. What in God's name were you about, woman? Did you think that I was giving too much attention to the Queen? Is that what it was?"

Katherine scrambled down from the window seat. "You great fool! Do you think I care what attention you give the Queen? For all I care you may go to Ireland and rot there in your bogs. Has it not even occurred to you that, while you were all humiliating me and naming me barren—I shall never, never forgive you for that, Brendan—"

"It was not I who called you barren."

"It was you who spoke of me as still being without child, wasn't it? That's the same thing as calling me barren. I could not believe my ears! To think that you would tell the Queen that you had to stay home so that you could serve me, as if I were a bitch in heat! And before the whole Court, too."

"Only a few people heard," Brendan muttered.

"In that den of scandalmongers one person hearing would be enough. What in the name of heaven and all its saints made you say such a thing?"

He stood over her, glaring down at her. "Because it is the truth. Because all I want in life is to stay at Radcliffe and raise fine horses and a fine family, with you by my side and in my bed. That is all I wish for. Is that so terrible?"

"It does not show much ambition on your part."

"Ambition? Do you know what I wanted to shout at the Queen when she ordered me back to Ireland? I wanted to say: 'What would happen to your fine country, Your Majesty, if all the young men were off pirating the high seas and pillaging foreign countries? Where would your England be without men who were willing to stay at home to oversee the farming of the land, the growing of the grain, the raising of cattle and horses?'"

"But you didn't say that to her, did you? You said nothing except a mealymouthed, 'Could I not serve my queen in Yorkshire?' God's blood, what sort of protest is that?"

Brendan folded his arms and sighed heavily. "My dearest Kate, when it comes to knowledge of the world, you are an infant. One cannot protest a queen's command, particularly in my precarious position. I am related to the family the Queen blames most for the devastation of Ireland. She has poured out thousands of pounds on trying to end the rebellion, and yet my kinsman, the Earl of Desmond, still lives and still rallies the few people who are not starved or hanged. Had I made more than a feeble protest, Radcliffe could have been taken from me. And I would remind you, madam wife, that if Radcliffe is taken from me, it is taken from you and your family, also."

Katherine opened her mouth, but then closed it again. Much as she hated to admit it, Brendan was right. "Then you are still going to Ireland? You were not able to change the Queen's mind?"

"I was not. She did give me an alternative, however."

"What was that?"

"Ralegh's suggestion. That I serve as captain on one of the expeditions to the New World his half-brother, Gilbert, will be undertaking."

Katherine's hand flew to her throat. "Oh, no, Brendan, you didn't accept it, did you?"

He took a step closer to her. "Ah, so you do care a little about me, then."

She glared at him. "I do not like to think of you drowned in the sea thousands of miles from here," she murmured.

"Well, there is no need for you to worry on that score, for I graciously declined the offer." He went to the bedside table to light another candle. "By the Mass, I could run Ralegh through for what he has done. The thought of having to remain beneath his roof until we leave for Ireland sticks in my gullet."

Katherine shivered. The breeze coming in from the open window was cool against her bare shoulders. "What do you mean, until *we* leave for Ireland? Do you mean you and your troop of soldiers?"

"Certainly not. The soldiers are already there. I mean us, you and me, my darling."

Katherine was imbued by an inner coldness now. "You surely cannot believe that I would accompany you to Ireland?"

Brendan turned from the bedside, half-in, half-out of his doublet. "I cannot believe you would not. It is perfectly secure and civilized within the Pale, I assure you, Kate. Why, even some of the governors have taken their wives and settled them in Dublin."

"Well, this is one wife who will not be settled in Dublin."

He came to her then, dragging off his doublet and letting it fall to the floor. "You are not serious, Kate. Tell me you do not mean it."

"I do mean it. Why do you think I have been packing tonight? I am leaving for Radcliffe tomorrow. I had hoped that you might have been able to dissuade the Queen and come home with me, but it seems that is not to be."

His face was almost as white as his lawn shirt. "Ever since the Queen ordered me back to Ireland, my one consolation, my sole source of hope was that this time it would be different, this time I would be returning to you in Dublin after the campaigning."

She turned away from him, unable to bear the stricken look on his face. "I leave for Radcliffe tomorrow."

"I could order you to accompany me to Ireland. As your husband, I have that right."

"Why, certainly you do. But you would have to chain me up to achieve your ends. Is that what you wish?"

"You know it is not. I swear to you, Kate, I would never force you to go somewhere that is not safe for you. Can I not be persuading you at all? Perhaps we could seek out some women who have lived in Dublin recently and you could speak to them about it."

He was pleading now, desperate. She could not bear to see him this way. She must put an end to it, for both their sakes.

"All that time the Queen was humiliating me for being barren and for being unwell in her royal presence, did it never occur to you why I was unwell?"

He looked bewildered by this sudden change of subject. "Perhaps it was the mussels you ate."

"Perhaps. I do not think so." She went to him and laid her hands against his breast, sliding one beneath his shirt to press it against his fast-beating heart. "It is still too early to be absolutely certain, but I believe I am carrying your child, Brendan."

She felt his heart jump against her hand and then his arms were about her. "A child? That is the most wonderful news."

He was about to kiss her, but she put a hand up to stave him off. "I cannot be certain, Brendan. But now you will understand why I must go home. My child cannot be born anywhere but at Radcliffe Hall."

His excitement died as quickly as it had been born. "I understand."

"At a time like this, I wish to be with my mother." Strangely enough, this was the truth. Since Katherine had returned to Durham House and come to the realization that she was probably pregnant, she had felt an overwhelming desire to be with her mother.

"That, too, I understand." His voice was flat, hopeless. "You must return to Radcliffe. I must beg for more time so that I may accompany you to Yorkshire before taking up my commission in Ireland."

"No, Brendan. There will surely be a party riding north I can go with. Perhaps Lady Scrope will be going home. If so, I would be willing to wait for her."

"It is such a long way for you to travel alone. Will it not harm the baby?"

"Of course not. How foolish you men can be about such things." Her laughter was hollow, but it was preferable to the tears that lay beneath.

"I would to God we had never come to London," Brendan said.

"Amen to that."

He stood in the shaft of moonlight that streamed in through the window, his face gaunt with despair. "I would to God I had never been born."

Chapter 26

When Katherine rose the next morning, the nausea had returned, making her almost certain now that she was carrying a child. A feverish desire to return to Radcliffe, to her mother, agitated her. She insisted that Brendan immediately make enquiries about parties traveling north. "Unless Lady Scrope is planning to leave by Friday at the latest, I shall not wait for her," she told him.

By the afternoon, he had been able to discover that Lady Scrope was not leaving London until the end of the month, but that a certain Sir John Bradshaw was traveling to York with his wife and family the very next day. That was good enough for Katherine. "I shall go with them," she announced.

"Are you certain you will not change your mind and come with me to Ireland?" Brendan asked. But she knew from the dispirited tone of his voice that he had given up all hope of that—and he would not force her to go with him against her will.

"I must go home," she said softly, and turned away from him to busy herself with the folding of bodices and kirtles and overgowns.

By midafternoon it was all arranged. When he told her, Brendan also shared the news that he had been commanded to attend at Court again that evening.

"So, Her Majesty has deemed that you shall not spend your last evening alone with your wife," said Katherine. "Very well then. I shall go with you to Court. With your permission, of course, husband."

He smiled. "My dearest Kate, you are the gamest lass I know. Will you not wish to rest before your long journey?"

"Not I. I intend to dance and enjoy myself tonight. The Court of Her Gracious Majesty shall see that Katherine Radcliffe is no weak, snivelling fool to be publicly humiliated."

Although she would never have said so, she was glad that they were not to spend this last evening alone together. She could not bear to see the terrible sadness in Brendan's eyes and dreaded to suffer more of the long silences that fell between them.

That evening, she swept down the long gallery on Brendan's arm, dressed this time in her shimmering wedding gown, her brown eyes flecked with fire. She danced with Brendan—and with Ralegh, although his attempts to press her body close to his during the pavane disgusted her. What kind of man would seek to philander openly with his supposed friend's wife?

She was also invited to dance a galliard with the Earl of Leicester. That was a definite triumph, for Lady Scrope later told her that Leicester rarely danced nowadays.

All this took place beneath the gimlet eyes of the Queen, who danced only twice—a pavane with Sir Christopher Hatton and a branle with the handsome Earl of Oxford. Her Majesty liked to surround herself with attractive men, Katherine noted. It was with Brendan and Ralegh, however, that she mostly spoke, keeping them at her side most of the evening.

By the time the evening was over, Katherine knew she had scored a triumph. Now she could turn her back on London and the Court. Despite the heady feeling of success, she would be perfectly content never to see the Court or its red-wigged, waspish queen again. Once again, she recalled all that her grandfather had told her of the Tudor Court. *You were right, Grandy*, she thought.

"I do not believe we shall meet again, Master Ralegh," she told their host in the hallway when they had disembarked from his barge and walked up the steps into Durham House. "I shall be up before dawn tomorrow."

"Ah, never say so, fairest lady," he said, hand on heart. "Surely you are not leaving us so soon." He looked genuinely surprised.

Seeing that they were alone, Brendan having gone to make arrangements for their horses for the morning, she did not try to hide her contempt. "I am leaving for Yorkshire tomorrow. Doubtless you think I should be grateful to you for your assistance in gaining my husband such largesse from Her Majesty, Master Ralegh."

"I gather you are not. But thus it is with all wives. They seek to bind us to them with silken threads. The female sex would give us everything but our freedom."

"Have you ever loved a woman, Master Ralegh?"

He stepped back from her, his blue eyes widening in mock horror. "You ask me, Walter Ralegh, if I have ever loved a woman, Mistress Radcliffe? Does the sun rise, the river flow?"

"Do not mock me," she said coldly. "I do not believe you have ever truly loved any woman. Lusted after them, perhaps. But loved? No. If you had, you might better understand my husband's sentiments at present."

He peered down into her face, his own expression suddenly serious. "I notice you do not say your sentiments, Katherine Radcliffe."

"I am too numb from what has passed here to know what my sentiments are," she told him. "And now, because of you, it is too late."

He was silent for a moment and then gave a little mirthless laugh. "And here was I, merely seeking to gain promotion for my old friend. Ah me, Mistress Radcliffe, your ingratitude strikes me to the very quick."

"My husband did not need promotion. He needed his own home and a family about him."

She realized as she spoke how true her own words were. She, who had always had the security of a home and a loving family—until recently, at least—had always taken these things for granted. Brendan, who had not had that security, felt a crying need, a desperate hunger for them. And just as he had found them, they had all been snatched away from him by this man and his vainglorious dreams.

"I hope you find whatever it is you are seeking, Master Ralegh: your Utopia, your Land of Heart's Desire. . . . It is too late now for Brendan, but I would remind you that there are many men who are content to search for these places nearer home."

The brilliant eyes held a dangerous light, and she knew that she had stirred him to anger. "Certainly there are, but your husband is not one of them. You have never seen him in the field, madam. I have. He is a natural leader of men, a fine commander. It would be a terrible waste to see such a man content to watch his oxen ploughing the fields, merely because he prefers to sleep in his wife's bed every night."

Katherine was about to make a heated response, but Brendan's return put an end to their conversation. Declining Ralegh's offer of a glass of Rhenish before he went up to bed, Brendan bade him a curt "Good night" and they left the Queen's favorite standing in the center of the hall, alone.

* * *

Dawn the next morning brought rain and rolling cloud. The spatter of rain against the window set Katherine shivering. She pulled her cloak more tightly about her and took one last look about the chamber. "If I have left anything behind you can send it on to me," she told Brendan.

Her eyes darted from the floor to the window to the bed, but she avoided looking at him. Difficult enough to sense his misery, without seeing it in his eyes as well.

They had made love in the night—if that brief, desperate coupling could be called lovemaking. After that, they had drawn apart, and lain at opposite edges of the bed, as they had used to do, divided by a great wall of bitterness spiked with splintered might-have-beens.

Now it was time to make their farewells. When the grooms had carried out the saddlebags and the two boxes, Katherine held out her hands to Brendan. "Time for us to take our leave," she said, hoping her attempt at a smile did not appear as false as it felt.

"Not so," Brendan said. "I shall ride to Aldersgate with you to see you safely stowed with Sir John and his wife."

"I beg you, Brendan, let us make our farewells here." She had vomited her breakfast already and her stomach was still churning. The thought of prolonging the time before their leave-taking made her feel even queasier.

Brendan was adamant, however. And so they rode over London Bridge and along Cheapside together, the street vendors' cries and ringing of handbells to clear the way and clatter of iron cartwheels on the cobblestones rendering speech between them impossible, which was a blessed relief.

They were just approaching the great stone gate with its timber-built additions when a horse clattered up to them, its fine trappings draped in black.

"Master Radcliffe!" called the horseman, his horse circling, made nervous by the throng of people.

Brendan reined in his mount and waited for horse and rider to come to them. His face paled. "God have mercy," he whispered. "'Tis the Sussex livery he is wearing. My father must be dead."

"Oh, no, Brendan." For one moment, Katherine was tempted to turn from him and spur her horse through the gate. She could not bear any more delays.

"I was told you would be here to meet with Sir John Bradshaw," said the groom. "I have a message from my lord of Sussex for you."

"Then he is not dead," Brendan muttered.

"The new Earl, sir. The late Earl died a little after three o'clock this morning, God rest his soul."

Brendan bent his head and made a sketchy sign of the cross. Katherine sincerely hoped that she was the only one to see the instinctive gesture.

"I am sent to bid you come to Bermondsey, sir."

"You were sent by Sir Henry, that is the Earl himself, to bring me thither?"

"I was, sir."

Brendan turned to Katherine. "If Sir Henry has sent for me, then I shall be expected at least." He smiled wryly. "Not like our last visit. I hate to be leaving you like this, Kate."

"Yes, yes, I know, but you must go." She was afraid that he would ask her to stay. She knew that he should not be left alone at such a time, that she should offer to remain with him in London, to be his comfort, but she did not do so. Besides, he had said all that there was to say about his father to her already.

"I see a group of people and horses approaching now," she said. "That must be Sir John's party, surely." Pray God, it is, she thought, her desire to escape like a fever in her blood.

"It is." Brendan bid the Earl's messenger wait and then hailed Sir John, a hearty red-faced knight astride a huge mount.

The return journey would not be as speedy as the last one, decided Katherine, looking at the robust Sir John and his even plumper lady. That did not matter. What mattered was that she end this agonizing delay here and now.

"You must not tarry any longer," she told Brendan, nodding towards the black-clad groom.

"You are right. And I shall have to stop off at Durham House to change my clothing." He looked down at his rain-sodden green trunk hose. "I cannot arrive at Bermondsey in this."

Yet still he made no move.

Katherine could bear it no longer. "Please go," she mouthed at him. She gave him a close-lipped smile, fighting to hold back tears.

He drew his horse close to hers, and leaned across to her. "Take care of yourself and our child."

"If there be one," she said hurriedly. The aroma of sandalwood mixed with the wet wool of his cloak came to her. His lips had barely brushed her cheek when his horse shied away.

"God be with you," she said.

"And with you, my love." His anxious face was wet from the steadily falling rain. "Send me word from Radcliffe the moment you arrive."

"I will."

He looked back once, and then disappeared into the milling crowd, so that all she could see through the grey curtain of rain, was his head with the jewel-green velvet cap bobbing above the mass of people.

By the time she was drawing near to Radcliffe, Katherine was close to exhaustion. The journey had taken almost three weeks. The weather had been appalling for riding; hot, thundery June days, interspersed with heavy rains, which churned the roadways and bridlepaths to heavy mud, delaying them further.

Each night, she had been forced to endure the company of a drunken Sir John and his empty-headed wife until she was able to retire to the rather dubious beds in the inferior hostelries Sir John had chosen. Each night, she found it necessary to spread borage ointment on her vermin-bites and on the raw saddle-chafing on her thighs.

Each morning, she had felt so ill she thought she would rather die than set out on another day's riding. But the thought of Radcliffe spurred her on, as, retching and shivering with nausea, she prepared herself to endure yet another day of plodding speeds and mind-numbing chatter.

How different matters would have been had Brendan been with her. His raillery and good humor would have kept up her spirits. And he would never have hired the spavined nags Sir John chose, nor stayed at such mean inns.

She was missing Brendan desperately. She would never have admitted such a thing to herself before. But she also blamed him for her plight, anger at him welling up inside her. It was Brendan's fault that their visit to London had been such a disaster. Brendan's fault that she was riding home alone on this miserable journey. Brendan's fault that she was pregnant and felt so unwell all the time.

At York, to her great relief, she parted from her companions and from thence rode with her horse groom, Brendan's valet, John Briggs, and a wool merchant and his son and daughter-in-law, who were making their way to Hawes.

The weather had changed to glorious June sunshine, the heat thrumming through the countryside, drying the roadways and the grain. As they paused on the rise above Masham, Katherine saw the great sweep of the fells sheltering the fertile valley lush with green trees and golden grain beneath them. She was in her own country. Nearing home.

The next day, in the rising heat of the forenoon, she rode down through the coppice above Radcliffe, her heartbeat quickening as, through the summer foliage of the trees, she caught glimpses of the slate-tiled roofs and ornate chimneys of the main Hall and its outbuildings.

The heat had quietened the birds. All that could be heard was the snorting of their horses, and the rumbling call of a wood pigeon, a drowsy sound in the warm wood.

The quietness was suddenly rent by shouts from below them. "Here she is!" cried Joanna's excited voice. And down the path from the gatehouse came her mother and Joanna and, hobbling as fast as she could behind them, Dame Joan.

Tears of joy and relief pouring down her face, Katherine slid from her horse and felt her mother's arms close about her and Joanna clasping both of them, so that all three were locked in one embrace.

"Welcome home, Mistress Katherine," said Tobias Ridley, who had followed the others down the pathway.

Katherine looked up. "I thank you, Tobias. I cannot begin to tell you how glad I am to be here."

"Tha looks nigh death," said blunt Joan. "What hast tha been doing to thyself, then?"

"Why have you come home so soon?" demanded Joanna.

So soon? So much had happened in the past few weeks that Katherine felt as if she had been away from Radcliffe for a year or more.

"Let the poor lass get inside before you besiege her with questions," said her mother quietly.

"Oh, Mother." Katherine's mouth trembled. "I am so glad to be home."

"Come away in, dearest, and you shall tell us all that has happened."

Katherine felt her mother's arm about her, supporting her, as they walked down the sun-dappled lane that led to her home.

At the very moment that Katherine stood before the entrance to Radcliffe Hall, gazing through misted eyes at its ancient walls, golden in the sunlight, Brendan stood ankle-deep in mud, surveying the ruins of the once mighty Fitzgerald fortress of Castlemaine.

Startled by the small troop of horses that had followed the two men into the courtyard, a flock of rain-drenched starlings flapped into the leaden sky.

"Desmond has no shelter but a tent left to him now," said the man at Brendan's side, Hugh O'Neill, heir to the O'Neills, who had been appointed a cavalry officer in Her Majesty's fight against the rebels. "All his castles, bar Askeaton, are down."

But if Brendan heard him, he made no response. His gaze was fixed on the now roofless walls of the castle that had once been the only home he and his mother had ever known.

Chapter 27

The search for Desmond and his ever-dwindling supporters was frustrating beyond belief. Reports of sightings came from all over Kerry and West Cork. As always, the warfare between the rebels and soldiers was utterly different from what the English-born officers were used to: sudden attacks from the hills at night; brief skirmishes in the deep, wooded glens, with their assailants disappearing back into the hills before they could be caught. . . .

It was only a matter of time now. Everyone knew that. Everyone but the Earl of Desmond himself, it seemed. Reports came in that he was suffering from his old wound, that he'd had to be carried across the bog by four of his men. Even his faithful wife, half-starved and exhausted, had given herself up to the Queen's army.

Yet Desmond, driven further west, would not surrender. He even had the audacity to write to his bitter enemy, Thomas Butler, the Earl of Ormonde—who had been recently appointed Governor of Munster by Queen Elizabeth—citing the wrongs that had been done to him.

Ormonde had tossed the letter, written two months before, to Brendan to read when he had first reported to Ormonde at Kilkenny Castle. "The man's a fool," he said. "He says he will submit to me, only on condition that all his land and his possessions go to his son."

Brendan scanned the hastily written letter. "And asks for a pardon and a passport so that he may move freely about the country."

Ormonde let out a great roar of laughter. "Not asking much, is he? Those Fitzgeralds have the nerve of the devil. If you'll forgive me for saying so, Captain *Radcliffe*." The dark eyes cast him a malicious look.

Ormonde was known as "Black Tom" by some. He was well-named. Dark of eye and hair and as swarthy as a Spaniard, he had been raised in England and was so close to the Queen that rumor said he had fathered a child on her. His leadership in Ireland had been fraught with trouble. He was impetuous, quick-tempered, but he was also sorely hampered by lack of money, good men and horses.

"By Christ, Radcliffe, whatever good there was in this Godforsaken country of ours, Desmond has destroyed. Even his own people curse him now. They've eaten all the best horses, and as soon as I offer pardon to the rebels and release them from captivity, they slaughter each other. We are fighting against savages."

The three men, Irish-born, the blood of three ancient Irish families in their veins—Butler, O'Neill and Fitzgerald—looked at each other, and then away. All three knew without saying it that they both loved and despaired of this beleaguered country of theirs. All three had been partly raised in England and felt that only the sanity of English law and English government could save Ireland from itself. And yet . . .

Ormonde shook his head. "The Queen has given me a thousand men, but most of them are newly come from England and know little of Irish-style warfare. I will leave that part of it to you, Radcliffe. Once Desmond is caught, it will all be at an end. While he is still free, he serves as a rallying point for the rebels. The plan is to fan out and push him westward, and then trap him in Kerry, making sure that he cannot escape by sea."

That was exactly what they had done. Hundreds more rebels had been slain and those that were not dead had surrendered, broken in spirit and starving.

Another letter from Desmond arrived, begging for a conference, but Ormonde returned word that he would offer no terms but those of unconditional surrender.

The leaves fell, the nights turned chill. Desmond was reduced now to eighty followers, reports said. There were murmurings against

Ormonde from other leaders in Ireland. His was the wrong way to deal with Desmond. The campaign had dragged on for several more months, with all the attending horrendous cost to the Crown. Food and fuel were growing more scarce all the time. The rebel Earl should be promised all he desired, it was suggested. Then, when he thought himself secure, he should be arrested for treason and executed.

"Never!" roared Ormonde. "If we let him go now, he will be over the sea to Spain, to return later with a vast army of Spaniards at his back."

So confident was Ormonde that he had Desmond trapped, he sent orders to the garrison at Castlemaine, where Brendan and Captain Stanley now held their troops, to move forward to trap him in the Dingle Peninsula. The Earl of Desmond's chaplain had been captured and had divulged—no doubt after torture of some sort—that the Earl was reduced to a bare handful of followers and was hidden in the mountainous glens near Tralee, not far from Castlemaine.

"You will take your troop of men to Dingle," Brendan told Stanley. "I shall remain here at Castlemaine. That way we shall have him trapped somewhere between us. He cannot get past you to Dingle Bay. He cannot pass me into the wider part of the country. We should have him before the week is out."

But Brendan's forecast was a trifle overoptimistic. Several days went by, October passed into November, and still his wily kinsman remained at liberty. The Earl of Desmond lacked food, shelter, warmth—all the comforts a man of his age particularly yearned for. Yet his pride—and his tenacious will to survive—would not permit him to surrender.

Each day, Brendan sent a troop of his kernes and foot soldiers to scour the ravines and glens west of Tralee, but somehow the Earl eluded them.

At night, lying in his rough bed in the cellars of Castlemaine, dank water seeping down the stone walls, Brendan tried to think himself into Desmond's mind.

Eventually, he must make an attempt to break from the trap. He and the few followers that remained must be near starvation. What was he waiting for? Brendan wondered. Possibly a Spanish vessel to come to his aid, but as yet nothing had been sighted.

Brendan did not like to admit, even to himself in the middle of the night, that he was praying that Desmond would make a break for Dingle Bay. That way it would be Stanley, not he, who would make the capture.

Brendan stared into the darkness, the rustle and coughing and curses from his men a background to his thoughts. During the day he was able to push all remembrances of Katherine to the back of his mind, but the nights were another matter. He had become inured to the stench of unwashed bodies and ordure, but although five months had now passed since he had last seen Kate, he had not grown inured to their separation. His body still ached for her. It was not merely their coupling that he missed, it was everything about her: the warm female smell of her in his bed; the brilliance of her smile; even the irrational changes in her mood that reminded him greatly of summer days in Ireland, teeming rain one minute, bright sunshine the next.

"Oh, Kate, my darling," he groaned into the rolled up cloak-bag that served as his pillow. "Shall I ever see you again?" She was six months gone with their child now. He felt a rush of longing to see her swollen belly, his fingers spreading as he imagined himself stroking it, pressing his hands against it to feel the babe's movements.

Unless Desmond was captured soon, he would never know that joy, not with this child, at least. "Damn you to hell, Fitzgerald," he whispered. Immediately he felt a shiver of foreboding, lest the curse be turned upon him, and hurriedly crossed himself beneath the wolfskin cloak that was his bedcover.

Before daybreak on November the tenth, Brendan was shaken awake by his lieutenant. "There is news of Desmond, Captain."

Throwing back his cloak, Brendan sprang up, instantly awake. "What is it?" he barked.

"A man named Maurice O'Moriarty has been robbed of forty kine and some horses."

"How can he be sure it was Desmond who robbed him?" demanded Brendan, as he marched ahead, dragging on his deerskin over-jerkin as he went.

"You may ask for yourself, Captain. His brother, Owen O'Moriarty is here, in the hall."

By the time he had heard O'Moriarty's story, Brendan was certain that it had been Desmond's followers who had committed the robbery.

"You say they actually entered the house?"

"They did that. And stripped my brother's wife and children of all their clothing, they did, God rot their souls." The man's eyes narrowed. "But they will be paying for it, to be sure. I know every inch of this land, Captain. They will not be hiding our cattle from me, I am telling you."

Brendan looked thoughtfully at the man before him, his fingers rubbing against his bearded chin. It could be a ruse to draw him from the castle, so that Desmond could slip by him. On the other hand, he could not risk sending the O'Moriartys on their own to search for Desmond.

"How many men have you?" he asked.

"Close to thirty. The entire O'Moriarty family will be at my back." He spat on the ground. "What there is left of it, no thanks to Desmond."

"Good. Lieutenant O'Kelly here will accompany you with a small troop of soldiers from the garrison." Brendan turned to the lieutenant. "Anything larger would be an encumbrance in the mountains. On the other hand, if we do not send enough men Desmond might be tempted to try an ambush on the company."

He drew O'Kelly aside to give him his final orders. "Desmond is to be brought back unharmed, you understand? Keep an eye on the O'Moriartys lest they decide to take the law into their own hands. Do not at any time forget that you are in command of this venture."

Once the company of soldiers and O'Moriartys bent on vengeance had left, Brendan set the rest of the garrison on alert, sending out sentries to several outpost positions so that every avenue of escape was closed.

Having done that, he readied himself for the long wait, first checking all the lookout points and then sending word to Captain Stanley that the end might be near, warning him to be prepared lest Desmond make a last desperate run westward to the coast.

The day dragged on, the tension of waiting coupled with inactivity making everyone in the garrison nervous. Tempers grew short and by evening Brendan had to step in to deal with several small flare-ups over such minor matters as cheating in a dicing game or a dispute as to whether or not a soldier had too large a portion of ale in his tankard.

Fortunately, for once the weather was on their side. Very little cloud. When night fell, the full moon shone brightly. If it remained thus, visibility even in the steep-sided glens would be excellent.

The possibility of having the rebellion at an end after so much misery was hard to believe. Four years had passed since the Fitzgerald rebellion had begun, four years that had brought utter devastation to Munster in particular, so that almost all its people had perished through famine or disease, in battle or by execution.

"Do you think the country will ever recover?" asked Lieutenant Barrow, who hailed from Somerset, as they dined on turnip stew that night.

"You mean will Munster ever recover? I doubt it," Brendan replied, between mouthfuls of the watery broth. "Or, I should say, it will never be the same again. If there is to be a harvest of any kind next year, they will have to import men from England and give them the incentive of their own land."

Barrow's face brightened. "That is what I am hoping for, sir," he said in his rich Somerset drawl.

"I expect you are."

That was Ralegh's favorite plan, of course, the plantation of Englishmen on Irish soil. Englishmen to own the land, run the country. "It is the only way Ireland can be governed," he had told the Queen during their conversation at Whitehall Palace. "From within." Desmond's rebellion and the subsequent famine its suppression had caused had made this plan eminently possible.

The next morning, there was still no word. Having made a full inspection of the garrison to ensure that the long wait had not made his troop lax in their preparedness, Brendan climbed up the spiral stone stairway that led to the upper floor of the castle. Acknowledging the salute from his lookouts posted on the curtain wall, he peered through the broken parapet, searching for some sign of movement in the hills that surrounded the castle. But all he could see or hear was the River Maine, swollen from the heavy rains that had fallen until now.

He turned to go down again, but something held him back. Since his arrival at the castle he had fought the urge to go to the top of the square tower, which was still standing. It was both a desire and a dread to him. Now he knew that he could no longer fight it.

Carefully, he mounted the winding stair, the steps so narrow that his feet could barely get a purchase on them. He used to be able to fly up and down them, he recalled, as fleet as any mountain goat. But the stones were not crumbling away then, and his feet were much smaller. The feet of a young boy.

His heart was pounding in his breast when he reached the top floor, but he knew that it was not from lack of breath.

For many weeks he had been avoiding this tiny chamber with its narrow window slits and uneven flagged floor. Now, with an end in sight, he sought it out. Perhaps it was a kind of justice that the man who had banished his lovely young cousin and her child to solitary imprisonment in this cell most likely would be handed over to that child, now a grown man, in this very castle.

He had never found out exactly how his father and mother had met. It was even remotely possible that he had been conceived in Castlemaine. Certainly it must have been on one of his father's visits to Munster as Governor of Ireland. The Earl of Desmond had not always been a rebel. He would have hosted the Earl of Sussex sometime at one or more of his castles.

All Brendan knew was that some spark of love or lust had ignited between Aileen Fitzgerald and the mighty Earl of Sussex, and that he had been the result.

The Earl of Sussex, having planted his seed, had ridden away.

When Desmond had discovered his young cousin's disgrace, he had banished her to this cell in Castlemaine, forbidding her to leave it, on pain of death. And here she had raised her son, tending to his needs by herself. Teaching him to read and write, to play the lute and pipe. But, most of all, she had taught him by example how to endure.

He, in his turn, sensing her longing to be free, had brought her the first primroses in spring, then the fluffy pussy willows—whose buds he joyed in rubbing up and down her soft cheek—and sheaves of wild white lilies, their flowers as pale as her skin.

One day, he remembered, he had burst into the tiny chamber, his arms laden with branches of hawthorn covered in frothy white blossom, but she had exclaimed in horror at this. Grabbing the branches from him, she had thrown them out the narrow window slit. "Never bring thorn blossom inside, my darling," she told him, when she had dried his disappointed tears. "It brings ill fortune."

Whether it was the hawthorn or not, fortune certainly had not smiled upon him or his mother. And yet in a way they had been happy together, living their strange secluded life in this cell, the wind always in their ears and about their feet.

Eventually, Brendan had been permitted to join in the life in the castle, but his mother remained shut away.

Only now, as he looked about the tiny chamber, which measured not much more than seven feet across, did he realize how devastating his going away must have been to her. For eight years he had been her sole companion, her one bond with the outside world. Yet she had been the one to write to Sussex to beg him to take his son and educate him as a gentleman.

He recalled now, through the haze of time, that he had been excited at the prospect of going all the way across the breadth of Ireland to Dublin. He had given her the present of a green linnet in a gilded cage. "So that you will have a friend," he told her. "And instead of me playing the pipe for you, she can sing for you."

She had wept then, he remembered. She had turned her face from him, the face he could no longer recall. But he could recall the tears welling up in her eyes and trickling down her cheeks. "I hate him, I hate him," he had shouted, tears flowing down his own cheeks. "One day when I am a man I shall kill him."

She had taken him into her arms, pressing him close to her breast then. "Hush, my darling. You must not be hating your cousin. He is a just man. I am the one to blame, not him. Most men would have killed their kinswomen for what I did."

But to young Brendan his mother was blameless. The Fitzgeralds and their leader, the Earl of Desmond, were to be hated for locking her away.

Now, with the wisdom of an adult man, he saw the truth in what she had told him. Compared to others, Desmond had indeed been merciful.

"My darling Mam," Brendan murmured, his head pressed against the damp stone wall, "what must it have been like when I left you here alone, your only companions your linnet and your books?"

The slimy walls, green with lichen, themselves gave back the answer. For the first time he knew the true extent of her sacrifice. Here, she had given birth to him and here she had died. Had she been alone at the hour of her death? he wondered. Had she been given the last rites of the faith that had been her one solace? Or had they left her to gasp out her last breath alone in the dark, windswept tower?

"Captain!"

The urgent call jerked Brendan back to the present. Someone was calling him from the foot of the stairs. He peered down. "What is it?"

Barrow's red-cheeked face appeared around the corner of the winding stair. He was grinning from ear to ear. "They've got 'im, sir. They've got Desmond. O'Kelly sent a messenger ahead to say that they captured him at daybreak this morning."

Brendan went down the steps to join him. "Where was he?"

"In the woods of Glenageenty."

"Holy Mother of God, how did he slip past Tralee, I wonder?"

"The Lord knows, but he's captured now, thank God. O'Kelly has sent word they're bringing him in to the castle."

So it was over, thought Brendan, as they made their way down to the keep. Soon he would be face to face with his kinsman. Not for the first time on this campaign, he thanked God that he had taken his father's name. Unless someone who knew told him, Desmond would never recognize in the tall captain with the English surname the little lad who had been his fair cousin's son.

Two hours later, the troop rode into the forecourt. Steeling himself, Brendan went out to meet them. His eyes scanned the faces of the few men on horseback, but saw none that was not familiar. He saw the grinning face of Owen O'Moriarty and Lieutenant Daniel O'Kelly's, strangely white.

"Where is Desmond?" he demanded, his voice sharp with anxiety lest something had gone wrong.

"He is here, or at least part of him, God curse his soul." Owen held up a bag of rawhide.

Even from a distance, Brendan could see the dark stain that smeared the bag. A roaring sound, like the pounding of the sea against the Skellig Rocks, filled his ears. Steeling himself, he strode forward to take the bag from O'Moriarty. Before he reached him, however, the man drew open the top of the bag and Brendan found himself looking down at the head of the Earl of Desmond, his mouth gaping wide in his bloodless face.

Chapter 28

Brendan looked up from the disgusting object in the bag. His eyes fixed on the ashen-faced lieutenant. "O'Kelly," he barked. "Get inside, and bring that," nodding to the bag, "with you."

"If it please you, sir," said O'Kelly, licking dry lips, "what about the body?"

Christ in heaven! Brendan had forgotten that where there was a head, there should be a body also. He was rigid with anger. "Where is it?"

"We have it on a cart outside, Captain," muttered O'Moriarty, his glee somewhat subdued.

"Bring it into the courtyard." At first, no one moved to carry out his order. "Now!" he roared. A group of his own soldiers broke rank and rushed from the forecourt to do his bidding.

With a raucous screech of unoiled wheels, the cart clattered in, drawn by an ancient nag, which had probably escaped being eaten because it would be too tough. Desmond's headless body lay wrapped in sacking on the flat boards.

"Unwrap it," Brendan told Barrow, loathe to touch the thing himself. "Be careful," he snapped, as Barrow tugged at the sacking.

Barrow gave him a surprised glance. It was not like a soldier to be squeamish about dead bodies, especially one with Captain Radcliffe's years of experience.

"The Earl of Desmond's body will have to be taken as evidence to the Earl of Ormonde at Kilkenny," Brendan said, as if to explain his qualms. "Therefore it must be treated with the greatest of care."

When Barrow had unwrapped the body, Brendan stepped forward. His gorge rose as he saw the severed neck vessels and the pool of blood. The clothes were stiff with filth, rank, as if they had not been changed for weeks. Beneath them he could see that the body of his kinsman was emaciated. The cattle he had stolen had come a little too late to ease his hunger, it seemed.

Fastidiously, Brendan drew back the matted cloak, the deerhide jerkin, to reveal a fresh swordcut on the right arm. "Who did this?"

"I did, sir," said O'Kelly from the rear. He seemed reluctant to look at the body. "The man—"

"You mean the Earl of Desmond?" asked Brendan. O'Kelly nodded. "Then say so."

"I will, sir. The Earl was reaching for his sword, so I cut him so as he could not use it."

"Why are there no other prisoners?"

O'Moriarty pushed forward now, determined to take charge. "There was only one other man there, sir, and he fled out the back of the hut where we found them. The others must have fled afore we came. 'Tis likely they went for help."

Brendan looked down again at the shrunken body. "Did Desmond say anything when you took him?"

"All he said was, 'I am the Earl of Desmond. Save my life,'" O'Kelly muttered.

O'Moriarty shouldered the visibly shaking lieutenant out of the way. "And I says to Desmond, says I, 'You killed yourself long ago, when you took up arms 'gainst the Queen's Majesty. Now you are our prisoner.'"

The man stuck out his chest and grinned about him at the other members of his clan.

Brendan turned to Lieutenant Barrow. "Bring the body and head into the armory. O'Kelly, O'Moriarty, I'll speak with you in my chamber. Privately," he added swiftly, when he saw the rest of the O'Moriartys prepared to follow their leader.

"Well now," he said, when they were alone. "Perhaps you would both be so kind as to tell me why you saw fit to strike off Desmond's head, when I particularly enjoined Lieutenant O'Kelly to bring him here unharmed."

"It was like this, Captain," began O'Moriarty. "You see, we—"

"I'll hear it from the lieutenant first, if you please, Master Moriarty," said Brendan, his voice soft as silk.

O'Kelly shuffled his feet and then lifted his bullet head, still clad in a steel helmet. "The Earl could not walk, Captain. We had to carry him through the glen. 'Twas slow going, to be sure. Then we caught sight of men through the trees on the other side of the glen. A great troop of them there was."

"There must have been, if you thought they would outnumber your forty or more men," Brendan said drily.

"We'd left our horses back on the hill and climbed down the steep side of the ravine, you see," explained O'Kelly. "So we were open targets for Desmond's followers. And—"

"And with Desmond to carry back up the steep glen," Owen O'Moriarty interrupted, impatient with O'Kelly's hesitant account, "we were trapped. I knew if they rescued Desmond, you'd have *our* heads, to be sure. What, says I to myself, would the Captain do if he were here? I prayed to the Holy Saint Patrick, and he gave me the answer. 'Strike off his head,' says I to O'Kelly. 'Strike it off with your sword.' That way, you see, the Fitzgeralds would see no point in attacking us. And if they did, we'd be able to fight them without Desmond to worry about."

"So Lieutenant O'Kelly struck off Desmond's head with his sword?" Brendan said, his words measured out slowly.

"He did that. Clean as a whistle, the sword cut through him." O'Moriarty winked at the anxious lieutenant. "A sweet sharp blade, that, O'Kelly. 'Tis a good soldier you are to Her Majesty. Then," he said to Brendan, "I raised the head on high so as the Fitzgeralds on the other side could see it, still dripping blood. 'Here is your mighty Earl of Desmond,' I shouts to them. You should have seen them run! Like rats from a burning haycock. With their leader dead, they'd no stomach for a fight. Poor fear-shitten knaves they were."

Brendan surveyed the two men, the one a preening braggart, the other a weak officer who had dithered in a crisis, and then caved in to the stronger man. At least that was how it looked on the surface. Who knew what story lay beneath? There was no doubt that O'Moriarty's standing with his clan would be much higher now than it would have been had he merely been instrumental in capturing Desmond and bringing him back alive to Castlemaine.

Personal vengeance ranked higher than service to Her Majesty in these parts, Brendan knew.

He paced around the rough board across a gun chest that served as his desk. God's wounds! He should have gone to take Desmond himself. He could just hear Ormonde now. "So you thought it best not to sully your hands with your kinsman's blood, Captain *Radcliffe*," with that emphasis on Brendan's new name that always made Brendan grit his teeth. Butler and Fitzgerald. There had been enmity between the two clans for centuries; since the days they had come to Ireland as Normans, in truth, before they were assimilated and became more Irish than the ancient Irish people themselves.

And whatever name Brendan chose to call himself, to Thomas Butler, Earl of Ormonde, he was still a Fitzgerald, and therefore suspect.

He drew in a long breath and let it out in a sigh. "Well, the attack on your brother and his family is now avenged, it seems, O'Moriarty. You may send the rest of your family home, but I wish you to wait at Castlemaine."

O'Moriarty's grin faded. "Can I be asking you what for, sir?"

"You can. I am sending to Dingle for Captain Stanley. When he arrives, I wish you to accompany him to Kilkenny Castle, to tell your story to the Earl of Ormonde. And, as I shall be writing down your present version of it, I advise you not to add any embellishments to it, unless you choose to change your story and advise me before you leave. You understand me?"

"I do, Captain, I do that."

"Good. Then go send your followers home. I've a wish to speak with Lieutenant O'Kelly alone."

The burly O'Moriarty strode out, glancing at the bag on the desk as he left.

Raindrops began to fall on the makeshift roof of tarpaulin stretched over cut tree branches above them. Brendan shivered. He hoped he would be relieved of his post here soon. It remained to be seen what would happen once the news of Desmond's death reached England. He dared not entertain the speck of hope that leapt in his breast at the thought that he might even be granted leave to go home. Better not to hope than to be disappointed.

He went to stand before the young lieutenant. "Now that we are alone, O'Kelly, I should like the truth from you."

"'Twas exactly the way O'Moriarty told you, Captain Radcliffe." The younger man's eyes met his, blinking rapidly.

"How many men would you say there were on the other side of the glen?"

O'Kelly licked his lips. "Ach, now you have me, sir. 'Twas dark and there were shadows. . . ."

"Guess at it, then."

"I would say about fifty or sixty men, sir."

"Would you, now? Yet the Earl of Desmond had only one follower with him when you entered the hut. Strange that so many could be gathered together in such a brief time."

"Most like they had been hiding in the glen from the start and only came out when they saw us take Desmond," suggested O'Kelly.

"Most like." Brendan rubbed at the back of his neck, feeling the tension there. "Your sword, if you please, lieutenant," he said, holding out his hand.

Anger flared in the soldier's eyes for a moment and then he took his sword from its scabbard and handed it to Brendan. The bright blade was stained as if it had turned rusty. "You would have done the same, Captain," he protested, "rather than have them release Desmond."

"Perhaps I would. But for now I am relieving you of your duties until I have made further enquiries."

"Am I to be placed under guard?" O'Kelly asked through stiff lips.

"That is up to you, Danny." Brendan smiled for the first time. "I doubt you'd fare very well here in Fitzgerald country if you were to leave the castle."

"May I go then, sir?"

"You may. But if you remember aught else about the incident, perhaps you would share it with me. I shall be sending you with O'Moriarty to Kilkenny, so I would advise you to get your story straight before you face the Governor, or he'll be far harder on you than I have been."

O'Kelly's expression grew even more miserable.

"Cheer up, man. You never can tell. Maybe he will offer you a reward for having rid him of Desmond and for having saved the Crown the expense and trouble of putting him on trial for treason."

The next morning, Stanley arrived from Dingle with a large troop of men at his back. Before noon, he left for Kilkenny, bearing Desmond's head, now wrapped in clean linen on Brendan's orders, and accompanied by O'Moriarty and O'Kelly.

Brendan had spoken the truth when he had told Daniel O'Kelly that Ormonde might be so pleased to have his enemy dead he would reward him. There was no telling with Black Tom. The man was utterly unpredictable.

One thing was certain, he thought, as he went back into the keep, his own judgment was decidedly clouded by his mixed feelings at the manner of Desmond's death. The child in him exulted at the death of the man who had imprisoned his mother. The solider in him exulted in the death of the enemy who had eluded them for so long. The man in him exulted in the death of a man who had caused so much misery to his own loyal followers, who had shown little mercy to his enemies, whose pride and tenacity had destroyed his country.

But the Fitzgerald blood in Brendan seethed with indignation at the Earl of Desmond's mean death, with no priest to shrive him, at the indignities afforded his body.

"What shall we do with the body, Captain?"

Brendan started. Lieutenant Barrow was at his elbow.

"The body?" Brendan repeated, as if he were stupid.

"Aye, sir. Someone said as how the rats might—"

"To be sure," Brendan said hastily. He thought for a moment.

"Should we bury it, think you, sir?"

"I think not. I must await the Governor's orders."

"He'll no doubt chop it up and have the quarters displayed somewhere," said the always practical Barrow.

"No doubt." More indignities. Brendan wished he *could* bury the body, here, in the woods near Castlemaine. In Fitzgerald country.

"Find a gun chest and put the body in there. But wrap it in linen first, as you did the head."

"Aye, sir."

"And then put it in the little chamber just off the great hall. It was once a chapel," he added, feeling an urge to explain.

It was soon done. Brendan wished he could secretly have found a priest to pray over his kinsman, to help ease his long wait in purgatory, but Catholic priests were even harder to find in Ireland than they were in England.

With the body in the gun chest and the top nailed down, Brendan felt a little better. But still, when night came, and he lay down on the unrolled bale of straw that was his bed, he could not sleep. He dozed off and on, but the horrific visions of Desmond's eyes in the trunkless head glaring down at him shocked him awake.

Eventually, he could bear it no longer and got up. Wrapping his mantle about him, he trod softly across the cellar floor, so as not to wake the other men, and mounted the short stairway to the keep.

He was about to go outside when something, a slight sound like a loosened stone, stopped him. The sound came from the direction of the old chapel. Drawing his dagger—and wishing he had thought to bring his sword with him—he moved silently along the screen passageway, halting just outside the crumbling archway into the chapel.

It was almost pitch-dark, but the moonlight shone intermittently through scudding clouds, affording a few streaks of light through the open roof of the castle.

Breathing lightly, Brendan flattened himself against the stone wall and then peered into the chapel. Six or seven men were busy trying to pry open the coffin. He was about to give the alarm, when the light from the lantern one man held illuminated the holder's face.

It was Colum, Brendan's groom.

Stifling a curse, Brendan crept closer, straining his ears to hear their whispers. They were speaking in Irish.

"Is it sure you are that he is in here?" one said.

"Haven't I been telling you the captain said to put the body in a gun chest in the chapel?" It was Colum's voice answering. "I could tell by the way he looked that he'd have ordered candles for his head and feet, too, if he'd been able."

Brendan cursed inwardly. Were his thoughts that easy to read?

"Jesus, Mary and Joseph," someone breathed, "but these nails are hard to move."

"Could we not carry the coffin out as it is?"

"And invite the sentries to the wake as well, is it?" said Colum. "Keep at it. You'll have it off soon."

Why am I standing here watching them? Brendan asked himself. *Why haven't I given the alarm?*

As if God-sent, his answer came.

"For the love of God, put your elbow into it, man. If you do not, the English will chop the chief of the Fitzgeralds into gobbets and set them up in London for people to spit upon."

The warning must have put strength into the man's elbow, for only a moment passed before Brendan heard the screech of nail against wood over and over again. He winced, holding his breath, certain that the sounds must have been heard by one of the lookouts. And in that moment he knew whose side he was on. There was still time to give the alarm, but he did not.

Excited whispers. "We have it now. Here it is."

Brendan glanced sideways into the chapel. They were lifting the body out with great care, with a sense of reverence that had been entirely lacking in the soldiers' and the O'Moriartys' treatment of it.

Now they were coming out. Brendan slipped into a niche in the broken wall, trusting that the light from Colum's lantern would not seek him out. But they were too intent on escaping with their burden to notice him. He waited in his hiding place for several minutes before moving, his heart beating hard against his chest, expecting at every moment to hear the alarm given. But all was silent.

He was about to make his way back down to the cellar, and actually had his foot on one step, when he heard a footfall behind him. Spinning around, his dagger poised, he came face to face with Colum.

"What the devil are you about, man?" he asked him.

Moonlight struck his groom's face through the open roof of the castle. Its expression bore a mixture of fear and bravado. "I saw you," Colum whispered, after a long pause.

"Saw me where?"

"By the chapel. I saw you when we carried the body out."

Brendan froze.

"If I had told them you were there, for sure the men would have slit your throat," Colum said.

"But you did not tell them," said Brendan.

"I did not. And you did not give the alarm, Captain."

Brendan ignored the unspoken question. "What will they do with the body?"

"They are Fitzgeralds. As we are. They will hide it until the search for it is stopped, and then they will bury himself in the Fitzgerald chapel in Tralee."

Of course. The Chapel of the Name, it was called. The place where nearly all the Fitzgerald chiefs were buried, in the Dominican Friary of the Holy Cross. The fitting burial place for the last Earl of Desmond.

"Get back to the horses," Brendan told him. "And do not be forgetting that, if at any time you might think of betraying me, I'll not hesitate to name you as the leader of the men who stole Desmond's body."

To Brendan's amazement, when he went into the chapel the next morning he found that someone had nailed the gun chest shut again. It was not until three days later, when it was raised in preparation to send it to Cork on Ormonde's orders, that the theft of the body was discovered.

The alarm was given, enquiries made, but the trail was cold by then, and despite an intensive search the body was not found.

Part 3
1584

Chapter 29

Christmas at Radcliffe Hall had been a melancholy time compared to the previous year. Now that the rebellion in Ireland was at an end, Katherine had hoped that Brendan would be able to obtain leave to travel home, but he had written to her at the beginning of December, to say that he could not leave Munster. The new Deputy-General of Ireland, Sir John Perrot, was about to take office and Brendan must be there for his arrival.

So the short gray days and long dark nights of January dragged by and Katherine grew slower and heavier. There were many things she resented about her pregnancy: not being able to run fleet-footed up and down stairs, to ride pell-mell across the gallops on Middleham High Moor—unless you could call being perched on the back of a barrel-bellied mule riding; but, most of all, she hated to look at herself in the long mirror of polished steel in her bedchamber.

"I am weary of wearing shapeless meal-sacks," she told her mother one morning at the end of January, as they sat sewing together.

Alyssa looked up and smiled at her. "It will not be long now, Kate. A few more weeks at the most."

Katherine smacked her hands down on the hummock that was her belly. "I shall never see my waist again."

Alyssa laughed aloud at this. "Oh, dearest, of course you will. I bore three children, yet I have a waist."

It was true, thought Katherine. Her mother had a waist and a very trim figure. For a moment she saw her as a stranger might see her and was surprised. Her mother was still a very attractive woman. Her nut-brown hair, coiled about her head with two smooth wings over her forehead, had little gray in it. Her skin, though pale, was soft and smooth. And her brown eyes were still gold-sparked when she smiled, which she did frequently.

"Have you ever considered marrying again, Mother?"

Alyssa looked up from her tapestry frame, her mouth open in astonishment. "Heavens, Kate, what made you ask such a thing?"

Katherine shrugged and gave her a sheepish smile. "I don't know. I was just thinking that . . . that you would make some man a good wife, that was all."

Her mother frowned. "At thirty-eight I am far too old and set in my ways to wed some stranger." She bent over the frame. "Besides, I have no desire to marry again."

The moment was there. They were alone. Katherine had only to open her mouth and the long-stifled questions would come pouring out. *Why did you hate my father? Were you and my grandfather lovers? Was he Richard's father? Did the two of you conspire to murder my father?*

But she could not do it. How could she ask such appalling questions of the little woman who sat before her tapestry frame, her small hands skillfully weaving the crimson silk thread in and out of the canvas? To disturb the even tenor of their lives now, when Katherine was feeling most vulnerable, most in need of her mother's comfort and reassurances, was unthinkable.

Once again the questions were stuffed away in some remote repository in her mind, the door closed, the key turned, but she knew that they would always be there, ready to spring out again like a hideous jack-in-the-box at some unexpected moment.

"Are you still planning to visit Aunt Isobel tomorrow?" she asked, after a long interval of silence.

Her mother continued to sew. "So long as it doesn't snow again. Tobias says that the roadway is clear as far as Middleham at least."

"I wish you would not go," Katherine murmured, her words almost inaudible.

"Why not?"

Katherine glared at her. "Because you might be snowed in at Colborne Place. What would happen to me then?"

Her mother stuck the needle into her needlecase, stood up and came to her. "My darling Kate," she said, putting her arms about her from behind. "It is hardly likely that I would be trapped at Colborne for three weeks, is it? And even if I were, you silly goose, you would be perfectly well looked after by Margery and Joan."

Katherine turned in sudden panic and snatched at her mother's hands. "Don't say that. I could not manage without you."

Her mother smiled down at her. "You could, you know, and very well, too. But you will not have to. I shall return from Colborne long before nightfall tomorrow."

She took Katherine's face between her hands. "Forgive me, Kate. I do not like to make you anxious, but Isobel has not been at all well recently. I haven't seen her since Twelfth Night, and she was looking terribly unwell then, so thin and pale. I am deeply concerned about her."

If she knew the dreadful things her sister had said about her, thought Katherine, she would probably refuse ever to see Isobel again. Yet another reason why she should not confront her mother at this time.

"I must get up. My feet are growing numb again." Leaning on her mother's arm for balance, Katherine stood up. "I am concerned about Aunt Isobel, too. Of course you must go, Mother. I am just being foolish."

Alyssa gave her a fond smile. "It is natural. We all feel that way when our time is almost upon us."

Katherine rubbed at her forehead. "It is strange. I both wish for it and dread it." She turned away. "I wish Brendan could have come home in time." Her mouth quivered. What in the name of all the saints was the matter with her? It was not like her to feel this way and she rarely spoke of her longing to see Brendan again.

"He would have been here if he had been able, you know that, dearest," said her mother.

"Was my father here for my birth?"

Her mother's hand, outstretched to caress her, froze in mid-air. "He was."

"And Joanna's?"

"Yes."

No little anecdotes, no fond tales of her father's excitement at the birth of his first child. Nothing. It had ever been thus. Her father denied to her, a blank page, the faceless figure of a phantom. Only

Aunt Isobel's few tales of him to fill in some of the gaps, and even she always held something back.

Part of her was missing, Katherine felt, and until she discovered it she would never be entirely whole.

"Well, I must be off to meet with Applegarth about the new shepherd," her mother said briskly. "Stay here in the warm. I'll send Joanna up to keep you company. She should have finished her lessons with Master Paget by now."

Katherine nodded and smiled at her mother as she left the solar, but inside she bristled with resentment. Since her return to Radcliffe, she had found herself relegated to the role of daughter of the household again. It was her mother who managed Radcliffe Manor, her mother and Tobias.

"But I am mistress of Radcliffe," Katherine muttered. She kicked the footstool. "And, by God, once this baby is born, I shall make sure everyone knows that."

She turned as Joanna burst into the room. "Lessons finished?"

"Aye, they are, thank the Lord." Joanna grimaced. "How I hate Latin! I keep telling Mother that I am too old now to be taking lessons with old Master Paget. Pah! He stinks of garlic."

"No doubt you also told Mother, as you always do, that she was already betrothed at your age?"

"I did, but to no avail." She came to sit beside Katherine on the settle. "Oh, Kate, I long to be married like you, with a handsome husband and my own home and a baby coming. How fortunate you are."

Katherine smiled wryly. "I see no husband about, do you? As far as a home of my own, I have no say in the management of Radcliffe. And, as for the baby, I cannot sleep at night for its kicking me, my ankles are all swollen and I feel like a prize cow."

"Oh, you are in a sorry state this morning." Joanna flung her arms about her sister and hugged her. "But you cannot put me off that easily. I would exchange places with you any day."

Katherine could not help smiling at Joanna's exuberance. Her sister could charm anyone out of a melancholy mood. "And have you a young gentleman in mind to help you fulfill this dream of domesticity?" she asked.

To her surprise, Joanna's plump cheeks reddened. She jumped up and pretended to examine her mother's tapestry in the wooden frame. "Promise me you will not tell Mother."

"Of course I won't tell her."

"She would only say I was still too young," Joanna hastened to explain. "It is Harry Seaton."

"Oh, Joanna. A younger son." Katherine shook her head. "You can do much better for yourself than that."

Joanna frowned. "You sound just like Mother, Kate." She lifted her chin. "I happen to love Harry."

"Nonsense. You barely know him. How could you possibly love him?"

"We have been meeting at the old tower on Melmerby Moor," Joanna muttered, turning her face away.

Katherine levered herself up from the settle and went to her sister. "You haven't done anything to be ashamed of, I hope."

Joanna's soft brown eyes flared with indignation. "Of course I haven't. And shame on you, Kate Radcliffe, to think such a thing of your sister."

"Forgive me, but it is so unlike you to be so secretive, I thought—"

"Well, you may think again. You dishonor not only me but also Harry to be even thinking such a thing."

Katherine hid a smile at the sight of her small, plump sister staunchly defending the honor of herself and her sweetheart. "I most humbly beg your pardon."

"Will you help us, Kate?" Joanna asked eagerly.

"How?"

"You could drop little hints to Mother about what a charming young gentleman Harry Seaton is."

"Rather difficult, considering I have exchanged little more than a 'good day' with him."

"Perhaps you could ride over to visit his mother and sisters?"

"In my condition? Do be serious, Joanna."

Her sister's face fell. "Of course not. That was foolish of me."

"It was, indeed. And so is this idea of marriage. You are only sixteen."

"Three of my friends are already wed at sixteen. And you were only seventeen when you were betrothed to Brendan."

"I was married five months after my eighteenth birthday, I would remind you," Katherine said coldly, determined to squelch this nonsense before it got out of hand. "You are a Radcliffe, Joanna. You must set your sights far higher than Harry Seaton. His grandfather was a mere yeoman."

"At least *Harry's* father married his mother." As soon as she spoke, Joanna clamped her hand over her mouth. "Oh, Kate," she whispered. "I never meant to say that. Forgive me."

Katherine glared at her. Her hand itched to slap her sister's pink cheek. "I would remind you, Sister, that I had no choice in the matter. You seem to have forgotten that I was forced to marry a stranger to enable you and the rest of the family to remain at Radcliffe. How was I to know he was a bastard?"

"But you did come to love Brendan afterwards, didn't you, Kate?" Joanna asked in a small, pleading voice.

"I have feelings of affection for Brendan. He is a kind man." Katherine chose her words with great care.

"But you do not love him?" Joanna's eyes were big with disappointment.

"You have been reading too many of Sir Thomas Wyatt's love poems, Mistress Joanna. Go, see if dinner is ready yet. I am starving hungry and smell roast onions."

Joanna crossed the floor, her head down. She paused at the door as if she would say something, but then opened it and went out.

Katherine remained staring at the door long after her sister had gone. She knew she had dealt badly with her. She could have been more kind, more tactful. The first pangs of love were always the sharpest.

And therein, she suddenly realized, lay the reason for her unkindness to Joanna. Why should her sister be encouraged in her desire to marry her first love, when she, Katherine, had been denied hers?

Thoughts of Edward had come less frequently to her during the first year of her marriage, but Brendan's absence and the forced inaction of the later months of her pregnancy had turned her mind inward of late.

Three years had passed since she had last seen Edward. All she knew of him was the news his mother imparted, and that was precious little. He was still in Rome and probably had taken holy orders by now.

However hard she tried, Katherine found it difficult to conjure up his face. She squeezed her eyes shut now, screwing up her face in an effort to see the beloved countenance, to remember the voice which had held such power to thrill her. But nothing was there, bar a halo of golden hair around a vague, ever-changing oval of a face, like a cloud-wreathed moon.

Sighing deeply, she crossed the floor and heaved herself up to sit in the window seat of the oriel window.

There was some commotion down in the inner courtyard. Grooms leading horses to the stables. She was not in the mood for visitors and hoped her mother would be able to fob them off. Perhaps she would send word down that she would take her dinner here, in the solar.

She heard feet on the stairs, raised voices on the landing. God's wounds, could she not be left in peace? She hated people to see her nowadays and was in no mood for chitchat.

Sighing, she slid from the window seat, smoothed down the wide skirts of her worsted gown edged with marten fur, and waited for the door to open.

When it did, it was to disclose a tall figure in riding clothes, the leather breeches and boots splashed with mud.

"Brendan?" Katherine whispered. For a moment, she thought it was some vision she was seeing.

The vision strode across the chamber, very real with his beaming smile and boots that squelched mud across the gleaming oak-planked floor.

"By God, it is good to see you, Kate."

"I cannot believe you are here. Why did you not send word that you were coming home?"

But all he could say as he stood before her was, "Let me look at you, Caitlin darling."

She gave an embarrassed little laugh. "No, no. Don't look at me. I am a terrible sight. Monstrous!"

"Not look at you? All during this damnable journey home I have been thinking of nothing else but being able to feast my eyes upon you."

"I am ugly. A great tub."

He shook his head slowly. "You are the most beautiful sight I have ever seen, my darling." His eyes drank in her face and then her body. "Our child," he said with an expression of wonderment. "May I?" he whispered, one hand tentatively stretched out.

She nodded, embarrassed and yet touched by the awed expression in his blue eyes.

First the tips of his fingers touched her belly. Then his entire hand circled the mound that was their child. And all the time his eyes shone with that sense of wonderment. Then he pressed both hands against her and stroked her belly back and forth. A jolt of raw pleasure ran from his hands to her loins.

"Oh, Brendan, how glad I am to see you," she said with a little sob, and threw her arms about his neck to kiss him.

His lips were cold against hers, but they soon warmed as he kissed her hungrily, straining her against his body as if striving to meld the two of them into one. "My darling, my darling, my darling," he whispered, his face wet against hers.

Then he suddenly jerked back. "What the devil . . . !"

For a second, Katherine wondered what ailed him. Then she laughed. "Did the babe kick you? You will grow used to that. He keeps me awake most of the night nowadays. Give me your hand."

He held his hand out and she took it in hers and pressed it firmly against her belly. Then the baby squirmed, its foot pressing against her in the delicious sensation that never ceased to amaze her. She saw her own amazement mirrored in Brendan's eyes.

"'Tis the babe itself kicking against my hand?"

"Of course."

"Our child."

"Yes, Brendan. Our child." She met his eyes and saw the unashamed tears swimming in them. "Soon to be born. Very soon, I hope."

"'Twas my one concern. That I would not arrive in time for the birth. I did not send word ahead of my coming because I knew no messenger could ride faster than I could. All the way from Dublin, on the boat crossing the sea to Wales, riding through snows and storms, I kept thinking. 'What if I do not arrive in time? What if something happens to Kate?'"

"What a Jonah you are. Nothing is going to happen to me. But I own I shall be glad to have it over with."

"My poor Kate. Here am I, thinking only of my joy at being home with you. Has it been a difficult time for you, sweetheart?"

She looked at him, seeing him properly for the first time since he had come in the door. "No, not difficult, merely tedious. But you, Brendan. You are grown so thin and you have lost all the color in your face. Have you been sick in Ireland?"

He turned his face away. "In spirit, perhaps, but not in body. There was not much food to go round. That should soon be changed, though. As for color, the sun does not shine much in Ireland, nowadays."

"Well, we can talk about all that later. For now, you must get those wet clothes off you at once. They are soaked."

They were, indeed. Steam was rising from him as he stood before the fire and a puddle had formed at their feet.

"How good it is to be home again." He looked about the solar, open hunger and love in his eyes.

"Why, I do believe you love Radcliffe as much as I do," said Katherine.

"It is my home, my only home," he said simply. "The very thought of leaving it again makes me heartsick."

Katherine felt a qualm about her heart. So he was not home to stay. She said nothing, determined to make his homecoming a joyous occasion, but his words had cast a shadow on her pleasure.

"First, fresh clothing, and then food," she said briskly, taking his hand. "I am famished, sir husband, and so is your child. Let us waste no more time in idle talk. Go, change those wet clothes and then let us celebrate your homecoming by eating dinner."

Chapter 30

Brendan had been given two months leave. After that he would have to return to Wales to escort the new Deputy General to Ireland. Now the weeks that Katherine had longed to see fly by also checked off the time that Brendan would be at Radcliffe.

His return brought color and laughter to their lives. Although Katherine was unable to walk far nowadays, and Brendan was busy about the estate, he would return frequently to spend time with her. Her heart lifted whenever she heard first his jaunty whistling in the hall and then his footsteps on the stairs.

Was this some sort of love, Katherine wondered as she waited for him in the parlor one day in mid-February, this quiet, warm feeling of comfortableness together, the joy of hearing the news of the manor and its people from him and seeing his pleasure in the telling of it? One thing was certain: It was not the burning fire-in-the-blood love she had once known. That she could never feel for anyone but Edward.

She sighed and returned to her embroidery. Doubtless it was nothing more than Dame Nature encouraging feelings of affection for her child's father in an impatiently expectant mother.

The first pains came in the middle of a Sunday night. She had felt vaguely uncomfortable the previous evening, but had put it down to an overindulgence in apple fritters with honey syrup. Although her mother had given her a posset, she had slept fitfully, waking several times. Now she awoke to a rolling pain that made her gasp.

"What is it?" Brendan asked, sitting up in the bed.

For a moment, she could not reply, the pain catching her breath. Then it receded. She could hear Brendan fumbling with the tinder-box and saw the candle flicker and then flame into warm light, illuminating his anxious face as he turned to her.

"Is it the baby?"

She nodded. "I believe so."

Before she could say any more, he had shot off the bed and was dragging on his bedgown.

She sat up, unable to withhold her laughter. "Oh, Brendan. I did not think that you, of all people, would act the anxious father-to-be."

He turned, already halfway to the door. "I fail to see any humor in the situation," he said, hurt at her laughter. "I was about to fetch your mother to you."

She swung her legs over the side of the bed and held out her hand to him. "Come back here. The babe will take its time. I wish to say something to you while I am able."

He fell on his knees before her. "Do not be saying such a thing. If anything were to happen to you—" He buried his face in her lap, pressing it against the child that was about to be born.

"By my life, Brendan Radcliffe, you are a cheery soul to have about me at such a time!" she said lightly, her fingers twining in his hair. "I assure you that nothing is going to happen to me, except that I am about to deliver our firstborn child." *God willing*, she added silently, not wishing the Almighty to think she was attempting to usurp His power.

Brendan looked up at her. "Pray forgive me, sweetheart, but—"

"You are afraid only because you do not know about such things. So it is with all men. I am not one whit afraid."

If only that were true. As the knot of pain began again in her belly, she experienced a longing to run away from what was before her. She took his hand, gripping it between hers. "Another pain is starting," she said in a surprised tone. "Let me say what I must and then you may fetch my mother. But first help me up, for I feel I would be more comfortable standing."

But when she stood, the wave of pain overtook her and she doubled over, her hands crossed over her belly, rocking back and forth.

"Oh, Jesu," said Brendan. "What can I do to help you?"

"You . . . can . . . stay here with me . . . until . . . this pain . . . is over," Katherine gasped out.

He did so, instinctively rubbing her back until the pain had receded. When it left her, Katherine looked up at him, breathing fast. "The pains are quite close together, which is unusual in a first child. I must tell you, Brendan, so do not interrupt me again, I pray you," she said, urgency sharpening her voice. "I have never thanked you fully for all you have done for me, for my family." Tears stung her eyes. "I can never thank you enough," she whispered. "I have not always been kind, I know, but—"

Brendan put his hand gently on her mouth. "Say no more. You have thanked me in a thousand different ways, sweetheart. You have given me Radcliffe. You are about to bring forth our child. I am here with you. What more happiness could a man want?"

His question hung in the air, yet still she could not say the words she knew he longed to hear. She was still not certain whether the emotion she felt for him was love or a mere warm affection. And though she feared that she might never have the chance to say the words, still, in all honesty, she could not utter them. Perhaps later, when the baby was born, she would, she told herself, just to please him.

"I hope I can give you a son. Then the future of Radcliffe will be secure."

"Son or daughter, I care not, so long as the child is whole and you are well."

His anxiety was palpable. She was about to offer him reassurance, when she felt a sudden gush of warmth down her legs. "Oh!" she gasped.

"What is the matter?"

"The waters have burst."

He looked utterly bewildered. "Go," she said. "Kiss me, Brendan, and then go fetch my mother." She was uncomfortably damp and wanted him gone now that the baby was coming in earnest.

He took her face between his hands and kissed her lips. "God save you, my darling," he murmured.

"Go fetch my mother," she repeated, pushing him from her, "and then go check on the lambing. There were several due to be born today, like our little lamb."

As he reluctantly left her, she thought of the ease in which many of the sheep gave birth and prayed to God and the Holy Virgin that her labor might be as easy.

It was not, of course. The hours passed, the respite between pains grew even less, until she knew nothing but the grinding pain and unimaginably hard labor of giving birth. Her mind blotted out everything but her own efforts and the encouraging voices of her mother and Joan and Margery.

And then came the last peak of pain and a great cry bursting forth from her and, in its wake, the first cry of her child.

"A lad!" cried Margery. "God be praised."

Her face streaming sweat, Katherine lay back against the pillow. Her mother bent over her to wipe her face with a refreshing cloth, soaked in rosewater, and to offer her a restorative drink. "You have a son, my darling Kate. A beautiful son. Oh, what a clever lass you are to give us an heir to Radcliffe."

Katherine found the strength to smile at her mother's face, which was beaming with pride. "He is whole, no defects at all?" she asked.

"None at all. A big lad with a big voice, as you can hear." Her mother's eyes were bright with tears.

They placed the baby, still damp from his washing, in her arms, so that she might see for herself. As he squirmed against her, red-skinned and indignant, she knew a sudden pang of affinity with her mother and realized what it meant to give birth to a being that was both part of you, and yet separate.

She knew also what her mother must have suffered to have her only son cut down after only ten years of life, as Richard had been.

"Richard," she said, watching as Joan swaddled the flailing little limbs in warm flannel. "We shall call him Richard." She met her mother's eyes and gave her a half-smile.

"I thought . . . that you and Brendan had decided to call a son Thomas in memory of both your fathers," her mother said hesitantly.

"We had. But now I think not. He shall be called Richard after the former heir to Radcliffe."

"Thank you, Kate." Her mother's mouth quivered. "You have given me the most precious gift imaginable," she whispered, and turned away.

"I must go tell Brendan," she said briskly, a moment later. "The last time I saw him, he had just ridden down from the moor. I don't know which was more exhausted from the ride, his poor mount or him."

Katherine closed her eyes, content to listen to the bustle of the women about her and yet no longer be at the center of it. She groaned softly as she shifted her legs into a more comfortable position. By St. Mary, she was sore! But though her body was weary, her mind exulted in the realization that the long period of waiting was over. She had delivered a son. Radcliffe was secure.

She pushed away the nagging remembrance that so must her mother have thought on the day of Richard's birth. "This babe shall live," she whispered, locking her hands together beneath the bed covers. "Gracious God, let this child live to manhood."

How many other mothers had prayed thus after their long travail, she wondered, knowing how disease could strike their sons down at any time or, if they escaped disease, the ravages of war?

She heard a floorboard creak near her bed and opened her eyes to find Brendan standing beside her, gazing down at her with an intense expression. He was still dressed in his riding boots and from him came the peaty smell of the wet moor.

They smiled at each other. Then she patted the side of the bed. "Sit down."

He hesitated. "Is it all right to do so?"

Her smile broadened. "I assure you I shall not break." Very gingerly, he sat down on the edge of the bed. "Have you seen our son?" she asked.

"I have. Joan showed him to me. A splendid lad with lusty lungs. Oh, Kate. What you have endured!"

She lifted her hand to brush the frown lines on his forehead. "It was easier than most. Only a few hours. I was fortunate."

"Fortunate? To suffer such pain?" He grasped her hand tightly in his. "And I am to blame for it."

"Dear Brendan," she said, laughing up at him. "We are both to blame. Enough of this maudlin talk. I have decided on a name for our babe."

He looked taken aback at this. "I thought we had decided on Thomas, if it was a son."

"Aye, we had, but I have thought again about it. It would please me greatly if we were to call him Richard," she said coaxingly, "after my dead brother."

"Richard." He thought for a moment.

"It would also please my mother." She caressed the back of his hand, running her fingers along the strong bones. "After the babe was born, I realized what it must have been like for her to have lost her only son. I thought it might help if we called our son Richard in his memory."

He lifted his left hand to brush her tangled hair back from her face. "It is a kind thought, Kate. Richard Radcliffe he shall be. The heir to Radcliffe Manor." His face was bright with triumph. "Radcliffe now has an heir and cannot be taken from us."

A shiver ran over her shoulders. "Do not tempt the gods," she whispered.

The lying-in period tried Katherine's patience sorely, for after only three days she felt perfectly able to get up and resume her duties about the house.

By the end of the fourth day, despite the protestations of her mother and the women servants, she insisted on rising and walking the length of the long gallery. The next day she dressed, rejoicing in her almost flat stomach and fast-returning waist, and descended to the parlor.

She had never been so happy as she was in the ensuing weeks. Spring was upon them. Below them, in the wide valley of the Ure, the river gushed and tumbled. The air was filled with the cries of birds, the bleating of newborn lambs.

Wrapping up Richard well in a fleece-lined bag, she carried him outside to show him his demesne: the orchard with its budding fruit trees, plums and pears, apples and cherries; the bowling green, its grass turning emerald-green again; the mews and stables, brewhouse and dairy. . . . And everywhere she went, Radcliffe servants flocked to see and exclaim over the new heir, so that Brendan, had he been a jealous man, might well have grown to hate his son.

But Brendan was prouder than any other person of his child.

"Do you not resent their attitude a little?" asked Katherine of him, after one of those excursions. She spoke tentatively, anxious not to hurt his feelings, but also curious. She would have hated to be usurped by a tiny infant of only a few weeks old.

Brendan smiled. "They see me as the guardian to the rightful heir to Radcliffe, I suppose. But, God willing, I intend to live a long and contented life. It will be many years before Richard Radcliffe will be the lord of the manor. Meanwhile," he said, with a shrug, "they will have to accept me as their lord, inadequate though I might be in their eyes."

"They respect you."

"They tolerate me," he said lightly. "I doubt they will ever accept me fully as their lord. It is natural. I am a foreigner."

"Tobias defers to you," Katherine insisted, anxious that his feelings should not be hurt.

"Tobias appears to defer to me. In truth, Tobias Ridley defers to no one. Was he thus with your grandfather, also?"

Katherine frowned and then smiled in remembrance. "They had a very special relationship. It was not like master and servant at all. More like that of two brothers, separated by several years, who respected each other greatly."

The idyllic days could not last. Although Brendan still whistled when he entered Radcliffe Hall, there was a tension about his mouth and a stiffness in his arms and shoulders that told Katherine he was no longer at ease.

Silently, she cursed Queen Elizabeth and Walter Ralegh for having forced him into service in Ireland again. Every few days papers and documents were arriving from London and from Sir John Perrot in Wales, bearing enquiries that must be answered immediately and returned posthaste.

The week before he was due to leave, Katherine returned from her first visit to her ailing Aunt Isobel since the baby's birth, to find the courtyard and house a bustle with activity.

Brendan greeted her at the door. "Thank God you have come. I was about to send for you." His face showed patches of white beneath the tan.

"What has happened?" she demanded, stripping off her riding gloves.

"I have been ordered to go directly to Wales."

"But you have another week of leave."

"The Earl of Ormonde has joined Sir John in Wales and demands my presence there."

"Can you not wait a few more days, at least?"

"Not even a few hours. I must go at once. I am commanded by Ormonde to do so." He held the letter crushed in his hand.

"May I see?" she asked him.

His hand closed even more tightly about the paper. "It is merely a military order," he told her. "I must go see that John has packed all I need," he said, turning from her.

But before he turned she had seen not disappointment but fear lurking in his eyes.

Chapter 31

As she waved halfheartedly to Brendan from the courtyard, Katherine was beside herself with anger. How dare he shut her out of his life, refusing even to show her the letter that had blighted their contentment! He had closeted himself away with Tobias and Master Applegarth all morning, giving them brusque orders about the management of Radcliffe, which ran itself perfectly well without him, anyway.

But most of all she hated him for leaving her with the dread fear that something more than a mere command to return to his post had been in that letter from Ormonde.

They were natural foes, she knew. He had told her a little about the old enmity between Butler and Fitzgerald. He had also said, briefly, that he hoped that their paths would not cross again, now that Ormonde was to be relieved of his post as Governor of Munster. It seemed that Brendan was not to have his wish—for the time being at least.

Her resentment against Brendan and his secrecy built up over the ensuing weeks.

"You are missing him, that is all," Joanna told her one sunny day in June, as they sat on a rug on the velvety bowling green, playing with the baby.

Katherine slammed down the baby's bone rattle. "I am missing him not one jot. Nor, it seems, is he missing me. He has sent me one brief note from Dublin, that is all. One note in three whole months!"

Joanna continued to string daisies together, piercing their stems with her nail and then threading the stems through the slits. She was making a garland for baby Dickon. "He said himself that he is busy with all the preparations for the new Governor's installation and—"

"And the survey of the Earl of Desmond's confiscated lands," intervened Katherine impatiently. "I know all that. But he is keeping something from me."

"That would not be like Brendan." Joanna leaned forward to festoon the baby with the tiny daisy garland.

"It would be like all men, who think that their wives are to be treated like fools or children. And talking of such," she snapped, "take that stupid thing off the baby. For the love of heaven, Joanna, he will eat the daisies and make himself sick."

Joanna leaned down to remove the garland, which young Dickon had grasped in his pudgy little hand. She had to prise his fingers apart to release it. "You are quite right, Sister," she said placidly. "That was foolish of me."

Deprived of his new plaything, Dickon's face crumpled and he began to cry. "Nay, my hinny," Joanna crooned, gathering him up to rock him against her breast. "Your auntie is here."

His hand grasped on a strand of her red-brown hair and his cry changed to a gurgle of contentment.

"You spoil him," complained Katherine. "All of you spoil him: Mother, the women, even Tobias."

"He is very precious to us all. And it is good for him to feel loved."

Katherine sat with her arms locked around her knees, gazing across the dale, which was bathed in a golden haze. Joanna's words had conjured up an image of Brendan as a young child, locked away in a tiny cell with only his mother for company. Joanna was right. Dickon was fortunate to have so many to love him.

"You look well with a child," she told her sister.

Joanna looked up and a tide of red ruddied her cheeks. She ducked her head to kiss Dickon's plump neck.

"Did you speak to Brendan about Harry Seaton?" Katherine asked her.

Joanna nodded.

"I thought you might. What did he say?"

"He said that when he returned he would discuss the matter with you and Mother." Joanna smiled. "He also said that it would not hurt us to wait just a little longer, to ensure that both Harry and I were still of the same mind."

"That sounds like Brendan."

"But he didn't say it was an impossible match," Joanna added eagerly. "He said time would tell."

Katherine couldn't help smiling. "That also sounds like Brendan. A man of patience, my husband." She studied her sister's flushed face. "So that is why you have been singing about the place again. Brendan has given you hope." She sighed. "The wretched man seems to have no sense of what is correct. Harry Seaton is not good enough for a Radcliffe of Radcliffe Hall. He is a third son. What future can he give you?"

"A contented one," Joanna replied softly. "A tiny stone cottage in the dalehead with Harry at my side would please me far more than a palace with some other husband."

"Well, don't expect your sister to come visiting you in the dalehead," snapped Katherine.

Joanna grinned. "I don't think you would have to. When I told Brendan he laughed and said that he thought he could find me something better than a tiny cottage."

"How like him to encourage you in your foolishness!" Everything about Brendan annoyed Katherine at present.

She was stopped from saying more by her mother's approach across the green. "So this is where you both are. Margery has been waiting this past half-hour for you, Kate. Apparently you wished to sort out the linen chests with her and she is afraid to start in on her own."

Katherine bridled at her mother's tone. She was heartily sick of being treated like a delinquent child in her own home. She scrambled to her feet. "I shall get to Margery in my own time," she retorted, angrily brushing grass from her skirts. "Did she seek you out to complain about me?"

Her mother's expression grew even more severe. "No, Katherine, she did not. I found her waiting in the main bedchamber and admonished her for wasting time, only to be told that she was waiting for you."

Joanna sprang up. "I can go help Margery. I have nothing else to do at present."

Her mother turned upon her. "I believe you were to gather herbs for me this morning," she said, her tone icy. "No, this is Katherine's duty. She must learn not to keep the servants from their work."

This was too much. Katherine's hands clenched at her sides. "I must learn, must I, my lady Mother? I must learn. It is time you learned that I am the true mistress of Radcliffe. It is *my* husband who is the Lord of Radcliffe and therefore *I* am its mistress."

"Kate, don't," whispered Joanna.

"Be mindful of your own business, Joanna, not mine. This is between Mother and me and is long overdue." She glared at her mother, whose small face had become as impassive as smooth, cold glass. "Well, what have you to say, madam my Mother?"

"I have little to say, but that you appear to have forgotten God's commandment to honor thy father and thy mother."

Disgust and anger rose like bile into Katherine's throat. "Honor! What know you of honor? I have heard such tales of you that would make Boccaccio's *Decameron* seem like some fairy story."

Her mother's face was now ghastly white.

Joanna gripped Katherine's arm. "That's enough, Kate. You have said more than enough. You are frightening the baby with your angry voice."

This was true, for Dickon was wailing, his mouth wide, his legs kicking in protest at this sudden disturbance in the even tenor of his day.

"I shall take him in," said Alyssa, bending down to hide her face from Katherine.

"I think we should finish this now," Katherine said, wishing with all her heart that she had not started it. Why, oh, why did Brendan have to leave? He had promised to help her clear up all the mysteries about her mother and father and the past before he returned to Ireland, but there had not been enough time. The excitement of the baby's birth had swept away all thought of what lurked beneath the surface, their joy covering it up like a bright-colored carpet over a filthy floor.

Now it had surfaced again, together with her resentment of her mother's usurpation of her role as the rightful mistress of Radcliffe.

Alyssa gathered Dickon into her arms and turned to face her. "Give the baby to me," said Katherine.

Her mother's eyes widened, but she did not relinquish her hold.

"I said, give him to me," repeated Katherine. "I do not wish you to touch him."

"Oh, Kate, how can you be so cruel?" whispered Joanna, tears filling her eyes. "I will take Dickon inside." She held out her arms and her mother placed the squirming, screaming baby in them.

"It is time we talked together," Katherine said, when Joanna had left them.

Her mother merely shook her head in reply and bent down to gather up the rattle and blanket from the green lawn. Then she bent again to pick up the tiny daisy chain. "I used to love making these as a girl," she said, as if she spoke in a dream.

"Mother, we must talk."

Alyssa avoided her daughter's eyes. "Yes, we must," she said, neatly folding the blanket into a square, before tucking it beneath her arm. "I am very concerned about your Aunt Isobel and wish to discuss—"

"I do not wish to discuss Aunt Isobel at present." Apart, that was, from her many insinuations about her sister, thought Katherine.

Her mother raised her eyes and Katherine saw that they were filled with tears. "I cannot talk now," she whispered, and, head down, she walked away across the green, letting the daisy chain fall as she went.

Another chance for enlightenment denied her, Katherine thought bitterly as she stared after her mother. It was ever thus.

An uneasy truce ensued, dictated more by Isobel's worsening health than any wish on Katherine's part to make amends. It was now known that the cause of her aunt's grievous sickness was a canker in the right breast. She was losing flesh from her bones so fast that her seamstress could not keep up. As soon as one of her rich-colored gowns was altered, she lost more weight, so that it was still too large and hung on her thin body like clothes on a scarecrow.

Katherine hated to visit her aunt nowadays. Young and healthy herself, she was terrified to see the woman who had once been the most beautiful woman in the shire reduced to a near-skeleton.

"Poor Lady Colborne," the gossips muttered, some crossing themselves beneath their shawls. "'Tis God's punishment for her sins."

What sins had her aunt committed, wondered Katherine, other than her violent repudiation of her sister's immorality?

But as Isobel grew weaker, Alyssa's desire to do everything in her power to help her sister grew stronger. "One last recourse we have," she announced at the dinner table one forenoon in early July. "We could take her to Buxton for the waters."

"I doubt she would be strong enough to undertake the journey," said Tobias, who, at Alyssa's insistence, had at last reluctantly agreed to dine regularly with them.

"It is her last chance." Alyssa blinked rapidly. "Even if she were to die on the road, at least we would have tried."

Katherine marveled at her mother's tenacity. It was evident to everyone else that Aunt Isobel had very little time left to her. Yet still her mother kept pouring into her sister various new physics she herself had compounded in the stillroom. "Would she not be more comfortable in her own home, at peace," she asked, "without all the rigors of traveling?"

Her mother looked through her, as if a disembodied voice had spoken. "We must try everything," she muttered.

"Are you not going against God's will by denying that she is near death?" Tobias asked gently.

"I must try. Miracles happen. Besides, Isobel wishes to go. She grew quite animated when I suggested it to her."

And so it was hurriedly arranged that Mistress Alyssa Radcliffe and her steward, Tobias Ridley, should accompany Lady Colborne, with sundry servants to wait upon her, to Buxton in Derbyshire, where she would take the restorative waters.

"After all," said Isobel to Katherine, when she was visiting her with baby Dickon one day at Colborne Place, "if the Scottish Queen regularly visits Buxton in the summer, why should not I?"

"Does she?" asked Katherine, her interest sparked. "I am surprised that she is permitted to leave her prison quarters in Sheffield Castle."

"Apparently her health is also failing and Queen Elizabeth is terrified she will be accused of poisoning her cousin," revealed Isobel in a whisper, so that her servants could not hear, "so she permits her to visit Buxton each year for her health. Indeed, there was talk of a meeting between the royal cousins there, but nothing came of it."

As soon as her aunt had uttered the words, Katherine knew that she must go with them. Although reason told her that there was little chance of an encounter with Queen Mary—no doubt she was kept from the public eye at all times—she would never again have even this slight opportunity to meet the woman who had played such a large part in her grandfather's destiny, the Queen whose pin and locket were hidden deep within the mattress on her bed.

And so she sought out her mother, hating to beg for favors, and also terrified that she would discover her true reason for wishing to accompany them to Buxton. So strong were her mother's feelings against Mary, Queen of Scots that even a hint of the Queen's possible presence in Buxton might cause her to cancel the entire expedition.

Having warned her aunt not to mention the likelihood lest her mother decide not to go, Katherine smiled her sweetest smile and spoke in honeyed tones. "I would dearly love to go with you and Aunt Isobel to Buxton," she told her mother.

Alyssa frowned. "And leave the baby? You could not take him on that long journey, you know."

"Of course not. Joanna and Margery will take good care of him, and he has taken well to Jane." Jane was Dickon's new wet-nurse. "I beg you, Mother, take me with you. I am miserable without Brendan and the baby's birth has left me listless."

Her mother peered at her, a small smile flickering about her mouth. "I have yet to see you listless, Kate. You have such an abundance of energy that I wish you could lend me some."

Katherine put on a sad face, which was not entirely playacting. "I would like to spend as much time as possible with Aunt Isobel. I fear—"

"Very well," Alyssa said hurriedly, evidently not wishing to be reminded again of her sister's impending death. "You shall come with us." She gave Katherine a wan smile. "In truth, it will be a great help to me to have you there. As you know, Isobel and I are frequently at odds with each other. It will be a relief to us both to have your company."

What is it about my mother that she always makes me feel imbued with guilt, whatever I do? thought Katherine, as she left her. Instead of feeling triumphant that she had got her own way, she felt despicable for having obtained it by deception.

The full flush of summer was upon them by the time they were ready to embark upon the long journey to Buxton. Everyone was in a festive mood, even Isobel, whose spirits had rallied with the prospect of several weeks away from the Dales—and her surly husband. She had confided to Katherine that she feared Lord Colborne might wish to accompany them, for Buxton was decidedly the fashionable place to be at this time of year, but the superior joys of coursing and hawking on the moors had prevailed.

Despite the fine weather and dry roadways and bridlepaths, it took them a week to reach Buxton. Isobel was too weak to ride and traveled in a horse litter, which slowed them down.

Their lodgings were at the quieter end of Chapel Street, a little way from St. Anne's Chapel and the Market Square. It was but a short distance from St. Anne's Well, the source of the medicinal waters, which stood at the base of a bleak, treeless hill.

The one house of consequence in the town was the Hall that the Earl of Shrewsbury had built recently, so that he might house the Scottish Queen—and his own family—in comfort when they visited Buxton. Four stories high, with great glass windows, it contained a score or so of apartments, but at present, to Katherine's great disappointment, these were occupied by Lord Shrewsbury's friends, not by himself or his royal prisoner.

By the end of her first week in Buxton, Katherine was wishing she was home at Radcliffe. She had always loved harvest time and missed the sight of golden grain in the fields, the songs of the harvesters as they wielded their scythes in unison, their clothing and sunburned faces coated with grain dust.

Instead, she walked the streets of this busy little town, the cobblestones hot and hard beneath the thin soles of her fashionable shoes, and drank the water from the springs, which was not too unpleasant—for medicinal water.

Although the visitors from London and York paraded in the latest fashions up and down the High Street each afternoon, there was still no sign of the Scottish Queen, and rumor denied that she would even be making her usual visit there this year.

"She is in disgrace, 'tis said," Mistress Sidbury, the hostess of their lodgings told Katherine. "For her involvement in the Throckmorton Plot."

"Ah, yes." Francis Throckmorton had been executed for his part in relaying letters to and from Mary regarding a Spanish invasion which would effect her release from prison.

"But, then," Mistress Sidbury leaned her head closer to Katherine, a strong smell of apple cider on her breath, "who can blame the poor lady? After all's said and done, she's been locked away sixteen years. Not that I blame our Good Queen Bess, mind," she hastened to add, lest Katherine suspect her of treason. "But it must be powerful hard for a mighty lady like the Scottish Queen to be locked away and watched and guarded night and day. I wouldn't exchange my life for hers for the world. You and me, we may not be queens, Mistress Radcliffe, but we do have our freedom to come and go as we pleases."

Katherine shivered. *Swear that you will do everything in your power to help Queen Mary regain her throne*, said her grandfather's voice in her mind.

She began to wish that she had never come to Buxton. At least at Radcliffe she was safe. All this talk of plots and prisons, and the reminder that Francis Throckmorton had been cruelly tortured before he was executed, brought home to her the dangers of meddling in the affairs of state.

That night she lay in bed, unable to sleep. It was stifling hot in the tiny upper chamber and she was sadly missing Dickon.

As she lay on her back, arms behind her head, she suddenly realized that in a strange way she was relieved that the Scottish Queen was not in Buxton. She had at least made the gesture of coming here. Surely that would placate her grandfather and fulfill her promise made to him on his deathbed. He could not expect her to do more than that, could he?

But still the uneasiness she felt about her heart would not let her rest. The brief conversation with Mistress Sidbury had brought back memories of the martyred Edmund Campion, which in turn reminded her of those wretched months she and her mother had spent in prison at York. She was taken by a fit of shivering and a griping of the bowels as she smelled again the prison stench that spoke of disease and despair and felt the dank walls close in on her.

A longing to hold her baby against her breast, to kiss the fine down on his head and feel his tiny hand grasping her finger overwhelmed her. This was followed by an even stronger desire to be held in Brendan's arms, to feel safe and secure against him, to hear his lilting voice tell her: "'Tis safe you are here, my darling Caitlin, here in my arms at Radcliffe."

But Brendan was in Ireland, hundreds of miles away. *Come back to me, before it be too late*, her soul cried out to him. Her only response was the screech of a night owl and the sudden rustle of a bat as it careered from beneath the thatch outside the casement window.

Chapter 32

Each morning Isobel was carried in a chair down the steep High Street to bathe in the warm, regenerative waters. The medicinal baths had been there since as far back as the days of the Romans, some said. But it was certain that people had been coming to Buxton to bathe in the miraculously warm waters that gushed up from some hidden spring, and to drink them, hoping so to cure whatever ailment they suffered, from time immemorial.

Whether it was the waters or the change of environment, there was no doubt that Isobel's spirits, at least, were improving and a little natural color had returned to her fine-boned cheeks.

On the morning of their ninth day in Buxton, however, when they neared the baths, they were prevented from going further by a retinue of men, garbed in livery, who stood in a line across the path and surrounding the building. They were all armed, some with drawn swords, others bearing pikes held menacingly at the ready.

The men carrying Isobel's chair set it down. "What is going on?" she demanded in a querulous tone.

"Must be the Scottish Queen, my lady," one of the men told her. "I heard tell she might be coming to Buxton this week. They's the Earl of Shrewsbury's men," he added, jerking his head in the direction of the guards.

Katherine's heartbeat quickened. She immediately became aware of her mother's tension.

"Pick up the chair," Alyssa told the men, her hands gripped together at her waist. "Let us come away before the crowds grow too thick."

"We cannot," said one of the chairmen. "See, mistress, the crowd is all about us."

It was true. In just a few minutes the handful of people that had drifted down from the marketplace to see what was happening had grown to an exuberant crowd of more than a hundred, pressing against them in the narrow street. Something akin to panic filled Alyssa's eyes.

"There must be a way through," she muttered to Katherine. "If we do not leave, Isobel could be crushed in this crowd."

"What nonsense, Alyssa," snapped her sister. "You can see by looking at them that the people are friendly."

"Quite right," said an old woman, whose face was as dark and wizened as a prune. "Queen Mary is always welcome at Buxton. A more generous, sweet creature you never will find this side of heaven."

Alyssa bit her lip. Her entire body was as rigid as an iron pike.

"You might as well be still, Mother, for we cannot do anything about it," said Katherine.

Her mother looked at her. In her eyes Katherine saw both terror and anger. "How can you bid me be still, Daughter," she said in a harsh whisper, "when you know well what your grandfather suffered for this woman? I cannot bear even the sight of her."

"It was his choice to do so," retorted Katherine. "You cannot keep blaming her for inspiring loyalty and compassion."

"I can and I will."

"Hush the both of you," said Isobel. "I believe she is coming. I wonder if she will remember us after all these years."

"She will not even see us in this crush," muttered Alyssa.

Katherine fervently hoped that her mother was wrong, for she was burning with a desire to meet the Queen whose name had been on her grandfather's lips on his deathbed, the woman for whom he had sacrificed his good name, his estates—and, but for the intervention of the Earl of Leicester, his life.

"Stand back!" came the command.

The crowd obediently parted and the narrow pathway they made was lined again with Shrewsbury's armed men. A cheer went up from the people nearest the small building that housed the baths and then a woman spoke, her voice both musical and compelling.

"Good people of Buxton, I give you thanks for your warm welcome. Once again, I have the joy of being released from my confinement to ease my pains in Buxton's soothing waters and to bask in its sunshine. For this I give thanks to God and to the kindness and benevolence of my dearly beloved cousin, Queen Elizabeth."

Another cheer. Katherine tried to peer over the shoulders of the guards directly in front of them, but she could see nothing apart from the throng of people on the other side of the path, and beyond them the soaring, green-clad hills that sheltered Buxton.

Several men appeared, shouting orders for the people to be held back. Behind them came another group of guards, in their midst several women dressed in black and, head and shoulders above them, Queen Mary.

Katherine had been a child of four or five when she had first encountered the Scottish Queen at Radcliffe. Her clouded memory of this had been fed by her grandfather, who had detailed to her every word the Queen had spoken to her and all she had said and done in reply. One memory was clearer than all others: that the Queen had gone down on her knees to play with her and the other children in the nursery.

But that queen had been beautiful, her face and red-gold hair brighter than the jewels she had worn about her neck and on her fingers. This one was heavy-jowled, clad in black, and moved slowly as if every step pained her. It was hard to imagine this woman being capable of even going on her knees to pray, let alone to embrace and play games with young children.

Then she smiled, and Katherine knew it was the same queen, the same fascinating woman, for the smile lit her face with a radiance that made her beautiful once more. She spoke soft words to a crippled man who leaned his gnarled hands on two sticks, smiled upon the old woman with the wizened face, and laid her hand on the head of a child whose back was grotesquely twisted.

"'Tis said she has the power of healing," muttered someone behind Katherine.

Alms were distributed from a black velvet pouch held by one of the Queen's attendants. Katherine watched, fascinated, as the Queen approached, passing slowly down the crowd, beckoning forth a child here, an old man there.

Two richly dressed men accompanied her. One, a man of about sixty with a long beard, frowned as he watched the Queen's progress, chewing at the side of his mouth as if he wished to put an end to this nonsense, but dared not. The other man, Katherine realized, with a start, was the Earl of Leicester, and he was looking directly across at them.

"It is the Earl of—"

Her mother interrupted her. "I know very well who it is," she whispered. To Katherine's surprise, her mother's cheeks were suffused with pink, which made her appear far younger than her years.

"He is coming over here," said Isobel, with a haughty lift of the head, as if she herself were a queen on a throne preparing to greet Queen Elizabeth's favorite.

The guards parted and Leicester was before them, bowing and flourishing his high-crowned hat in response to the ladies' curtsies. "Mistress Radcliffe," he said in his deep, rich voice. Katherine was about to respond, but then she realized that it was her mother the Earl was addressing.

"My lord," Alyssa said, curtsying again. "I am amazed that you would remember me after all these years."

"You have changed very little. I would have recognized you anywhere." Leicester was about to say more, but became aware of the Earl of Shrewsbury's evident impatience and anxiety at this further delay. "I beg your pardon, but I cannot stay now. Do you remain in Buxton for long?"

"For another week at least. My sister, Lady Colborne, is—"

"Good," he said brusquely. "Then you must dine with us. I shall arrange it with my lord of Shrewsbury. Where are your lodgings?"

"In Chapel Street. Mistress Sidbury's house," replied Alyssa, with a bemused half-smile.

"We are guests of my lord Shrewsbury at the Hall," he nodded to the magnificent house nearby. "I shall send word as to the day and time. Your servant, Mistress Alyssa." A strange, secretive smiled touched his lips and then was hidden as he made his bow. Had he been a younger man, Katherine would have said he was being flirtatious with her mother, but that was impossible, of course. The Earl of Leicester was a man of fifty, corpulent and gray-haired. And her mother was a matron, albeit a slim one, of near forty.

In a moment, the Scottish Queen's entourage had disappeared from their sight, as the crowd pressed in behind them.

"How ill-mannered of you, Alyssa, not to present me to my lord of Leicester," Isobel complained.

Alyssa turned, her expression vague, as if her sister's voice had drawn her from some distance. "There was no time. It was evident that my lord of Shrewsbury was ill at ease. As well he might be," she added severely. "In this crowd anyone could have rushed forward and tried to rescue her. I am amazed that she should be permitted to be seen thus in public."

"If you mean Queen Mary, surely she has as much right as anyone else to take the waters," Katherine said indignantly. "You could see how it pained her even to walk, poor lady."

Her mother pressed her lips together. "Then they should bring her here in the middle of the night, so that she might not create a danger. After all, the Hall is but a few paces from the baths."

"There's a private passage from the house to the baths," said a toothless old man. "But the Queen likes to see the people of Buxton, and us her. Even when she uses the private entrance, the people gets to know about it, see? Last year, they took her there at night, and within ten minutes the baths was surrounded by a great crowd and the doors almost broken down. And in that darkness—black as pitch it were—anyone could have spirited her away, if they'd 'ad a mind to do it. Old Shrewsbury made sure that were the last time Queen Mary went to the baths at nighttime. Scared witless, he were." The old man cackled with laughter, displaying his pink, moist gums.

Alyssa's lips pressed even tighter together. "The crowd is dispersing. Perhaps now we can get into the baths."

"I didn't know that you were acquainted with my lord of Leicester, Mother," Katherine said, as the chairmen lifted Isobel's chair.

"Your mother has many secrets hidden away from you," Isobel said maliciously.

Alyssa turned her back on her sister. "You forget that it was my lord of Leicester who was instrumental in arranging the release of your grandfather from prison," she reminded Katherine.

"I knew that, of course. But I thought it was merely a matter of his approving Grandy's release or advising Queen Elizabeth to do so, or some such thing."

"No, it took a little more than that to gain your grandfather's release," her mother said enigmatically. She cast a hurried look about her. "It all happened many, many years ago. Besides, this is neither the place nor the time for private conversation," she warned.

Katherine was left with several unanswered questions hovering on her lips. The crowd flowed away, leaving the entrance to the baths open to them, and they moved forward.

By next morning, Isobel had forgotten her anger at not being presented to the Earl of Leicester and was eagerly awaiting his invitation to dine with him, although Alyssa told Katherine that she was sure the Earl would have forgotten the invitation as soon as he had left them.

They had discovered from Mistress Sidbury that he was visiting Buxton to take the waters for severe gout and was to spend another week or so at the Hall with the Earl of Shrewsbury and Queen Mary, before he returned to Queen Elizabeth's Court.

"They are strange companions, to be sure, Leicester and Queen Mary," said Isobel. "I wonder what Queen Elizabeth would think of that."

"You can be sure she knows about it," replied Alyssa. "Perhaps it was even her idea. My lord of Leicester would not risk her anger again, not after having been banished from Court for so long after his secret marriage."

"I still cannot see why Queen Elizabeth would want her favorite to spend time in Queen Mary's company," said Katherine.

Alyssa bent her head over the small embroidery frame she took everywhere with her, for inactivity—or sloth, as she called it—made her agitated. "My lord of Leicester is still a handsome man. No doubt Queen Elizabeth hopes that Queen Mary will be tempted to confide in him."

"You mean that he is acting as some sort of spy?" said Katherine.

"It would not be the first time."

"I think that is monstrous." Heat rushed into Katherine's face.

Alyssa lifted her eyes to confront her daughter. "Not half so monstrous as using one's undoubted charms to lure men—and women, for that matter—into a hopeless cause, luring them to their torture and imprisonment and the terrible death that awaits those who commit treason."

"I hate to hear of such things," Isobel said, her voice shaking.

Alyssa was immediately all concern for her sister. She set down her frame and went to her. "Forgive me, Isobel. I was not thinking. What would you like to do today? Shall we go riding in Corbar Woods or perhaps another visit to Ashwood? It is so beautiful there, with all the meadows ablaze with flowers."

But they were to do neither for, to the surprise of mother and daughter, at least, a groom in Leicester's livery arrived at their lodging in the midmorning. He bore a message from my lord of Leicester, inviting Lady Colborne and the two Mistress Radcliffes in the name of himself and my lord of Shrewsbury to a musical entertainment accompanied by a light repast that very evening.

All thoughts of excursions to Ashwood Dale or Corbar Wood were forgotten in a flurry of "What shall we wear? Is the blue silk too formal, do you think? My tawny overdress or the green . . . ?"

Seeing Isobel's flushed face and the thin hands trembling with excitement, Alyssa confided in Katherine that she was concerned it would all be too much for her sister. Perhaps they should politely decline the Earl's invitation.

"That would break her heart," Katherine told her. "Can you not see how happy this has made her? You know how Aunt Isobel loves to consort with nobility."

Mother and daughter exchanged wry smiles in a rare moment of understanding.

Alyssa sighed. "You are right, of course. But I cannot pretend to be easy at this meeting with Queen Mary. I know you do not understand my feelings about her. I cannot expect you to, considering your grandfather adored her."

Although she was tempted, Katherine decided that this was not the time to engage in a heated argument about Queen Mary or her undoubted rights to reign as the Queen of Scotland and to be the appointed heir to the throne of England. "Perhaps she will not be there," she said lightly. "Mistress Sidbury told me she usually dines in her own apartments."

When they were ushered into the upper chamber of the richly furnished mansion, however, the Scottish Queen was in full view, seated beneath her canopy of state on the dais. Although she was garbed in black, as before, her gown was of the finest silk and she wore over it a mantle of transparent gold tissue, which was attached to her large white neck ruff. Her only jewels were earrings of gold filigree and the golden crucifix with pendant pearls that lay on her breast.

Her women attendants devotedly hovered about her. It was evident that they held her in deep affection, and she them. For many years they had shared their queen's long exile and imprisonment and had become her family. So, too, had her pet dogs, one of which crouched in the comparative safety of her skirts, shivering at the discordant noise of the musical instruments tuning up for the entertainment.

Leicester had presented Katherine, her mother and aunt to my lord of Shrewsbury when they first entered the mansion. The old Earl had a nervous habit of stroking his long beard and then tugging at it. He greeted them with a marked lack of enthusiasm, affording them the courtesy required for acquaintances of the powerful Earl of Leicester, but no more than that.

It was evident that new faces troubled him. The strain of having been Queen Mary's jailer for more than a dozen years had exacted its toll. No one, not even an acquaintance of the Earl of Leicester, was to be trusted.

Katherine wondered how the lugubrious-faced Shrewsbury would react if he knew that, less than three years before, she and her mother had been imprisoned for harboring the famous Catholic priest Edmund Campion in their home. The thought amused her. It was unfortunate that the only other person there who might be similarly amused by it was Queen Mary herself.

When they were presented to the Queen, she cried out with pleasure, tears starting in her amber eyes. "You are my dear Sir Philip Radcliffe's Alyssa," she said, holding out her hands in an impulsive gesture of welcome. "How could I ever forget you and those happy days in Wensleydale? But this cannot be your little Kate, surely."

"It is indeed, Your Majesty," murmured Alyssa, forcing her mouth into a semblance of a smile.

The Queen turned her own smiling face upon Katherine. "Sir Philip's beloved little Kate. He spoke of you frequently when he was at the Scottish Court, always saddened that he had not returned to Radcliffe to see his first grandchild." She held out her hand to Katherine. "And now that shy little lass with the big, dark eyes has grown to be a beauty. Come, Kate, let me kiss you in remembrance of your grandfather, one of my most loyal followers."

Aware of her mother's eyes like rods of hot iron upon her back, Katherine mounted the dais step to kneel before the Queen. Bending forward, Mary kissed her on both cheeks, the sweet fragrance of exotic flowers emanating from her.

In that suspended moment, Katherine was caught, hopelessly snared by Mary's impulsive warmth, the loving esteem in which she held Grandy. Also, the very fact that a captive queen, with all her fears and sorrows, would remember a little child she had met only two or three times a full sixteen years ago was amazing to Katherine.

She was imbued with a flood of loving warmth for this woman. No wonder her grandfather had been willing to lay down his life for her!

She thought of Queen Elizabeth's callous mockery at Whitehall Palace, when she had been overcome by nausea. The contrast between the two queens was so extreme that Katherine felt like screaming it from the rooftops. *Cannot you see, you blind fools? Queen Elizabeth is a cruel hyena, a grotesquely painted gargoyle in comparison with Queen Mary.*

God in heaven, she prayed. *Give me the opportunity to be alone with her so that I might swear to help her, in my grandfather's name.*

Naught of this was spoken, of course. Katherine took the Queen's hand, pressing her lips to it in a fervent gesture of loyalty.

And all this time she was uneasily aware of her mother's hot eyes boring into her back.

Chapter 33

Ironically, it was Alyssa herself who provided the opportunity for Katherine to be alone with the Queen. All evening, during the dancing and madrigal singing, she had stuck like a leech by Katherine's side. Her knowledge that Katherine was growing increasingly incensed with her fed her fear that her daughter was already entrapped by the Queen's dangerous charm.

Christ Jesu, save my daughter from her snares, she prayed, as the music of the saltarello increased its hectic pace, *or we shall all be lost.*

They should never have come. She should have used Isobel's frail condition as an excuse to decline the invitation. But in her heart she knew that it was a desire to renew her acquaintance with the richly dressed nobleman who now stood before her that had persuaded her to accept the invitation.

They paced the length of the presence chamber, exchanging little conversation until they turned into the small gallery adjoining the upper chamber. "I was sorry to hear of Sir Philip's death," Leicester said, looking down at her from his superior height.

Alyssa dipped her head, her hands gripping the silver pomander that hung from her girdle. "I thank you, my lord," she murmured.

"I was sorrier still to hear about your son."

This time her eyes met his and she halted in her walking. "It was a great blow. I am not sure I shall ever recover from it."

His fingers brushed across her hand in a tiny gesture of condolence, and then he turned from her and began to pace again. "But you were content in those few years you had?"

A small smile escaped her. "Truly content, thanks to you, my lord. I shall be able to live on the memory of those years for the rest of my life."

"A melancholy prospect. You are still a vibrant, healthy woman. Would you not consider marriage again?"

She gave him a direct look. "I am almost past the years of childbearing. What use would I be to any man now, my lord?"

"When you look at me like that, with your head to one side, daring me to answer you, I am tempted to tell you, Mistress Alyssa, what use you could be to a man."

Alyssa felt the blood rush to her cheeks. Damn him for having drawn her into this strange conversation and damn him also for making her feel desirable again. She did not wish to experience the stirring of sensations that she had forced down for so many years. At her age it was indecent to feel one's heart jump at the thought that a man would wish to have her in his bed.

"You blush like a girl, still," he said, highly amused.

"But I am not a girl," she retorted. She rounded upon him. "And you, my lord, are you content in your marriage?" She had meant the question to be a riposte to his taunting, but regretted it immediately when she saw the flicker of hurt in his eyes.

"As content as I am ever likely to be, I suppose," he said brusquely.

This time it was she who touched his hand. "Forgive me," she whispered. "I had sincerely hoped that you were content. I had forgotten that you, too, had lost your only son."

"We are alike in that, too," he said with a wry smile. "She was kind when she heard."

"Queen Elizabeth?" she asked, knowing the answer already.

He nodded. "She has never forgiven me my marriage, but she spoke kind words on the death of my son."

What was it between them that they could speak so openly of such secret matters, as if they were old friends long kept apart? And yet, despite their widely disparate worlds and natures, that was how she felt about Leicester and, she was sure, how he felt towards her.

"Enough of this sad talk," he said. "You have created a beautiful daughter. That much, at least, your husband gave you. What think you of young Brendan, your son-in-law?"

"Why, of course, you met him at Court, did you not? Katherine told me how kind you were when she was unwell. I thank you for that. It seems I am to be always in your debt, my lord."

She was about to tell him how much she liked Brendan, despite the fact that he was Sussex's son, but her anxiety for Katherine disturbed her. "Should we not return to the main chamber?"

"Are you concerned about your sister?"

"No, not Isobel. She and my lord Shrewsbury were deep in conversation about the building of his new house when I left them. It is Katherine. I . . ." She did not continue. How could she tell the man closest to Queen Elizabeth that she was deeply afraid her daughter might do something both foolish and dangerous? How could she explain her inordinate fear of the Scottish Queen, when Leicester himself was paying court to her, to ensure that Queen Mary would remember him if ever she were appointed heir to the throne of England?

"Katherine? She was speaking with one of Queen Mary's attendants when we left the chamber. Do not be so concerned. Your daughter is quite safe with the Queen. Despite all the plots that surround her, and all the letters she has written back and forth to Spain and France and Scotland, Mary seems to engage only those who are already active in her service in her treasonous pursuits." He shrugged. "Shrewsbury watches her like a hawk. There are few letters to and from her that we do not intercept. In that way we are able to discover who, in England, is a traitor, as we did with Throckmorton."

That was what Alyssa was afraid of! An involuntary shiver ran across her shoulders. Leicester looked down at her, frowning. "That reminds me. What in the name of Christ was Edmund Campion doing in your house? I have never come closer to writing to you than I did three years ago when I heard you were in prison."

"I am glad you did not." Alyssa's eyes opened wide at him. "Whatever happens in my life, I ask you never again to become involved in it, my lord. You obtained Philip's release for me. For that I am evermore in your debt. To have written to me in prison would have been the height of folly."

He smiled ruefully. "So, reluctantly, I decided for myself. Fortunately, Sussex sent his bastard son to the rescue."

"In truth, he did not. Although Sussex sent his approval of our release, it was Brendan's idea to come to our rescue, not his father's."

Leicester gave a low whistle. "Was it, indeed? I did not know that. I am impressed. Despite the fact that Sussex was my arch-enemy, I liked his son. But I deplore his lack of ambition. The English Court is not a place for the squeamish."

"Which is why he is not there, I suppose."

"He could have been. Her Majesty was much taken with him." Leicester's gray-flecked brows lowered. "Have you had news of him recently?"

"Brendan? No, we haven't. He has written Katherine only one letter and there was one to Tobias, our steward, also. That is all." Now it was Alyssa's turn to frown. "It is not like Brendan to write so infrequently. Why do you ask, my lord? Is there some trouble in Ireland?"

His eyes evaded hers. "Not that I know of," he said lightly. "The new Governor, Perrot, has at last left Wales with Ormonde. By now, your son-in-law will doubtless have attended Perrot's installation. But we have changed the subject, Mistress Alyssa, no doubt to your great relief. I asked you why Campion was at Radcliffe."

She looked up at him. "For the reason I gave in my answer to the tribunal, my lord. Philip was dying and wished for a Catholic priest. Father Campion was in the district and ministered the final rites to him."

"But he returned to visit you after Sir Philip's death, did he not?" pressed Leicester.

Alyssa looked away. "I received him for one reason only: because he was the one to be with Philip at the very end. It was Philip's dying wish that he visit me."

"Did you turn Catholic to please your Philip, too?" Leicester's voice was smooth as silk.

"Good Lord, no," Alyssa shot back indignantly. "He would never have asked me to do so."

"I am glad to hear it. Now, cease agitating yourself about Queen Mary and your daughter and tell me all you have been doing at Radcliffe in these many years since we last met."

But, despite Leicester's assurances that Shrewsbury watched the Scottish Queen like a hawk, he had not taken into account Lady Colborne's still-potent ability to both charm and flatter men. While the Earl of Shrewsbury was engaged in regaling Isobel with tales of the frustrations of being jailer to the most famous prisoner in the world, Queen Mary had bidden Katherine to sit on a stool at her feet, and asked her to tell her all about her marriage and her baby son.

Basking in the warmth of her interest, Katherine found herself forgetting that this woman was a queen and answered her questions eagerly, telling her about Brendan and little Dickon.

The Queen sighed. "How fortunate you are to be able to be with your son."

For one appalling moment, Katherine remembered that the Queen had been parted from her son for sixteen years. How callous she was to have mentioned Dickon! What would the Queen think of her? "I humbly beg your pardon, Your Majesty. I did not think. I . . ."

Queen Mary touched Katherine's head reassuringly. "I love to hear talk of children. There is nothing that pleases me more. Do not be sad for me, for I hope soon to be reconciled with my own son."

From the corner of her eye, Katherine saw her mother and Leicester reenter the chamber. It was now or never. "Your Majesty," she whispered. "There is little time for us to speak. I have your locket and pin."

The Queen looked bewildered and shook her head, with a puzzled little smile. "I do not know—"

"You gave them to my grandfather," Katherine explained hurriedly. "When he was dying, he passed them on to me for safekeeping."

"Ah, *je comprends.*" The Queen touched her white forehead with long fingers. "The locket, I remember. I gave it to him when he left the Scottish court, I believe."

"Yes, yes. And the pin at the time of your wedding." Katherine leaned close to the Queen's knees. "Your Majesty, I would serve you," she whispered. "I am yours to command for any service, however small. When my grandfather gave me the pin and locket, I made a solemn vow to him on his deathbed."

Now the Queen really did understand. Her amber eyes glowed with lambent fire. "Sit back a little on the stool," she said softly. "Do not make it appear as if we are speaking secretly. Elizabeth, Barbara, draw a little closer, if you please."

To anyone watching, it would appear that the Queen was making light conversation with the daughter of an old friend and drawing her attendants into it. It was evident to Katherine that she had learned to become expert at conducting secret conversations in the presence of her jailer.

"There is something you can do for me," said the Queen.

"Yes, yes." Katherine leaned forward, her heart beating as fast as the tabor that had accompanied the wild leaps of the dancers who had entertained them earlier.

"Sit back," she was ordered peremptorily, and hastily obeyed the command. "We are in need of a friend in the North Riding for messages to be carried to Scotland. The Bulmers' home is too closely watched nowadays."

Katherine saw that her mother's eyes were fixed upon them. "My mother is coming," she whispered.

"There is nothing more to say. May we rely upon you to help us?"

"You know that you have my absolute loyalty," Katherine replied fervently, her heart pounding in her breast. "I swear to serve you and help you to regain your throne in Scotland in whatever way I can."

To Katherine's surprise, the Queen leant her head back and laughed merrily. "And that is exactly what my son did at the same age," she said, raising her voice. "You will receive a message in the next few days, either at your lodgings or the baths," she whispered and then looked beyond Katherine. "My lord of Leicester, I was about to send for you. You gave me your word that we should make music together before it be too late. Take up your lute and I my harp and let us begin."

Katherine marveled at the Queen's poise. She switched from secrecy to public cajolery without one moment of hesitation. But then, she thought, the poor woman has had many long years in which to perfect the art of deception.

Having been musically entertained by Queen Mary and Leicester for half an hour, Alyssa made their excuses. Isobel was beginning to slump in her chair with weariness and must be taken home to rest. Besides, Alyssa was so agitated by her thoughts that she had found it difficult to remain still on her stool.

They were escorted back to their lodgings by two of Leicester's servants and Tobias, who had been content to remain in the downstairs hall and act the faithful servant for the evening.

When they arrived, Isobel was straightway put to bed.

"I think I will go to my bed, also," said Katherine, yawning. "I will bid you good night, Tobias. Will you be coming up soon, Mother?"

"Soon. I must speak to Tobias first. There is no need to leave the candle burning for me. And you may go to bed too, Margery," she told her servant. "I can undress myself."

"Nonsense," said Margery. "I'd like to see thee undo all that lacing by thyself."

Alyssa gave her a faint smile. "Very well, then. You may help me off with my gown and I shall put on my dressing gown to speak with Master Ridley."

When she returned to the parlor, she found that Tobias had thrown another log on the fire to set it blazing merrily up the chimney. "Sit down, Tobias." She nodded to the leather-cushioned stool and herself sat in the high-backed settle that fronted the hearth.

For a few minutes, she stared into the fire, fascinated by the leaping flames, but her fascination was an uneasy one, for the bright colors spoke to her of blood and horror rather than comfort. A violent shiver ran over her.

Tobias leaned towards her. "Something is amiss." Although he did not touch her, his concern was palpable. "What is it?" he asked eventually in his soft voice.

Alyssa drew in a deep breath and released it in a sigh. "You may think me foolish, Tobias, but I fear for Katherine."

"With regard to Queen Mary?"

How astute he was. One rarely had to explain matters to Tobias. A man of few words himself, it needed few to make him understand.

"Am I letting my imagination overcome me, do you think?"

He pondered the question for a moment. "The Scottish Queen is a dangerous woman. Of that there is no doubt."

"And Katherine? Do you think she would be foolish enough to become enmeshed in Mary's web?"

"That depends."

Alyssa waited, but nothing more came. "Depends upon what?" she asked impatiently.

"Upon what transpired between them this evening. Were they alone together at any time?"

Alyssa felt a tide of warmth flood over her. "Alas, they were. The Earl of Leicester and I walked for a few minutes in the gallery." She lifted her head to meet his eyes. "We were speaking of Sir Philip and of Brendan," she told him, suddenly the haughty mistress addressing her steward.

"But what of my lord of Shrewsbury? Was he not there, in the presence chamber?"

Alyssa twisted her hands together, catching up the green silk girdle of her worsted dressing gown. "He was engaged in conversation with Isobel. When I returned to the chamber Katherine was on a stool at Mary's feet and their heads were together."

"Jesu!"

Tobias's exclamation chilled her blood. "So you do not believe these are merely womanish fears on my part?" she whispered.

"You have never been one for womanish fears." His eyes expressed warm approval.

"What are we to do?" she asked him. How often in the past had she asked him that question. As always, he gave her the answer she needed.

"You say they had only a few minutes together? Probably not enough to exchange more than a few words then. It is unlikely that Katherine and Mary will meet again. While we remain at Buxton, however, I believe you should watch Katherine day and night. Never let her out of your sight."

"It will not be easy," Alyssa said with a sigh. "As it is, she is fiercely resentful of my authority. In truth," she added, her voice sinking, "I think she hates me."

For once Tobias did not seek to reassure her. Although she was not looking at him, she sensed that his entire body had grown rigid. He knew about her and Philip, of course. He had always known. But never by one word had he betrayed his knowledge.

She raised her eyes to his and caught a flicker of emotion in his gray eyes. Then it was gone. "Mistress Katherine has much of the good side of her father in her," Tobias said. "She has his strong streak of independence coupled with his stubborn nature. She is also intelligent, but not always as wise as her mother. She is impulsive and longs to be engaged in some activity where she can feel useful."

It was a long speech for Tobias. "In other words," said Alyssa. "She has not enough to occupy her mind."

"Exactly so."

Alyssa twisted the girdle round and round her clasped hands. "She should be mistress at Radcliffe, that is what you are saying," she said, her words almost inaudible.

"That is what I am saying."

"But she is not wise, you said so yourself," Alyssa protested. "She is impulsive. How will she manage a large estate like Radcliffe, especially with Brendan away?"

"She will learn to do it, as you did, as Lady Laura did before you. Katherine is fortunate to have her mother close by her to advise her."

"And she has you, Tobias."

"And me, Mistress Radcliffe."

Alyssa pulled the girdle tighter, so that it cut into the backs of her hands. "Dear God, what a fool I have been. By shutting her out of participation in the management of Radcliffe, I may have caused her to involve herself in great danger."

"It is unlikely."

"I told you that Philip had given Mary's locket and pin to her on his deathbed?"

"You did. And that you asked her not to keep them in the house."

Alyssa unwound the girdle, rubbing one hand with the other. "I believe she still has them."

"That was unwise of her," Tobias said calmly. "But consider this: What can a young mother living in the remote North Riding of Yorkshire do to assist the Queen of Scotland?"

"Nothing, I hope and pray," Alyssa said fervently.

"Keep watch over her. Observe anyone who might come near her, in case a letter or note be passed between them. I doubt anything will happen, though." Tobias stood up, putting an end to their conversation. "Now, I think it is time you retired. You look weary. It is not easy for you being with Lady Colborne all this time, I am sure."

She smiled ruefully. "You are right, as always, my friend. My sister and I do not make good companions, I fear. But she is a little improved in her looks, don't you think, Tobias?" she asked him eagerly.

"The change of air and, doubtless, the waters have raised her spirits, to be sure." He smiled. "She has certainly resorted to her usual haughty manner."

"But she is not any better in health, is she?" asked Alyssa with a sinking heart.

"No. I regret to say, she is not. But these days at Buxton have given her a great deal of pleasure," he added, his voice gentle. "Now, set your mind at rest about Katherine, and try to get a good sleep."

Alyssa laid her hand on his arm, and felt the muscles tighten beneath her fingers. "What would I do without you, my dear friend? God keep you, Tobias."

"God be with you, mistress."

Chapter 34

For the next few days nothing untoward happened. Katherine seemed particularly lively, speaking quite openly of her meeting with Queen Mary, excited about their forthcoming visit to Poole's Cavern. Could this volatile child of hers really be capable of committing treason? wondered Alyssa. For that matter, was she capable of managing an estate like Radcliffe, as Tobias seemed to think?

These questions seethed through her mind, so that she had them, as well as her restless sister, to worry over each night. *I am beginning to look positively hagridden from lack of sleep*, she thought as she peered into her silver-backed hand mirror on the morning of their visit to the cavern.

Isobel was not well enough to accompany them. Indeed, Alyssa had already decided that it was time to make their plans to return to Yorkshire. Isobel had slept little in the past few nights. The pain in her breast and, now, throughout her body was growing worse, so that Alyssa had to increase the dosage of laudanum the physician had prescribed. Tobias was right. The revival had been more of the spirit than the flesh. Alyssa began to fear that her sister might even die before they reached Wensleydale.

"I have spoken to Tobias," she told Katherine, as they were dressing in their riding clothes for the excursion. "We will leave here on Monday."

"Monday," exclaimed Katherine. "But . . . but that's only four days away."

Alyssa held her breath for a moment and then turned slowly to face her. "I would have thought you would be happy at the thought of seeing little Dickon again."

"I am. I cannot wait to hold him again. It is only that . . . that we have been here such a short time."

"And your aunt's health has worsened, alas," her mother said sternly. "We leave Monday."

Was it her imagination or was there a flash of panic in Kate's eyes? Alyssa turned away. Lack of sleep was making her as tense and fretful as a lute string and oversuspicious.

Having dined lightly on a herb custard and cheese, they rode out with a party of ladies and gentlemen who were residing at the Hall as guests of the Earl of Shrewsbury. To Alyssa's great relief, Queen Mary was not of their party. Nor was Leicester. Doubtless he would be taking advantage of their brief time together to assure the Queen of his friendship. Insurance against the future.

It was a small party, not much more than a dozen or so. But to Alyssa they were all strangers and, therefore, suspect. As they rode through the wood, she kept her mount pressed as close as possible to Katherine's, so that she was able to hear all that passed between her daughter and the young man with a winning smile at her side, who was patently attracted to her.

When they dismounted near the mouth of the cavern, it was not a groom but the same handsome young man who helped Katherine down from her horse. She flashed him her brilliant smile and thanked him prettily.

Alyssa pressed her lips together. The girl was incorrigible. Then she thought of her own behavor with Leicester the previous week and smiled ruefully to herself.

Still, said her sterner self, Kate is married. Not for the first time in the past months, Alyssa sighed heavily, wishing to God that Brendan were the one lifting his wife from her horse, not some unknown young man.

The cave was set in an abutment of rock in the steep hillside. Once inside, they were led down a passageway by guides carrying flaming torches to light the way as the daylight dwindled—and then disappeared.

A shiver ran over Alyssa's back and shoulders. As they progressed further into the cave, it became even as she imagined the netherworld to be: dark, mysterious, the sound of dripping water and their muted voices echoing about the dank, stained walls.

Her heart began to pound, and her head took up its beat. Merciful heavens, don't let me become faint at this crucial time, she prayed. She must have all her faculties about her to watch Kate. But the pounding grew louder and the walls began to close in on her, depriving her of breath.

I cannot go one step further, said her trembling legs. *You must*, admonished her stronger self. *You cannot leave Kate.* The walls tilted and swung about her.

"Are you not well, Mother?" Kate asked her.

Her voice sounded a long way off, distorted by the echo. Alyssa felt as if she were in a world of distortion; familiar sounds and sights, including her beloved daughter's face, seemed to ebb and flow, expand and contract, so that nothing remained safe.

"I am just a little faint from the lack of air," she told Katherine.

"Perhaps you should go back."

"No, no, I cannot," Alyssa said, her panic increasing. "Give me your arm to lean upon and I shall manage very well."

She gripped Kate's arm and, head swimming, found herself being led into a vast chamber with strange rock growths that looked like huge icicles shooting upward from the slippery cavern floor and downward from its roof.

As she stood there, the flickering torchlight created grotesque shadows, so that everything—the walls, people's faces—seemed to be in motion, dipping and swaying in a diabolical dance.

The shivering spread to her entire body. The boom of voices increased, echoing now inside her head, the air of unreality stealing her senses away from her. "I must get out," she whispered to Katherine, hoping not to betray her weakness to everyone there. But the echo picked her voice up and bounced it from one wall to the other. *Must get out . . . must get out . . . must get out . . . out . . . out . . . out . . .*

People turned to look at her. "Us'll be done in a moment, mistress," said one of the guides.

But Alyssa shook her head and turned, wild-eyed, towards the darkness which, she knew, led eventually to air and light.

"Permit me to help," said an elderly man with gray hair and beard.

"This lady is not well," he told one of the guides. "One of you come with me so that I may escort her and her daughter outside."

"May I be of assistance?" asked a woman whose thin face wavered in the torchlight. Alyssa did not like the way the woman pressed against Katherine, but she was beyond speech by now.

"How kind," Alyssa heard Kate say. "But I think we shall manage very well if this gentleman—"

"Sir Miles Vincent," offered the man.

"If Sir Miles would assist me," finished Katherine.

Alyssa was to the point now where she wished she would swoon. That way she would wake up and find herself outside. She felt Kate's arm about her waist and, on her other side, the kind old gentleman gave her his arm to lean upon.

Impelled by nameless terror, Alyssa hurried forward, following the torch held by the guide, who grumbled beneath his breath. Her feet stumbled on loose stones, caught against clefts in the rocky path, but still she pressed on, dragging Sir Miles and Katherine with her.

At last she saw, beyond the shimmering smoke of the torch, a shaft of light and, within a minute or so, they were outside. Shaking uncontrollably, Alyssa drew in great gulps of air. Never had the sight of a few stunted trees, the pulsating song of the lark seemed so sweet. Never had a pale blue sky flecked with clouds offered such a welcome. She had returned to reality.

But with this return came a flood of both embarrassment and fear. "I am ashamed to have behaved so foolishly," she told Sir Miles, pressing her handkerchief to her lips. "I cannot think what came over me."

"It is a strange, unnatural place," said her rescuer kindly. "I can understand how it could affect someone of a particularly sensitive nature."

"I am under somewhat of a strain at present," she said, seeking to excuse her strange behavior. "My sister is very sick." Alyssa gave him a faint smile—which immediately died upon her lips, for from the corner of her eyes she had seen a flash of white in her daughter's hands. Her sight blurred for a moment. When it cleared Kate was coming towards her.

"I was just paying the guide a little extra," she said. "He was complaining at having to leave all the people to the other guide. Meaning, of course, that he would lose out on his payment."

"You should have permitted me to see to him," said Sir Miles gallantly.

"It is done," said Katherine.

Pray God she was referring merely to paying the guide, thought Alyssa.

When they returned to their lodging in Chapel Street, Alyssa toyed with the idea of confronting Katherine, demanding that she empty out the contents of the purse at her waist, but to what avail? Her daughter would refuse and, if her suspicions were based upon nothing but her overwrought imagination, the rift between them would grow even wider. Better to keep a constant watch on her, at least until they left Buxton. For now, at least, she would not even confide in Tobias.

But throughout the ensuing days, when she was first preparing Isobel for the journey home and then undergoing it, the flames of suspicion licked at her mind, so that she slept little and ate even less.

"You must try to eat and rest," Tobias told her, his thin face creased with worry. "Otherwise you yourself will fall sick and what use will you be to your sister, then?"

He was right—except that he did not know that her concern for Kate was even greater than her concern for Isobel.

They had to journey so slowly, halting frequently to allow Isobel to rest during the day as well as at nighttime, that it took two days to reach Doncaster and then a further eight days from there to the lower reaches of Wensleydale.

When they arrived at Colborne Place, Isobel clung to Alyssa. "Don't leave me here alone," she begged.

"You are not alone. You have your family to take care of you. Ingram, your sons, little Bess."

But her little Bess had hung back when Isobel had held out her wasted arms to her, until Alyssa had to pinch her hard on the arm and thrust her forward to embrace her mother.

"So, you are back," had been Lord Colborne's greeting to his wife. He did not even try to hide his shrinking disgust from her. "I thought you were to be away another two weeks at least. You should have sent word ahead of your coming."

So that you could better smuggle your wench or wenches from the house before Isobel arrived, thought Alyssa, who had not missed the consternation on his face when they had first ridden in. He had looked like a lad caught stealing apple tarts from the larder. His already ruddy face was even redder with fury and chagrin as he gave them his boorish greeting.

"I must go home," Alyssa told Isobel gently. "There is Joanna . . . and the harvest to see to. But I shall return as soon as possible."

"To remain for a while? Not just for a few hours. You will stay with me." Isobel's sapphire eyes glowed unnaturally in her gaunt face. She gripped Alyssa's hand, her nails digging into her flesh. "I have much to say to you," she said feverishly. "Do not fail me. Come soon or it may be too late."

"I will come soon," Alyssa promised, gently disengaging her hand. She bent to kiss her sister, trying not to flinch from the fetid breath, the skin that felt like hot parchment.

Oh God, the pity of it. To think of her sister's vanished beauty: the lustrous golden hair had become dry hay on her scalp, the swan-white complexion sallow. The facial bones were so close to the surface they looked as if they might break through the skin.

What would Thomas say if he saw his beautiful Isobel now? Alyssa wondered for a moment, and then pushed the thought away, despising herself for even thinking it.

Her eyes dwelt on dark-haired Bess, biting her lips to hold back tears, and then, after a moment's hesitation, she went to her. "Come, darling," she said putting her arms about the distressed girl. She felt Bess's body stiffen at first and then she raised her arms to hug her aunt against her, her hands clutching at her.

"You will come back, won't you, Aunt Alyssa?" she begged, raising her troubled face, the dark eyes ringed with long black lashes.

"I give you my word in God's name that I will return as soon as possible."

She said little to Kate as they rode the last part of the journey home. Her mind was filled with thoughts of the past and what might have been had Fate not taken them all up and tossed them about to be her plaything.

She looked up from her dark musing to see on her right the ruined limestone walls of Jervaulx Abbey turned to gold by the sunshine. How often had she and Philip ridden here to walk through the once-mighty abbey within whose precincts he had been born and raised. "Here was the great church where I used to sing each morning," he would say. "Now it is the birds who raise their voices to heaven. Here, the novices and I played at bowls," he told her, as they paced along the cloisters, the once smooth green a riot of daisies and celandines. And in the neglected churchyard he would kneel before his grandfather's tombstone and read aloud the inscription: *Thomas Thomson, Horsemaster of Jervaulx 1485 to 1537. Servitor Fidelis.* "A faithful servant," he would murmur, with a proud, loving smile.

As they rode past the ruins, Alyssa remembered, too late, where this bridlepath led. "We should have crossed at Ulshaw Bridge," she murmured to Tobias, her heart pounding into her throat.

"Why?" said Katherine, catching what she had said. "We should only have to cross the Ure again further up."

"Your pardon," muttered Tobias to Alyssa. "I had forgot."

Alyssa would never forget. As the trees remaining from this part of Jervaulx Forest closed about them, shutting out the sun, a chill of horror ran over her. The leaves rustled and she imagined them to be men stealthily closing in on them. She spurred her horse, but the trees were so dense that it was impossible for the poor animal to respond to her urgency.

Tobias cast an anxious look at her. "Soon be out," he murmured.

Alyssa cursed herself for not having gone another way, as she and Philip had always done, but her mind had been dwelling on Isobel and then upon Philip himself, until it was too late to turn back without having to explain herself to Kate.

"What on earth is the matter with you, Mother?" demanded Katherine, as Alyssa bent her head to avoid seeing the clearing in the center of the wood.

"Robbers. I am afraid of robbers," she murmured.

"What nonsense. We have six of our own men and three of Lord Colborne's to guard us. Surely you are not afraid that we shall be robbed in the middle of the day," Katherine said scornfully.

But Alyssa felt too sick to reply. She saw again the flash of knives, heard again the sound of many men breathing heavily and Thomas's cries as the blades repeatedly struck home, and then, more fearful than all the rest, Philip's anguished cry, "Thomas!"

She bent her head over her mare's neck, breathing in the warm animal smell of her, and felt Tobias's hand upon her bridle. She said nothing, but permitted him to guide her, forbearing even to raise her eyes until the glint of sunlight on the mare's silver trappings told her they were out of the wood.

When she lifted her eyes, it was to see Katherine, her eyes large and dark in her white face. "That was where it happened, wasn't it?" she said accusingly. "That was where my father was murdered."

Alyssa did not reply.

"Answer me, my lady Mother," Katherine cried. "Is that where my father was killed?"

Alyssa nodded. "It is."

Katherine turned her horse's head. "I wish to go back there."

Tobias released Alyssa's bridle. "We are riding home to Radcliffe, Mistress Katherine."

"You may do as you please, but I am returning to see the place where my father was murdered."

"Oh, Kate. Not today," Alyssa said wearily.

"You cannot stop me."

Tobias's hand shot out to grab at Katherine's reins. "Another day you may return to the wood. For now, you will ride home with your mother."

"How dare you tell me what I may or may not do. You are but a servant, and may not give me orders."

Alyssa's hand clenched on her birch whip. "Never again let me hear you speak thus to Tobias," she hissed at Katherine. "Turn your horse and cease making a fool of yourself before the servants."

Katherine's eyes filled with tears. "He was my father. You have never permitted me to know things about my own father."

Alyssa drew her mare close. "You shall know all you wish to know," she said in a low voice. "You may return to this place with Tobias, who was there at the time, and he will tell you all that happened. But first you must ride home with me. If you do not I shall leave you here without even one groom to protect you."

Katherine hesitated and then reluctantly turned her horse's head. "Very well, but I demand to know the truth about my father. I am no longer a child to be fobbed off with inventions."

It was true, thought Alyssa. One day she must be given the truth. But not today. Today she was bone-weary from the long journey, the scene with Isobel at Colborne Place and now this confrontation with Katherine. She was losing her strength to stand up to her daughter, as had Philip with his son, Katherine's father. She exchanged a glance with Tobias and saw his expression of concern and sympathy. Oh God, she thought wearily, all I want is a little peace and rest. Is that too much to ask?

The joy of returning to Radcliffe, seeing Joanna's bright, cheerful face and the dear, familiar sunbathed walls of the house that had been her home for twenty-two years sustained her for the remainder of the day and for several days thereafter. But then her overriding fear for Kate engulfed her again. Isobel was sending messages to her every day, begging her to come to Colborne Place. Yet how could Alyssa leave Radcliffe when she was still so unsure about her daughter's involvement with Queen Mary? Her suspicions were tearing her apart.

Chapter 35

One morning, a week after their return home, Alyssa went into the solar to fetch her prayer book. She had left it in the window seat. As she leant forward to pick it up, she saw from the window a man she did not recognize slipping through the orchard.

Almost immediately thereafter, she saw a flash of murrey-red. She narrowed her eyes, and saw that it was Katherine approaching the orchard from the courtyard wall. Something about the stealthy way she was moving alerted Alyssa. She was walking slowly through the orchard, nodding her head as if she were counting. Then she paused before a damson tree, its branches laden with purple fruit, and suddenly lifted her skirts to kneel down and scrabble with her hands at the base of the trunk.

Alyssa watched her, barely daring to breathe. Then she scrambled down from the window seat and, picking up her skirts, raced from the gallery. She sped down the stairs, across the hall, past the surprised servants, and out into the courtyard just as Katherine emerged from the orchard.

When she saw her mother, she turned as if she would retreat back into the orchard, but then she stood her ground, trying to hide her earth-covered hands behind her back.

Alyssa hurried across the courtyard, her heart racing. When she reached her daughter, she grasped her arm, fearing that Katherine might suddenly run from her. "Give me whatever it is you have dug up in the orchard," she said, panting for breath.

Katherine blanched, but she lifted her chin defiantly. "I have not one jot of an idea what you are talking about."

Anger and terror roared together in Alyssa's head. "If I have to call Tobias to deal with you, I will. Give it to me."

"The steward," scoffed Katherine. "What will he do to me? If he lays one hand on me I shall dismiss him, in my husband's name. You seem to forget that I am mistress of Radcliffe now," she said, but there was a shrinking fear in the depths of the eyes she fixed haughtily upon her mother.

Alyssa's grip tightened. "If you continue to do whatever it is you are doing, there will be no Radcliffe. No Radcliffe to hand over to little Dickon when he is grown, or to his children."

"I do not know what you are talking about, my lady Mother. Go lie down. You must be sick again. This is but another of the spells you have been having recently."

"For the love of Christ Jesu, Kate, cannot you understand where this will lead?" Alyssa choked back the sob that rose in her throat. "They will burn you at the stake if they find you guilty of treason."

Katherine's body tensed. "I do not know what you are talking about," she said again. "You are imagining things."

Alyssa shook Katherine's arm. "I swear before God and all His saints that if you do not give me what you dug up, I shall call the servants to hold you and wrest it from you. Is that what you wish?"

"You would not dare."

Alyssa looked up at her daughter, fixing her eyes upon hers. "To save you from the fire I would dare anything. I would stop at nothing, *nothing*, to save you and Radcliffe."

Katherine glared at her, her breast heaving. Then her eyes wavered and, slowly, she brought one soiled hand from behind her back and reached into the bodice of her gown. She drew out a twisted piece of paper and handed it to her mother.

Alyssa took it from her, releasing her arm to smooth the paper out. *Deliver this letter as you did the last*, she read. She looked up. "Where is the letter?"

"I will not tell you."

Alyssa held out her hand. "Give me the letter, Katherine."

"It is not mine to give. I would rather die than show it to you."

Alyssa's heart was beating so hard, she felt certain it would burst. "You speak lightly of dying, my daughter. But the death of a traitor means not only prolonged pain, but the loss of all we have won back: our home, our good name. Your child will be not only motherless but homeless and destitute as well." She took Katherine's arm and shook it hard. "For the love of God, Kate, think! Is that woman worth all that: your life, your home, your child?"

"What woman?"

Alyssa sighed. "You must think me a fool. Mary, Queen of the Scots. The black spider who entices innocent people into her web and then devours them."

Katherine raised her chin. "She has been wrongfully imprisoned by Elizabeth. She begged for her aid in regaining the throne of Scotland and Elizabeth clapped her into prison." She flung off her mother's hand. "She was a beautiful young woman when she first came to England. Look at her now. She looks more like a woman of sixty than forty-two. That is Elizabeth's doing."

"Oh, Kate. What have we to do with queens? Let it alone, for pity's sake. Give me the letter and I will destroy it. Pray God, that will be the end of it."

Katherine's face was pinched and drained of color, so that her dark eyes looked enormous. She stepped back. "I gave Grandy my word. He made me swear on his deathbed that I would help Mary."

Alyssa felt as if she had been struck a tremendous blow. "He had no right to lay such a burden upon you," she whispered through dry lips.

"Right or no, he gave me the Queen's gifts into my keeping and had me swear to do everything in my power to help her."

Oh, Philip, Philip. Even on your deathbed she was in your mind. Alyssa felt drained of all her resources. How could she fight a sacred oath made to Philip? As before, Mary had defeated her, but this time Radcliffe would be gone forever and her firstborn child would die a dreadful death.

She racked her brain to think of some way to make Katherine see reason. "Have you considered how your act of treason will affect Brendan?"

"Brendan?"

"Aye, Brendan, your husband. Whom you seem to have forgotten quite in your wilful conduct."

"Brendan seems to have forgotten me." Katherine's lips quivered. "I thought that perhaps there would be a letter waiting when we came home. It is more than three months since he wrote to me. Why should I consider him, when he pays no heed to me?"

Alyssa tried to summon up reasons for Brendan's uncommon neglect. "It is not like him. Perhaps he is not well," she suggested. "Perhaps he has been posted to some wild part of Ireland where he cannot send out messages."

"God's wounds, Mother. There are dispatches sent from Ireland to England every day."

"Dearest Kate, we cannot continue on this way. Give me the letter," Alyssa pleaded. When she saw that her daughter was intractable, her voice hardened. "If you persist in this tomfoolery, I say, I shall send for servants to help me search you."

Katherine gave a wild laugh. "And while you send for them, I shall have run from here and hidden the letter where you will never find it. Have done, Mother. I intend to play some small part in seeing that justice is at last done to Queen Mary."

"Which means a plan to kill Queen Elizabeth, no doubt. Your queen, I would remind you. Or a plan to have the Spanish invade so that they may set Mary on Elizabeth's throne. Treason, Kate. Treason."

"What nonsense you talk, Mother. Mary means no harm to her cousin. You heard what she called her at Buxton: 'my beloved cousin.'"

"You are not only headstrong, Katherine, but also a gullible fool."

Katherine's face grew hard as granite: "Whatever I am, I am no longer under your thumb, my lady Mother. You do not rule me."

Oh God, how history repeated itself. It could have been Thomas there, standing before his father, defying him. Alyssa folded her trembling hands before her. "That is true. But there is one person who has the power to exercise control over you. I shall write to Brendan immediately and beg him to come home. Pray God, your husband will be able to save you from yourself, and us with you."

Chapter 36

Brendan did not receive Alyssa's frantic letter in Ireland. By the time it arrived there, he had sailed to England, ordered to London by the Lord High Treasurer, William Cecil, Lord Burghley, himself.

The Earl of Ormonde had waited until Perrot had been installed as the new Governor of Ireland before sharing with him his suspicions about Brendan's involvement in the disappearance of the Earl of Desmond's body. By then it was common knowledge that the body—apart from its head, which graced the south gate of London Bridge—had been secretly buried in the Fitzgerald chapel in Tralee. The new Deputy General, whose business it now was to reconcile the rival factions and bring peace to the beleaguered country, decided to hush the matter up and to leave Desmond's body where it was.

When Brendan was questioned on the matter, however, he remained stubbornly silent.

"God's wounds, man," Perrot had roared, his face crimson with rage. "All you need do is name names, so that we may punish them. Your involvement in sanctioning the removal need never be mentioned, but I must have names to satisfy London."

Ormonde looked on, his face registering severe disapproval of the Deputy General's leniency.

Perrot struck the table before him with his fist. "We have need of you in Ireland, Radcliffe. God's blood, I am leaning over backwards to keep your name out of this. If Burghley were to hear of it, you'd be stripped of your commission and hauled back to London. Then where would you be? Probably facing a charge of high treason."

But nothing Perrot did or said could move Brendan to divulge names. Nor, for that matter, would he admit to his own involvement in the theft of Desmond's body.

In the end, it was Ormonde, he knew, who had written directly to Lord Burghley about him.

The result was a summons to come to London directly.

Not for him the hero's farewell when he left Ireland. "You are a damned fool, Radcliffe," were Perrot's last words. "You have thrown your entire future away for a dead body."

Brendan's reply to this had been a brisk military bow to the Lord Deputy of Ireland, nothing more.

The final humiliation was to be placed in the charge of a lieutenant and two men from his own troop. The only man to mourn his departure from Ireland was Colum, who wept as Brendan took leave of him. "I have a good mind to be telling them the truth," he whispered, scrubbing at his eyes with the back of his hand.

"Do that and you'll be joining Desmond," warned Brendan, replying in their native tongue. "Keep your mouth shut."

"Will you be back, do you think?"

Brendan had just shrugged and given Colum a faint smile in reply, but as he stood on deck watching the blue-misted hills of Ireland fade from his sight, he had asked himself the same question. Although part of him delighted in the thought of never seeing his blighted country again, he could not deny the aching in his throat and the pricking of tears as the land he had always called home receded into a wet mist.

Squaring his shoulders, he turned his back upon it and set his face to England.

"Burghley has delegated me to deal with your case."

To Brendan's surprise, when he reached London he had been ordered to Durham House to appear before Walter Ralegh.

"I am considered somewhat of an expert on Irish affairs," Ralegh drawled, his heavy-lidded eyes mocking Brendan, "and you were acting as my deputy in Ireland." Resplendent in his doublet of stiff black silk laced with gold, he leaned back in his velvet cushioned chair, his legs stretched out informally before him.

Brendan gave him no reply, but remained ramrod straight between his two guards.

"You may go," Ralegh said, nodding to the lieutenant.

"My orders are to remain—"

Ralegh's eyes widened, effectively silencing the lieutenant. "And my orders to you are to leave and take your men with you." He slapped the flat of his hand down on a document before him. "Her Majesty's orders are that Captain Radcliffe be turned over to me. You have done so, and may now go. My steward will see to your billet and comfort while you remain in London."

"Your servant, Captain Ralegh." The lieutenant made a stiff military bow and, nodding to his two men, marched them from the chamber.

Ralegh smiled. "Captain Ralegh—it seems another age since I was called thus. Yet it is but three years since you and I were together in Ireland."

Brendan stared at the painting of a long-dead Bishop of Durham above Ralegh's head.

"God's bones, Radcliffe, take that doomed look off your face and sit down," Ralegh said impatiently. He nodded towards the chair across the wide table from him and Brendan sat down. Ralegh pushed a blue bowl containing crushed dry tobacco leaves towards him. "Will you take a pipe with me?"

Brendan shook his head.

"Nay, I recall now that you did not take to the habit when you were last here."

Ralegh filled his long-stemmed pipe with the tobacco, tamping it down with his finger, and then lit it with a spill from the candle on the table. The tobacco glowed red as he pulled at the pipe and then he leaned back, blowing a cloud of smoke from his mouth. "Why the devil did you do it, Brendan? And for the love of God don't deny that you did. I know full well the strange loyalty the Irish have to members of their clan."

Brendan looked at Ralegh, his eyes hard. "If you know that, why be asking me why I did it?"

"Because I thought your noble English blood—and therefore your loyalty to your queen—would have prevailed. But it seems that the tribal instinct runs deep," Ralegh said contemptuously.

"One cannot be loyal to one's queen and to one's family, then?"

"Not when that family consists of a bunch of rebels who have caused the death of thousands of their own countrymen and, what is more, cost England thousands of pounds to put down. God's teeth, Radcliffe! The Fitzgeralds are vermin. They have caused the utter devastation of their own once-beautiful land. Desmond was no hero. He saw his own people reduced to eating each other and yet he would not submit. How could you bring yourself to pity such a man?"

"Can we not pity the hunted fox?"

Ralegh took out his pipe and spat into the rushes on the tiled floor. "A good metaphor. Foxes too are vermin."

Brendan sat very still and straight, his clenched hands hidden beneath the table. "The Earl of Desmond was my kinsman. Ormonde had his head. I considered that was enough for him to sport with. I preferred not to have my kinsman chopped into gobbets and distributed about Ireland."

"Why not? I hear it is a favorite pastime of the Irish with their enemies," Ralegh's mouth smiled at him above his pipe.

Brendan's smile was equally cynical. "Ah, but then there is my noble, English blood, which deplores such savagery. The English, of course, prefer to partially hang a man and cut him down to disembowel him before his own eyes, as they did with Campion. So much more civilized, don't you think?"

"You are speaking to the wrong man if you think I relish killing for killing's sake, Radcliffe. But what must be done, must be done. There is no place in the army of life for the squeamish. Besides, better to die by the sword than to wither away into old age. Highborn or lowborn, princes or paupers, of dust are we born, and dust will we become, until the Lord raises us up."

A long silence ensued while Brendan stared at his wavering reflection in the highly polished table and Ralegh puffed complacently at his pipe, watching him with half-closed eyes. "What is to become of me?" Brendan asked at last, no longer able to bear the strain of silent waiting.

"That depends upon you. As it is, you are fortunate not to have been clapped in the Tower on your arrival in London."

Brendan gave Ralegh a faint smile. "I have you to thank for that, I believe."

"You have. And damnably ungrateful you have been for it, too."

Brendan met the fire in his eyes and then looked down at the table. "I crave your pardon. That was churlish of me. I am most grateful for your intervention. But I still refuse to divulge names to you or to anyone else who asks me."

Ralegh sighed and then took a long draw on his pipe. "Answer me this one question and I shall not trouble you for any names: Was there any other man of rank involved in the theft of Desmond's body?"

Brendan lifted his head to meet the piercing blue eyes. "There was not. I swear to that in the name of the Lord Almighty."

"Good. Then we need have no concern for treachery amongst the officers."

"Nor amongst the men themselves, in truth. Would you not do the same if it were your brother?"

"Desmond was not your brother."

"He was my kinsman. That was enough. I considered that having his head displayed to be abused by all the ragtags of London was indignity enough."

"Was it your idea to steal the body away?"

"It was not."

"So you caught the culprits at it and turned a blind eye, was that it?"

"Something like that."

Ralegh shook his head slowly. "God's wounds, Brendan. Did you not realize that in that one moment of blindness you threw away a promising career, perhaps your chance of making a fortune? Desmond's lands are to be forfeited to the Crown, as you know. As the son of Sussex, albeit a natural one, you would doubtless have been granted a tidy parcel of land in Munster."

Brendan smoothed the pleats of the linen ruff at his wrist with one finger. "I doubt I shall be permitted to return to Ireland."

"I doubt you will. The Queen is as mad as a hornet. She liked you, you know. To receive the Queen's regard is to bask in the golden sun."

Brendan looked up as he caught the edge of sarcasm in Ralegh's voice. His eye ran over the heavy golden chain studded with sapphires, the hands laden with bright-jeweled rings, and thought how difficult it would be to wield a sword handicapped thus. "But it has not made you content, has it?" he ventured.

Ralegh's eyes flared. *You are presumptuous*, they said. Then he shrugged and grimaced. "I admit to you that I am damnably frustrated mewed up here at Court. My new ship is as strong as Noah's ark, which God himself invented. But I fear I shall never be permitted to sail in her to the New World. Others will do so, but I will not." He set his pipe down in the silver bowl with a clatter. "She still will not let me from her side."

Brendan had heard this from him before, but now the bitterness was harder, as if permanently engrained. "I hear that you have successfully established a colony in the Americas."

Ralegh's face brightened. "Aye, Captain Barlow has returned to

Court with tales of fertile soil, abundant fishing and a warm climate. He also brought back two Indian warriors with him, which pleased Her Majesty mightily. The land he took possession of is to be named 'Virginia' in her honor."

Seeing that Ralegh was warming to his favorite subject and might not be turned from it if he went further, Brendan broke in. "Will you tell me what is to become of me?" he asked again.

Ralegh frowned, irritated at the interruption. "You will not be permitted to serve again in the Queen's army in Ireland. Even I could not persuade Her Majesty to change her mind on that score. Burghley and she say you could no longer be trusted there."

Although a part of him flinched at this slur upon his honor, Brendan could not still the leap of his heart. But he said nothing, waiting for Ralegh to continue.

"By God, Brendan, you chose the worst time possible for your act of petty treason."

Brendan stiffened, but he did not dispute the term.

"Not only is the Queen mourning the death of her last suitor, Alençon," Ralegh continued, "but the assassination of the Prince of Orange has both appalled and terrified her. She has lost her only Protestant ally and feels herself alone in a sea of Catholics, all bent upon her destruction, with those supporting Mary, Queen of Scots in the very heart of her kingdom. So the news of your involvement in the disappearance of Desmond's body came as yet another blow. The son of her most loyal councillor, Sussex, working against her in Ireland!"

"'Fore God, Ralegh, I have never been anything but unfailingly loyal to Her Majesty," Brendan protested. "Surely you believe me."

"I believe you, but to the Queen, who envisages Spaniards pouring in on her from Ireland, it was an act of abject disloyalty. Only her love for your father prevented her from ordering your imprisonment, if not death."

"Christ Jesu," Brendan groaned, putting his hands over his eyes.

"Courage, my friend. You will live to fight other battles. I have been able to persuade the Queen that you would be a good man to help colonize our new lands in North America."

Brendan could not hide his start of anxiety at this. Dear Christ, was he never to be allowed to return to Katherine and Radcliffe, then? Was this his fate, to be marooned in some faraway alien land, perhaps never permitted to return to his home?

"You do not like the idea?"

Brendan shoved back his chair, scraping the legs on the tiled floor, and stood up. "You know full well that I have no wish for adventure," he said harshly. "Is this to be my punishment?"

Ralegh sprang up, to glare at him across the table. "Your punishment? Christ Jesu, man. Here I thought to be helping you to an even better life than you had before, the chance of riches beyond measure, gold and silver and pearls, and you call it your 'punishment.' But for my intervention, you might be lying in some evil jail at this very moment. God's bones, Radcliffe, you are an ungrateful cur!"

Brendan closed his eyes for a moment and then opened them to look steadily at Ralegh. "If you wish to please me rather than punish me, my friend, you will send me home to Yorkshire and my wife and child. I have told you before that we cannot all be out on the open seas discovering new worlds and gathering jewels for Her Majesty. Some of us must remain behind to guard our land against the Scots, to till our soil and breed our sheep and horses and beget a new generation."

"And is that the height of your ambition, Radcliffe, to breed sheep and horses and lie every night with the same woman?" Ralegh did not even try to hide his contempt.

Brendan released a deep sigh. "Although you will never comprehend it, that is my ambition. If your desire is to punish me for my part in Desmond's burial, then send me to the New World in one of your great ships. But if you seek to take from me my position and yet make me content, send me home to Radcliffe Manor."

"I shall never understand you, Radcliffe. By appearance, you might be my brother. Both of us are of the same build, with the same air of authority and pride. Yet temperamentally we are like the proverbial chalk and cheese. What irony! Do you realize that were I of your temperament I might be content to remain in my velvet prison at Court."

Brendan smiled. "I doubt that. If you were of my temperament, Her Majesty would have had little interest in you."

Ralegh threw back his head and laughed at this. "How right you are. You would have bored her to death with talk of horses and sheep. Whereas, she thrills to hear my tales of exploration and adventure."

He strode around the end of the table to stand eye-to-eye with Brendan. "So, that is your wish, my friend? A discharge from her Majesty's army and permission to retire to your manor in the wilds of the North?"

Brendan's heart was beating so hard he thought it would rise up and choke him. "That is my wish. An honorable discharge, for the sake of my children."

"Those many children you intend to father, eh? Lucky dog, to have such a woman of fire to warm your bed. But is it possible that one woman can suffice?"

"When you meet such a woman, you will understand better. Then you will say, 'Now I am at one with Brendan Radcliffe.'"

Ralegh grimaced. "God grant I never have to say so. I prefer to cull all the flowers I fancy, not just one. But enough. An honorable discharge, you say?"

Brendan nodded. "If that is possible."

Ralegh cocked his left eyebrow at him. "I will say this for you, for a man accused of treason you have the devil's nerve."

"If you grant me what I wish, I shall prove myself the truest Englishman that ever lived. I shall help guard Her Majesty's kingdom in the North against all invaders, be they Scots, French or Spanish."

"Or papist priests," Ralegh reminded him softly.

"Or papist priests." Brendan hesitated. "To own the truth, Ralegh, that is another reason for my desire to return home. You know the history of Radcliffe Manor and of its family. Better for me to be there as lord of the manor, ensuring that there be no return to its former ways."

Ralegh held up his hand, his great ruby and pearl ring flashing in the sunlight streaming in from the oriel window. "Enough! I am persuaded. I shall seek out Lord Burghley and make out that this will be your punishment: banishment to your estates in the North, where you will seek to prove your loyalty for the remainder of your life." His smile was ironic. "To me, that would be a sentence of living death. Heigh-ho, how different we mere mortals are from each other," he said, with a shrug. "Meantime, you will lie low here until I receive word of Her Majesty's pleasure regarding your future. I regret that you would not be a welcome sight at Court at present."

Next morning, Ralegh brought news of Brendan's release—and the letter from Alyssa, which had been sent on to him from Ireland.

"It is from my wife's mother," Brendan told Ralegh. He frowned. "I trust my wife or son is not unwell." He set the letter down, but his eyes kept straying to it.

"Open it now, if you wish," Ralegh told him.

"It can wait. I must first find words to convey my gratitude to you for all you have done for me." Brendan held out his hand. "You have acted as a true friend on my part."

"Most reluctantly, I assure you. I should prefer to be putting a commission as a captain of one of my ships into your hand." Nevertheless, he took Brendan's proffered hand and gripped it tightly in his. "May God's good fortune go with you, my friend. Although I think you a fool, I cannot help envying you that folly. At least you are gaining your heart's desire, unworthy though that desire might be."

"I have the feeling that you, too, will one day gain your desire to see the New World, Walter, and you will gain the love of a good woman."

"Ah, the Celtic second sight, is it?" Ralegh said.

Brendan shrugged good-naturedly, not at all deterred by Ralegh's sneers. "Second sight or no, it is my wish for you."

"Will you remain for a few days yet?"

Brendan set his hand down on the paper that gave him his honorable discharge. "I think not. Better I leave London before someone changes his or her mind."

"Very well. Best take one of my grooms with you for the journey. I have business to attend to and must return to Greenwich this evening, so I shall not see you again. Whatever needs you have for your journey north, bid my steward attend to it."

Ralegh turned on his heel as if he would leave without any further word.

"My thanks again," Brendan called after him. "God bless you for it."

Ralegh turned to grin at him, his even white teeth gleaming above the dark, pointed beard. "It was my pleasure. God go with you."

"And with you." Brendan made him a deep bow. When he raised his head again, he was the only man in the chamber.

He stretched out his hand for the letter from Alyssa, but some fear kept it unopened in his hand. He turned it this way and that, and then drew his dagger from his belt and slid it under the seal to break it.

The letter was brief. Only a few lines, written hastily in an uncharacteristically careless hand, with blots and crossings out.

> *Return home as soon as possible*, he read. *K is in great danger and I am powerless to control her. Please come home lest something terrible happen to her and to us all!*

The stark message was signed with a simple *A. Radcliffe*.

For several minutes Brendan perused the three lines, as if by rereading them he might be able to change their meaning or, at least, gain some sense from them. But he gained nothing but a slow chilling of the blood, so that he was actually shivering, despite the warmth of the autumn sun upon the colored glass windows.

What appalled him even more than the lines Alyssa had written was the date at the foot of the page.

> *Written this day, the tenth of August.*

Almost a month had elapsed since Alyssa had sent the letter. Only God knew what had happened at Radcliffe since then.

Chapter 37

As Brendan rode northwards, fear rode at his heels, urging him on. If only he had one of Radcliffe's fleet-footed horses between his thighs, he would have been able to ride like the wind down the great northern road, leaving Ralegh's groom way behind him. But he had to make do with hacks borrowed from the various inns on the way and cursed at their plodding pace, their spavined hocks and ill-kempt hooves.

He felt no sorrow at the thought of leaving London, perhaps never to see the great city again. His entire being was fixed on one place only: Radcliffe. And as the distance between him and London increased, his great fear of the unknown peril that lay before him was slowly eased by the vision of Radcliffe Hall itself that beckoned him ever on.

Plains and forests and rivers flashed by him, but he saw them not, for his mind was filled with the mirage of honey-colored limestone walls, the asymmetrical gables that sheltered casement windows whose panes were the eyes of the house, issuing a shining welcome to weary travelers.

I am going home. The unspoken words echoed in his head, accentuated by the rhythmical beat of his mount's hooves. *Home, home, home.* Tears rushed to his eyes as he experienced this entirely new feeling composed of love for his wife and child and for the earth they lived upon and the air they breathed and the house in which they lived. *Home.*

And with this upsurge of emotion came a grim determination that he would allow nothing to take that home from him. Whatever had happened while he was away, he would not permit anything or anybody to wrest this newfound happiness from him. To protect his home and family he would take up arms, lie, steal, cheat . . . even kill.

Armed with this steely determination, he set aside all those conjectures about Katherine's peril that had tortured him throughout the journey. He was nearing its end now. The great plain of York lay at his back. Before him lay the rolling lands that heralded the dale country and, in the distance, the outlines of the craggy, flat-topped hills that sheltered the towns and villages he had grown to love in the brief time he had dwelt amongst them.

If he had his way, he thought later, as he rode up the rise from Middleham to the moor, he would be content never to leave the North again. Even as he registered the thought, a small pang squeezed his heart at the realization that this would mean never seeing his homeland again, never again to hear the gentle voices, nor see the soft green land and hazy-blue hills of Ireland, but he pushed these thoughts aside. His heart lay here, in this remote, rugged land, with its rough-voiced, forthright people, for this was where his Caitlin was, where Radcliffe was.

A large flock of golden plover suddenly wheeled and swooped above him, their cries an "Amen" to his thoughts.

It was a little less than three years since he had made his first entrance into Radcliffe, but how different was it now to that first sight of it. Then it had been deserted, with its inhabitants hiding from the despised new master that had been foisted upon them. Now it was bustling with the activity of autumn: Outside the walls, the rich ground was being tilled by teams of oxen before the frost bit into it; and in the outer courtyard, with the smells of fermenting ale and stable manure mingling, people went about their business tending to the horses, the birds in the mews, the dairy and the laundry.

"Good day to thee, master," said the old gatekeeper, as if Brendan had been from Radcliffe but a day.

Brendan grinned to himself. If he was waiting for a warm welcome, he'd have to wait another few years, he was thinking.

His heart thumped in his breast as he rode into the inner courtyard. Waving aside both the groom from the previous night's hostelry—for he had long since sent Ralegh's groom home—and Barnaby, who had run from the stables to greet him, he swept his leg over his mount and sprang down.

As he drank in the sight of the shadow-dappled house, the heavy, nail-studded door swung wide and Alyssa ran out, hands outstretched to him. "Oh, Brendan, God be thanked, you are here at last. I saw you ride in from the window. I thought you would never come."

He went on his knees to her and felt her hand on his head. "I was called from Ireland to London," he explained, when he had risen. "Your letter did not reach me there until I was about to leave, last week. Where is Kate?"

Alyssa's small fingers grasped his arm. "She is playing on the bowling green with little Dickon. Do not tell her I wrote to you, I pray you, Brendan."

"I must," he said gently. "But tell me quickly what is going on. I have been sick with apprehension since I had your letter."

"Walk with me around the side of the house and I will tell you."

Brendan paused to give orders for his saddlebag to be unloaded from his mount. "The remaining baggage is being sent on by carrier, some of it from Ireland," he told Barnaby, "so 'twill be a while before it gets here." He tucked Alyssa's hand within his arm. "Now, my lady Mother, your news before I see my beloved Kate again," he said in a low voice.

As they walked around the house, Alyssa kept her eyes bent to the ground. "She has undertaken the role of an emissary for letters to and from the Scottish Queen," she told him baldly, when they were out of the earshot of the outdoor servants.

Brendan halted in the lee of the west wall and swung around to confront her. "May the Saints preserve us! Surely you must be mistaken. Kate could not have been so foolhardy as to jeopardize her life and that of us all for Mary, Queen of Scots."

Alyssa met the anger gathering in his eyes without flinching. "She admitted it to me, said that she intended to play some part, however small, in seeing that justice was done to Queen Mary. Oh, Brendan, I have been utterly terrified for her these past weeks." Her lips trembled. "Night and day, I am tormented by the image of her at the stake, the flames licking about her body. I have been unable to sleep at night for it."

He saw now that there were deep pockets like bruises beneath her eyes and she had lost weight.

"Does Tobias know?"

"He knows there is something the matter, but I refuse to tell him what it is. Had I done so, he would have had Kate locked in her chamber until you came home, I am sure."

"Which is exactly what should have been done with her. You should have told him."

"Katherine is the daughter of the house," she said, drawing herself up haughtily. "Tobias is our steward."

"Tobias is a loyal friend and a gentleman, as you know full well, my lady Mother."

Alyssa chewed on her lower lip. "I am weary of fighting with Kate. She carries so much anger towards me already, I could not bear to cause more."

"Better angry at you, than dead." He took her hands in his and squeezed them tightly. "Go back inside the house. I will deal with her."

"Be kind," Alyssa begged. "She thinks because you have not written that you have forgotten her."

"I have not forgotten her, not for one second. But this is not the time for kindness. Go inside and send for Margery to fetch the baby immediately."

Brendan gave her a little push in the direction of the screen-entrance door, and then strode around to the north front of the house, his mouth setting into a tight line. His delight at the prospect of seeing Kate again had faded away, replaced by a cold fury that she should have endangered them all for a mere whim.

He walked around the corner, crossing the stone-flagged terrace, and then paused, momentarily enchanted by the sight of his Kate, lying on her back on the smoothly scythed bowling green, holding Dickon above her. The baby was chuckling at her, his plump fists reaching down to her radiant face.

Brendan's heart turned in his breast. God, how beautiful she was and how he loved her! Even now, when he was riven with cold fury at her hazardous folly, she had the power to entrance him. He raised and lowered his shoulders, both physically and mentally shaking himself. If he succumbed now, it might be the end of them all.

Lightly, he ran down the steps and strode across the green. So immersed in playing with their child was she that she did not hear Brendan approach until he was standing beside her. "Oh," she said, as his shadow loomed above her, one hand instinctively clutching the laughing child to her breast, the other smoothing down the skirts that had ridden up to her white thighs.

Then she saw who it was and her apprehension changed to a dawning joy that would have dissolved Brendan's resolution—and his knees—to jelly had it been any other time but this.

"Brendan! Is it really, truly you? Oh, Brendan, I had begun to think you dead." Still clutching Dickon to her, she sprang up, her arm extended to Brendan. When he made no move towards her, her smile faded and she tilted her head in a little gesture of enquiry. "What is it, what is the matter?"

"I have asked your mother to send Margery out for the baby. I wish to speak alone with you."

She lifted her chin in the old defiant way. "Well, that is a fine greeting after having been away without writing for almost six months. You haven't even glanced at our son. Isn't he a darling?"

"I shall have an abundance of time to make my son's acquaintance later," Brendan said, holding himself rock-still. To his relief, he heard the jingle of Margery's keys behind him and turned to receive her greeting.

"Well, tha'rt home at last, master, and not afore time, I might say." The look she shot at Katherine beneath lowered eyebrows told him that Margery, too, was aware of some trouble between Katherine and her mother. "Give me the babe." She scooped the baby from Katherine's arms, before she had time to protest, and marched him away to the house with a flurry of starched petticoats.

"I think I will go inside, too," said Katherine, avoiding his eyes. She bent to gather up the blanket and the baby's bone rattle and teething ring.

"Leave those," Brendan ordered her.

She ignored him, tucking the rattle and ring into the pocket of her white apron, then carefully folding the blanket, end to end, corner to corner.

"By Christ, Kate, you will obey me."

She looked up at him then, her dark eyes wide at this uncommon anger in him. He dragged the blanket from her hands, throwing it on the ground, and grabbed her upper arms.

"You are hurting me." She put up her hands to loosen his, but his grip merely tightened.

"I shall hurt you far more than this if you will not be still and listen to what I have to say to you."

Her hands dropped to her sides, but still she gazed up into his face with a look of stubborn defiance. "What lies has my mother been telling you?"

"Your mother does not lie, as you well know, madam wife."

She gave a harsh laugh. "My mother's entire life has been a monstrous falsehood."

"Enough. I am weary of these tales about your mother. You are a grown woman now, responsible for your own life . . . and that of our son and any other children we may have."

"If you remain at Radcliffe long enough to father any more."

He put his face close to hers. "Oh, I shall be at Radcliffe for the rest of my life, sweetheart, have no fear. That is, unless it is too late to undo your arrant folly." He took her face between his hands, the pulse in her temples quickening against his fingers. "Why did you do it, Kate? Why did you endanger everyone you love, and who love you? Why would you hazard Radcliffe, our home and Dickon's inheritance, for such a lost cause?"

"It is not a lost cause," she screamed, dashing his hands away and springing back from him. "Mary is the rightful heir to the English throne. We mean to make Elizabeth see that."

"By killing her? In truth, that will make her see it very well."

"We have no intention of killing Elizabeth. We intend only to ensure that she names Mary as her heir."

"Oh, Kate, Kate, how gullible you are."

Her breast rose and fell fast. "And how insufferably arrogant you are. You, who have no notion at all of what loyalty to an ideal might mean. You, a man without a true country, a mercenary who fights against his own people for silver. What would you know of loyalty, bastard?" She spat out the last word with relish, as if it had hung on her lips since they had parted and she was glad to say it at last.

"Your words have a smattering of truth," he said, his face impassive. "But you must know that the plots regarding Mary's escape are all backed by Spain. Spain is now England's most dangerous foe. You must know that. Every day there is increasing talk of an invasion of England by Spain's mighty armada of ships. By passing letters to and from Mary, you are subscribing to that invasion."

Fine beads of sweat stood out on her upper lip. "She should at least be restored to her rightful place as the Queen of Scotland."

Brendan recognized this as a small token of retreat. "That is for her son, King James, to arrange. Not for you, a woman with a busy household to manage."

She made a grimace to hide the trembling of her mouth. "I have no household, you must know that. My mother is mistress of Radcliffe and will remain so for the rest of her life." She dashed away a lock of dark hair that had fallen from beneath her cap. "All I am good for is sewing hems on pillowcases and putting labels on the bottles of physic she makes up for the stillroom."

"I mean to be changing that, now that I am home permanently. But first you must make peace with your mother."

She turned away. "That will never be."

He took her chin in his hand, forcing her to look up at him. "Have faith in God's mercy, Kate. Your mother's judgment is for Him to decide, not you. Meanwhile, I demand your promise that you give up this foolhardy game of yours."

"It is no game to me, Brendan."

The intensity of her expression made him far more fearful than had her defiance. "You are right. It is no game, but a perilous enterprise that could end in your death at the stake."

"I do not care," she whispered.

"You do not care!" he roared. His hands turned to fists. Never had he come closer to striking her. "You do not care about being burned alive. Well, *I* care if you do not." He beat his right fist against his chest. "I care for Radcliffe Manor and all its retainers. I care for your mother and Joanna and Tobias and our son, Dickon." He grabbed at her as she stepped back from him. "But, most of all, I care about you," he cried, shaking her hard. "I love you, Kate Radcliffe. You are my life and my light. Without you I am nothing. And if I have to beat this out of you and starve it from you, I swear in the name of Almighty God I shall do so, for I'll not have you burn for the sake of that damnable witch who's cast a spell over you."

She was weeping now. "Oh, Brendan," she sobbed, her arms hanging limp at her sides. "I must. Don't you see, I must. I gave him my word."

"Gave who your word?" He glared down at her. "Was it that man, Edward Carlton?"

"No, no, not Edward, Grandy. I gave Grandy my word."

"Your grandfather?" he said, astonished. "When was this?"

"When he was dying. He gave me the locket and the pin, the gifts Queen Mary had given him, and made me promise that I would do all I could to help her." Her eyes were dark pools. "He said that he had failed her and that I must do it for his sake."

"He had no right to ask such a thing of a young girl."

"He had every right," she said indignantly. "I loved my grandfather more than anyone else in the world. Besides . . ." She fixed her eyes upon the gilt and pearl buttons of his doublet.

"Besides what?" he demanded.

She lifted her tearstained face to his. "Give me your word you will never divulge this to another soul," she begged.

"I swear it," he said solemnly, trying to stem his impatience.

"He had me and Joanna secretly baptized by a Catholic priest when we were infants."

God damn you, Sir Philip, thought Brendan, not so much for having it done, but for telling Kate and for laying this tremendous burden on her.

He gave a light laugh. "And so was I baptized. So were many of us. But our religious practice since that time has washed away all the holy water."

"Do not treat me like a child," she said coldly.

"That was not my intention. 'Twas my intention to make you stop acting like one."

"Make me?" Her dark eyebrows arched upward.

"Make you. It surely has not escaped your attention that you are my wife, Madam Radcliffe."

"The promise I made to Grandy was a sacred promise, made on his deathbed."

"And the promise you made to love and obey me was made before the sacred altar in the house of God. Naturally, that supercedes any other vows you may have made before then."

"Do you truly think so?"

"I know so. Besides, can you truly believe that your grandfather would have intended you to risk your life and that of your family and the future of Radcliffe for the Scottish Queen?"

"He risked his own life in her cause."

"Perhaps he did," Brendan said hurriedly. "But he cannot surely have expected the same of his granddaughter? From the little I know of him, it does not sound like him at all. Doubtless, when he was dying, he was racked with guilt for not having accomplished more for Queen Mary."

"He was. There were other things, too, that troubled him. That was why he begged for a Catholic priest and why Edward brought Father Campion to him." She clapped a hand to her mouth. "Oh! I should not have told you that it was Edward who brought him."

Brendan's mouth flickered into a tense smile. "I guessed at it."

A flock of crows flew low above their head, their raucous cawing startling them."

"It is time we went in," he said gently. "I am weary from the long ride—and filthy." He showed her his hands, grimy with dust. "I need a good bath."

She made no move towards the house, but looked up at him with eyes suddenly wide with fear. "Pray God, it be not too late for me to extricate myself from this mess, Brendan, without it causing lasting harm."

He took her hands between his and then put his arm about her, pressing her against his side. "So long as you do not become further embroiled in anything more, I am certain the danger will soon be past," he told her, mentally praying to God to make it so. His eyes held hers. "Swear to me, my darling, that there will be no further communication with Queen Mary or her emissaries."

"I swear it," she whispered. Her troubled eyes met his and he smiled, seeking to set her mind at rest.

"Now, my sweet, I believe it is time for this travel-weary husband to receive a kiss of welcome from his wife."

She gave a little sob. Then all thoughts of treason and sacred oaths and secret letters were forgotten, as their lips met and touched and then clung, and Katherine's pliant arms slipped about his neck to draw him even closer, obliterating everything but the sweet, violent rush of desire.

Chapter 38

Katherine awoke to find herself alone in the bedchamber. She had no idea what time it was, for when they had come into the room Brendan had slammed the shutters shut and latched them, muttering something about, "It may be day outside, but for us it is night." All she remembered after that was much laughter, cursing as they struggled to help each other get their clothes off, Brendan's apologies for going to bed with her without washing the dust of travel from his body, and the ecstasy of their bodies merging.

It had been as easy as that: no courtship, for the long period apart had been courtship enough. Just the coming together for which they had both pined for so long, the culmination of all the tension and desire that they had been forced to sublimate since the baby's birth and Brendan's departure for Ireland.

Later, when they had slept for a while in each other's arms, Brendan took her again, this time so teasing her by his maddeningly slow strokes, that she cursed him and rolled on top of him to determine their concerted movements herself.

"My little Roman," he told her, his eyes laughing up at her.

It was quiet now in the shuttered chamber, but from outside came the clip-clop of hooves, the lowing of cattle and clanking of pails. Must be milking time, she decided. She giggled to herself, thinking how shocked the servants would have been by her sudden disappearance upstairs with Brendan. Doubtless, her mother, too, would consider her guilty of conduct unbecoming to a gentlewoman.

She swept back the bedclothes and jumped from the bed, to do a few steps of a courante across the chamber floor. "Your pardon, my lady Mother," she said, curtsying to the ornately carved cupboard, and pretending to simper, "but now that my husband is home, I shall be the mistress of Radcliffe and may do exactly as I please here."

"Well," said Brendan's voice from the door, "a fine household this will be if its mistress is to dance about naked all day."

"Oh, you gave me a start, coming in like that." Suddenly shy, she tried to cover herself from him with her hands.

"Too late now for modesty. You are discovered for the wanton you are." He crossed the room, fully clothed, the aroma of some spicy scent emanating from him.

"You are all dressed," she said.

"That I am. Dressed and bathed and my hair trimmed." He made her a flourishing bow. "Ready for the homecoming feast your mother is having prepared for me."

Katherine put a hand to her mouth. "Oh Lord. I should have thought of that."

He put his arm about her. "*Your* homecoming feast was infinitely preferable to food, my darling one."

She darted away from him. "Lord in heaven, I must get dressed before the entire neighborhood is in upon us."

"Many of them are." Brendan strode to the window and folded back the shutters. "Here's your Uncle Piers riding in with Giles Challoner," he said, sitting down in the window seat.

"And here am I, determined to be mistress of Radcliffe, only to be discovered abed in the late afternoon by everyone in Wensleydale! God's wounds, Brendan, stop laughing and give me my bedrobe that I may get some water to wash."

"I will have Grace bring some up and shall make your apologies to our friends by telling them that you were overcome by the unexpectedness of my arrival home."

"Which is the truth." She wrapped the bedrobe about her and then, frowning, sat upon the bed and studied him. "Why haven't you written to me all this time?"

Her question seemed to take him by surprise. He hesitated for a moment and then said, "We were sent up to the wildlands of Ulster, far from any source of communication, to investigate a complaint of a Scottish invasion."

"And then you had to go to London?"

"I did. I had to report to Walter Ralegh, who seems to be fully in charge of Irish affairs nowadays."

Although it was a likely enough story, something about Brendan's demeanor while telling it troubled her. His tone was a little too light, his stance a little too stiff.

She knelt up on the rumpled bed. "I thought you were so invaluable to the English army in Ireland that they would never let you go."

He gave her a faint smile. "Friendships can be useful at times."

"Ralegh, you mean?"

"Just so. He was trying to persuade me to captain one of his ships to help settle the land his explorers have just discovered in the Americas."

"Oh, Brendan, not again."

He smiled. "Again? Ralegh never thinks of anything else. Even his relentless pursuit of wealth is so that he can pay for his vessels and their men and supplies."

"But you told him you would not go, of course."

"That I did." He turned to look down into the courtyard. "I grasped the bull by the horns and told him that, if he were truly my friend, he would obtain my release so that I might go where I am most content to be."

"And he was able to do so."

He turned to her, a dull red smoldering in his cheeks. "I am here, amn't I?"

She shook her head. "I am surprised that the Queen assented, knowing how she felt about your father. She wished you to make a success of your life."

He stood up, breathing heavily, as if his heart were racing. "My father has nothing to do with it," he said, his voice harsh. "And I consider being the Lord of Radcliffe Manor all the success I need."

Now it was Katherine's turn to flush. "There is no need to bark at me. I would much rather have you here than away in Ireland."

The next moment he was beside the bed and on his knees before her. "I never thought to hear you say that. You will not regret it, sweetheart. I swear in the name of God and all His saints that I shall do everything in my power to make you happy." He looked up into her face with an intensity that made her afraid. "God, how I love you, my precious Kate, my Caitlin."

He buried his face in her lap and she entwined her fingers in the crisp dark hair curling at the nape of his neck. But still she held back from words of love and she knew when he looked up that she had disappointed him yet again.

Although Brendan's return brought laughter and dancing and music back to the house, the move to make Katherine the true mistress of Radcliffe was shelved for a while.

"Your mother has too many worries about her ailing sister and mother for us to turn her from her usual routines," Brendan told her when she broached the subject.

"My mother will always have concerns about someone," cried Katherine. "She is that sort of person. She must be busy about something or she would pine to death."

"Leave it to me," Brendan told her. "I shall devise something that will bring contentment to all of us."

As the busy weeks of autumn passed, with sides of beef and bacon to be salted, and fruits and vegetables preserved and pickled, and eggs sorted and stored, Katherine's resentment built again as her mother slipped into her old ways of telling her daughter what must be done and giving orders to the servants.

Before Brendan had come home, Katherine had had the perilous excitement of playing a role—albeit a minor one—in assisting Queen Mary to her rightful throne. Although, in truth, the excitement had been more in the anticipation than in fact, for in the entire three months since she had returned from Buxton only two letters had passed into her hands. Now the knowledge that she was useful to Mary's cause, that she held some small position of importance, was gone. And though she was in many ways relieved to have put an end to the concern that she was endangering not only herself but her entire family and Radcliffe by her actions, the flat feeling of not being truly important to anyone increased. Not even the prospect of becoming the true mistress of Radcliffe in the near future could alleviate her boredom.

"I will come with you to visit Aunt Isobel," she said one day in the middle of October, as her mother was preparing to ride out to Colborne Place.

"It is a wretched day," said her mother. "Better that you avoid a long ride in the rain. You still have a cough left over from that cold in the lungs you had."

"Oh, Mother, for the love of heaven, stop treating me like an infant," snapped Katherine.

Her mother sighed. "I was merely pointing out that it was a cold, wet day. If you are not wholly well you should avoid riding out in such weather."

"I've a good mind to take Silver Moon up on Melmerby Moor and gallop her as hard as I can."

Again, her mother sighed. "Oh, Kate, Kate. How like your father you can be sometimes," she said in her maddeningly mild voice.

"I wouldn't know about that, would I, Mother, considering you never tell me anything about him."

Alyssa drew on her riding gloves and then looked down at them, flexing her fingers. "I am in need of new gloves. That new kestrel of mine has torn the backs of these with his talons."

As always, she had changed the subject when Katherine had spoken of her father. "Give Aunt Isobel my love," she said, knowing from experience that she would never beat down her mother in this avoidance of discussing her father.

"I will." Alyssa bit her lip. "I can hardly bear to see her now, Kate. She is like a skeleton and has not the strength to speak more than a few words at a time. Pray God, it will not be long now. A few weeks at the most, the physician says. In truth, he feels she should have died a long time ago, but that something is keeping her from relinquishing her hold on life. I wish I knew what it was, so that I could help her."

She smiled sadly at Katherine, her eyes filled with tears.

"Oh, Mother." Katherine flung her arms about her mother's shoulders. Brendan was right. This was not the time to cause more upheaval in her mother's life. Time enough for that later.

"Must you go today?" she said, going to peer through the tall window in the great hall. The rain was lashing down, the wind gusting it against the walls and windows of the house. "You will be soaked to the very skin."

"Rain does not trouble me. In truth, I like it. Besides, I gave Isobel my word that I would come today. I cannot disappoint her."

Knowing that nothing would change her mother's mind, Katherine did not try further to dissuade her. She would take advantage of her absence by speaking to Margery about the deplorable state of some bed linen she had discovered in a chest, their creases scored with mildew.

She was in the stillroom, putting away the jars of calf's-foot jelly the cook had prepared the day before, when Sally, the little scullery maid, crept up to her. "Yes, Sally, what is it?" she asked sharply, wondering what the girl was doing away from the kitchens.

"If it please thee, mistress, there's a person here to see thee," the girl whispered, rubbing her red hands up and down the apron of sacking that covered almost the whole of her small body.

"A person? Do you mean a tradesman, Sally? Tell him he must speak with Cook or Master Ridley."

"Nay, mistress, he's no tradesman. 'Tis a gentlemen he is and asking for thee. Nobody else but Mistress Katherine, he said, and bid me go secretly about it."

A hand of iron squeezed Katherine's heart. Oh God, it appeared she was not to escape from Mary's secret service after all.

"Where is this man now?" she asked the agitated maidservant.

"He said to tell thee he'd be at the bottom of the orchard, mistress, by the mulberry tree."

The orchard. She was right, then. It was in the orchard that Mary's letters had been hidden. For a wild moment, she thought of going to Brendan and asking him to deal with it. But the moment of weakness was gone as soon as it came. This was her dilemma. She must settle it herself.

"You know the cloak stand by the screen entrance?"

Sally nodded.

"My old winter cloak is hanging there. Fetch it to me, and mind you say nothing to anyone about this man. Not now or at any time." She bent down to look into the lass's eyes. "Can I trust you, Sally? This is to be a secret between us two only."

The child's eyes shone. "Aye, mistress. I swear on the prayer book I'll not betray thee."

Jesu, now the girl was probably imagining a romantic assignation with another man. Oh well, thought Katherine, better that than the truth. "Go, then. And make haste."

Sally returned a few minutes later, the cloak bundled in front of her. "I'd to hide a bit," she explained. "Master Ridley was coming from the buttery, but then he went away." Her eyes were two round coins as she watched Katherine put on the cloak.

"Now, off you go, back to the scullery, Sally. And, mind, not a word of this to anyone."

The girl gave her a huge wink and dashed out the door.

Katherine waited in the doorway for several minutes to ensure that no one was about, and then swiftly crossed the passageway, her head and face hidden in the cloak's hood, and went out the servants' door.

She halted for a moment, the onslaught of rain and wind tearing at her breath. Then she bent into it and hurried across first the inner courtyard and then the outer. The gate was open, as it usually was at midday to permit the laborers to pass through. In a few minutes she was within the orchard, sheltered a little by the rows of fruit trees, which shivered in the wind now that they were denuded of their last leaves.

Katherine shivered with them. Her gown and kirtle were soaked through already, the wind having flung open her cloak to let in the driving rain. She looked about her, but could see nothing but the angular limbs of trees. There was barely any light in the orchard; the rain-filled clouds loomed dark and menacing above her.

A feeling of terror overcame her. The familiar forms of pear and apple and plum and quince trees seemed to have become stunted and grotesque in the wind and gloom, their gnarled branches reaching out to her like the withered arms of witches. She was wishing now with all her heart that she had not come.

Not daring to call out, she approached the tall mulberry tree, its fallen fermented fruit squishing unpleasantly beneath her feet. At first she could have sworn that no one was there. Then a tall man stepped from behind its trunk, his face, like hers, masked by the folds of a black hood.

She peered at the cloaked figure, but could not recognize it. Then it spoke. "It is good to see you again, Katherine."

She would have known that sonorous voice anywhere. She stumbled forward, propelled by surprise and excitement . . . and some other emotion, which she could not think about now.

"Oh, Edward," she cried, "you have come home at last!"

Chapter 39

Edward stepped back from her outstretched arms, his raised hands staving her off, palms facing her. It was a strangely feminine gesture, like a woman repelling a man's advances.

Katherine suddenly became a child once more, a child who had run to her father with outstretched arms, only to be thrust aside and cursed for being in his way. A tide of warmth spread from her neck up to her face. "Have you been in England long?" she asked, determined to keep a tight rein on her emotions.

"For a while. Are you well, Katherine?"

Her name sounded peculiarly formal on his lips. Then she remembered that Edward had always called her by her full name, unlike Brendan, who called her Kate or Katie or Caitlin, but rarely Katherine. She had liked the way Edward had spoken her name in those bygone days; it had made her feel like a grown woman instead of a child. But now it merely sounded cold and formal, matching his demeanor.

"I am very well." She gripped her hands together beneath her cloak.

God in heaven, was this to be the conversation between them after almost four years apart: a mere exchange of polite niceties as if they were barely acquainted? She had dreamed of this moment of reconciliation, of how he would take her in his arms and tell her that he had given up the priesthood because he could not live without her. "I have thought of you . . . often."

"And my thoughts have been with you and your family." His voice was snow-cold.

Anger rose up like bile, spilling over in words. "Have they? Have they, indeed? And were they with me when my mother and I were thrown into prison because of the priest you brought to Radcliffe? Or when I wrote to you in utter despair because I was being forced to marry a stranger against my will? Do you recall what you wrote back to me?" she demanded.

He smiled a faint, pained smile and shook his head.

She stepped forward, so that they were less than a yard apart. Her eyes dared him to move back from her. "You told me in that cruel letter—which was not even addressed to me, but to my mother—that my letters had caused you great embarrassment, that I should consider you as one dead."

"I wrote nothing but the truth. You were acting impetuously, as you always did." He sounded like a stern parent. "You did not take into account the fact that I was a man in the throes of taking holy orders, Katherine. You were thinking solely of yourself."

Miraculously, his rebuke cooled her fury. In truth, she had never felt so physically cold as she did now, standing close to the man she had loved since childhood, the bitter rain falling on them. She shivered. "Yes, I was thinking of myself," she said with a proud little smile. "You had broken my heart, Edward."

"You must not exaggerate, Katherine," he said. Had he changed so much since their last meeting or had Edward always been this patronizing?

"I do not exaggerate, Edward," she said, her voice perfectly calm. "In breaking the promise of everlasting love you made to me, you broke my heart. And you did it quite callously, without any forewarning."

In the gloom, his face grew hard as white marble. "God had called me. I could not place a woman before God."

"Of course not," she said briskly.

"And you recovered swiftly, no doubt. You have a child now, my mother tells me."

"I have. A son who will become the new Lord of Radcliffe. We named him Richard after my brother."

"So all is well with you now. You are settled into marriage with your husband. He is a good, kind man, my mother tells me."

"What would your mother know about my husband? He has been away in Ireland during a great part of our marriage and when he is home we receive few invitations to visit our neighbors. Brendan is not one of us, you see, Edward. He is an incomer, a foreigner and, therefore, unacceptable to the gentry of the North Riding."

He lifted his cloak further forward on his shoulders. "Again, I believe you exaggerate."

"Perhaps." She summoned up a slight smile. "But we manage very well, I assure you. Brendan is not one to be downcast over little slights and rebuffs. And Lord Scrope is very kind, although he is rarely in residence at Bolton nowadays, of course."

"So, you are content." He seemed anxious to receive her assurance of this.

"Oh, my heart is quite mended now, if that is what you mean," she said lightly. "Even if you examined it very closely, I swear you could barely see the crack."

"You speak nonsense."

"To you it must seem so." She half turned from him, suddenly unutterably weary. She longed to seek out her chamber, close the door against everyone, and sleep. Then she turned back again. "Why are you here, Edward?"

He hesitated and then said, "I am in need of your assistance. I did not like to place you in jeopardy by my presence, but my mother assures me you have reverted to Catholicism and have, in fact, been helping Queen Mary." His voice had dropped to a whisper, although the only possible eavesdropper could be the blackbird piping its sweet, sad song on the branch of a plum tree.

"Your mother knows that I gave up all connection with Queen Mary when Brendan came home. She had no right to tell you about it," she said indignantly. "Pray God, she has told no one else."

It was Edward's turn for indignation now. "I am sure she has not."

Katherine lifted her head to look directly into his eyes. "It was a mistake to embroil myself in such a dangerous game in the first place, but when I discovered that your mother was one of the other conspirators in the district, I should have reneged immediately."

"So you should . . . and advised my mother to do so also. I was appalled when she told me she and then you were employed in such a perilous game, as you so rightly call it. I have ordered her to advise whosoever she must that she is no longer able to continue. In her mistaken belief that by joining in the conspiracy against Queen

Elizabeth she was helping the Catholic cause, she has caused great danger to her household and family. If my father knew about it, he would disown her." Edward's mouth, the mouth that had kissed her with such passion that last time, twisted. "As he has disowned me for joining the priesthood."

Katherine longed to have this meeting at an end. The rain was even heavier now and she was shivering violently with the cold. "What is it you want of me?"

"I am here to minister unto the needs of all Catholics. To say Mass, to baptize, to administer the sacraments to those who have long been deprived of them. We missionary priests have returned to England not to engage in political warfare but to feed our starving flock." Even in the slanting rain she could see the light shining in his eyes, the light of a lover for his beloved.

"And?" she said impatiently.

"I am in urgent need of a place to stay, a place where the faithful can gather in secret to hear Mass and receive the sacraments."

Her entire body stiffened as if it had been turned to stone. "Not Radcliffe. I cannot hide you at Radcliffe."

"Of course not. It must be some place where the entire family is Catholic. But until such a haven is found, I need shelter for one or two nights. Have you an outlying barn or an abandoned shepherd's hut in which I could hide?"

Now her tongue too was frozen. All she could think of was Brendan's warning that she would be in extreme danger if she became embroiled in further offenses against the state. She had sworn to him in God's name that she would not. Why, oh why, hadn't Edward stayed in Europe! "I do not think so," she murmured.

He put back his hood, to reveal the thick, barley-gold hair she had so loved to gaze upon, to touch. She looked away, her fingers flexing as she recalled the first time she had touched his hair.

"For the love of God and His work, think, Katherine. If I am discovered now, before I begin my mission, all my years of work, all those sacrifices I have made, will have been wasted."

She tried to resist, but the voice, throbbing with stifled emotion, still held the power to thrill her.

"There is an old ruined tower on the slope of Coverdale, near Melmerby Beck," she said, after pausing to think for a while. "You ride up Penhill and over Melmerby Moor to reach it. Joanna and I discovered it when we were children visiting our grandparents at Harcourt Hall. I haven't been there for years. For all I know, it might well have fallen down."

He did not appear particularly pleased. "A tower? Would that not be too conspicuous?"

"It is not on the high moor, but on the lower slope of the fell, with trees about it."

"That might be suitable."

"It is all I can think of," she said sharply, annoyed at his lack of enthusiasm.

He moved closer to her. "My mother was able to provide me with a basket of food and flask of wine. Could you find me some blankets for warmth? Mother was so terrified that my father might catch her she did not dare smuggle them from the house."

He smiled at her, the old warm smile that turned her heart. Her eyes flashed back at him. "How the devil am *I* to smuggle blankets from Radcliffe?" she demanded. "What if Brendan were to catch *me*?"

"Ah, my dear Katherine, you were always so resourceful." Again, the warm smile.

And so gullible, she thought. How easily he manipulated her, but now it was different. Now she knew that he employed his undoubted ability to charm to gain his own ends.

"Have you a horse?"

"Aye, I have. A friend lent me one so that I might ride here from the coast. I landed at Whitby two nights ago and have been making my way here ever since."

"You must be weary."

He smiled ruefully. "I am, but it is nothing that cannot be remedied by a good sleep."

How she longed to be able to invite him in, to show him to their guest bedchamber, as she would have done any traveler who needed rest and refreshment on his journey. But here was one person who must be kept from the confines of Radcliffe at all cost.

"I will get you some bedding. The Lord knows how, but I will do it."

"The Lord will show you the way."

"I trust He will," she said caustically, "for only He knows how I shall gather up an armful of blankets and march past my servants and husband and my ever-watchful steward and get them to you."

"God will provide the way," Edward said in his maddeningly assured manner.

It seemed that Edward was right, for it was easily accomplished. When she reentered Radcliffe it was to discover that the heavy rain had burst through the roof in the second bedchamber, spilling onto the covers of the bed there. There was such a great toing and froing, with people scurrying about with buckets and tubs and armfuls of wet bedding, that no one thought twice about Mistress Katherine running downstairs with two blankets and a pillow, wrapped in a quilt.

Folding her cloak about them, as far as it would go, she dashed back across the inner and outer courtyard and into the orchard.

"Go, now," she told Edward, thrusting the bedding at him. Her heart was hammering with the expectation that at any minute someone would come upon them.

"Will you do one more thing for me, Katherine?"

"What is it?" she asked abruptly.

"My mother must know where I am or she will be sick with worry. Would you be able to send her word?"

She nodded. "I'll send my groom to your house today. But will it be safe to do so?"

"Fortunately, my father rode over to my uncle's estate in Arnecliff this afternoon. He will not be back before nightfall."

"I shall take care to write a message that would seem perfectly innocuous were it to fall into hands other than your mother's," Katherine told him.

"I thank you. Once she knows where I am, she will be able to send further provisions and to advise me when she has found a house where I may shelter more permanently."

She met his eyes, gazing at him as if she could not get enough of him. "Pardon me for not hiding you in Radcliffe," she said eventually. "I dare not."

"I understand. God bless you for what you are doing." He gave her his sweet smile and blessed her awkwardly with his right hand, at the same time trying to keep a hold on the bundle of bedding.

"Go!" she said again and, turning from him, left him standing there amongst the trees, the rain spilling down his face.

She was running across the outer court when she saw her mother ride through the gateway. "God's death!" she muttered and shrank back against the washhouse wall, hoping that her mother would think she was one of the laundresses. But this time God must have been keeping His eye fully on Edward as he escaped, for her mother recognized her and hailed her.

"Katherine. What in the name of heaven are you doing out here?"

Katherine thought quickly. "There's been a leak in the roof. I couldn't bear all the noise and rushing about, so I came outside to clear my head."

Her mother drew her horse up close to her. "In this weather?" she asked, her voice rising.

Katherine shrugged. "I know, I know. I must be out of my mind," she said sheepishly. "It was a whim, Mother. You know how I was longing to go riding with you to Colborne Place." She put a hand up to her mother's bridle. "How is Aunt Isobel?"

Her mother's face became even more pinched than before. "Come inside to the warm and I will tell you."

Katherine followed her mother into the inner courtyard, silently giving thanks to God that her mother had not ridden in a moment sooner. When she had dismounted, Katherine took her arm and they entered the house together. They went straight to the parlor, and closed the door, ignoring the disturbance outside.

"Oh, Mother, you must be wet through. Take off that wet cloak at once lest you fall ill from an ague." Katherine helped her remove the sodden cloak, but as she drew it away, her mother grasped her arm.

"You are just as wet as I am, Mistress Kate," in a mock-stern manner. "Come, your cloak off, too."

Katherine swung hers off, the water from the two cloaks soaking the sleeve of her gown as she went to the door. She opened it, and shouted to one of the passing servants, bidding him take the cloaks to the kitchen to dry. Then she came to join her mother before the fire.

For a moment, they both stood silently before the hearth, watching the bright flames leaping up the chimney, breathing in the sweet scent of apple logs.

Relishing the feeling of well-being as the warmth permeated her body, Katherine did not speak. It was one of those rare moments of companionship between her and her mother and therefore to be treasured in silence.

Her mother sighed and rubbed her hands together. "That is better. I don't think I have ever felt quite so cold." She sat down on the settle and folded her skirts back to her knees, so that the sodden hems would not press against her legs.

"You should change your gown immediately," Katherine told her.

Her mother looked up and gave her a wan smile. "I should, but I am too comfortable at present to move." She patted the place beside her on the tapestry cushion. "Come, sit with me, Kate."

Katherine hesitated, and then came to sit next to her mother, forced to touch thighs and elbows with her in the close confines of the high-backed seat. "Aunt Isobel is worse, isn't she?" she said softly.

"I doubt she will last the week out, Kate." Alyssa's eyes filled with tears. "I would welcome it as God's mercy, if it were not that her spirit is being torn apart with the struggle to stay alive. I have never seen anyone quite so terrified of death as Isobel is."

Katherine covered her mother's agitated little hands with hers. "Is there aught I can do to help?"

"I must go back to her in the morning, but this time I shall stay with her until the end. Pray God it will come soon, for her sake. Yet I would give the world to have her die in peace." She closed her eyes, the tears squeezing from the corners to run slowly down her pale face.

"When you are warm, we shall go and pray for her in the chapel."

"Aye, and later we'll gather the entire household together to pray for her. She is in such anguish that we shall need many prayers to help her in her struggle."

"What else can I do to help?" Katherine asked.

Alyssa gave her her habitual, direct look. "I do not like to ask this of you, particularly with this appalling weather, but Isobel has asked to see you—and Joanna, of course. She asked that you come as soon as possible to visit her."

"I shall ride with you in the morning. Joanna and I can ride back with our grooms, for I admit I have no wish to remain overnight at Colborne Place." Katherine wriggled her shoulders as a shiver passed over them. "I cannot bear even to be in the same room as my uncle. Poor Aunt Isobel, imagine having to share a bed with the man."

Her mother stiffened, her chin lifting a little. Katherine was surprised. It was not like her mother to be narrowly prudish. Indeed, when she was younger, she had often been shocked by her mother's outspokenness.

Shaking her wet skirts down, Alyssa got to her feet. "I must go and change. You should do so, too. Then find Joanna and meet me in the chapel so that we may pray for your aunt."

Katherine watched her mother leave the parlor. The spring had gone from her step. For the first time she could have been mistaken for an old woman. Her sister's imminent death had drained her of her usual energy, but there was something more. Since Isobel's illness the ancient enmity between the two sisters had been set aside—by Alyssa, at least. But the questions still hung there, as maddening to Katherine as the food and drink had been to Tantalus of Phrygia.

Now she had thoughts of Edward also to torment her. But she thrust them aside. Those thoughts she would take out and contemplate later, when she lay in bed, for she knew that what had happened this day had changed her entire life. There was no time now, however, to think about it. She must put on dry clothing and then seek out Joanna, who was doubtless playing with Dickon.

Later tonight she would think about this great change in her life, but for now she was too busy.

Chapter 40

Despite Katherine's promise to herself to think about Edward later that night, by the time she climbed into bed and settled into that most comforting position, lying on her side, with Brendan's body pressed against her back, his hand cupping her breast, she was too weary to distinguish one thought from another.

But as she drifted into a welcome sleep, one insistent thought became paramount, that Brendan must never know about Edward. She had given her word to him never again to place Radcliffe and the family in jeopardy. Nothing would make her break that promise.

When they rode out from Radcliffe the next morning, the rain had ceased, but the wind was still raw and penetrating. As they cantered over the High Moor, Katherine glanced over her shoulder in the direction of Coverdale, wondering how Edward had fared during the night. For all she knew, he might no longer be hiding in the tower near Melmerby Beck. His mother had merely acknowledged receipt of her hastily penned message and sent her thanks. That was all. She bent her head for a moment, clasping her hands on the reins. *God keep him safe,* she prayed.

Tobias had accompanied them on the ride. For most of the time he had ridden at Alyssa's side, his slight figure inclined to her whenever she spoke to him. Katherine smiled to herself as she watched the familiar face with its rare smile. Dear wise, loyal Tobias. Whatever would they have done without him all these years? she wondered.

Now, as the towers of Colborne Place came in sight, he slipped back to ride in the inferior position, behind Alyssa. Throughout the journey, Joanna had talked to Katherine about this and that, the constant chatter an annoying background to her thoughts.

As they rode down the broad clearing lined on both sides by great lime trees, she was brought back to the present by Joanna's insistent, "Did you hear what I said, Kate?"

"What?" snapped Kate.

"Oh, Kate," wailed Joanna, "I swear you have not listened to one word I have said to you."

"Then you would be wrong, for you have spoken of little else but your precious Harry all the way here."

"Will you do it, then?" Joanna turned her sweet moonface towards her sister. "Say you will."

Katherine grimaced. "Now you do have me. Were you asking me to do something for you?"

"I knew it," Joanna said triumphantly but with no hint of vexation. "I was sure you hadn't been listening." She cast a wary glance at her mother's back. "You gave me your word you would discuss our betrothal with Brendan when he returned."

"Why don't you speak of it to him yourself? You know my opinion: that a Radcliffe could do much better for herself than Harry Seaton. Why not speak to Brendan first, so that he will hear your side of it before I throw my bucket of cold water over it?"

"Oh, Kate, please don't. I love him so much." Joanna's eyes filled with tears.

"God's wounds, Joanna, don't start weeping now, especially in front of Mother. Speak to Brendan about it. We will let him make the decision as to whether this match should even be thought of. Now, no more talk of Harry Seaton. We are here. For the love of God, dry your eyes before we dismount."

They were greeted in the large inner courtyard by Isobel's elder son, Robert Colborne, who informed them in an offhand manner that his father was out somewhere with the bailiff and steward.

Katherine was greatly relieved to hear it. A welcoming embrace from her boorish uncle by marriage usually meant a great pinch on the bottom or, worse yet, on the breast. If he were to do that today, lord or uncle, she swore she would slap his red face hard for him.

They found Isobel sitting up, propped by pillows, in the large bed with its massive oak posts. The tester above was so heavily carved that it seemed to Katherine to quite overwhelm her poor aunt. She bent to kiss her dry cheek.

"You look much improved, dearest Aunt," she lied, trying hard to hide her dismay at the appalling change in the few weeks since she had seen Isobel. She looked like a hag of eighty, her sallow skin stretched thin over her bones. Only her eyes, those wondrous sapphire eyes, blazing in her head, were alive.

She was able to stretch her cracked lips into a glimmer of a smile, but in her eyes was a look of constant fear. "Send Bess and Joanna away," she said to Alyssa, plucking at her sleeve.

Bess, who had sobbed piteously and thrown herself on her Aunt Alyssa's breast upon her arrival, broke into loud protests. "I won't go. I want to stay with my mother," she screamed.

But Joanna put her arm about her cousin's waist, kissed her wet, rosy cheeks and, drawing back the wing of dark hair to whisper something in her ear, led her quietly away.

"She's a good lass, your Joanna," Isobel said, lying back with a heavy sigh. "She is good for my Bess."

She looked at her sister and niece for a moment. Then she raised her hand. "Draw up two stools," was her command. "You will sit here, near my head, Alyssa. And you, Kate, will sit at my feet."

She was still Lady Colborne, giving orders for the disposal of her guests.

Alyssa bent over her. "Will you not rest, Sister? We can sit by the fire whilst you sleep."

"I did not ask you to return with Kate so that you could watch me sleep. Do as I ask." As Alyssa hesitated, Isobel struggled to sit up higher in the bed. "Polly, are you there? Set up two stools by my bed for my sister and niece."

It was done over Alyssa's protests. Then the women servants were dismissed and the three women were left alone together in the cavernous bedchamber.

At first the only sound to be heard was the harsh breathing from the bed. A shiver ran like a mouse across Katherine's shoulders. She looked up from contemplating the fine stitching in the bed curtain beside her, to see that her mother's face had grown very pale. She sat straight-backed as always on the stool, but her hands picked at the silver embroidery on her sleeves, her nail pick, pick, picking until Katherine felt like screaming.

At last Isobel spoke. "We must talk, you and I, Alyssa."

Her sister smiled and leaned forward to pat Isobel's hand. "Of course we must. What shall we talk about?" Another false smile.

"I have little time left. I will not waste it. We shall talk about Thomas."

Katherine started. Her mother's body went rigid. "If that is your wish, dearest Sister," she said, "but first I must send Kate away."

"No!" Isobel's voice rang through the chamber. "You have run away from this for too long, Alyssa." She paused to catch her breath and then lifted her bony finger to point it directly at Katherine. "Kate is a woman now. Thomas was her father. It is time she learned the truth about not only Thomas, but Philip, also."

Alyssa sprang to her feet, her skirts knocking over the stool. "No, Isobel, you cannot do this to her. I will not permit it. Until Kate leaves the room I forbid you to speak."

Isobel was struggling for breath now, unable to reply, but her eyes blazed eloquently at her sister.

"For the love of God, Mother," cried Katherine. "Can't you see that this must be what is troubling Aunt Isobel? This is why she cannot die—" She clapped her hand to her mouth.

Isobel sank back, strands of her faded golden hair spread out on the pillows. "Why I cannot die in peace," she panted. "Say so, Kate, for you speak the truth."

Alyssa stood rooted to the floor, her eyes downcast, as Isobel sought for more breath to continue.

"I have committed terrible sins in my hatred for you, Alyssa, but you have compounded them by never being able to share the truth with me or, even more important, with Kate."

"I wished to protect her." Alyssa's words were barely audible.

"By trying to protect her from the truth you turned her love for you to hatred. That is why I want you both here with me today. Even if it is too late for us, Alyssa, it is not too late to heal the wounds between you and your daughter. If I can accomplish that, my sister, perhaps I shall be able to partially atone for my grievous sins against you and your family."

"Sit down again, Mother." Katherine's voice was as commanding as her aunt's had been. "For Aunt Isobel's sake and for mine, none of us shall leave this room until questions are answered and the truth is told."

Like one in a dream, Alyssa picked up the stool and sat down upon it again, her hands folded resignedly in her lap. "I cannot think this wise, Isobel," she murmured.

"It is my dying wish."

The sisters' eyes met. "And for that reason only I shall not deny you," said Alyssa. "Which one of us shall start?"

"First, let Kate ask her questions," said Isobel. "We shall answer them as best we can. Then you and I shall have our say, Alyssa."

Both women fixed their eyes upon Katherine. At first she did not say a word. It had all happened too fast. For so long she had thrust the questions down, as if she had been hiding them deep in the bole of a tree. Now she had to dig deep to find them again. Then she recalled the sinister wood near Jervaulx and knew that that was where she must begin.

She sat bolt upright on the stool. "Who murdered my father?"

A great sigh escaped Isobel. "Ah, you begin with the one question I burn to ask."

They both turned to Alyssa.

Isobel's mouth stretched into a hideous smile. "The truth, mind. We must have the truth, dear Sister."

Alyssa hesitated, and then said, "The truth is that although I was there, I do not know for certain exactly who all the men who attacked Thomas were. But I did recognize many of those who had supported the rebellion or whose brothers or fathers had been hanged after it." Her eyes met Isobel's. "You asked for the truth. The truth is that every man present in that band of masked men struck a blow in Thomas's body. He was hated not only for having taken the Queen's side against the rebellion, but also for arresting and imprisoning his own father, Sir Philip, who was beloved throughout the Dales."

"So Grandy did not kill my father," said Katherine, "or arrange to have him killed?"

Her mother's head whipped about, fury in her eyes. "Your grandfather drew his own sword and fought beside his son to defend him. When Thomas lay slain on the forest floor he wept over his body."

Katherine looked at Isobel accusingly. "But you said—"

"My first sin," her aunt acknowledged with a tiny shrug. "I was not certain. It seemed to make sense that Sir Philip would kill the son he despised."

Alyssa rounded upon her sister now. "Philip did not despise Thomas, as you well know, Isobel. He—"

"Enough." Katherine held up her hand. "It will be better if we can avoid confrontation between us. It is not good for Aunt Isobel to be upset."

She thought, almost with amusement, that from the look on her mother's face, upsetting Isobel was what she would most like to do.

She turned again to her aunt. "Why are you so interested in my father, Thomas Radcliffe? No one else seemed willing to speak to me about him. Yet you seemed to gain special pleasure from it. Why?"

"Because I loved Thomas," Isobel replied softly, "and he loved me."

Katherine let a small sigh escape her. Of course. That would explain a great deal. Katherine looked at her mother, but her head was bent in contemplation of her tightly clasped hands.

"Was this before my mother's marriage to him?" she asked her aunt.

"It was. But—"

"But Isobel was already betrothed to Ingram Colborne, Lord Colborne's eldest son," interposed Alyssa. "So the marriage between Thomas and me was arranged."

Isobel glared at her sister. "And if you had refused to wed him, as I had begged you to do, we might well have been able to persuade Father to permit me to wed Thomas."

Alyssa passed a trembling hand over her forehead. "Oh, 'Belle, we have been over this so many times. You were already lawfully contracted to Ingram. It was impossible for you to break that contract to wed Thomas."

Isobel opened her mouth to reply, but Katherine intervened.

"So Mother married Thomas Radcliffe. I take it that you never forgave her for it, Aunt."

"You take it correctly. From the time of their betrothal, I hated the very sight of my sister and was determined to do her whatever harm I could for the rest of our lives." The blue eyes blazed with a steely light. "She had stolen my Thomas from me."

Alyssa closed her eyes in exasperation. It was evident that the old argument would never be fully resolved.

"What kind of man was my father?" Katherine asked, determined now to hear the full story. "I can remember him only as tall and loud. A man who hugged me too tightly when he embraced me. There must be more to him than that."

Both sisters opened their mouths to speak, and both fell silent.

"Mother? The truth, mind."

"The truth sometimes hurts."

"Then, let it hurt. Better that than leaving it to the wild imaginings of the mind. Was he kind, cruel? Did he beat you?" *Did he love me?* Katherine longed to ask, but did not.

"He was like a young colt at first, all legs and action," said Alyssa.

"He was beautiful to look upon," said Isobel.

"He could be unkind, impatient," said Alyssa.

"He was gentle and strong at the same time," said Isobel.

It was not difficult to tell which sister had truly loved Thomas Radcliffe. Yet is was for her mother that Katherine's heart ached. To be wed to a man who loved your sister must have been a dreadful burden.

"Was he angry that his firstborn child was not a son?" She knew how delighted Brendan had been with his son, yet she was sure he would not have minded a daughter. Something told her, however, that the man her father had been would have wanted only sons.

Her mother looked at her, lips trying to form the right words.

"The truth, remember?" Katherine reminded her.

"He was—" Alyssa began.

"He was furious when Joanna was born, I can tell you that," burst in Isobel. "Two daughters and no son. He rode directly to me and—"

Her eyes met her sister's and she said no more. Katherine was left to ponder the warning look that had flashed from one to the other. She was beginning to feel a mixture of strong dislike and reluctant admiration for the shadowy figure of her father. She was also beginning, in just this short time, to understand her mother far more than ever before.

But there was still the main, most compelling question to be asked, and she did not think she could bring herself to do so, not even in this rarified atmosphere of her aunt's deathbed.

Her aunt read her mind. Having drunk some of the barley water that Alyssa had offered her, she lay back again and said, "You have said nothing about your mother and Sir Philip, I notice, Kate."

Alyssa set the green-glass pitcher down with a thud on the sideboard. "I think we have answered more than enough questions for one day."

"This is the one that must be answered for Kate's future peace of mind, Alys. Sit down. This time I shall ask the question, so that Katherine will be spared from doing so. Were you and Sir Philip lovers?"

Alyssa shook her head. It was not denial she indicated, but a wish not to have the question asked. Yet it hung in the air, its sound reverberating: *lovers, lovers, lovers* . . .

And Katherine, too, now wished that the question had not been aired. She longed to clap her hands over her ears and dash from the room, to avoid hearing either the answer or the sound of her mother's silence. But it was too late now. Her mother was opening her mouth. . . .

"I had loved Sir Philip Radcliffe since I was a child," she heard her mother say, the words sounding as if she were speaking from a deep hollow in the ground. Then her voice strengthened. "I continued to love him, my love growing deeper, throughout my marriage. Until his wife's death, he never knew, never guessed. I believe she knew, but of course she and I never spoke of it. How could we? When his wife, Laura, died, he and I grew closer, particularly with Thomas away at Court. But he never behaved towards me in any way but as a father to a beloved daughter. Then we were alone together at Radcliffe for a winter. People began to gossip." She gave her sister an enigmatic smile. "My mother told me word was going about that we were lovers." She twisted her silken girdle about her fingers. "Philip left Radcliffe and went to the Scottish Court for three years."

"But were you lovers?" Isobel's insistent voice broke the ensuing silence.

"I loved him, as I said. He was growing to love me. No doubt only because of his loneliness and the loss of his wife."

Isobel was not going to let it go at that. "But you had not lain together? The truth, Alyssa, remember?"

"The truth? No, we had not lain together."

Isobel was disappointed. Katherine could see that she had hoped for a different answer.

"Not then, anyway. We lay together but once in our entire lives."

Her mother's statement made in her cool, clear voice astounded Katherine. It was not only the admission of what she had so long suspected that shocked her, but the fact that she had not, even now, expected her mother ever to admit it.

"Only once," her mother repeated. "And that, not until *after* Thomas's death."

"So," Isobel hissed. "I was right in my thinking. Richard was Philip's son."

Alyssa shook her head. "You were wrong, my sister, as you were wrong about so many matters. I was pregnant with Richard when I lay with Philip. I had told the Earl of Sussex that I suspected I was pregnant when he attended Thomas's funeral."

"You expect me to believe that?"

Alyssa shrugged. "Believe what you please. You asked for truth. That is the truth."

"Did you seduce Grandy?" The words burst from Katherine's mouth.

A little smile. "I suppose in a way I did. But it was his wish."

The frank admission silenced Katherine. What more was there left to say? It was all clear now; her suspicions confirmed, and yet not confirmed, for with the admissions had come an amazing insight into the plight of the two sisters, both in love with men they could not have.

As she looked from one to the other of them, she wondered which would be worse, to love a man and live beside him as his daughter, or to have your lover dead, never to see his dear face again, nor to hear his voice.

On the whole, she thought her mother had suffered less than Aunt Isobel, for her mother did not have Ingram Colborne for a husband.

"It did not happen at Radcliffe, Kate." It was so long since her mother had last spoken that Katherine started at the sound of her voice.

"Probably in the old Melmerby Tower," Isobel said dryly.

Again, Katherine started. How ironic that would be.

"That was where Thomas and I used to meet," explained Isobel. "Before either of us was married," she added.

"No, not in the tower," said Alyssa. "Where it happened is no one's business. All that matters to Kate is that it was not at Radcliffe, and that it happened only once."

How strange it was to hear her decorous, almost staid mother talk so openly about lying with her husband's father!

"Only once." Isobel's voice echoed her sister's words.

Katherine looked up, embarrassed, and intercepted the look they were exchanging. To her surprise, both of them were smiling.

"Once?" said Alyssa.

Isobel nodded. Then the smile faded and she turned her gray face into the pillow. "I am so weary," she whispered. "And yet there is more."

Alyssa bent over her, tenderly stroking back the strands of hair from her forehead. "Rest now, dearest. We have all said enough for today."

"No, no. There is more." Isobel tossed her head from side to side on the damp pillow. "I must confess. I must have a priest to confess."

"Has the rector been to see you?"

"No, no, a Catholic priest. I must confess. If I die unshriven I will burn in hell's fire forever for what I have done."

Alyssa caught her restless hands to hold them fast within hers. "Hush, dearest, there are no Catholic priests in England anymore. Besides, you are not a Catholic now."

"Only a priest can absolve me. Then I shall be able to die in peace."

"Why not tell me what it is you wish to confess? Perhaps that will make you feel better."

"I will, but that is not enough."

"But it may help to set your mind at rest for tonight, at least." Alyssa cast a frantic look at Katherine.

"I betrayed you," Isobel cried out. "It was I who told Ingram about Edmund Campion's visits to Radcliffe."

Katherine sank back on the stool, limp with horror.

Isobel's eyes blazed at her sister, waiting for her response, but none came. "Can you not speak to me, at least?" she cried. "Tell me how it feels to have been thrown into prison with your daughter because your sister betrayed you? Are you not appalled, shocked to hear such a thing?" She fell back, gasping for breath.

"Neither appalled, nor shocked," said Alyssa's cool voice. "I knew it must have been you. No one else hated me enough to do it. But why Kate, Isobel? Why include my innocent daughter? What harm had she done you?"

"It was a mistake," Isobel cried. "Somehow the Council included Kate in the order. And Ingram, damn his soul to hell, would do nothing to have it changed. He wanted Radcliffe for our son. He said, Robert shall be Lord of Radcliffe."

Katherine had heard more than enough truth for one day. She longed to go home to the peace and safety of Radcliffe, to hold her baby against her breast and to kiss his downy head. Most of all she longed to have Brendan's arms wrapped about her to stave off any more truth.

"Now you see why I must have a priest." Isobel's voice rose on a note of anguish. "I am so tired. I am weary of pain and suffering and sadness. I long to die, but how can I with so many sins on my conscience?"

Alyssa bent over her. "Let me send for Parson Bennett. He will set your mind at rest and pray with you."

Isobel dashed her sister's hands away. Finding new strength, she struggled to swing her legs, thin as birch twigs, over the side of the bed. Tears ran down her seamed cheeks. "A priest," she screamed. "I must have a priest. Only a Catholic priest can absolve me of all my sins."

"Oh, Isobel." Alyssa's own eyes filled with tears as she struggled to calm her sister.

Katherine rose slowly from the stool. "Be at peace, Aunt Isobel," she said. "Get back into bed and lie down again. You shall have your Catholic priest."

Her mother gave her a little warning shake of the head. "Do not lie to her," she said in a low voice. "Not now."

"No, Mother, I am not just saying it to calm Aunt Isobel. This is the time for truth, remember?" Katherine smiled, but she felt more like weeping. She wished she could be anywhere but here. She wished she were home with Brendan. "I know where there is a Catholic priest," she said. "And I shall have him here with Aunt Isobel by tonight."

Chapter 41

Isobel ceased her struggling and fell back upon the bed amidst a tangle of bedclothes. "The Lord bless you, Kate," she whispered, and closed her eyes.

Alyssa did not speak. She did not need to. Those large, dark eyes spoke eloquently to Katherine of her mother's immense sorrow and disappointment.

She made a little move towards her. "It is not what you think, Mother."

Her mother bent over her exhausted sister, gently straightening her legs, smoothing the bed linen about her. "You told me it was all finished," she said to Katherine in a low voice, when she had made Isobel comfortable again.

"It is. I swear in God's name that it is. I gave Brendan my word."

"Yet you are able to find a Catholic priest for Isobel."

"I cannot explain. This involves another person's welfare."

Her mother grasped her arm and drew her from the bed. "And what about our welfare, the safety of all those at Radcliffe?" she demanded, thrusting her face close to Katherine's. "Does that mean nothing to you?"

"You know that it does. I am doing this for Aunt Isobel, for you. I thought it would please you that your sister will be able to die at peace with herself at last."

"Not if it means risking the lives of my children and grandchild. They come first with me; they always will."

"Well, it is too late now," Katherine said in a dull voice. "I cannot disappoint her now."

"And where will you find this priest of yours?" As she waited for Katherine's answer, Alyssa's eyes widened. "Jesu, never tell me you've hidden him somewhere at Radcliffe."

"Of course not. He is hidden where no one will find him. I am going to fetch him now, while Uncle Ingram is away from home. Pray God, I can smuggle him in without my beloved cousins seeing him."

Her mother's hands twisted together. "It is too dangerous, particularly in this house. If Ingram were to find out—"

"He will not. But we may have to take Tobias into our confidence to accomplish it. He could keep watch for us."

"If Tobias has even the smallest inkling of what you are about, he will forbid it."

"Forbid it! How many times must I remind you, my lady Mother, that Tobias is our steward, our servant."

"And I would remind you, my daughter, that Tobias was your grandfather's dear friend and is now mine and I will not have you belittle him thus."

Katherine knew that dangerously soft tone of her mother's. It was useless to protest further. "Then, unless you wish your sister to remain in anguish, fighting death, you and I must work together alone to accomplish this."

Their eyes met, locked, but her mother said nothing.

"Is that, in truth, what you want, Mother? That your sister suffer in hell's fire eternally for all she has done to you, for her adultery with your husband, her betrayal of you?"

Her mother's eyes blinked rapidly. "She does not need a Catholic priest to confess her sins."

"We know that. The point is that at this moment she believes she will be cast into hell if she is not shriven by a Catholic priest. I know where I can find one. I leave the final decision to you, madam my Mother."

"Who is this priest? I thought there had been no papist priests in the Dales since Father Campion."

"It is not necessary for you to know who he is. I will bring him here and you will not see him. That way you will not be implicated."

Her mother gave a harsh laugh. "How brim full of confidence are the young."

"And how cowardly are the old," retorted Katherine. "Come, Mother, I am waiting for your answer."

Alyssa chewed on her lip. "Go, fetch your priest," she said at last. "I will not have my sister's damnation on my conscience."

Almost three hours had passed by the time Katherine rode back through the gates of Colborne Place with Edward at her side. At first she had thought she would never get away, for Tobias had been extremely suspicious of her leaving with only her groom for protection. Indeed, he had suggested that he should go on whatever important errand it was she was bent upon. But her mother had managed to draw Tobias off by reminding him that if Isobel died she would need him to assist her in dealing with Lord Colborne.

Now, as Katherine rode in, her heart beating fast, she felt ready to drop with weariness. Her chest was raw and she could not stop shivering. The rain was falling steadily. She wondered if she would ever be warm again. Beside her, Edward crouched low over his mount in an attempt to disguise his height, but as soon as he dismounted, of course, that would be impossible.

Edward was right, thought Katherine. She was impetuous. She must have lost her wits completely to begin an adventure that could only bring disaster to them all. But it was too late now to have second thoughts.

As they were dismounting, she saw, to her dismay, her cousin William coming from the stables. "Who is this?" he demanded of her.

"The apothecary from Masham," she replied quickly, for that was the story they had decided upon. "He has brought your mother some new physic for the pain." Edward made a low bow, trying to keep his face partially covered.

But William was not interested in him or any other person at present. "Curse this filthy weather," he muttered. "Haven't been able to hunt for three days." He strode away from them, cursing under his breath, his brachet hounds slinking behind him.

For once Katherine was grateful for her cousin's rude manners.

Explaining again, this time to Lord Colborne's steward, that she had fetched the apothecary from Masham, she was led up the wide stone staircase to her ladyship's apartments, with Edward following close behind.

His relaxed manner infuriated her. She was terrified at the thought of his discovery, but from the time she had hurriedly explained the situation to him in the tower, he had been calm and confident. "We are in God's hands," he told her. She felt like commenting acidly that so had been Edmund Campion, but did not. This was decidedly not the time for a confrontation with Edward.

"Wait here," she told him in the antechamber and went through the door into her aunt's main bedchamber.

Her mother sprang up from the stool as she came in.

Katherine drew her aside so that Isobel's women could not hear. "I have brought him," she said in answer to Alyssa's unspoken enquiry. "Will you go out the other door, Mother? I do not wish you to see him. That way, if we were questioned, you could truthfully say you saw no man enter your sister's chamber."

"You will send for me, as soon as—"

"As soon as he is gone, I shall send for you." Katherine turned to the two women who sat sewing by the fireplace. "I wish to have a few minutes alone with my aunt," she told them haughtily. "Leave with Mistress Radcliffe, I pray you."

The two women glanced at each other and then at Alyssa. Seeing that she already stood waiting for them, the door open, they had no alternative but to leave.

When the door closed behind them, Katherine stood for a moment, drawing in a long breath and releasing it slowly to ease her tension. One hurdle over.

She went to the large bed and bent over her aunt. For one dreadful moment she thought she was dead, that all her efforts had been wasted, but then she saw that the covers over her aunt's upper body were rising and falling very slightly.

She hated to wake her, to draw her back from a sleep induced by poppy juice to wracking pain, but it must be done.

"Aunt Isobel," she whispered. "Aunt Isobel, wake up."

Her aunt groaned and then her eyes flickered open. She stared at her, as if trying hard to recognize her, and then said in a thick voice, "Kate? Is that you, Kate?"

"Aye, it's Kate. I have brought you your priest, Aunt Isobel."

The blue eyes opened wider. "A priest? A Catholic priest? Bless you, Kate." The thin fingers scrabbled on the coverlet until Katherine gently pressed hers about them. "Bring him," Isobel gasped. "Make haste."

Katherine left her and crossed the floor to open the door to the antechamber. Edward was contemplating the hunting scene that was painted in brilliant colors on the plaster wall. "She is ready for you now," she told him.

He picked up his small bag of rough leather, which contained, he had told her in Melmerby Tower, not only his stole and the small box holding the sacred host and the wine, but also several packages of different herbs and small phials of liquid physics to confirm that he was, indeed, an apothecary. He had also assured her that he was as learned as any true apothecary in the science of herbs and medicines.

When she had shown her skepticism he had smiled. "You would be surprised to learn how many trusted physicians there are now in England who are actually priests."

As they entered the chamber, she turned to lock the door, but he shook his head. "A locked door would only cause suspicion. Remember, if anyone enters, I am the apothecary from Masham."

She could not help smiling. The tall figure with the golden hair and well-shaped hands did not quite fit her image of the usual old apothecary; not like the one at Richmond, for instance, his black apron covered in stains and dotted with holes where he had dropped acid on it.

When Edward reached the bed, he put back his hood. From his bag he drew out the stole and put it on beneath his cloak, so that, if necessary, it could be easily hidden. All his movements were quiet and graceful, with no sense of hurry or fear. Watching him, Katherine marveled at the aura of peace and contentment he exuded.

"Lady Colborne."

Isobel opened her eyes and struggled to focus them upon the figure by her bed.

"You have asked for a Catholic priest to attend you. I am here."

"Your face," she whispered. "Your face seems familiar to me. What is your name?"

"There is no need for names. 'Father' will be sufficient."

"Father," she breathed. Her hand moved beneath his. "I must confess to you. Where is Alyssa?" She tried to drag herself up in the bed.

"Mother will be here soon," Katherine told her. "Let me help you."

She lifted her aunt up against the pillows. She did not like to touch her. It was like gathering together a bunch of thin, dead branches that might snap in her hands. Then she retreated to watch from the center of the room as Edward bent his head to listen to Isobel's confession.

As the time passed, Katherine felt like screaming out her impatience and fear. It was taking too long. Several times she was tempted to put a halt to it, but the sight of her aunt's face, the poignant sound of her sobbing followed by Edward's voice, speaking in low, assuring tones, stopped her. Although her very life might depend upon it, she could not interrupt such an ancient, sacred ritual.

And as she watched Edward giving her aunt the last rites, anointing her with the sacred oil and chrism from tiny pewter boxes, Katherine knew that she was participating in a ceremony that would heal their wounds and soothe their bitterness. Not only for her aunt and mother, but for herself. She knew, also, that it was meet that Edward should be the one to perform the ceremony, for he was at the very center of her own healing. She knelt down on the Turkish carpeting and bent her head in prayer.

It was over at last. Isobel lay back on the pillow, the sheen of the holy oil upon her forehead, her hands clasped on her breast. As Katherine stood up and went to them, Edward removed his stole, kissed it, and carefully folded it.

Their eyes met. "She is at peace at last, thanks to you," Katherine told him.

He shook his head. "It is to God, not me, you owe your thanks."

Isobel opened her eyes. They were dull now, their color strangely faded. "Alyssa?" she said in a thin, wavering voice. "I want Alyssa."

"I shall bring her to you immediately." Katherine hesitated, and then bent to kiss her aunt's cheek, but if Isobel was aware of her she showed no sign. Her eyes were closed, her mouth agape to draw in air.

Having ushered Edward out one door, Katherine sped across to the other and opened it. Her mother darted forward. "Is it over?" she whispered.

Katherine nodded. "I must see that he gets away safely. I shall return as soon as that is done."

Her mother's face was creased with anxiety. "Take great care. I shall not feel secure until he is well away from here."

"Do not concern yourself. I mean to take him down the servants' staircase. So far everything has gone smoothly." Katherine smiled at her. "Now, go to your sister and make your peace with her, so that you will be able to remember her with affection when she is no longer here."

"Oh, Kate."

Katherine gathered her mother in her arms, as if she were the child and Katherine her mother. A few months ago, before the birth of her own child, she doubted she would have been capable of doing this. Just a few hours ago, she could not have done so without feeling ill at ease. But a new bond had been forged between her and her mother. Now, it felt right to take her in her arms and comfort her.

"I love you, darling Kate," said her mother, lifting her flushed face up to Katherine's.

"And I love you, dearest Mother."

They exchanged embarrassed little smiles and then parted, Alyssa to go to her sister, Katherine to join Edward.

"We must leave by the servants' entrance," she told him.

"Won't that give rise to suspicion? It is not likely that you would leave the house thus."

"Suspicion or not, it is far safer than a chance encounter with one of my cousins or, worse still, Lord Colborne. Besides, I could hear Tobias's voice in the main hall a moment ago. I dare not let him see me with you."

Reluctantly, Edward followed her down the narrow, winding stairway to the servants' hall. "I wish to arrange for refreshment for the apothecary," she said boldly to one of the servants who, most unfortunately, was standing directly at the foot of the stairs. He was obviously astounded at the sight of Lady Colborne's niece walking down the servants' stairway.

"With your permission, madam, I will arrange for that for you," the servant replied, bowing low.

"Thank you, no," Katherine replied haughtily. "I must also speak with the cook about a hot custard for Lady Colborne."

If the servant thought it highly unusual for her ladyship's niece to be going into the kitchens herself, instead of sending one of her ladyship's women, he said nothing.

"Wait by the door," Katherine ordered Edward. Her heart thudding, she was forced to conduct a discussion with the startled cook about the respective merits of a custard versus calf's-foot jelly. The combined aromas of sage and boiled rabbit and garlic on her churning stomach were almost her undoing. Imperiously demanding a rabbit pie for the apothecary, she fled from the kitchen, to join Edward.

"Here." She thrust the pie wrapped in a cloth at him. She peered out into the kitchen yard, beyond it the large herb garden. It had ceased raining and was almost dark now, the shadows moving eerily across the torchlit ground.

"All safe," she said, stepping into the yard.

"It is best that you come no further with me," he told her. "We must part here."

They stood very close to each other by the open doorway. She could hear his quickened breathing and sensed that he was not entirely unaware of her as a woman. She was glad of it.

"I shall never be able to thank you enough," she told him. "I cannot explain why exactly, but I feel that your coming here to Isobel has caused a great change in the lives of us all. I thank you for it."

"There is no need. To serve God is my reason for being here."

"I understand that, but I can still give you thanks."

They stood together in the pool of light from the lantern hanging above them. "God bless you, dear Katherine," Edward said. "God keep you and your family in His loving care at all times."

Stepping back from her, he held up his hand and blessed her, making the sign of the cross in the air.

The light fell on his face and hair, making them shine like burnished gold. Katherine went on her knees before him and, taking his hand, kissed it. "God keep you safe, Father Carlton," she said. Then he was gone, melting into the night.

She remained on her knees for a moment, and then stood up, her legs trembling so hard she was forced to lean against the wall. It was over. She had accomplished what she had set out to do. Now it was all over.

As she turned to go back into the house, a feeling of such dejection swept over her that she felt like stretching herself out on the doorstep and never getting up again.

"Don't be so ridiculous," she told herself and set her hand on the door latch to go back inside.

"Good even to you, dear Niece." The voice came from close by.

Katherine spun around. Out of the darkness stepped her uncle, Lord Colborne.

Chapter 42

Resisting the impulse to run from him, Katherine sank into a respectful curtsy. "Good even to you, my lord Uncle."

"Shall we go inside the house?" His hand closed about her arm and he opened the door and went inside. "Holla!" he roared.

Three servants came running at the sound of their master's shout, their expressions showing their amazement that he should arrive by the servants' entrance.

He still retained his grip on Katherine's arm. She tried to ease it away, but the grip tightened. She knew then that he had seen Edward.

He released her arm as his cloak was removed and then took it again, to lead her into the main hall. "Who was that man?" he demanded.

"Which man was that, my lord?"

"The man you were with outside a moment ago."

"Ah, you mean the apothecary," she said, seeking to placate him with a little smile. "He was here to attend my aunt."

He nodded his bull head. "The apothecary." The pale eyes fringed with sandy lashes did not blink. "A strange-looking apothecary, wouldn't you say? An apothecary with a gentleman's stance and voice."

Katherine met his eyes, trying not to show her fear of him. "A gentleman fallen on hard times, perhaps, my lord Uncle." She must delay him as long as possible so that Edward would have time to get a head start.

"Hard times, indeed, Niece." His voice roughened. "'Twill be hard times for that scurvy priest when he's slit open at Tyburn and his guts spilled out."

Katherine steeled herself not to react. "Priest, my lord Uncle? I don't understand. What priest?"

His hand shot out. She cried out at the stinging shock of the blow across her face.

"Perhaps that will loosen your tongue, you whore's daughter. Tell me the name of the priest you and your whore-mother brought to my house."

She confronted him, eyes blazing. "How dare you strike me, sir. And how dare you speak thus of my mother, your own wife's sister."

"Aye, to my cost. I rue the day I allied myself with your whoreson family. Radcliffes!" He spat at her feet.

From behind her came sounds of feet on the staircase. She did not turn around.

"Katherine, was it you who cried out?" said her mother's voice. "I heard a dreadful cry from upstairs."

"Are you hurt, Kate?" Joanna ran to her and flung her arms about her waist. "Your face is all red. What happened?"

Katherine turned to meet her mother's horrified gaze. "It is nothing," she said, trying to smile down at her sister. "I only—"

"Your daughter only smuggled a priest into my house, madam," said Lord Colborne. "That is all. She dared to bring papist filth into my house. By Christ, I have you all now, treacherous Radcliffes. Caught red-handed. But before I turn Mistress Katherine Radcliffe over to the authorities I shall have the name of this priest from her. Even if I have to take my horsewhip to her myself."

"I think not." The voice came from the shadows by the great carved screen that separated the servants' hall and offices from the main hall. "You will not touch her."

At first Lord Colborne stiffened at this interruption, his hand flying to his sword, but then he relaxed. "'Tis only the steward. Get that old man out of here," he barked.

Tobias Ridley stepped forth, the candlelight glinting on the small dagger he held poised in his right hand. "The first man that touches me shall have this in his gullet."

The servants halted.

Alyssa went to him and put her hand on his arm. "I pray you, put the dagger away, Tobias," she said softly. "It will do no good."

"How touching," sneered Colborne. "Another of your paramours, madam? Your steward this time. You have come down in the world."

Although a nerve jumped in Tobias's cheek, he did not make a move. But Katherine saw how tightly her mother had to grip his arm to hold him beside her.

It was too late for her now, Katherine knew, but she could try to stall for time, so that Edward would not be found. "How could you possibly think the apothecary bringing physic to my aunt was a priest?" she demanded of Lord Colborne.

"Because, my pretty deceiver, I saw him bless you and saw you kiss his hand and curtsy to him in return. And though I could not hear your conversation for the blowing of the wind, even a fool could guess that the man you were bidding farewell to at my back door was a papist priest."

Oh Edward, Edward, why did you have to bestow a blessing upon me?

"Ah, you hang your head at that. You see, you cannot wriggle your way out. And this time I'll make sure you and your haughty mother do not escape the fire that awaits treacherous bitches like you. Now, tell me the priest's name."

He moved to grab at Katherine. As he did so, Tobias darted forward, but it was Joanna who leapt at Lord Colborne like a mad thing, raking at his face with her nails, yelling, "Let my sister alone. Don't you dare touch her again!"

"Holla! To me!" roared Lord Colborne. He thrust Joanna aside and dashed across the hall to sound the alarm, pulling the bell rope that set the great bell in the roof timbers clanging.

As the sound reverberated in their ears, the hall suddenly filled with servants, streaming in from the kitchens and stables.

"What the devil's going on?" cried Robert, the falcon he had been tending still strapped to his wrist.

"Tie Ridley up," his father ordered him. "Watch him, he's got a knife."

"Give my nephew the dagger, Tobias," Alyssa said calmly. "We are too few against so many." She turned to her brother-in-law. "It is not necessary to bind my steward, my lord. He was merely trying to protect us, as any gentleman might when he sees ladies being attacked."

Lord Colborne's face turned scarlet.

"God's wounds, will someone tell me what's happening here?" demanded Robert again, as his groom jerked Tobias Ridley's arms behind him and bound them with his belt.

"I'll be happy to do so," said his father. "Our fair cousin Kate here has turned traitor again. But this time she's gone too far. This time she brought a papist priest here, to your mother. And there's no doubt your Aunt Alys was in it, too."

"No."

"What was that, Niece?"

Katherine lifted her chin to look defiantly at Lord Colborne. "I said no, my mother was not involved. She knew nothing about it."

"So you do admit to bringing a priest here."

"I admit nothing. All I said was that my mother was not involved in anything I might have done."

Lord Colborne raised his bushy eyebrows at his son. "You see? It remains for us to get the name and whereabouts of this priest from Cousin Kate."

Robert grinned. "I shall be happy to do that myself." He proffered his arm to his groom, who unstrapped the falcon from it.

Katherine's head swam. She had been alone only once with her eldest cousin. She had cause to fear him far more than she feared her uncle.

"Good. Take her to the armory and be quick about it. I'll send men out to scour the immediate countryside, but we must discover exactly where the priest is hiding lest he escape to another region in the darkness."

"Does he know that he was seen, do you think?" asked William, who had joined them now.

"Nay," said his father. "I kept very still until he had left. He'll go back to his hole, thinking himself safe."

Robert put his arm about Katherine's waist and dragged her to his side. "So all we need to know is his hiding place and we have him, right?"

"Aye, that's right."

"You'll not . . . hurt her, will you?" William nodded rather shamefacedly at Katherine. "After all, she is our cousin."

"Nay, I'll not hurt her, little brother." Robert gave a braying laugh. "Off you go, Will, and get the men together to start the search."

Katherine could smell his ale-breath on her cheek.

"I believe you are forgetting one person in all this, my lord," said Tobias's cool voice.

"And who might that be, sir steward?"

"Master Radcliffe. I believe he might have something to say about the treatment his ladies have received here this evening."

"Master Radcliffe? Ah, you mean the Irish bastard, Fitzgerald, who reigns up at Radcliffe Hall under the guise of a gentleman. I doubt he will remain Lord of Radcliffe long. The Council of the North, in its wisdom, will see that a foreigner from Ireland whose wife has been burnt at the stake for harboring priests doubtless was himself involved in plots of treason against Her Majesty."

"You have always coveted Radcliffe for yourself, have you not, Ingram?" Alyssa's voice carried throughout the hall, so that everyone could hear. "And you would go to any lengths to obtain it. But in your excitement to have the Radcliffes in your clutches at last, you and your sons seem to have completely forgotten one thing: that upstairs your wife of more than twenty years—mother of your sons and daughter—lies dying, and not one member of her family is with her, bar her daughter, Bess."

She flung out her arm, pointing it directly at her brother-in-law. "Shame on you, Lord Colborne. And shame on you, Robert and Will, that you should be so warped by greed that you would forget the mother who gave you birth." Her voice rang out, clear and carrying, so that no one in the hall or the gallery above it could fail to hear her.

A murmur went up from the servants, but it was drowned suddenly by piercing shrieks from above. "She's dead! Mother's dead!"

Alyssa's hand flew to her throat. "Oh, God in heaven. I was not there with her." She looked at Lord Colborne, her eyes narrowing with hatred. "I shall never forgive you for this, sir. Never."

"Wait here. I forbid you to—"

But she paid him no heed. Picking up her skirts, she ran to the staircase and mounted it as fast as she was able, Joanna at her heels.

Katherine was about to follow them, but Robert barred her way. "Keep her and the steward here and watch them," Robert said curtly to one of his men. With a jerk of his head to his brother, he ran across the hall and up the stairs.

After a moment's hesitation, Lord Colborne followed his sons, his eyes fixed on the floor to avoid the suddenly hostile eyes of his servants.

All this time, Katherine's mind had been trying to deal with several dilemmas at once. The most immediate one, how to escape her interrogation by Robert, seemed to have been postponed, for a little while at least, by her aunt's death.

God rest her soul, she prayed silently. She closed her eyes for a moment, heartsore that Aunt Isobel should have died while members of her family were, literally, daggers drawn with each other below.

Then she remembered the aura of peace Edward had brought to her and thanked God for that, at least.

It was of no import to her whether or not her aunt had been shriven by a Catholic priest. What was important was that she had died with her mind and soul at rest. And she knew instinctively that this would make the world of difference to her mother's peace of mind, also.

She went now to Tobias. He stood, his back against the wall, his face disconsolate. "Are you all right, Tobias?"

He gave her a twisted smile. "Aye, Mistress Katherine. As right as I can be in the circumstances."

"Would you loosen the belt a little?" she asked the servant who guarded him. "It is biting into his wrists."

The servant muttered beneath his breath, but the request had been accompanied by a sweet smile and he had known Mistress Kate for many a year, so he loosened the belt and permitted the steward to sit on the stool Mistress Kate herself brought.

"There, that is better," she said.

But it seemed that it was not, for Tobias suddenly groaned and bent over, coughing and gasping for breath. "Drink," he gasped.

"Get him a drink," snapped Katherine, terrified that the ordeal had been too much for him.

The man ran to fetch a mug of ale, but as Katherine bent over Tobias she looked into eyes that were alert and free of pain. "I was able to send a message to your husband," he whispered. "Hush, say nothing," he warned, as the servant returned.

As Tobias thanked the servant courteously for the ale and drank it down, Katherine stood watching him, her heart racing against her clasped hands.

Brendan. Tobias had somehow contrived to get a message to Brendan. Oh God, she would give the world to see him walk through the heavy, iron-studded doors now. Surely Brendan would think of some way to get them out of this danger.

But her surge of optimism soon died. What could Brendan do against a man as powerful as Lord Colborne? Her uncle was a respected member of the mighty Council of the North. A word from him and, as had happened before, they would be clapped into prison. And this time there was no Earl of Sussex to send them a savior.

For a long while she paced across the floor, her mind going over all that had happened in the past twenty-four hours. So much. Pacing back and forth, back and forth, she examined each episode minutely: Edward's arrival at Radcliffe, her aunt's dying demand for a priest, her frantic ride to Melmerby Tower to fetch Edward, Edward with her aunt. . . .

Eventually her thoughts narrowed to focus on the two men: Brendan and Edward. Although a speck of hope remained, she knew in her heart that Edward would be discovered. If only she could get a message to him, but it was impossible. Even as she leaned her aching back against the wall, she could feel the eyes of Robert's groom fixed upon her, following her every move, as he had done in the past hour or so.

She straightened up. "I should like to go to my mother," she told him, "so that I may pray with her over Lady Colborne's body."

But the man shook his head. "My orders are to keep thee here, mistress." All the servants, she sensed, were embarrassed at having to deal thus with the relatives of their dead mistress, but none would dare to disobey their master or one of his sons.

She heard sounds from upstairs, voices and footsteps. Dear God in heaven, they were coming down. At any minute now Robert would appear to drag her off to the armory. He would have to drag her or carry her, for she would be damned before she would walk there with him. If only she had the bodkin she usually carried with her when she went from home, but she had not expected to need it on a visit to her dying aunt.

She turned to face the staircase, head up, eyes bright. As she waited, she became aware of more noises, this time behind her in the courtyard outside: the clatter of horses' hooves, men's voices shouting—followed by a pounding on the door and the sudden joyous, wondrous sound of Brendan's voice shouting, "Let me in. I demand entry."

Chapter 43

By good fortune, Brendan had intercepted Tobias's messenger long before he reached Radcliffe. He was riding along the bridlepath from Jervaulx with Master Applegarth and their two grooms, when Alyssa's horse groom galloped up behind him.

"Praise God," cried the groom. "He is with us today, to be sure. This'll save us an hour at least."

Brendan turned his horse's head and bore down on him. "What's the matter?" he barked, fear rising in him.

"Master Ridley sent me," gasped the groom. "He says to tell thee there's danger at Colborne Place, danger for Mistress Kate. He bids thee ride there as fast as tha can, and bring men along of thee."

"Jesu! What sort of danger? Did he say?"

"Nay, Master. He said nobbut to hasten and to bring men."

"From where does this danger arise. Did he tell you that?"

"I believe 'tis from Lord Colborne hisself, master. And he said bring plenty of men so tha can get inside."

Brendan groaned inwardly. What the devil was that swine Colborne up to now? By Christ, if he had harmed Kate or any of the women he would . . . "We haven't enough men at our backs to storm the house," Brendan said to Applegarth. "Master Metcalfe and Master Challoner's houses are nearby. We'll ride there."

Saying no more, he wheeled his horse and galloped off, without even checking to see that the men followed him.

By good fortune, both Piers Metcalfe, Kate's great-uncle, and his good friend, Giles Challoner, were at home. It needed little persuasion to have them mounted, with a troop of retainers at their backs, in a short time. Lord Colborne might be powerful, but he was not popular and despite their ages both men vowed they would be prepared to fight to the death for the ladies of Radcliffe.

Brendan sincerely hoped it would not come to that. His show of power was intended mainly to ensure that he not be barred from entering Colborne Place.

As it was, once he arrived at the gates to the great mansion, he and his men were permitted to enter without further challenge, for there was but a handful of men guarding the courtyard.

"Where is everyone?" he shouted to the gatekeeper.

"Inside, or gone searching for the priest," the man replied.

Priest? His heart lurched. Pray God, Kate had not become involved with Catholic priests again, for if she had not even a thousand men at his back would be able to save her.

He dismounted, as did Giles and Piers. "A dozen men only come with us," was his order. "The rest of you stay mounted and at the alert. Applegarth, remain out here, but report to me inside if there is any change."

The burly bailiff nodded his head. "As you say, sir."

Brendan strode to the immense door of oak, which was barred and studded with iron, and hammered on it with the hilt of his sword. "Let me in. I demand entry."

No answer.

He hammered and shouted again, and this time there came the screech of bolts being drawn back and the doors slowly opened.

Before he entered, he turned to check his companions. "Ah good, you have your swords at the ready. Pray God we have no need to use them," he said, and strode into the hall.

As soon as he was inside, his eyes raked the great beamed hall, trying the assess the situation in the time it took to take a few paces. It was an ability he had learned in his many years of service in Ireland.

There were two score or so people in the hall, most of them servants and grooms. In the center, by the long table, stood Lord Colborne and his two sons, swords drawn. Alyssa and Joanna and Bess stood at the foot of the stairs, huddled together. To his immediate left, against the wall, sat Tobias on a stool, his hands tied behind his back with a belt. Their eyes met, and Brendan gave him a little nod.

To his left, beneath the tall window stood Kate, her great dark eyes fixed upon him, her body straining towards him as if she had stopped herself at the very last minute from flying to him.

"Good even to you, my lord," Brendan said in a jovial voice, as if he had just arrived to dine with his wife's kinsman. He turned to Piers and Giles. "Go to Kate, will you, Metcalfe?" he said softly. "And you, Challoner, to the other women."

As Giles Challoner went to pass by him, Robert stepped in front of him to block his way.

"I think you should permit Master Challoner to pass, Cousin Robert," Brendan said. "I must tell you that I have a sizeable troop of men outside, eagerly awaiting my signal to ride through those doors."

At last Lord Colborne spoke. "And what will that avail you, Radcliffe? You cannot kill us all. You dare not kill me. All you will have accomplished will be to have willful murder added to the counts against you and your family."

"I have no desire at all to kill anyone, I assure you, my lord. I am here to defend my womenfolk and to demand a reason for their kinsman treating them with such rank discourtesy."

"Reason enough, as you will soon discover."

"Then, pray tell me what it is, my lord."

"First, put up your swords." Lord Colborne glowered about him. "Challoner, Metcalfe, I am amazed to see you, of all people, storming into Colborne Place, swords in hand, when you should both be at home before your fires."

Giles Challoner's round face shone like a rosy-red apple with anger. "And I am amazed to see such evident rancor in a house where its mistress lies seriously sick," was his reply.

Lord Colborne's expression grew hard as granite. "Lady Colborne is dead. She died but a short time ago."

"I am sorry to hear it," said Giles. "May her soul rest in peace." His left hand moved upwards, as if he were about to make the sign of the cross, and then fell to his side again.

"And therein lies the crux of the matter," said Lord Colborne, turning back to Brendan. "You asked for a reason for my discourtesy. I have great cause. Your wife," he jerked his head in Katherine's direction, "secretly brought a papist priest to Lady Colborne, a priest she has been harboring in some secret hiding place."

Beneath his doublet, Brendan's heart hammered in his chest. Christ in heaven, let it not be true, he prayed. "And what proof have you of this, my lord?" he asked scornfully.

"The very best, sir. Mine own eyes. I saw her bid him farewell at my back door. Saw him bless her. Saw her curtsy to him and kiss his hand."

Brendan's eyes went to Katherine. He did not have to ask her if Lord Colborne spoke the truth. It was written in her face, in her half-defiant, half-pleading expression. He also saw how her Great-Uncle Piers stepped away from her, to set a distance between them.

If it were true, Kate was already condemned to the fire, and nothing could save her.

Then a woman's voice spoke, clear and decisive. It was Alyssa. "It was my sister's dying request."

A surprised murmur ran through the people gathered there.

"Isobel begged us to find a Catholic priest to shrive her before she died."

Lord Colborne rounded upon his sister-in-law. "You lie," he growled. "My wife could not abide papists. It was she—" He stopped, his face turning brick-red.

"Aye, my lord," said Alyssa. "It was she who betrayed me, was it not? She told you and you informed the Council. She told me so herself on her deathbed. You see, Ingram, there are no secrets between us now."

"Aye, she betrayed you, as you call it. She knew you to be a traitor to your Queen as well as a whore who lies with her own—"

His words were cut off by Brendan's sudden leap across the hall and the prick of his sword point against his throat.

"One more word, my lord," Brendan ground out in his ear, "and I swear it will be your last."

Colborne's pale eyes met his. Brendan could smell fear in the sweaty stink from him. Then the man laughed, but he was careful not to move one inch. "The only possible proof that my wife asked for a papist priest would be from her mouth alone. And I regret to say she is unable to provide it," he said, with a smirk in his sons' direction.

"She did ask for a priest," cried a shrill voice.

Brendan turned in surprise at the cry.

"I heard her myself," Bess said, and then shrank back against her Aunt Alyssa when she saw the expression on her father's face.

"Come hither, Bess," said Brendan, smiling at her. "Do not be afraid."

Clinging to her aunt's hand, she came to the center of the hall.

Brendan lowered his sword and held out his left hand to her. "Tell us what you heard, Bess."

"Open your mouth again, daughter, and I'll take my whip to you," growled her father.

"I will not let him hurt you," Brendan assured her. "Just tell us the truth."

The young girl looked from her father to Brendan, her brown eyes wide with fear. Then, encouraged by Brendan's smile, she said, "Aunt Alyssa sent me into the next chamber with Gertrude and Jane, my mother's women. We could hear my mother weeping, and then she kept screaming, 'A priest. I must have a Catholic priest to absolve me of my sins.'"

Now Giles Challoner stepped forward. "Are you absolutely certain that is what she said, Bess? A Catholic priest?"

She turned to him. "Oh yes. But it wasn't the first time. During the past week, I often heard her beg the women to find her a Catholic priest."

"By Christ in heaven, daughter, you'll rue the day you spoke against your own father." Lord Colborne's hand reached out for her.

But his son Robert suddenly stood before him. "Do not touch her, sir. I'll not have my sister harmed." Father and son stood glaring at each other, but Lord Colborne's hand dropped.

"It seems we are at somewhat of an impasse," Brendan said. "I would suggest that you dismiss your men, my lord. Then we shall put up our swords and discuss what is to be done next, like gentlemen."

"Gentlemen, pah!" Lord Colborne spat at Brendan's feet. "Call yourself a gentleman. You are nothing but an Irish bastard."

Brendan towered over him. "I am both proud to be an Irishman and to be the bastard son of the Earl of Sussex, whose surname I now bear, at his behest. I would remind you, sir, that, when you insult me, you insult the name of one of Her Majesty's most beloved and trusted councillors."

Robert gripped his father's arm. "Have done, sir. Doubtless he still has powerful friends at Court." Without waiting for his father's permission, he turned to the gathered men and dismissed them. "To your posts, the lot of you. And one word of warning before you go: anybody that speaks of this will have his tongue slit. Understand?"

They understood, all right. Most of them had at some time or other felt Master Robert's boot or whip and would heed his warning.

As the men filed through the screen entrance, Brendan turned back to Lord Colborne. "I would suggest that the ladies retire to the parlor. They must be perished with the cold, standing out here all this while." He knew he certainly was.

But Alyssa stepped forward. "I would prefer to sit in vigil with my sister, if it please you, my lord."

"A good thought, Aunt," said William. "All the ladies shall go upstairs."

"I shall not," said Katherine, chin raised. "I wish to take part in these discussions, as it is my life that is at stake."

Brendan winced. It was a singularly unfortunate choice of words. "I wish to speak privately with you first, my sweet," he said.

She looked warily at him. "Very well, but then I shall—"

"Then you shall go upstairs with your mother, my lady wife," he said firmly.

She opened her mouth to protest, and then shut it again.

"Your pardon, sir," Brendan said to Lord Colborne. "This will take but a moment."

He drew Katherine into the parlor, closing the door behind them. "Where have you hidden this priest?" he demanded.

Her eyes flew to his and then away again. "I cannot tell you."

His hands gripped her upper arms tightly. "'Fore God, Kate, you must and you shall. To save you, the priest must be sacrificed. Tell me where he is."

"Never." She tried to drag her arms away from him, but he would not let her go.

"By Jesus, 'tis a horsewhip I should like to be taking to you, you stubborn woman." He glared down at her averted face. "Don't you see, Kate? If they have the priest, they'll maybe not bother any further with you, especially after what Bess said."

"I cannot betray him."

"Why not?" His voice was harsh. "Isn't it for that reason the priests come to England: to die the glorious death of a martyr for their faith?"

"I cannot betray him," she whispered.

A coldness swept over him. "Who is he?"

"I cannot tell you."

But Brendan knew now without being told. It was what he had always dreaded. The man she had loved all these years, the man who had rejected her to join the priesthood, had returned.

"Edward Carlton, your faithless lover that jilted you, that's who it is, isn't it?"

She nodded, the tears sliding from beneath her lowered lids.

He released her, to pace across the chamber and then back again to confront her. "You would risk your life and those of everyone at Radcliffe for this man?"

"I refused to hide him at Radcliffe," she said in a low voice. "I sent him away. Then Aunt Isobel was begging for a Catholic priest. I thought of Edward."

"You thought of Edward," he repeated. "But you did not pause to think of the incredible folly of bringing a papist priest into the house of the man who, I gather from your mother's words, was responsible for imprisoning you and her at York."

"Oh, Brendan," she said piteously, "if you had but heard Aunt Isobel, you would have done the same. There is no time now to tell you why, but it involves important matters that happened in the past. Matters that have caused all the troubles between me and my mother."

She raised her eyes to his and he saw that whatever had happened behind those closed doors of Lady Colborne's bedchamber had created a profound change in his wife.

"Will you save him for me?"

He had to hold himself in check not to recoil physically from such a monstrous request. But so strange was the entire situation that all he said was, "Do you still love him?"

A radiant smile lit her face, so that his heart plummeted until the meaning of what she was saying sank in. "My darling Brendan, it wasn't until Edward appeared that I realized it was you I loved. That I had probably loved you since the first moment I saw you in that wretched prison. That I would always love you."

He stood, thunderstruck by her words.

"Don't stand there like a great noddy with your mouth agape." She flung her arms about his neck and planted great kisses on his mouth, his cheeks, his forehead and then his mouth again.

He pushed her away, holding her at arm's length. "Be still for a moment, Kate." He blinked several times, fighting the tears that had gathered at the back of his eyes. "Is it the truth you are telling me? You're not saying this so I shall help you with Carlton?"

"Of course not, you foolish man. I love you, Brendan. I love you, husband. I love you, father of my darling little Dickon. There," she said breathlessly. "Is that convincing enough?"

He beamed down at her. "Utterly. Then, my darling, sweet Caitlin, I shall try to save your Edward, but only with Lord Colborne's contrivance."

Her happiness faded to an expression of dismay. "Lord Colborne? You must have lost all your wits. He would never agree to it."

He smiled. "I think he will. Where is Carlton hidden?"

She hesitated. "You will not tell Lord Colborne?"

"I will not. But if I am to save Edward Carlton, you must tell me where he is."

"He is hidden in the old tower near Melmerby Beck. Do you remember, I showed it—"

"The one you played in with your sister when you were children?"

"That's the one. Edward should have been back there ages ago, unless he was going elsewhere after he left here."

"You do not think he realized he had been seen."

"I swear he didn't. Lord Colborne waited until Edward had gone before he showed himself."

Brendan frowned. "Melmerby Tower. Surely that place is falling down."

"It was the only place I could think of that would be safe and yet keep him well away from Radcliffe. I had given you my word that I would not engage in anything dangerous ever again. You can imagine my feelings when Edward appeared."

He gave her a searching look. "In truth, I cannot imagine your feelings, but we shall not go into that now. He must be plaguey cold in that tower. If I remember aright it has hardly any roof left."

She hung her head. "His mother gave him provisions and I gave him blankets and a pillow."

He shook his head at her. "Oh, Kate, Kate, what shall I be doing with you? But I forgive you everything after hearing those wondrous words from your fair lips. Say them again before I go to Colborne."

"I love you, Brendan." And he saw from the look in her eyes that she spoke the truth.

Reluctantly, he put her from him. "Of all times for you to declare your love for me, this must be the worst. Go to your mother now and think no more of Edward Carlton. I will ensure that he is safely disposed before the night is out."

Chapter 44

The plan was forming in Brendan's mind as he walked from the parlor to request that Lord Colborne and he discuss their business in private. After consultation with his eldest son, Lord Colborne reluctantly agreed to his request.

"I will be brief, my lord," Brendan told him, as the door closed and they were alone. "You would be ill-advised to pursue this matter with my wife further."

Lord Colborne kicked one of his blue-mottled Gascon hounds away from the hearth and stood with his back to the fire. "Aye, you'd like that, Radcliffe, wouldn't you? To have your bonny Kate get off scot-free."

"What I would like is to have no scandal at all attached to either the Radcliffe or the Colborne family."

Colborne bristled. "There's no scandal attached to my family, sir."

"Indeed? You do not think that the Council of the North might be interested to hear that Lady Colborne of Colborne Place insisted that a

Catholic priest be brought to her, so that she might be shriven and receive the sacrament from him?"

Lord Colborne's hands opened and shut at his sides, the firelight glinting on the red hairs on their backs. "Damn you to hell, Radcliffe."

Brendan smiled. "Exactly so, my lord. It appears we understand each other better than we thought. I have a plan that might solve the problem. I believe that Her Majesty is complaining about the large amount of priests filling our prisons at present. If I were to rid her of one of these pesky priests, even if she were not aware of it, would not that be best?"

"You mean, you'll kill the wretch?"

"If I kill him there'll doubtless be some sort of enquiry and our ladies' involvement will be discovered. I have a better plan. If I escort him over the border to Scotland, he can plague the Scots or be hanged by them. Either way he is not troubling us or our families again."

"You'd have to catch him first."

"I think that can be managed." Brendan gave him a knowing half-smile.

"Ah. A man after my own heart after all. You'll beat it out of your wife, eh?"

"Something of the sort."

"And you'll undertake to see him over the border yourself?"

"That's the safest way, I'm thinking. Otherwise he'd likely try to bribe the guards who escorted him. If I take him, you'll know I will not risk the chance of his slinking back to Yorkshire."

"Do you know who he is?"

"Not yet. I mean to find that out from my wife tonight."

Lord Colborne opened his mouth in a laugh. "I'd like to be there to see it. She's a hellion, that Kate of yours."

"She is, indeed." Brendan took his riding gloves from his belt and began to draw them on. "One thing I will need from you."

"What's that?"

"A safe conduct for us both for the journey, lest we be challenged."

Lord Colborne looked at him with suspicion. "That would get my name involved in this. If it were discovered that—"

"Your name is already involved, my lord," Brendan said softly. "More than a score of people heard your daughter say that your wife begged for a Catholic priest to be brought to her. No doubt her women would also confirm what Bess said."

Lord Colborne jerked away from the fireplace. "God's blood! If she were not dead already, I'd break her scrawny neck for her."

Brendan busied himself with pulling the gloves over his wrist ruffs to avoid Colborne seeing from his expression how vile he thought him.

Before he left Colborne Place, he had one last person to speak with. He strode out behind Lord Colborne and went up to Tobias. "Release him," he ordered the groom who was guarding him.

The man looked past him to his master.

"Do as he bids you," said Lord Colborne.

Tobias was released. Brendan helped him to his feet, for the poor man was stiff from having sat so long on the stool, and led the way into the parlor for his third meeting there in the past half-hour.

"We have precious little time, Tobias," he said, after he had given him the gist of what he had agreed with Lord Colborne.

He drew him to the window seat, so that they might be as far away as possible from the door, and told him what he had learned from Katherine. "It is of vital importance that Colborne not discover who the priest is, or he will suspect me of conspiring with my wife. In addition, I wish to protect the Carlton family from charges of harboring a priest, if I can."

"What can I do to help?" asked Tobias.

"Two things you can do. You can ride to Radcliffe with Barnaby and prepare horses and saddlebags with provisions for the ride to Scotland."

"Where are you going, sir?"

"I am going to fetch Carlton immediately, before Lord Colborne changes his mind."

"And the other thing you wish me to do?"

"You know all about Sir Philip's friends in Scotland. Where can I safely send an English Catholic priest?"

"That's easily answered. To Sir Thomas Kerr, Laird of Ferniehirst."

"What? The Warden of the Middle Marches?"

Tobias's lips twitched. "Aye. He's an ardent Catholic. And if you but mention the name of Sir Philip Radcliffe he'll do anything for you."

"Good." Brendan was already edging towards the door. "I'll get the details from you when I return to Radcliffe."

He was reluctant to leave Katherine and her mother and sister at Colborne Place, but he could not prevail upon Alyssa to leave. "My place is with my sister and with poor Bess," she told him. And her daughters refused to leave her there by herself.

Brendan had to be content with Lord Colborne's word that, so long as he carried out his part of the bargain and got the priest out of Yorkshire at once, his ladies would be safe.

"Be sure to find out who he is, though, so we can haul in his family on some pretext or other," Lord Colborne warned him. "These missionary priests always return to their own regions to spread their filth."

Brendan made a mental note to work out a story of some priest from Essex having been blown off course and landing on the Yorkshire coast, or some such tale. He would have time a'plenty to invent stories while riding to the Scottish border with Edward Carlton.

His belly muscles squeezed at the thought of having to spend time with the man who caused Kate so much anguish. He thought again of that cruel letter Carlton had written to her, dwelling over such words as he could recall. 'Her letters have caused me great embarrassment. . . . Consider me as one dead.'"

By the time he was riding along Melmerby Beck to the tower, he had worked himself into a perfect lather of hatred against Carlton. Perhaps it would be better to kill the wretch after all and bury him up on the moor.

The tower stood amongst a clump of stunted trees on the slope above the beck. So well was it hidden that even the searching moonlight did not pick it out. Had it not been for Barnaby, Brendan would never have found it by himself.

"Hold the lantern higher," he bade Barnaby as he dismounted. Taking care not to make a sound, he went to the tower, listening outside for a few moments. Then he rapped on the boards held together by rusty hinges that had once been a door. He smiled grimly to himself, imagining the puny priest quaking in a corner. "Come out, Carlton, I know you're in there."

"You are seeking me, sir?"

The voice came from behind Brendan. He pivoted around, hand on the hilt of his sword, to find himself facing a man almost as tall as himself. He was dressed simply in gentleman's riding garb of leather breeches and jerkin, but nothing could disguise the golden hair touched to silver in places by the moonlight.

Jesu, Mary and Joseph, thought Brendan. *No wonder she loved him.*

"I am Carlton," the man said in his deep, sonorous voice.

"Are you alone?" demanded Brendan.

"I am."

"I thought you would be in the tower. Where were you?"

Carlton's brows lowered in surprise at the question. "I was washing in the beck. Why?"

"No reason. You must gather your things together immediately."

Suddenly Carlton was all action. "You should have said so from the first. Where am I needed?" he asked, already striding back to the tower. "Is someone sick?"

Brendan caught up with him and gripped his arm from behind. The man's arm muscles tightened and Brendan sensed his instinctive reaction to reach for his sword. But he wore no sword. Brendan heard the deep intake and slow release of breath, and then the muscles beneath his fingers relaxed, as Carlton turned around to face him.

"You must prepare to ride with me," Brendan told him, "but first I must speak with you."

Carlton inclined his head slightly, waiting for Brendan to continue.

Had he not known otherwise, Brendan would have taken him for a normal gentleman, but he had a singular quality of stillness that set him apart. The tension in Carlton's arm when Brendan had gripped it told him that this had not been an easy lesson for him to learn.

"I have ridden here directly from Colborne Place."

Again, tension in the body, but the face remained expressionless.

"You were seen by Lord Colborne."

"And you have come to arrest me, I take it," Carlton said.

"You take it incorrectly. I have come to escort you out of danger."

"Perhaps I should know who it is I am addressing."

Damn his coolness! "Perhaps you should. I am Brendan Radcliffe, husband of Katherine Radcliffe. Who, but for a whim of Dame Fortune, might now be clapped in irons because of your stupidity in involving her in your quest to become a martyr."

Carlton's face tensed in the moonlight. "Dear God in heaven," he breathed. "Is she harmed?"

"No thanks to you, she is not. My steward sent a message to me and, by great good fortune, I met the messenger on my way home. Otherwise, I might have been too late."

"You can be certain it was not fortune's hand but God's that was in this."

"God cannot keep His eye solely on you all the time, Carlton, so we are going to give Him a helping hand. I managed to persuade Colborne to permit me to see you over the Scottish border."

Carlton lifted his chin so that his face looked like some finely chiseled marble monument. "I cannot leave the Dales."

Brendan spoke through gritted teeth. "You have no choice."

"A priest does not run from his assigned duties."

Brendan fingered his sword hilt. "He does and he will if my wife's life hangs in the balance."

Carlton's eyes widened.

Brendan smiled. "Ah, I see you begin to understand the situation. Colborne has released Kate—as we ride, I shall explain the exact reason he did so—in exchange for my warranty that you will never again set foot in England."

Carlton gripped his arm. "You must understand, sir, that I have a higher calling, which transcends all fear of imprisonment, torture or even death."

The undoubted radiance in his expression, enhanced by the silver moonlight, did nothing to dissuade Brendan.

"You appear to be so caught up in the greater glory of God, Carlton, that you seem not to have heard what I am telling you. It is a case of your life or Kate's."

Edward Carlton's eyes shifted beneath Brendan's glare. "I find it hard to believe that Lord Colborne would harm his own wife's niece."

"You have lived too long out of this world then. I have no time now to explain, but I give you my word as a gentleman that it is so."

Carlton looked about him in despair. "I have waited so long for this. So long. All these years of training, waiting to return to my own land, to minister unto my own people."

Brendan felt a twinge of sympathy. "Are not all people brothers in Christ's eyes?" he asked him.

"In truth, they are," replied Carlton, his brusqueness betraying his impatience.

"Then you will be able to minister unto the Catholic Scots, who are even more sorely persecuted than the English."

For the first time, Carlton permitted a small smile to escape him, a smile that lit his eyes. "You have a most persuasive manner, Master Radcliffe."

For a brief moment, the thought struck Brendan that at another period in time they might well have become friends. But he immediately hardened himself, lest Carlton slip through his fingers. "Most of all, Carlton, you owe this to Kate."

The gray eyes widened at this, but Carlton said nothing.

"You callously abandoned her, knowing how much she loved you. Even when you knew she and her mother were in prison in York you did nothing."

"I could not. I had taken my vows." He flinched before Brendan's pitiless expression.

"And then to write that cruel letter, after all that time. By God, if that is what it means to be a priest, I am heartily glad I shall never be one."

"In having to abandon her, I suffered as much anguish as she did."

Brendan's fists itched to batter his saintly face. "I doubt that very much."

"You may choose not to believe me, Radcliffe, but I had never loved another woman as I loved Kate."

Looking into the other man's anguished eyes, Brendan began to believe him. "Prove it then. By coming with me to Scotland you will both save Kate and live to save the souls of the poor beleaguered Scots."

Carlton looked at him wonderingly. "You will come all that way with me, risk being caught with a papist priest?"

"I do it for Kate. And you, Father Carlton, must in turn swear that you will never again return to England, for the moment you set foot over the border, Kate's life will be in immediate danger."

Carlton hesitated for a long while, closing his eyes in what Brendan took to be silent prayer. Then he drew forth a crucifix from beneath his jerkin and kissed it. "I swear upon the crucified body of Christ that I shall never again return to England."

Brendan knew an overwhelming sense of relief. A living Edward he could conquer, but he had no desire to live the rest of his life with his wife's memories of a handsome, saintly Father Edward Carlton who had been tortured and martyred for his faith.

Epilogue
1585

Alyssa stood before the portrait of Sir Philip Radcliffe, her entire body rapt in contemplation of the aesthetic face, the faraway gaze of the penetrating blue eyes. As he watched her, it occurred to Brendan that mother and daughter had been attracted to the same kind of man.

"Why do you not take it with you to Harcourt Hall?" he asked, from behind her.

She started and turned to him with a wry little smile. "I did not hear you come in. No, no. Philip belongs here, at Radcliffe."

Brendan took her hands in his. "You will not change your mind, then?"

She shook her head and gave him one of her disconcertingly direct looks. "You would not truly wish me to, Brendan. Kate is mistress of Radcliffe Hall now and a worthy one she is, too. Besides, my father is ailing and needs me at Harcourt." Her brown eyes danced. "You would not believe the plans I have for the house. Ever since my mother died I have been longing to take it in hand and tear down all those dull curtains and throw away those shabby cushions and start anew. Now I shall be able to do so, with Joanna to help me."

"You mean to keep her with you, then?"

"Why, certainly. Once she and Harry Seaton are wed, they can help me manage Harcourt Hall. Harry will run the estate and Joanna and I the house itself."

"You are a very self-sufficient woman, Mistress Radcliffe."

"Not quite so self-sufficient that I shall not be pestering you for your aid a dozen or so times a week."

"I shall always be there for madam my mother," he said, executing a flourishing bow to her.

Her heart-shaped face grew serious. "As you have always been there for me and my family, Brendan. I shall never be able to thank you enough."

He turned from her in embarrassment, to study the portrait above them. "You do not know what it means to me to have a wife and family of my own to cherish," he murmured.

"And one that cherishes you in return," she said softly. She touched his arm and drew him to the window.

Below them, Katherine sat on a turf seat by the herb garden, holding out her arms to Dickon. With a squeal of glee, he tottered towards her, to be swept up and kissed soundly. She suddenly looked up at the window and, seeing Brendan, waved and threw kisses to him. Nearby, Joanna slowly paced along the path bordered by blooming lavender bushes, her hand clasped by the earnest-looking young man at her side.

Alyssa smiled down at her daughters and then moved away from the window. "I shall miss Radcliffe. When I came here as Thomas's bride I was younger than Joanna."

"Would he have approved, do you think?" Brendan nodded at Sir Philip. He remembered asking her the same question a long time ago.

"Of you? Certainly he would. When I came to Radcliffe it was not entirely a happy house, mainly because of Thomas. Even afterwards. . . ." She blinked and hurried on. "Now you have changed that. It is as if you have thrown open the shutters and let in sunshine and air. Kate loves you and you know how to manage her. You have the respect of the entire North Riding."

"Despite I'm a foreigner," he said, with a smile. "However, I believe Sir John Carlton is partly responsible for that."

"Perhaps he is. He told me he would never forget what you had done for the Carlton family."

Brendan grimaced. "I did it for Kate."

"But you were also thinking of the Carlton family name, I am sure."

Brendan shrugged.

Alyssa smiled, raising her delicate eyebrows at him. "Very well, I shall say no more on that subject. But to have Tobias Ridley eating from your hand is definitely a matter for congratulation, sir."

"You have decided to take him with you to Harcourt, as I suggested?"

"I have. Although I did not tell him what you said, that at his age he needs a rest from the strain of managing Radcliffe. I told him I could not manage at Harcourt without him and he then said, if that were the case, he would agree to come, so long as he could spend half his days at Radcliffe to oversee the new steward for the first year."

"Poor man," Brendan said with a heavy sigh. "Whoever he is, his life will be made a misery with Tobias looking disapprovingly over his shoulder all the time."

Alyssa smiled. "Poor man, indeed. So you see, Brendan, Lord of Radcliffe Manor, you have nicely organized us all into our rightful places. How could Philip fail to approve of you? Ever since he first came here as his grandmother's heir almost fifty years ago the happiness of those at Radcliffe was his main concern."

As Brendan turned to look again at the portrait of his son's great-grandfather, he thought how strangely the wheel of fortune spun. Four years ago, the name of Radcliffe had meant only one person to him: the remote Earl of Sussex, who had been his patron—and his father. Now the name of Radcliffe had come to symbolize love and home and family.

"I have it," he exclaimed suddenly, drawing Alyssa's arm through his and patting her hand. "I shall engage a painter to make a copy of the portrait and it shall be a gift from Kate and me for your new home."

"Would you do that?" Gratitude and love shone from her eyes.

"It shall be started immediately. Tobias will know the right man for it."

They looked at each other and laughed, both with the same thought, that Tobias knew the right man for everything. Still chuckling, they left the gallery, arm in arm, to seek out the rest of the Radcliffe family.

In the doorway, Alyssa turned to look at the portrait again and fancied that Philip's lips had parted in a slight smile, to join in their amusement. Then she closed the door.

Author's Note

Although this is a work of fiction, the historical background is factual. The Radcliffes, their relatives, retainers and some of their friends are imaginary characters, but readers will recognize several famous historical figures in these pages.

Apart from the manor houses, all the places mentioned can be found on modern maps of both England and Ireland.

Of the three main historical personages left alive at the end of this book, only Queen Elizabeth died of natural causes.

Mary, Queen of Scots was beheaded at Fotheringay Castle in 1587, after twenty years of imprisonment. Her son, James VI of Scotland, united the two kingdoms when he ascended the throne of England in 1603.

Sir Walter Ralegh eventually found his true love, Bess Throckmorton, and secretly married her. At the end of the sixteenth century he embarked on his quest for El Dorado, landing at Trinidad and Guiana, but when Queen Elizabeth died he fell out of favor with the new king, James I. The famous explorer and poet was executed in 1618.

My chief source for the history of Ireland in the Elizabethan age was Richard Bagwell's *Ireland under the Tudors*.